T0363351

THE BEAST'S GARDEN

KATE FORSYTH

THE BEAST'S GARDEN

VINTAGE BOOKS

Australia

A Vintage book
Published by Penguin Random House Australia Pty Ltd
Level 3, 100 Pacific Highway, North Sydney NSW 2060
www.penguin.com.au

Penguin
Random House
Australia

First published by Vintage in 2015
This edition published in 2016

Copyright © Kate Forsyth 2015

The moral right of the author has been asserted.

All rights reserved. No part of this book may be reproduced or transmitted
by any person or entity, including internet search engines or retailers, in any
form or by any means, electronic or mechanical, including photocopying
(except under the statutory exceptions provisions of the Australian *Copyright
Act 1968*), recording, scanning or by any information storage and retrieval system
without the prior written permission of Penguin Random House Australia.

Addresses for the Penguin Random House group of companies can be found at
global.penguinrandomhouse.com/offices.

National Library of Australia
Cataloguing-in-Publication entry

Forsyth, Kate, 1966– author
The beast's garden/Kate Forsyth

ISBN 978 0 85798 041 0 (paperback)

Man-woman relationships – Fiction
World War, 1939–1945 – Underground movements – Germany – Fiction
Berlin (Germany) – History – 1918–1945 – Fiction

A823.3

Cover design by Nada Backovic
Cover images: young woman, Trevillion; Brandenburg Gate, Corbis; barbed wire,
the letter 'B' and the rose, Shutterstock
Typeset in 10.5/15.5 Goudy Old Style by Midland Typesetters, Australia
Printed in Australia by Griffin Press, an accredited ISO AS/NZS 14001:2004
Environmental Management System printer

Penguin Random House Australia uses papers that are natural, renewable
and recyclable products and made from wood grown in sustainable forests.
The logging and manufacturing processes are expected to conform to the
environmental regulations of the country of origin.

'The government has no right to dominate men and restrain them by force or by fear of force . . . no right to transform them into wild beasts or machines . . . no right to demand unconditional obedience or blind faith . . .'

Helmuth James Graf von Moltke
Executed 23 January 1945 by the Third Reich

Part I

The Singing, Springing Lark
November 1938 – March 1939

As the man began to climb the tree, a lion leapt up and roared till the leaves on the trees trembled. 'I will devour anyone who tries to steal my singing, springing lark!'

'The Singing, Springing Lark', the Brothers Grimm

The Night of Broken Glass

Ava fell in love the night the Nazis first showed their true faces to the world.

It was winter. The sound of smashing glass woke her. Ava sat up, still half in the shadowlands of sleep, thinking: *it's just a nightmare*. Then she heard a huge explosion. Her bedroom was lit up with orange glare. The colour of D major, the key of glory and war rejoicing.

Ava stumbled out of bed and made her way, barefoot and shivering, to the window. The streets were full of dark figures, running. Over the rooftops, fire ate the night sky. It was so bright Ava could read the hands of her watch. It was after two o'clock in the morning. Angelika was wailing. Ava wrapped her robe about her and ran out into the corridor. Her sister Bertha paced up and down, jiggling her weeping daughter in her arms. 'Why won't you stop crying?' Bertha pleaded.

Ava's other sister, Monika, stood at the end of the corridor, her dressing-gown tied neatly about her, one hand holding the curtain up so she could look outside. Her fair hair was cut in an angle to her cheekbone.

'What is it, what's happening?' Ava cried.

'The synagogue's on fire,' Monika answered.

3

'On fire!' Ava looked out the window and could see the synagogue's gilded dome silhouetted against the sky. A crowd of dark figures jostled in the street below.

'Someone is wrecking the houses of the Jews,' Monika went on. 'Look! They've broken all the windows in Herr Benowitz's shop.'

Shards of glass littered the road. Someone was painting 'Jew' in bloody red letters across the wall. Someone else was beating and kicking a bundle of old rags in the gutter. Ava saw an arm flop. She caught hold of the window-sill, suddenly unable to take a breath.

Bertha said tremulously, 'It'll be the Hitler Youth. Or the Brownshirts. Or both.'

Ava was hardly listening to her. 'Rupert!' she cried. 'Oh, do you think the Feidlers will be in danger?'

'They're Jews, aren't they?' Monika retorted.

'Frau Feidler is only half-Jewish,' Bertha said, glad to have caught her in an imprecision.

'I have to go and help them.' Ava ran back towards her room, but her father's voice stopped her. 'Ava, no. Stay here. I will go.'

Herr Doktor Otto Falkenhorst came out of his bedroom, hastily dressed, his grey hair and beard dishevelled.

'Father! What are you going to do?' Ava cried.

'I don't know. Franz is a decorated war hero. Surely that must mean something.' As he spoke, Otto finished buttoning up his shirt. He went down the stairs, saying over his shoulder, 'Keep the door locked. Let nobody in.' Then he pointed one squat finger at Ava. 'Stay here, Ava. Do you hear me?'

'Yes, Father,' she replied.

Her father took his coat from where it hung on the hook by the front door, put on his hat, and went out. Ava heard the snick of the lock.

'I wish he wouldn't go,' Bertha said. 'It's far too dangerous.'

'He's not Jewish,' Monika said.

Ava cried hotly, 'He has to do something! He can't just stand by and do nothing.'

'That would be the smart thing to do,' Monika answered, sharp as shale. Angelika began to wail again.

'Must you shout so?' Bertha bounced her daughter up and down. 'I have such a pounding headache. Ava, can't you take her?'

Ava shook her head. 'I'm sorry. I can't.' She laid one hand on her niece's hot cheek, then hurried back to her room. She pulled on a woollen frock and her warmest stockings, her fingers trembling as she tied her bootlaces. Then she ran back into the corridor.

'You told Father you wouldn't go out,' Bertha accused her.

'No, I didn't. I told him I heard what he said.' Ava ran down the stairs to the front hall, her sisters following behind, arguing with her.

As Ava put on her red coat and beret, Monika cried, 'Ava, don't be a fool.'

'I can't stand by and watch it.'

'You'll be hurt!' Bertha wailed.

'Why would they hurt me? I'm not Jewish.' Ava mimicked Monika's voice with bitter sarcasm.

'No-one could tell that by looking at you, gypsy girl,' Monika retorted at once.

This was an old bruise. Ava was dark-haired and olive-skinned, while both her sisters were blonde and blue-eyed, perfect Aryan specimens. They were only Ava's half-sisters, and already in their thirties while Ava had just turned nineteen. When her mother had died giving birth to Ava, Bertha and Monika had been expected to help raise her. Ava understood that it must have been a chore.

She did not answer. She unlocked the door and went out, slamming it shut behind her.

Oranienburger Strasse was full of men. Most wore jackboots under their trousers or brown collared shirts under their coats. They carried bottles of beer, and sang Nazi songs as they pushed and shoved. Ava remembered that yesterday had been the anniversary of Hitler's failed Beer Hall Putsch.

Ava drew her coat close around her and tried to slip through the crowd, all converging on the New Synagogue, just down the street from her family's apartment. Its great dome, buttressed with gilded ribs and flanked on either side by two smaller domed pavilions, rose high into the flaming sky. The synagogue's arched doors stood open. Many of its tall windows had been shattered. Men threw furniture and books and scrolls onto a fire kindled before the great doors. Flames leapt up, casting a dancing demonic light on the faces of the cheering crowd. It was a scene from Liszt's Inferno.

'Stop! Stop!' a policeman shouted. All Ava could see of him was his round helmet, bobbing above the heads of the crowd. 'This is a historical landmark! You can't smash it to pieces.'

No-one paid him any attention. He pulled out a gun and shot into the air. People stampeded away. Ava was knocked off balance. She grabbed at someone to stop herself from falling. She was afraid of the broken glass beneath her feet. It glittered red. Coughing in the smoke, she ran on down the road. The buildings were like rows of flaming torches, lighting her way. Ava could have made her way in darkness, however. She had been running this way ever since she was a little girl.

She had to go through the tunnel under the bridge. It was a dark mouth. For the first time, Ava wished she had chosen to buy the sensible, sober clothes her sister Monika had suggested. Her red coat and beret felt like warning flares in the fire-wracked night. Ava could not stop now, though. She crept into the tunnel, hoping it was empty. It was so dark in there she had to feel her way with both hands.

On the far side, the river was red as a rush of lava between its stone banks. To her left, Ava could hear glass smashing, wood splintering. The sound of terrified screams. She ran faster, her breath staccato. Soon she had a stitch. She stumbled on, running a few steps, then slowing, then running again. Glass cracked under her foot. Ava tried to step more lightly.

Rupert lived with his parents and his younger sister, Jutta, just off the Unter den Linden. Ava and Rupert had often joked that they should swap houses, since the Falkenhorsts lived near the synagogue and the Feidlers lived near the cathedral. Not that Ava's family ever went to church, or Rupert's family to the synagogue.

Ava could see the little bridge guarded by two squat obelisks and, on the far side of the river, the cathedral's grand domes outlined darkly against the crimson sky. The Feidlers' apartment was beyond a small park. Ava hurried under the shadow of the bare-twigged trees, her breath ragged in her throat. A woman cried out. Piano keys crashed, *acciaccato*. Then Ava heard a scream of pain.

She broke into a run again, dashing her hand across her eyes. Suddenly she collided with someone in the darkness under the trees. He caught her, holding her steady. Ava was weak-kneed, barely able to catch her breath. She cried something out, she hardly knew what.

'Quiet now.' He spoke low, close to her ear. His voice was deep, his arm strong about her waist, pulling her close to him. Ava struggled to be free. Flames leapt up, illuminating her face but keeping his in shadow.

'Sssh, I'll not hurt you,' he said. 'I can't promise the same of the Stormtroopers, though. Keep quiet.'

'My father . . .' Ava panted, pulling against his hand. 'My friends . . .'

He looked back towards the road. The sounds of the night were terrible. 'You are a Jew?'

'No!' She was angry now. 'You think I'm Jewish just because my hair is black? I'm as German as you. And so are the Feidlers, I'll have you know, Jewish though they may be. Now let me go!'

'You won't be able to save them.' His hand on her waist tightened.

'I can't stand by and do nothing!'

'Are you not afraid?'

His arm was still firm about her waist. Everything seemed still and poised, like that moment between the end of one dance and another, when the dancers stand waiting for the music to once again whirl them away.

Ava did not know why she answered him so truthfully. Perhaps it was the darkness. Perhaps it was the strength of the arm that held her, when she was trembling so much she could scarcely stand. Perhaps she simply needed to confess her terror.

'Yes,' Ava said. 'I'm so afraid I can scarcely bear it. Not just of what those thugs are doing to my friends, or what they might do to me.

I'm afraid . . . of everything. The whole world seems to be going mad. I feel like I am stepping into a void, and there is nothing . . . nothing beneath me.'

'Yes.' He answered so quietly that Ava could barely hear the word. His breath was warm on her cold skin. She shuddered, and his arm tightened about her, keeping her from falling.

'What is to become of us all?' Ava whispered. 'My father says we are being driven towards war. I cannot bear the thought. Surely, surely, we can stop it? If we all spoke out . . . if we refused to let them act like this . . .'

'I fear it is too late.'

'So you think it right to stand by and do nothing?' Her voice was sharp.

'No . . . but should we sacrifice ourselves senselessly? If we cannot change things?'

'If war comes again, many millions will be sacrificed senselessly. And we will probably die anyway. But it'd be a death without honour, without conscience. I'd rather die now trying to stop it!'

It was such an odd conversation to have with a stranger, in the dark under the winter-bare trees. It was as if the terror of the night had cracked something open in her, so that she had to speak out.

Ava went on, words tumbling out of her. 'Besides, it's more than that. To stand by and do nothing is to help them. So you see . . . I cannot stand by . . . no matter the consequences. Because the alternative is too awful.' As she spoke, she put both hands on his chest and pushed him away.

His clasp tightened, holding her close to him. Ava was aware of the strength of the muscled body pressed against hers. She tried to pull away, but he would not let her go. Flame exploded high above the rooftops. In its light she saw his face – ice-blue eyes, hollowed cheeks, a nose twisted awry – shadowed by a grey peaked cap. For a long moment, they simply stared at each other. It was a strange sensation, Ava thought, like the moment just before a glass smashes once it has fallen from your hand. You reach for it. You cannot catch it.

Then Ava saw the emblem on his cap. A golden eagle carrying a swastika. He was one of them.

A sharp stab of fear. She tried to wrench herself free.

He caught her wrists in his hands. 'Don't be a fool,' he said in her ear. 'Don't you realise what they would do to you if they saw you?'

'Because I look like a Jew?' she said with savage sarcasm.

'No, you idiot. Because you are so beautiful.'

Ava stared up at him. He shook her. 'Stay here. I'll do what I can to help.' Then he let her go so roughly she almost fell.

Ava stumbled to a nearby tree and clung on to its trunk. He strode off through the chiaroscuro of flame and shadow, pulling his pistol from his holster. 'Be careful!' she cried, hardly aware of what she said. He glanced back, raising his other hand to her. Then he stepped into the road.

A thunderous crash. The Feidlers' grand piano hit the ground in a shower of glass. Broken in half, the piano slowly folded in on itself. Strings twanged discordantly. Outrage brought new strength to her legs. Tante Thea had loved that piano so much. Ava ran and crouched beside the piano, picking up a cracked ivory key. She cradled it as if it was a hurt and living thing.

The man she had met in the darkness had barely broken stride. He disappeared inside the doorway, and Ava heard his boot heels drumming on the wooden stairs. Then she heard shouting.

Some minutes later, a troop of soldiers stamped down the stairs. Their coats only half-hid their brown uniforms. Truncheons and axes swung from their gloved hands. 'Abwehr pig,' one growled to the other. 'Who does he think he is?'

'One of Admiral Canaris's pups,' the other replied. 'Canaris is a friend of Heydrich's. Best not get on his wrong side.'

'Deserves a good kicking,' the first soldier said.

'Maybe so, but in the dark, when he doesn't know who's hit him. He's seen our faces now.'

'Let's go find another Jew to bash,' another said. 'I'm angry now.'

They did not see Ava, crouched in the shadow of the broken grand piano, as they strode away through the firelit darkness. As soon as they were out of sight, she ran across the road and up the stairs to the Feidlers' apartment. It was a mess. Every single window smashed to smithereens.

The antique mirror in glittering shards on the rug. Furniture broken and tumbled on the floor. Every cushion and pillow slashed to shreds. The Nazi officer stood at the window, looking out into the dark street below. He turned as Ava ran in, and she felt herself flush at the intensity of his regard. In the glare of the electric light, he seemed tall and stern and terrifying in his perfectly tailored grey uniform, the cap with its swastika badge shadowing his eyes. She tried to ignore him, gazing about her in utter dismay.

Jutta was on her knees, picking up shards of glass and throwing them in a bucket. She grimaced at Ava as she came in. She was a thin girl with sharp elbows and knees, her black eyes set just a little too close to her nose. Normally her face was full of such lively energy that one hardly noticed her plainness, but now her face was sallow and pinched. She was dressed only in an old pair of men's pyjamas and a shabby old dressing-gown, her short black hair sticking up any which way.

Herr Doktor Feidler sat hunched in a chair, blood pouring down the side of his face and matting in his full beard. Ava's father was trying to blot it away with his handkerchief. Rupert knelt on the floor beside them, holding a cold compress to his father's head. He looked much like his sister, with a long nose and brilliantly black eyes, but on Rupert the strong features were attractive, even handsome. His jaw was shadowed with stubble, and his face was marked with bruises, his lips puffy and torn. He wore loud paisley pyjamas, and a red velvet smoking jacket. He looked round at Ava as she came in and tried to smile, then winced with pain.

There was blood on his face, and on the floor, and on her father's handkerchief. Dizziness washed over her. Ava put out a hand, hanging on to the door for support.

'Ava!' Tante Thea rushed to her with arms outstretched. 'You shouldn't be here. Those Nazi swine have gone mad. Look what they've done! My grandmother's china! My piano.' She began to weep.

Tante Thea was dressed in a nightgown and slippers, her long iron-grey hair in a tousled plait down her back. Ava tried to comfort her, but had no words. She could only rock Tante Thea back and forth as she poured out the story: the banging on the door at the dead of night, the stampede of men with ugly faces and swinging truncheons, Rupert's futile attempt to stop them.

Across Tante Thea's bony shoulder, Ava saw the Nazi officer watching her. It was hard to read his expression. His jaw was set hard, his eyes inscrutable. His nose was formidable.

'But why?' Onkel Franz said. 'I don't understand. Why have they done this to us?'

'I imagine they'll say it is a spontaneous uprising in response to the assassination of the German diplomat in Paris yesterday.' The officer had an oddly formal way of speaking, his voice clipped and marked with a faint accent. Although he had answered Onkel Franz, his eyes were on Ava. They made her uncomfortable. She looked away.

'But what has that to do with us?' Onkel Franz gazed at him in bewilderment.

'Nothing. Apart from the fact that it was a young Jewish man who shot him.'

'But we don't condone that,' Tante Thea said, turning to stare at the officer. 'We are as shocked as any other German.'

He crossed the room, glass crunching under his boots. 'You should get out of Germany, if you can. This is only the beginning, I promise you.'

He stopped a pace away from Ava and bowed his head with a little, practised click of his heels. 'Fräulein.'

Then he was gone.

2

Tuning Fork

The night sky had faded to the violet of violins.

Shards of glass glittered all over the pavement. Every step sounded like cracking ice. Ava and her father and friends struggled along, laden with suitcases and boxes, through streets that should have been sleeping.

Ava could not believe what she saw. Ordinary Germans, people just like her, were smashing shop windows and taking what they could. Faces grinning with glee as they grabbed fine paintings in gilded frames, nine-branched silver candlesticks, white linen tablecloths, fur coats. Red scrawled paint along one wall proclaimed, 'Jews are filthy pigs! Jews are bloodsuckers! All Jews out!' A woman with a black scarf tied over her hair sat in the gutter, rocking back and forth, her arms crossed over her stomach. A teenage boy with a round skull-cap and dangling sidelocks did his best to comfort her. The brazen sky was dirty with smoke.

As they turned into Oranienburger Strasse, Ava saw a Jewish man in a tall black hat and a prayer shawl, surrounded by drunken louts. They pushed and taunted him, then one grabbed his beard, twisted it hard, and cut it off with a knife. Such grinning contempt in his face. Ava dared not protest. Like her friends, she turned her face away and hurried past, hoping no-one would accost them.

It was stupid of her to be so shocked. Ava had always known the Nazis hated the Jews. It was impossible to ignore when her best friend was Jewish.

Ava was three and a half hours older than Rupert. They had been born on the same day in the same hospital, from mothers who had been best friends. Ava's mother didn't live for very long, however, so Rupert's mother had taken on a great deal of the care of the motherless infant. They had been raised almost like twins, spending all day together in the Feidlers' beautiful old apartment overlooking the green lawns and gilded domes and cupolas of Museum Island. Every morning, Otto would push Ava in her pram along the path that ran beside the River Spree till they reached the street where the Feidlers lived. Ava would be left for the day with Tante Thea while Otto and Onkel Franz walked to the university together. They were old friends, just as Tante Thea and Ava's mother had been.

Rupert and Ava began school on the same day, ate the same lunch, did the same classes, read the same books, and spent their afternoons banging out tunes on Tante Thea's treasured grand piano. Ava knew, of course, that the Feidlers were Jewish and her family was not, but it did not seem to make much difference.

Then, when Rupert and Ava were fourteen, Hitler was elected Chancellor. Everything changed. Swastikas moved from a few people's armbands to vast scarlet banners that hung from every streetlamp and window. Everyone had to start throwing their right arm up into the air and shouting 'Heil Hitler' every time they met anybody. Suddenly everyone was saying it two dozen times a day. Little Hitler dolls were made with a moveable right arm so that small children could practise the gesture. Everybody greeted each other with it, even the desiccated old woman who took Ava's pfennig when she used the public toilet.

Jews, however, were not permitted to say it.

Every morning Ava stood with the other children in the school hall, her right arm raised to the ceiling till it ached, mouthing the words, 'Germany, awake from your nightmare! Give foreign Jews no place in your land. To the swastika devoted are we, Heil to our leader, Heil Hitler to thee!'

Rupert and Jutta and the other Jewish children would have to stand alone, raised hands striking towards their faces, the song beating the air about their ears. It was horrible. And there was nothing Ava could do about it. The punishment for refusing to salute was a caning across the hand, and sinister unspoken threats against her father for not teaching her to behave properly. Ava could not bear the possibility of her father being called in and reprimanded. And she could not bear to be whipped in front of the whole class. The very thought made her feel sick. So Ava saluted and sang with the others, not looking at Rupert and Jutta.

Tante Thea begged her husband to take them away from Germany, but Onkel Franz was adamant that the family must stay. 'Are we cowards, to run away from our home because of a few high-stepping fools? Where would we go? What would we do? No, no, Berlin is our home and here we shall stay.'

Tante Thea called him an obstinate fool, but Onkel Franz only closed up his book and walked out of the room, his lips folded firmly.

The Feidlers did all that they were ordered to do, hoping the Nazis would be satisfied and leave them alone. And things seemed to get better. As the Führer prepared for the Olympic Games, the newspapers stopped printing their hate-filled headlines. The posters warning against the Jews disappeared. The whole world came to Berlin for the Games, and the city was humming with music and laughter. In the crowds, it was easy for Ava and Rupert to slip in and out of the stadiums. Although there were men in uniforms everywhere, they were all smiling and affable. They did not grab anyone and start beating them up, even though there were people of all races and colours in the stadium, in all kinds of strange outfits.

The audience went wild when Germany won eighty-nine medals, thirty more than any other country. Rupert and Ava jumped up and down, arms around each other, almost crying with excitement. Ava had been so proud to be German in that moment.

She had not felt that way since.

Smoke nettled her eyes.

As Otto unlocked the front door, Monika hurried down the stairs. 'Father, Ava, where have you been! It's dawn already. You've been gone for hours.' Then she saw the Feidlers on the steps, bruised and bandaged, and laden with boxes and suitcases. She frowned. 'Are you mad? They can't stay here. We'll get into trouble!'

'They've nowhere else to go,' Otto replied in his gentle way. 'It will not be for long.'

'Aryans and Jews aren't meant to fraternise,' Monika protested.

'Franz is my oldest friend,' her father replied, holding the door wide so the Feidlers could come in. 'Where else would he go?'

'I'm very sorry,' Tante Thea said, putting down the suitcases she carried so she could scrub at her eyes with her crumpled handkerchief. Onkel Franz said nothing. He looked down at his box of books. A copy of Kafka's *The Trial* lay on top. He went into the study and put the box on top of the desk, then drew the book out, cradling it in his hands. He stood, reading silently, his hat and coat still on, his back turned. Ava's father moved to comfort Tante Thea. He put his arm around her, and she pressed her unhappy face into his shoulder. Her body shook.

Just then, a stout woman in a brown coat and hat stumped up the stairs. It was the family's housekeeper, Frau Günther. She had her key in her hand and was surprised to find the door open, the lobby full of people. She took in the sight of Otto comforting Tante Thea, and Rupert and Jutta standing by an untidy pile of belongings, and her mouth and eyes narrowed. 'Herr Doktor Falkenhorst! What is going on here?' she cried.

Otto looked at her in surprise. 'There has been a little trouble . . .'

'Big trouble, if you ask me,' Frau Günther snapped back. 'Haven't you heard the news? Now's not the time to be harbouring Jews.'

'I am so sorry.' Tante Thea stepped away from Otto. 'It's only for a few days.'

Frau Günther snorted. 'Better get all this mess out of the vestibule. Herr Doktor Falkenhorst's patients will be arriving soon and it's not at all the thing for him to be seen like this.'

'Of course.' Tante Thea cast Ava a look of appeal.

She settled Tante Thea and all her parcels and suitcases into the spare room, and made up beds for Rupert and Jutta on the couches in the sitting room. 'We've none of us had any sleep. Try and get some rest,' she told them.

'It's like we're kids again and sleeping over at each other's houses,' Rupert said, folding his arms behind his head and looking up at the ceiling. 'Shall we raid the pantry at midnight?'

Ava tried to smile. 'Midnight's long gone. It's almost breakfast time. Hopefully Frau Günther can whip something up for us.'

Jutta sat cross-legged on the couch, her black brows drawn together. Her short hair stuck up in five different directions. 'Will it cause trouble for you, having us here?' she asked abruptly.

'No, no, of course not . . . at least, I hope not. I don't know.' Ava took a deep breath. 'It doesn't matter. This is our private home. What we do here shouldn't concern them.'

Jutta made a rude noise.

Ava tried to smile. She was so tired the world seemed to waver about her. All she wanted to do was lie down and think about what had happened that night, and the stranger who had held her in his arms as they talked so candidly in the darkness. But her sisters were waiting for her in the front hall, Bertha with her daughter on her hip as always. Angelika was grizzling in a low, monotonous tone, her fists in her eyes.

'How long are they going to stay?' Monika demanded.

'I don't know,' Ava replied. 'As long as they need to, I suppose.'

'What shall we do about feeding them all? You know we have barely enough for the week's groceries as it is.' Her foot was tapping on the floor, her arms folded.

'We'll just have to manage somehow,' Ava answered wearily.

'But how, Ava?' Bertha protested. 'It's not fair. We have so little as it is. And my angel is a growing girl.' She squeezed her daughter close. Angelika responded by screaming in rage and throwing herself backwards so violently that Bertha almost dropped her. Her round face was hectic, her shrill voice soaring up to a perfect high C. It was enough to crack monocles, shatter champagne flutes, or explode a chandelier. Lucky Ava's family did not have any of those things.

'I can't bear it anymore! All she ever does is cry!' Bertha put Angelika down on the floor. Angelika drummed her heels.

'She's tired.'

'Well, so am I! So tired.'

'I'll take her.' Ava bent and picked up her niece, who kicked her legs and flailed her arms. 'Sssh, sssh.' She began to hum the little girl's favourite lullaby. Angelika put her thumb in her mouth and quietened, staring at her aunt with an anxious, cross-eyed gaze. 'Good evening, good night,' Ava sang, taking her weary niece upstairs to her room and tucking her up into her bed. Behind her, the two elder sisters continued to argue, Monika's sharp voice cutting across Bertha's softer, more plaintive tones.

'Lambie?' Angelika asked in a quavering voice. Ava passed her the bedraggled toy lamb, then went to fetch her battered copy of *Grimms' Fairy Tales* from her own room. The front cover was decorated with a silhouette of a little girl playing with a wolf in a field of flowers. It had been her father's childhood favourite book, and then Ava's. Otto had always said more wisdom was to be found in that collection of tales than in any textbook. Ava certainly had always found comfort in it, and the beautiful words consoled her now as much as they did Angelika.

Ava read her niece her favourite tale, 'The Singing, Springing Lark'. It was the story of a girl who had asked her father for the gift of a lark. The father had found the little bird in a castle garden belonging to a lion, and had been forced to give up his daughter in payment for it. The lion was only a beast by day. By night he was a man. He had been cursed by an enchantress. If any light touched him when he was in human form, he would be transformed into a dove. The girl persuaded him to come to her sister's wedding, and there a crack of light fell upon him. Her lover flew off in the shape of a bird, and the girl must follow a trail of blood and white feathers that he left behind him before she can outwit the enchantress and save him.

Ava's father believed that myths and fairy tales – like dreams – opened a window into the unconscious. By listening to the language of dreams and old tales, he said, all humans could learn to understand themselves, and the world, better. When Ava had been a little girl – not much older than Angelika – her father had read her a fairy tale every night before she went to sleep. Afterwards, he would light his pipe, the small bowl of embers glowing as he sucked upon its chewed stem, and ask Ava what she thought the story meant.

'It's about never giving up,' Ava had said the first time he read 'The Singing, Springing Lark' to her. 'It's about being brave,' she had said another time. Then, when she was a little older, she had thought the tale was about true love.

'And what do you think true love is?' her father had asked her.

'Loving even when all hope is gone,' she had answered.

He had smiled sadly and bent to kiss her on the forehead. Then he had tucked her up more warmly and left her to sleep, the book of fairy tales hidden under her pillow.

'. . . and from that time on, they lived happily until they died,' Ava read, then slowly closed the book. The little girl's damp eyelashes had fallen, and her breathing had deepened. She was asleep, one hand beneath her rosy cheek.

Ava thought about the Nazi officer. His voice had been deep and golden, like the song of a cello. He had told her she was beautiful. No-one had ever told Ava that before. Her sisters called her a grubby little gypsy. Rupert said it was a shame she was not a boy. Ava's father had always been more interested in her dreams than in her face.

Ava remembered the feel of the officer's arm, so unyielding about her waist. She felt a sharp twist of fear in her belly, a leap of her pulse. She remembered their conversation. What a fool she had been, to talk so freely to a Nazi. She kept seeing his face, with those ice-blue eyes and the strong nose. Her stomach lurched again. Her pulse thrummed in her fingertips. She was both hot and cold, light-headed and heavy-limbed. It was as if her soul had been struck by a tuning fork, all of her vibrating to a single pure note. Ava wondered what his name was, and if she would ever see him again.

Resolutely she closed her book of fairy tales and put it away on the shelf in her bedroom. She put on her nightgown and plaited her wild curls.

I'll never fall for a Nazi, she vowed.

3

Winter Frost

'Can you believe it? They want us to pay for all the damage!'

Ava gazed at Tante Thea in consternation. 'But . . . how can they do that? It wasn't your fault your apartment was destroyed. Surely the Stormtroopers should be made to pay?'

Tante Thea wrung her napkin in her hands. 'And we cannot claim anything on insurance. The government has confiscated all the insurance money. How can Herr Hitler do such a thing?'

'He's a criminal,' Jutta cried. 'He should be charged with theft and made to pay all the costs of our repairs.'

Onkel Franz pushed a piece of sausage around.

'I suppose he thinks the Jews can afford it.' Monika ate in small, angry bites. 'I mean, after all, why should the Reich pay for the damage? It wasn't their fault.'

'Oh, come on!' Jutta burst out. 'As if the whole thing wasn't planned by Hitler and his henchmen!'

'The Reich has announced it had nothing to do with it,' Monika snapped back.

'And you believe them?' Jutta asked.

Rupert laughed. He was smoking with jerky movements, keeping his cigarette well away from the cut on his lip. Otto, frowning, puffed on his pipe. Bertha sat silently, her fingers pressed to her temples. Angelika in her high chair was the only one happy. She was absorbed in banging her fork against her little wooden table. Her round face was covered with jam.

'The thing is, we cannot afford it,' Onkel Franz said in a low voice. 'We shall lose everything.'

There was a long uncomfortable silence, then Monika said, 'Well, somebody has to pay and I don't see why it should be us. If the Jews hadn't been so greedy for so long, they'd not have brought this storm of protest down upon their own heads.'

Otto looked troubled. 'Now, now, Monika, you cannot believe that . . .'

Monika made an impatient movement. 'Come now, Father, you must admit the Jews have been running things long enough!'

'That's strange,' Jutta retorted in a hard voice. 'I had no idea we were running things. If so, you'd think we'd have arranged things a little better. We'd be the ones in government and it'd be Herr Hitler and his crew locked up in concentration camps.'

Monika clicked her tongue against her teeth. 'For heaven's sake, Jutta, I don't mean you.'

'Why not? We're Jews, aren't we?'

'Well, yes, but you're not real Jews, are you? I mean, not like . . .' She gestured vaguely.

'We are real Jews, Monika,' Onkel Franz answered quietly. 'But not like that, no. No Jews are.'

'We should have gone from here when we could,' Tante Thea said to her husband. 'I told you! I told you we should go.'

'Where?' Onkel Franz asked wearily. 'Where should we have gone?'

'Anywhere,' Tante Thea shouted.

There was a long, fraught silence.

'Excuse me,' Monika said, pushing back her chair with a screech. 'I need to get back to work. I can't afford to lose my job.' She left the room, her heels tapping sharply. Bertha followed after her, whisking Angelika out of her high chair and out of the room. The little girl was not pleased to be taken from her impromptu drum. Her wails drifted back to the silent dining room.

Tante Thea looked at Otto. 'I'm so sorry. We're a great trouble to you.'

'Not at all,' he replied courteously. 'We are glad to have you. When do you think your apartment will be repaired?'

Tante Thea shrugged eloquently. Onkel Franz laid down his fork. 'You're very kind,' he said. 'It is just . . . we have the problem of paying for repairs. You know I can no longer take non-Jewish customers . . .'

'What Jew can afford a psychoanalyst now?' Tante Thea cried.

'Even if they could, no-one wants to talk in case they're overheard by a Gestapo spy,' Rupert interjected.

'These are hard times,' Otto said. 'I am losing customers also. Even clients that have been coming to me for years are no longer making appointments.' He sighed and finished the last of his sausage, then noticed that Jutta had eaten very little.

'But, Jutta, you do not eat. What is wrong? You must keep up your strength.'

'She's not hungry,' Tante Thea interjected swiftly.

Jutta spoke over the top of her. 'I cannot eat it, I'm sorry. I don't know how it was made, or what's in it.'

Otto was puzzled. 'How it was made? The usual way, I expect. And today I think the sausage is pork. Cooked with caraway seeds and allspice, if I'm not mistaken.'

'That's why I can't eat it,' Jutta replied.

Sudden comprehension dawned on Otto's face. 'Ah! Is it because it's not . . . what is the word? Kosher?' He looked at Onkel Franz. 'I'm so sorry, I didn't realise that you observed the rules of kosher.'

'We don't,' Onkel Franz replied with a strained smile and a shrug.

'But we should,' Jutta cried. 'It is part of the covenant . . . part of the Torah.' Her voice shook, and Ava looked at her in surprise. She had never thought of Jutta as being particularly religious. She had not gone to a Jewish school, or attended the synagogue.

Now Jutta gazed at her father. Her face was set and resolute, her black eyes imploring. 'Father, can't you see? It's part of *tikkun olam* . . . part of our mission to repair the world. Don't you think the world needs fixing now more than ever?'

He looked at her sadly. 'Yes, *bubbala*, indeed it does. And I wish that it was as easy as choosing not to eat pork.'

Jutta pushed her plate away, her jaw set. 'Well, I choose not to!'

Tante Thea looked embarrassed. 'I'm so sorry . . . please excuse her. Jutta doesn't mean to be rude. It has been a difficult week.' She tried to smile, but Ava could see the effort exhausted her.

'It doesn't make sense,' Rupert said to his sister. 'Of all the times to start worrying about what's in a sausage!'

'If we're to be persecuted and beaten up as Jews, we may as well live like Jews,' Jutta flashed back.

As she spoke, the door swung open and Frau Günther shuffled in. She wore a capacious apron tied on over her vast flowered dress, and shoes that seemed too small for her feet. She went around the room, clearing the plates. When she saw Jutta's untouched meal, the sausage congealing with fat, she stopped short, frowning.

'I'm sorry, I can't eat it,' Jutta said, in a clear, hard voice.

'What a waste of good food!' Frau Günther picked up the plate and banged it down on top of the others so hard it almost broke. Jutta went red.

Rupert lit a fresh cigarette, blowing a plume of smoke away from the table. Frau Günther glared at him. 'Smoking at the table! Filthy habit. Typical of you Jews.'

Otto hastily hid his pipe under the table. Clearing his throat, he said, 'Now, now, Frau Günther, no need to speak like that.'

Rupert waved the smoke away laconically. 'I'm just trying to help Herr Hitler along by poisoning my own body.'

Frau Günther pointed one squat finger at him. 'Don't you be so disrespectful, boy.'

Rupert looked away, his face set in an expression of surly rebellion that masked a deeper hurt. It made Ava angry. When she and Rupert had finished school a few months earlier, both had had high hopes of being able to study at the famous Berlin Conservatory of Music. But Jews were not permitted there anymore, and few women either. And their families were both too poor to pay the fees. Ava and Rupert had been hunting for jobs ever since. Ava had managed to get casual employment in a big department store on the Kurfürstendamm, modelling hats and dresses. It did not pay much, but at least it brought some money in and gave her something to do. Rupert, however, had had no luck.

Ava got up from the table, saying, 'Rupert is going to play for me and Angelika, Frau Günther. You know how much she loves to hear me sing.'

Frau Günther grunted. She had a soft spot for Angelika, and was always making her pastries bulging with cream and dusted with sugar. As a result, both Angelika and her mother were rather plump, as Bertha invariably took a quick bite – or two – of her daughter's treats.

Tante Thea got up. 'We are making a great deal of extra work for you, Frau Günther. I am sorry. Shall Jutta and I come and help you wash up?'

The housekeeper looked horrified. 'No, thank you!' She waddled away, her tray clinking with plates. Tante Thea flushed, and Jutta put her arm about her waist.

'Frau Günther likes to keep her kitchen to herself,' Otto said. 'She did not mean to be rude.'

'It is hard . . . all these extra people in your house . . . we cannot thank you enough.' Tante Thea's voice shook.

'It is only temporary.' Otto got up and tapped his pipe out absent-mindedly in his saucer. 'Franz, since you are here, I thought I'd get your opinion on a difficult case of what I think may be narcissistic mortification . . .'

'Is that a euphemism for masturbation?' Rupert whispered in Ava's ear.

'Sssh! Come and play for me.' She caught his hand and led him out into the hallway.

The two friends ran upstairs, and Ava knocked gently on her sister's door.

'Bertha!' she called. 'Do you want me to sing to Angelika?'

Bertha opened the door at once. 'Oh, would you? She's still so unsettled. Having all these people banging about the house at all hours has just ruined her routine. I don't think either of us got a wink of sleep last night.'

'I'm sorry,' Ava said. Rupert did not say anything, though the look of surliness settled back down over his face.

Angelika had heard Ava's voice and crab-crawled swiftly across the rug, smiling. Bertha had washed her daughter's face, so Angelika's pale hair hung in soft, damp ringlets. Ava picked her up. Her niece grabbed hold of her curls and pulled. 'Sing?' she asked.

Ava began to sing 'Twinkle, Twinkle, Little Star' while trying to free her hair. Angelika let go so she could croon along, making the gestures to the song with her pudgy little hands. Ava carried her down the hall, Rupert close behind.

In the music room, the big windows were all blurred with frost. Outside Ava could see the cupola of the telegraph office lit up against a darkening sky, its crowning spire as green as pistachio ice-cream. Dark leaves whirled past in a bitter wind from the east, and the road was slick with ice.

Rupert sat sideways on the piano stool and began to play the tune with great dramatic flourishes. Angelika struggled to get down, and so Ava put her on the floor. The little girl at once crawled over to Rupert, dragged herself up on his leg, and began to bang on the keys with both hands, mimicking him. Ava shook her hair loose and opened the window, letting the fresh damp air of the November afternoon press its cold hands against her hot skin.

'Will you play me "Bye, Bye, Blackbird"?' she asked. 'Angelika heard me singing it last week and seemed to really love it.'

Obediently Rupert began to play the tune, golden-green like new spring leaves in a ruffling wind. As Ava began to sing, Angelika swivelled around and stared at her. Then she slid down from Rupert's knee and crawled towards her aunt in her usual clumsy way. Uttering shrill cries of delight, she staggered to her feet, hauling herself up on Ava's leg.

Still singing, Ava drew the little girl on to her lap. Her soft body sagged into Ava's, and she put the thumb of her other hand into her mouth.

Ava hugged her closer. Angelika was the sweetest thing to cuddle. As Ava reached the end of the chorus, Angelika sat up, took her thumb out, and sang along. 'Bye-bye!' she sang.

Ava was thrilled. This was a new expression for Angelika. Though there was no doubt 'bye-bye' was easier for a little girl to say than 'Auf Wiedersehen', it was still exciting to hear Angelika speak a new word.

'Can you start again?' Ava asked Rupert.

Rupert obliged. Ava stood up, and began to dance slowly about the room, Angelika on her hip. Ava sang the first lines, then paused, allowing Angelika to sing the chorus alone. She sang, clear as a bell. 'Bye-bye, blackbird!'

'She's singing it!' Ava cried. It felt like a breakthrough. Angelika was almost three years old. She had all her baby teeth, yet she could say only a few mumbled words. Other children her age were running about and naming everything they saw, but not Angelika. The doctors said she had mongoloid imbecility, and there was no cure. This news had cast Bertha into the blackest depths of despair, made even worse when her husband was killed by a car only a few weeks later. Bertha had always refused to admit the doctors' prognosis had been right. She tried to pretend all was well with her daughter, when anyone could see that was not true.

Angelika and Ava sang the chorus again, dancing about the room, then Ava began to experiment with scat singing. This was something black singers like Ella Fitzgerald and Louis Armstrong did, and could only be heard on records smuggled in from America. Ava loved to improvise with her voice as if it was a trumpet or a saxophone. Angelika clapped her hands and tried to join in, singing, 'da-da-dah-doo!' at the top of her voice.

Bertha opened the door and said crossly, 'Have you not seen the time? It's Angel's nap time!' She took her daughter from Ava's arms. Angelika did not want to go at all, and began to fight her mother. Her wails grew softer as she was carried away down the hall.

Rupert sat sideways on the piano stool, hitting the one key over and over. His long face was melancholy, his mobile mouth downturned. He had lit another cigarette. Smoke wreathed about his head. Ava stood by the open window, looking out at the street below. 'You feeling blue?' she asked.

'So blue, baby,' he replied. 'I don't know what we're to do.' Then he grinned. 'I sound like a blues song.'

His fingers strayed into a tune Ava recognised. Softly she began to sing the Ella Fitzgerald song 'Under the Spell of the Blues'. It was a favourite tune of Ava's and Rupert's. They often performed it, though Rupert would much prefer to have been playing it on his trumpet, in some smoky basement somewhere, where his face could not be seen.

Gazing out the window, Ava saw a man standing in the shadow of the telegraph office, looking up at her. He was tall and dressed in field grey. Her stomach somersaulted. She leant forward, wondering: *is it him?*

It was.

Ava would know that aquiline nose anywhere. She stepped back from the window, one hand flying up to her throat. The song died away.

Rupert let his hands still, turning towards her inquisitively.

'I think he's out there,' Ava told him. 'That Nazi who threw the Storm-troopers out of your apartment.'

'Why would he be here?'

'I don't know,' Ava answered, though part of her felt she knew.

Rupert got up and came to look out the window, despite Ava's pleas not to. 'There's no-one there,' he reported. 'You must have imagined him. Don't tell me you're turning into a brown goose, swooning over Nazis like all those other idiotic girls.'

'He's not a Brownshirt. His uniform was grey, not brown. Those Stormtroopers at your apartment said he was with the Abwehr, whatever that is.'

Rupert turned pale. 'A spy? That officer of yours is a spy? Why would he be spying on us?'

'A spy? What do you mean?'

'The Abwehr is the secret intelligence service. Don't you know anything?'

'Not about spies,' Ava answered.

'It's not really meant to exist. But it does. And it reports direct to Hitler.'

Ava sat down. Suddenly she desperately wanted a cigarette. She picked up the one Rupert had left smouldering in the ashtray and took a deep drag. Smoke wreathed about her head, hiding her face.

'Why would he be here?' Rupert said. 'Did he follow us from our apartment? But why? Does he have a file on us?'

'We should be more careful,' Ava said. 'We shouldn't have been playing jazz.'

Rupert jerked one shoulder irritably. 'I'm sick of being careful. I don't want to spend my life creeping around, looking over my shoulder all the time, afraid people are listening to what I say. Life is for dancing and singing and falling in love, not living in little boxes like tin soldiers, everyone the same.'

'I know.' Ava tried to smile at him. 'But you don't want to draw attention to yourself, Rupert. Or me! They hate German girls that hang out with Jewish boys, you know that.'

'Even if the Jew is German too?' He twisted his mouth in a familiar bitter shape. 'Besides, Mama is only half-Jewish. And Father fought in the Great War. He's a decorated war hero. That should mean something, even to that Stormtrooper of yours.'

'He's not a Stormtrooper,' Ava said again, though she did not know why she should defend him. 'Anyway, what does it matter? He's gone now.'

Just then they heard a knock on the front door.

Ava's heart moved painfully. She looked at Rupert. 'Is it him?' she whispered. *Stupid, stupid*, she thought. *You've got to learn to mind your tongue!*

Angelika begin to wail as she was woken from her sleep.

Ava stood frozen. There was no-one else home. Otto and Onkel Franz had walked to the river to feed the ducks, as they did every afternoon. Frau Günther had gone to the butcher's. Tante Thea and Jutta were spending each day cleaning out the Feidlers' apartment, and trying to sell its contents to help raise the money for the Atonement Tax. Monika was at work.

The knocking came at the front door again. Bertha sighed noisily, and got out of bed. Ava heard her sister make her way down the stairs, and ran to try and stop her. Rupert loped along at her heels, saying, 'Ava's gone red! Is she soft on the Nazi, I wonder?'

'Shut up.' Ava turned to punch him, hard, on the arm.

Bertha had reached the ground floor. 'Don't answer it!' Ava called.

'Why ever not?' she replied, and opened the door. Angelika was on her hip as always, grizzling noisily. Ava heard the clipped aristocratic tones of the Nazi officer asking after her. Fräulein Ava Falkenhorst, he said. Ava felt a flare of panic. How did he know her name?

'I'm sorry,' Bertha said in that sweet vague way of hers. 'What do you want with Ava? I do not think I know you, sir. Do I?'

'Ava, Ava.' Angelika clapped her hands.

'I have not yet had the pleasure of meeting you,' the officer answered. 'I met your sister briefly the other night, during the . . .' He hesitated, then went on smoothly, 'disturbances.'

'Ava should not have been out in that madness,' Bertha said.

'No,' he agreed.

'Ava sing?' Angelika asked. She gazed up at the soldier with blue eyes, her plump tongue protruding from her mouth. 'Ava sing now!' She began to try and mimic Ava's scat singing, 'doo-doo-da-da-dah-doo,' waving her arms around as if conducting.

'Sssh, Angel,' Bertha said, her cheeks colouring.

'So is Ava . . . is your sister at home?'

Bertha shifted Angelika to the other hip. 'I don't know. I suppose . . .'

She turned indecisively. She saw Ava and Rupert hanging over the balustrades, and raised one eyebrow. Ava shook her head, moving her hands in a sharp negative gesture.

Bertha turned back to the soldier. 'I'm so sorry . . .'

Then she retreated a step, then another.

The Nazi officer stepped inside the doorway and looked up at Ava. He held his cap under his arm. His hair was fair and cropped close, his eyes as pale as winter frost. Tall and athletically built, the severe lines of his uniform accentuated his broad shoulders and narrow waist. If it had not been for the crooked line of his nose, his face would have been the very ideal of masculine beauty, with slightly hollowed cheeks below strong cheekbones. Ava heard Rupert give a little sigh of admiration, while Bertha surreptitiously patted her crown of braids to make sure all was neat.

'Fräulein Falkenhorst. I am glad to see you have suffered no lasting harm,' the Nazi officer said, then added with a sarcastic edge to his voice, 'despite the company you keep.' He glanced at Rupert, then moved his intense gaze back to Ava's face. 'I was wondering if you would like to accompany me for a walk in the Tiergarten?'

Ava coloured. 'No, thank you. I . . . I'm afraid I'm busy right now.'

His gaze moved back to Rupert, and he frowned. 'Tomorrow perhaps?'

'I'm busy tomorrow too.'

For a moment, he stood still, looking displeased. Ava felt her stomach muscles clench. The very sight of his uniform was enough to make anyone nervous, but it was the chill in his eyes that most unsettled her. Ava set her jaw, determined not to be intimidated. He bowed, clicking his heels together, then turned and walked out, shutting the door crisply behind him.

'Hot diggedy dog!' Rupert said.

The Hot Club

Most of the broken glass had been swept up, but empty shop windows gaped from behind hastily tacked-up boards. Everything was eerily quiet. A few people scurried along, their heads ducked down, hats pulled low. It was cold, and the sun had left only a smear of red along the square shapes of the university buildings. Brown leaves skittered along in the wind, and the few trees held up a tracery of black twigs against the leaden sky.

'Maybe we shouldn't have come,' Ava said.

'Rubbish! Don't you see, if we spend our days skulking about inside, too scared to put our noses outdoors, we're letting the Nazis win.' Rupert twirled his black umbrella. He wasn't carrying it because of the fear of rain. It was part of the English dandy look he was trying to emulate. He wore a baggy suit with a cravat, a long white silk scarf, and an old fedora on his slicked-back hair. Sometimes he carried a pipe and a rolled up copy of *The Times*, if he could get hold of one. Ava thought he secretly longed for a monocle.

'Why was Jutta so cross about us going out?' Ava asked.

Rupert shrugged. 'She thinks I should take things more seriously. Just because she's spending all day at the Jewish Cultural Centre and taking Hebrew lessons, she thinks I should too. It's all so frightfully boring.'

He spoke the last few words in English, in what he thought was an upper-class accent.

'It sounds very serious,' Ava said doubtfully. Jutta had always been both bookish and mulish, but lately she had taken it to whole new levels, studying all day and being difficult about doing chores on Saturdays. It was hard on Tante Thea, who was very much suffering from the pressure of trying to be a good house-guest.

'No fun at all,' Rupert agreed. 'But don't you worry, Ava, we'll have a good time tonight. I think Hans Kaufmann will be there, the one who's sweet on you.'

'Him! He's just a boy.'

'Particularly compared to that handsome Nazi of yours,' Rupert teased.

'I keep telling you, he's not mine.'

'Shame about his broken nose. He'd be one "Heil Hottler" otherwise.'

'I like his nose,' Ava protested, then turned red, knowing she had given herself away. Rupert laughed.

They came to the corner and turned down it. The smell of smoke stung Ava's nostrils. There, on the right, was the burnt-out hulk of what had been a Jewish kindergarten. Nothing was left but blackened timbers and charred rubble.

'They even fired the kindergarten?' she said in disbelief. 'Poor little kiddies, coming in the morning to find their school burnt down.'

'You think the Nazis care about Jewish kids?' Rupert returned.

Ava felt an ember of fury burning in her breast. She wished there was something she could do, but she was just a girl. What could she possibly do?

A few blocks later, Ava and Rupert came to a narrow lane between two high buildings. Looking about to make sure they had not been followed, they slipped down the alley. They passed a doorway in which a small boy sat huddled in a coat much too big for him. He gave them a thumbs-up sign as they passed; he was the Hot Club's lookout.

Opposite him, set low in the wall, were two steel doors. Ava tapped softly three times, then heard the rusty grating sound of the bolt being lifted and the doors being pushed open from within.

Rupert held the doors open as Ava climbed down a steep set of stairs into a cellar. It was lit with only a few candles stuck in saucers and the glow of rusty old hurricane lanterns, and was full of dark, jostling figures. This cellar was the secret headquarters of the Hot Club, a group of jazz lovers and swing dancers that met every Monday to play and sing and dance. Rupert passed down his trumpet, then clambered down himself. The doors were hastily pulled shut, and the bolt drawn again.

'Hey, Hot-Lips! Hey, Swing Doll!' Hans Kaufmann called, lifting one hand.

'Hey, jazz cats!' Rupert responded. 'Ready to cut loose?'

'Yeah,' a few people responded. Most were subdued. Ava looked around. Rupert was not the only one with a black eye and cut lip. One boy had his arm in a sling; another had a nasty bruise on his forehead; and another's hand was wrapped in bandages. All the talk was of the Night of Broken Glass. Many of the members of the Hot Club were Jewish, or had Jewish blood, which made them Mischlinge, or cross-breeds, in the Nazis' eyes. Many had had their homes invaded, their parents' businesses raided and wrecked, or members of their families arrested and deported.

'Let's not talk about it, it's all too awful,' said a pretty Jewish girl named Stella Goldschlag who used to go to school with Jutta. She had been told many times that she looked like Jean Harlow, and so she wore her hair in the same stiff blonde curls and plucked her eyebrows till they were almost non-existent. 'Let's get swinging.'

Rupert put a record on the gramophone, and the familiar music of 'Sing, Sing, Sing with a Swing' rang out. Ava danced with Rupert, who was the only boy tall enough to really get her swinging. They spun around and around and up and down till she could scarcely catch her breath. Someone had brought some jitter-sauce – gin mixed with 'pink' bitters. Ava had hers with tonic, but Rupert and most of the boys drank it straight. The cellar was blue with cigarette smoke. Hitler hated cigarettes, so all the jazz cats of the Hot Club loved them on principle.

Listening to jazz and swing was banned, of course. Herr Goebbels, the Reich Minister of Propaganda, called it 'niggerjazz' and 'jazzbazillus', as if it was some kind of disease. Ava and Rupert loved it passionately. Whenever they could, they sneaked out to watch Hollywood movies like *Swing Time* with Fred Astaire and Ginger Rogers, or *Day at the Races* with the Marx Brothers. There was one scene in that film which Ava just loved, where black male dancers threw their short-skirted partners up into the air and spun them in deft somersaults. All the dancers skipped and swung and spun as if they were so full of joy they were just about ready to burst out of their skins.

Ava had never seen anything like it. She and Rupert had been determined to try it. Singing at the top of their voices, they had hopped and kicked and swung all over the Feidlers' living room, knocking over a lamp and breaking a vase along the way.

Ava loved the way old-fashioned opera and new-fashioned jazz reeled together in that movie. Tante Thea always said one had to cancel out the other, and that Ava was ruining her voice by singing jazz. When Ava sang opera, Tante Thea would say, 'Your mother would be so proud.' When Tante Thea caught Ava singing jazz, she'd say, 'What would your father say if he heard you singing such trash?'

Ava's father loved opera. *La Traviata* was his favourite, and would move him to tears every time he listened to it. As a little girl, Ava would lie in bed and listen as he played the Violetta aria again and again, and she knew he would be drinking schnapps and weeping. Ava would wonder if he was thinking of her mother. He had first seen her performing in *La Traviata* as one of the gypsy girls. 'She was the most beautiful thing I had ever seen,' he told Ava once, much to her sisters' displeasure.

Ava wanted to make her father proud of her. She wanted to sing as her mother had once sung, in all those big gaudy dramas of love and despair. She wanted to be part of the world that Tante Thea described with such yearning. Yet . . . yet . . . It all seemed so serious and grown-up. It made Ava feel restless and defiant. She wanted some fun, some freedom, first.

So Ava and Rupert spent all their spare time listening to American records and trying to sing the songs. They were all sung in English, of course. Both Ava and Rupert had studied English at the Musikgymnasium, along with French and Italian, for languages were important for anyone who wished for a career in music. However, even though they were quite fluent in English, many of the songs simply didn't make much sense. (*Why would anyone sing about hot nuts?* Ava wondered.)

Her favourite song of all time was Billie Holiday singing 'Summertime', with Artie Shaw on clarinet and Bunny Berigan on trumpet. Billie's voice was not perfect by any means. It was tremulous, even weak. There were no astonishing vocal acrobatics, no extraordinary range. Yet it raised all the hairs on Ava's arms. As Billie Holiday sang, Ava saw in her mind's eye a sad-eyed black woman with her head wrapped in a kerchief, rocking a drowsy child in her arms. The endless flat cotton fields stretched away to the horizon, sharp-etched thorns snagging blowsy white balls like clouds hooked from the sky. The light was golden, thunderous. White-winged birds soared high. But the black woman must stay, pinned to the spot, to that life. Her voice broke. She could sing no longer. So the two voices of the trumpet and the clarinet sang for her, giving her the strength to lift her voice again, to spin out that thin thread of hope to the sleeping child.

Listening to that song, Ava felt it in every cell of her body. It made her want to cry, thickening her throat and burning her eyes. It made her want to dance, a slow sun-worshipping sway, lifting her arms to the sky. It made her want to sing.

Ava played that song till it was a wonder she did not wear the record through. She taught herself to mimic Billie's voice, though never could she quite manage that quaver of deep-felt emotion, that weariness at life. Rupert bought himself a battered old trumpet from some jumble sale, teaching himself to play so he could accompany her as she sang.

And so Ava's dreams changed. She no longer wanted to stand on a stage in a great dark cavernous hall, dressed in some elaborate dress, her voice as controlled as clockwork. She saw herself leaning on an old piano in some candlelit bar, her hair loose, her voice breaking as she sang out all she truly felt in the hidden recesses of her soul. Her voice and the voice of Rupert's trumpet would croon together and, somewhere in the audience, someone's breath would catch.

Ava and Rupert loved jazz because it was all about celebrating the individual. Jazz was improvisation, innovation, inspiration. Nazism was all about subjugating the individual. It was control, constraint, constipation.

And so they defied it the only way they knew how by singing and dancing and swinging.

When Ava grew weary, she sat and cooled herself with a fan made of sheet music, drinking another pink fizz, and listening as Stella sang 'My Lucky Valentine' in a sweet, breathy voice. Stella's voice was not wonderful, but she looked like a film star. She was even wearing lipstick and Ava couldn't help but wonder where she had got it from. Like most of the other girls, Ava had had to resort to sucking red lollies to get some colour into her lips.

Then Ava sang another love song, trying hard not to think about the Nazi officer.

Stella and her boyfriend, Manfred, stood kissing and calling it slow dancing; a few others spooned in the dark corners. Rupert did a long and virtuosic solo of 'The Very Thought of You' on his trumpet. A beautiful boy with a melancholy face and a halo of black curls sat gazing up at him. When Rupert had finished, he put his trumpet away and sat beside the curly haired boy. He put two cigarettes in his mouth and lit them both, then passed one to the boy, who took it with a shy smile. They smoked and talked for a while in low, intense voices. When Ava glanced over later, it looked as if the boy was crying. Rupert comforted him, one arm about his shoulder.

A boy Ava knew named Heinz Joachim played something beautiful and melancholy on his saxophone, then Ava sang again. Rupert pulled the curly headed boy up, and they began to dance a languid foxtrot together, cigarettes hanging from the corners of their mouths. When Ava had finished, Rupert pulled the boy over.

'Ava, this is Felix. Can you sing "Body and Soul" for us?'

'If you like,' Ava said, smiling at Felix. He did not meet her eyes, but ducked his head shyly in greeting. He was one of the prettiest boys Ava had ever seen. Inwardly, she sighed. Whenever Rupert was in love, he was lost to her for a few weeks. And, by the look on his face now, he was well and truly smitten.

Rupert and Felix danced together. Gradually they pressed closer into each other's arms. Then a girl named Irmgard Zarden sang. Irmgard's father had been some bigwig in the government, but had been forcibly retired because he was Jewish. It made Ava feel sad. She was dancing with Hans Kaufmann. When he tried to kiss her, she let him.

She felt nothing.

Suddenly there came a frenzied knocking on the steel doors. Ava snatched the record off the gramophone and shoved it into its brown paper slip. Rupert grabbed his trumpet. Everybody else blew out candles and lanterns, and gathered up their coats and musical instruments. Rupert caught Ava's hand, and they all made a rush for the stairs that led out of the cellar. In the alley outside Ava could hear the tramping of boots, then the rattling of the steel doors. Stella sobbed in terror. Manfred tried to shush her.

Upstairs, the windows were boarded up. It was dark. Ava heard broken glass splinter under her shoes. 'Sssh,' someone hissed. Someone began banging on the boards, shouting, 'Attention! Attention!'

Ava ran as quietly as she could up to the next floor, following Rupert. He drew aside a board that had not been nailed down properly. Ava crept out first, then Irmgard, then Felix, everyone scrambling away over the rooftops. Ava looked back anxiously, and saw Rupert's tall, lean shape as he clambered awkwardly out the window, his trumpet wedged under one arm.

'Dammit, I left my umbrella behind,' he grumbled.

'Come on!'

'Stop them!' someone shouted. Ava heard a pistol shot. Timber splintered.

'Run!' Rupert yelled. Everyone bolted away, slipping and slithering on the roof tiles, then jumped over a narrow laneway, the boys helping catch the girls.

The only way down was via a rusty drainpipe at the far end of the building. When Ava stumbled to the ground, she found herself in one of the university quadrangles. A statue of the Führer brooded in the centre. Behind her, she heard the sound of jackboots running.

'We have to get away,' Felix panted.

'Down here!' Irmgard pointed down a long archway. Everyone ran.

Rupert's white scarf had slipped and fallen. On impulse Ava seized hold of it and ran to the statue of the Führer. She clambered up the base of the statue and wound the scarf round and round Hitler's mouth, tying it tight. 'That should shut him up for a while,' she cried.

'You're crazy,' Rupert cried. He was laughing. 'Come on!'

Ava raced after him, glad of her rubber-soled plimsolls. She made it into the shadow of the archway just as black-clad SS soldiers ran into the quadrangle. They did not see her, though Ava could hear them cursing as they saw their Führer had been gagged.

'Find them!' their leader ordered.

Ava bolted into the darkness, her ears filled with the pitiless march of jackboots.

5

Her Mother's Chest

Ava sat at her father's desk, typing away as well as she could using only four fingers. Otto lay on his couch, his old tabby cat Muschi asleep on his stomach like a huge furry blanket. He was dictating: 'In order to clarify the investigation of such irrational mass psychological phenomena comma it is necessary to understand that the Oedipus spelt O-E-D-. . .'

'I know how to spell Oedipus,' Ava answered, banging away at the typewriter keys.

'Good, good, now what was I saying?'

Ava read him back the sentence and he went on, 'That's right . . . "the Oedipus complex most often arises from the repression of childhood sexuality born out of the natural fear of castration . . ."'

'What about girls?' Ava asked.

Otto was surprised. 'What about them?'

'Well, they can't have a natural fear of castration, can they? And lots of girls are brown gooses; they're always fainting at the sight of Hitler.'

'That's a whole different psychopathology,' Otto said.

'But interesting, don't you think?'

'No doubt . . . but now I've lost my train of thought . . .'

'So do you think Hitler has castration anxiety?'

'Perhaps, perhaps,' Otto said cautiously. 'He certainly has eroticised homicidal megalomania. It may be born out of castration anxiety.'

Ava rested her hands on the keys of the typewriter as Otto expounded on this theory. She could remember when her father had thought the Führer nothing but a clown. 'No-one can take Herr Hitler seriously,' he had said. 'He'll be laughed out of the Reichstag.'

Ava and Rupert had been fourteen when the Nazis came to power. They had certainly thought Hitler a funny little man then. They used to practise the high-kicking march they called 'the piercing step', and turn it into a can-can. Then Rupert would make Ava laugh as he mimicked the Führer giving a speech, the Charlie Chaplin moustache drawn on with charcoal. He'd thump the table, and shout, 'We will be the one and only power in Germany! The one! The only! All the rest of you, go screw yourselves!'

One day, a few months after Hitler was elected Chancellor, Ava and Rupert were at his apartment when they heard distant shouting and singing. It was a drizzly May evening. Although the sun had already long set, the clouds to the west were lit up with a brilliant tangerine glow. Their fathers were late coming home from the university that night, and Tante Thea was busy teaching a student whose voice was as awful as a yowling cat. Laughing, Rupert and Ava had pulled on their coats and sneaked out to see what was happening. They ran across the bridge and past the Old Museum, following the sound of cheers and roars of excitement. The air smelt of smoke. Ava saw red sparks flying in the wind. 'It's a bonfire,' she cried. 'But it's not Walpurgis Night.'

They ran towards Unter den Linden. People were everywhere, excited faces lit red by the flames which could be seen above the Crown Prince's palace. Then Ava could hear a man shouting, the sound amplified by loudspeakers. She stopped, feeling a sudden creeping dread. 'Come on!' Rupert had shouted.

Ava hurried after him, towards the Opernplatz. The crowd was too thick to run now. She had to squeeze her way through. They came into the square, lined with stately buildings – the State Opera House, St

Hedwig's Cathedral with its vast turquoise-green dome, and the massive stone bulk of the university's law faculty. In the centre of the square was a huge bonfire, flames clawing upwards. Rupert took Ava's hand, and they wriggled through the hordes of cheering people. Ava could hear amplified shouting, echoing off the buildings. Straining over people's shoulders, she saw Herr Doktor Goebbels. He stood at a table draped with a swastika flag. Brownshirts massed all around him, waving more of the scarlet and black flags. It was hard to hear Goebbels' words, because everyone was cheering so much. Ava managed to squeeze to the front, Rupert beside her.

They were burning books. Thousands of them. Young men hurled them into the fire, their eyes lit with tiny red dancing flames. People were running out of the university library, tossing more books into the hungry maw of the bonfire. Some students even trundled wheelbarrows full.

'This is a strong, great and symbolic deed ... from this wreckage the phoenix of a new spirit will triumphantly rise,' Goebbels yelled. People cheered, their right hands slashing upwards.

Ava was puzzled and upset. 'But why?' she asked Rupert. 'Why are they burning all the books?'

Rupert took her hand. 'Let's go home,' he said. 'Father would not want us here.'

They hurried away, pushing against the crowd. The sound of chanting rang in Ava's ears, making her head ache. Her hair smelt of smoke. She could not get the images of those cheering young men with their red glittering eyes out of her mind.

The two crept into the apartment as quietly as they could, and washed the smuts from their faces and hands. The smell of smoke hung around them.

When Otto and Onkel Franz at last got back to the Feidlers' apartment, they were grave-faced and silent. Ava's father's white hair stuck up from his head as if he had tried tearing it all out. He had two bags of books with him, so heavy Ava could see the handles cutting into the flesh of his hands.

As Ava and her father walked home through the fire-lit streets, he told her that he had resigned from the university. 'They've sacked Franz, and all my friends too. Instead, the Nazis are setting up a new department of racial sciences. Ava, the whole of Germany seems gripped in some kind of perverse collective pathology.'

'They're burning books in the Opernplatz,' she told him.

He nodded. 'I know. I've saved what I could.'

'But why, Father? I can't understand why.'

He stopped, dropping his bags at his feet so he could seize her by the shoulders. 'Because books are dangerous! Nothing opens up the mind and the heart like books do, and so they have the power to change the whole world. That's why they are burning books, Ava. To stop us thinking, and feeling, and imagining . . .' He could not go on. Pulling his handkerchief from his breast pocket, he mopped his eyes and blew his nose. 'That is why we must do all we can to resist them. They would make us robots without a soul.'

He had picked up his heavy burden, and walked on in silence.

'What are you going to do?' Ava had asked at last. She was amazed and troubled. Her father loved teaching at the university.

He had tried to smile. 'Perhaps I shall write a book.'

Otto no longer called Hitler a clown. The Führer had, he said, a dangerous case of narcissistic personality disorder. It was the subject of his book, which he called 'The Abnormal Psychology of Fascism as Repressed Oedipal Fixation'. He had few patients anymore, perhaps because everyone was too afraid to speak openly about their fears.

It was quiet and warm in Ava's father's study, the firelight dancing over his bust of Herr Doktor Freud and Otto's prized Kandinsky painting. Ava's laboured typing, her father's soft voice, and the loud purring of the cat were the only sounds. Ava was tired, with aching feet, after a day spent selling gloves and hats in the pre-Christmas rush, but she treasured this time alone with her father and knew that his book – impossible to publish – made him feel as if he was doing something worthwhile, some kind of protest against the collective madness that gripped Germany.

The phone rang. Ava looked up in surprise. It was not a sound she heard often anymore. She went out into the hall to answer it, hoping it was someone wanting to make an appointment to see her father. To her astonishment, it was someone named Frau Wirth ringing to ask if Ava was free to sing at a Christmas concert later that week. Ava said, with as much composure as she could muster, that she believed she was free. After she rang off, Ava looked across to her father, standing in the study doorway, and managed to tell him the news. She was breathless with excitement.

'Frau Wirth just discovered that the singer she had booked has a Jewish grandmother,' Ava explained. 'She says I was recommended to her!'

'Who by?' Otto wanted to know.

'I didn't think to ask,' Ava confessed. 'I was too excited. Maybe someone from school.'

She rushed across to the sitting room to tell Tante Thea, who was sitting by the fire, mending stockings. Both Ava's sisters sat on the couch nearby. Bertha was knitting and Monika was manicuring her nails. The radio was on, filling the room with tinny sentimental music. Angelika sat playing on the floor, banging two wooden animals together over and over again. She was delighted at the noise she was making, but Monika looked annoyed.

Jutta sat at the table with a great pile of books. She spent all her time studying, though she knew better than anyone that there was no hope of her ever being allowed to go to university. Her eyes were stormy and her cheeks flushed, and Ava hoped one of her sisters had not said something to upset her. Monika in particular took pride in always telling the brutal truth. Sometimes Ava thought it was the brutality that Monika was proud of, rather than the honesty.

'I've been offered a singing job!' Ava spoke as gaily as possible, hoping to ease the tension in the room.

'Will you be paid?' Monika wanted to know.

'A little. It may lead to more work, though,' Ava answered.

Monika snorted. 'That would be helpful.' She went back to filing her nails.

'Oh, Ava, this is a wonderful chance for you,' Tante Thea said. 'Who is the concert for?'

'Some government bigwigs. Oh, what do you think I should sing?'

'You must do "Ave Maria", of course, and some of Schubert's lieder,' Tante Thea replied, putting down her darning.

'And maybe a few carols, since it is Christmas time,' Bertha suggested.

'Have you not heard?' Monika said. 'The Party has banned Christmas carols and nativity plays. There's to be no Christmas this year, only celebration of the midwinter solstice.'

Bertha was distressed. 'No Christmas? But I was so looking forward to decorating the tree with Angelika. She's big enough now to really love it.'

At the sound of her name, Angelika looked up and smiled. Her soft blonde ringlets were tied back in two little pigtails, and she was wearing a blue-checked dress that brought out the starry colour of her eyes. Had it not been for her cross-eyed gaze and her sticky-out tongue, she would have been the prettiest little girl imaginable.

'We're still allowed a Christmas tree,' Monika said. 'We just shouldn't put angels and stars and things on it.'

'Oh, all right then,' Bertha answered in relief. 'I wouldn't like Angelika to miss out.'

Angelika crawled over to her mother and dragged herself up. Bertha lifted her up on to her lap and Angelika pressed her plump cheeks between her hands. 'Mama, mama,' she babbled. Bertha's eyes filled with tears. 'We don't need tinsel angels when we've got you, do we, darling?' She cuddled her daughter so tightly that Angelika began to struggle to be free. With a sigh, Bertha put her down.

'What, no Christmas carols at all?' Ava said. 'It's a Christmas concert!' Monika shrugged.

'Whatever shall I wear?' Ava clasped her hands together anxiously.

'Your good white frock?' Bertha suggested.

'It makes me look about twelve, and it's far too short.'

'Well, don't expect me to pay for a new dress,' Monika said. She seemed to take any opportunity to remind the family that she was the only one earning a steady income. She worked as a secretary for some officer at the Schutzstaffel, wearing tight dark suits as close to a uniform as she could get, and walking every morning to Prinz-Albrecht-Strasse, where the SS offices were located next to the Gestapo.

Bertha folded her arms, leaning back in her chair. 'Well, you can't borrow my blue dress, Ava. You know it wouldn't fit and I can't have you letting it down, it's my only good dress.'

Clothes were an ongoing problem for Ava. As the third daughter, many of her clothes were hand-me-downs. Since she was taller than her sisters, their dresses had to be remade to fit her. Ava hated sewing more than anything else in the world, but Tante Thea was a fine seamstress and so she altered most of Ava's clothes for her. Hand-me-downs were rarer than ever, though, and so Ava felt she had been wearing the same clothes since she was about fifteen.

'I need an evening gown,' she said, troubled.

Otto had followed her into the sitting room, and was bending over by the fire to tap out his pipe on a log. He looked at Ava. 'I kept all your mother's old clothes. I'm sure you'd find something in there if you look.'

'What a good idea!' Tante Thea exclaimed. 'Clementina had some beautiful evening clothes. It was very important for us to always appear at our best.'

'Really?' Ava gazed at her father in surprise. She had never known he had kept some of her mother's clothes, and wished she had known earlier.

'I only kept a few of her favourite things,' he answered. 'They're in an old chest in the back of my dressing-room.'

Just then, Rupert and his father came in, looking chilled and unhappy. They went to stand by the fire, holding out their hands to the blaze. Ava jumped up to pour them some coffee.

'I've had some good news.' She told Rupert about the singing job. 'Do you want to come and look through my mother's old dresses? Father thinks there may be something in there I can wear.'

They found the chest at the back of Otto's dressing-room. It was a veritable treasure trove. Folded neatly in tissue paper were two of the most beautiful dresses Ava had ever seen. Both had a designer's label sewn carefully into the inner hem. *Fortuny*, she read.

One was made of pleated golden silk, with straps of glowing glass beads in the same colour. It looked rather like a sack when Ava held it up, but once she slipped it over her head, it clung to every line and curve. The colour suited her warm olive skin, and changed the colour of her eyes to that of sunlight in a forest pool.

'Hot diggedy dog, Ava!' Rupert said, sitting on the bed. 'You'll be breaking hearts.'

Ava gazed at herself in the mirror in amazement.

'Try the next one on,' he said.

The second dress was made of glimmering silver satin, cut very simply, and delicately embroidered with the most exquisite designs in silver thread. The back was so low that Ava could see the little dimples just above her buttocks.

The chest also contained two pairs of shoes, one silver and one gold, with matching beaded bags; glittering strands of crystal beads; several pairs of long white gloves, a little stained around the fingertips; a fan of white ostrich feathers; and a white velvet mantle lined with silk. At the very bottom of the chest was a small, hand-sewn pouch of black velvet. Inside was a bunch of twigs tied together with green thread, an acorn, a shell with a hole Ava could put her finger through, and a white feather. Ava only glanced at the contents. She was far more interested in the clothes.

'Why did Father never tell me about this before? Think of the fun we could have had dressing up!'

'That's probably why,' Rupert replied dryly. He took the fan of ostrich feathers and fluttered it to and fro. 'Your mother must have been a bit of a doll.'

'If so, then so was your mother,' Ava flashed back. 'She introduced my parents.'

'Hard to believe,' he answered. 'Try the shoes, Ava.'

She sat down on the edge of the bed and pulled on the golden shoes. They too fitted perfectly.

'Try on the silver ones,' Rupert said, lying on his side, supporting his head with one arm. Ava bent and took off one shoe, and unbuckled the next.

At that very moment Frau Günther came into the room, laden with folded clothes. She gave a cry of horror. 'What are you doing in here!'

'I'm just trying on my mother's old clothes,' Ava explained.

Frau Günther pointed a squat finger at Rupert. 'With him watching?'

'Oh I don't mind,' Rupert answered. 'I've seen Ava naked before. We had baths together when we were babies.'

Ava cast him a look of exasperation, and tried to explain that she had not changed in front of him but in the dressing-room.

Frau Günther did not listen. 'Out, out, both of you!'

Ava got to her feet, puzzled by the old housekeeper's vehemence. Rupert looked at her sardonically. 'You afraid that we're getting up to hanky-panky, Frau Günther? I think you may be transferring your own desires onto us.'

Frau Günther cast him a look of loathing and hustled them both out into the corridor. 'Your father will have to hear about this,' she said.

'Hear about what?' Ava said in exasperation. 'He told me I could try on my mother's things!'

Frau Günther would not reply, and so Ava said angrily, 'I'll tell him myself!' She marched down the hallway and down the stairs, holding up the silver satin dress so she would not trip on its trailing hem. She knocked hard on Otto's study door, Rupert hanging back with a look of wry amusement on his face.

'Father!' Ava cried, opening the door.

Otto and Onkel Franz were sitting by the fire, playing a game of chess. They both looked up in surprise as Ava and Rupert came in, Frau Günther trying to barge in front of them.

'Father, you said it was all right for me to go and try on my mother's dresses, didn't you?'

'Why, yes . . .'

'Then can you tell Frau Günther so?'

'They were lying on your bed, Herr Doktor!' she cried.

'I was not! I was sitting on the bed, trying the shoes on!' Ava retorted. 'What a fuss about nothing.'

Her father looked from her to Frau Günther, then at Rupert who shrugged and spread his hands. 'You must admit, Onkel Otto, that if Ava and I wanted to get up to anything, we wouldn't choose your bedroom to do it.'

Ava looked at her father incredulously. 'Father! As if we would!'

'Very well. Perhaps you could leave me to chat to Frau Günther, and we can speak about it later.'

'There's nothing to speak about,' Ava retorted.

As she led Rupert out, Ava heard Frau Günther say, 'Herr Doktor, that Jew boy should not be here, hanging about with Fräulein Ava all day long . . . you know they are filled with lust and spite . . .'

'She's been reading *Der Stürmer*,' Rupert said, his face darkening. 'I told you she was a Nazi.'

Ava's father must have felt the same, for next thing she knew Frau Günther was coming out of the study with a very red face. She put on her coat on top of her frilled apron, and pinned her hat on askew. 'I wouldn't work in this house for another moment, anyway,' she shouted as she opened the front door.

Otto came into the hall, looking sterner than Ava had ever seen him. 'Then it is a good thing that we have decided to part our ways. Please leave the house keys before you go.'

Frau Günther took the keys from her apron pocket and threw them at his feet. Then she went out, banging the door hard behind her.

Otto bent with a little wheeze to pick the keys up.

'Father, I'm so sorry!' Ava cried. 'We never meant to cause any trouble.'

'I could not afford to keep her on, anyway,' Otto replied. 'I've been trying to think of a way of telling her for a while.'

'Whatever shall we do?'

He shrugged. 'You three girls shall need to take over her duties.' He tried to joke. 'It's about time you all learnt to cook.'

Ava could only stare at him in dismay. She hated cooking almost as much as she hated sewing.

6

Swastika

The Christmas concert was being held at the Hotel Adlon, the most luxurious hotel in Berlin.

Otto had decided he must accompany his daughter as her chaperone. He got out his good black suit and Ava brushed it for him and aired it by the fire. She wore her mother's silver satin dress, white velvet mantle and silver shoes. Since it was a clear night and they could not afford a taxi, Ava and her father walked together through the frosty winter evening. She was not used to walking in heels, and had to take care on the little cobblestones as they walked across the bridge and past Museum Island. All the domes and spires were silhouetted against the star-pricked sky.

Ava's breath plumed white. They passed the immense statue of King Frederick on his immense horse, and the row of ponderous buildings lined up along the Unter den Linden. When Ava was a little girl, she had thought Berlin must have been built by giants. Everything was so massive, it hurt her neck craning to try and see it. She had asked her father if giants had once lived here. He had smiled rather sadly and answered, 'No, my child. Only men.'

It had snowed all day, casting a white shroud over the streets. As Ava and her father made their way into the Pariser Platz, she looked down to the triumphal arch of the Brandenburg Gate, all lit up with spotlights. The chariot drawn by four enormous horses looked as if it might spring down and gallop towards her.

Hurrying out of the cold, they found their way to the ballroom, where many small tables were set up before a podium. A glossy black grand piano stood upon it, lid propped open. A huge Christmas tree stood at the far end of the room. It was hung with red baubles. It took Ava a while to realise, with a weird hop of her heart, that each red bauble was marked with a black swastika. A golden eagle with the emblem in its claws was perched at the top of the tree, where an angel normally stood.

She began to feel sick with nerves.

'You've gone rather green.' Otto put his hand under her elbow.

'I'll be fine once the music starts,' Ava whispered back. She hoped she was telling the truth. She had never sung in public before, only at school concerts and with friends at the Hot Club.

Ava found Frau Wirth, the event organiser, looking frazzled in a too-tight gown. Ava was given a long spiel about what important people were going to be there tonight, and how careful she must be to play only good German songs.

'So no Mendelssohn?' Ava asked innocently.

Frau Wirth looked shocked. 'Of course not!'

She then warned Ava that she must be careful to only sing approved Christmas carols, and gave her a sheaf of song sheets. On top was a new version of 'Silent Night'. Instead of 'Mother and child, holy infant so tender and mild', the first verse read, 'Only the Chancellor stays on guard, Germany's future to watch and to ward.' The second stanza read, 'Adolf Hitler is Germany's star, showing us greatness and glory afar.' Ava dropped the songs on top of the piano, revolted.

People were streaming in. Most of the men were in the sinister black uniforms of the SS, and Ava felt her nerves being screwed tighter and tighter. Otto got out his empty pipe and sucked on the stem, a clear sign he was feeling under pressure too. Frau Wirth found somewhere for him to sit, and he bought himself a schnapps and settled down to listen to the orchestra. Ava conferred with the pianist – a suave young man with glossy fair hair and a very stiff collar – while couples waltzed smoothly past.

Then the doors to the ballroom opened. In came an amiable-looking man with thick white hair and shaggy eyebrows, dressed in a shabby naval uniform with an Iron Cross at his breast. With him was a small elderly man with alert eyes behind pince-nez, dressed in a dark suit and sober tie. Ava hardly paid the two men any mind, though, for behind him stood a tall figure she remembered well. A highbred aristocratic face, ice-blue eyes, a broken nose.

Her heart did a somersault at the sight of him. He was wearing his field grey uniform again, a golden eagle carrying a swastika embroidered on his right breast. His grey jodhpurs had a red stripe down the outside of each leg, and he wore high black boots.

Suddenly he looked straight at her. Ava felt colour scorch her cheeks. She looked away, pretending to be busy with her music. A moment later, she stole a glance at him. Their eyes met. Then Ava looked away again, her whole body hot and tingly.

'Leo!' an imperious voice called. A woman in a clinging black dress with a great many diamonds around her neck swished up to him. Her red-gold hair was set in stiff waves and coils all over her head. 'Whatever are you doing here? Don't tell me you have decided to join the Schutzstaffel at last?'

'Not at all,' he answered coolly. 'I have come on other business.'

'Still with the Admiral?'

He indicated the man with the shock of white hair and the shaggy eyebrows. The redhead slid her arm through his, saying, 'Well, now you are here, you simply must come and meet the Reichsführer.' She led him away towards a group of men in black uniforms standing near the Christmas tree. Ava heard the redhead introduce him as Leo von Löwenstein.

His name is Leo, she thought. Leo von Löwenstein.

It suited him. Leo was a lion name, in shape and colour as well as in meaning. The word itself looked like a proud, tawny-coloured cat, sprawled across a sun-baked rock, its tail swinging lazily.

As long as Ava could remember, words and songs and stories had conjured imaginary pictures for her. When her father read fairy tales at night, Ava saw the dark forest leaning over her bed. When she sang 'Bye Bye Blackbird', she saw a thin black woman creeping away through a forest, carrying all that she owned tied up in a red scarf, hoping to find freedom, hoping to find love.

People's names were like flashes of brightly coloured pictures in her mind's eye. Her father's name, Otto, was a railway tunnel through a hill of pine trees. Monika's name was steely-grey and sharp-toothed, like a trap. Bertha was shaped just like her name, soft and billowy and yet capable of stinging. Rupert's name was a drag on a cigarette, the first mouthful of smoke, the hit at the back of the throat. Jutta was one of those feisty little black terriers, always barking at bigger dogs.

Ava's mother's name had been Clementina. It was a joyous name, full of sunshine and sweetness, yellow-gold as C major. There was nothing sharp or black or cruel about the name Clementina. Ava had never known her mother, but when she whispered her name she saw her, golden-skinned and smiling.

Her own name was white-winged, like a bird leaping into the sky. AVA. Then there was Nazi. A word with claws.

And Ava was surrounded by them on all sides. Men in black uniforms, with hair slicked close to their skulls. Boot heels clicking, hands flying out as if to strike. Women who cried 'Heil Hitler', when once they would have kissed each other's soft, scented cheeks. Giant black swastikas as clawed as the word.

The table nearest to the dais was occupied almost entirely by SS men. They were drinking and laughing. Quite a few raised their glasses to Ava, or looked her over with open appreciation. One was a tall man with a pale, refined face and fair hair slicked close to his skull. His eyes were narrow and deep set, seemingly too small for the long aquiline nose, and his chin seemed to recede in comparison to the broad pale forehead. Ava felt she knew his face. Then she glanced at the man who sat beside him. He was short, with round glasses, and looked like an ineffectual clerk. Ava recognised him at once. Heinrich Himmler, Chief of Police, and one of the most feared men in Germany.

Her stomach muscles clenched. She did not look at the table again, although she felt conscious of the blond man's fixed gaze. Ava thought she knew who he was now. Reinhard Heydrich, the head of the Gestapo.

She felt as shaken and afraid as if the red banners had been dipped in blood.

At last, people were seated, the first course was brought in, and it was time for Ava to sing. She filled her lungs with air, determined to show none of her fear. As soon as the first notes flew out of her mouth, Ava knew she was singing better than she ever had before, as if all the tumult of her feelings had given her voice new depth and purity. Many people looked up from their meals to gaze at her. Ava saw the elderly man in the pince-nez frown slightly and tap his fingers together, his head slightly tilted. She let herself fill with music like a lamp with light, shining out into the room. She was afraid no longer.

When Ava had finished, she saw Leo von Löwenstein lean in to the bespectacled old man and ask a question. He nodded his head very slowly. Then Leo glanced at her. Their eyes met. Ava's whole body grew hot with embarrassment. She looked away, determined not to be caught looking at him again. She sang Tchaikovsky's 'None But the Lonely Heart' and let her voice quaver with melancholy. Then she sang a few of Schubert's more sentimental love songs. The crowd loved them. Ava swept the ballroom with her gaze, seeking to connect with every person in the audience.

The music ended, and Ava turned to confer with the pianist. Her palms were damp, and nerves fluttered in the pit of her stomach. He began to play the song Ava had requested, Schubert's 'Death and the Maiden'. It was a perfect choice for her low contralto voice, and one that allowed her to show off her virtuosity. As the first dramatic notes rang out, Ava thought of Rupert. He had twice as much skill and talent as this suave and heavy-handed young pianist, but because of his Jewish blood was not permitted to play anywhere. She thought of kind-hearted Tante Thea, apologising every few minutes. She thought of Onkel Franz, facing humiliation and ruin. She thought of Jutta, her eyes bright with passion, crying, 'Is it not our mission to repair the world?'

Anger flashed through her, incandescent as sheet lightning. When the song finished, Ava turned to the pianist and said, 'Play me "Silent Night".' He obeyed, banging out the familiar opening chords.

Ava did not sing the new words the Reich had introduced.

She sang the old words, the words everyone had sung since they were children. She sang and she smiled, and she gestured to the audience. One by one, the audience joined in. The beautiful old carol filled the room, everyone singing of heavenly peace.

Ava was conscious of Leo's intent gaze on her face. He was leaning forward, his brows knit. The elderly man with the pince-nez was smiling. He turned and whispered something to the Admiral, who was regarding Ava thoughtfully.

Reinhard Heydrich also had his narrow eyes fixed upon her. He did not sing.

Ava's voice shook. Her heart was beating so hard she felt dizzy. The song came to its last sweet chord. A small storm of applause arose. Ava bowed and then turned to move away from the piano. Her legs did not want to work properly. Frau Wirth rushed up to her, looking harassed. 'My dear,' she said. 'You sang the wrong words? Did you not know?'

'I'm sorry,' Ava replied. 'I forgot.'

'Oh dear, oh dear, I do hope the Reichsführer is not angry!'

Ava smiled stiffly, and moved away. Reaction was setting in. The world wobbled. Leo brought her a glass of champagne. He clicked his heels, bowed and presented it to her.

'In compliments to your bravery,' he said.

Ava flushed and dropped her eyes. As she brought the glass to her lips, he bent even closer and said, with a hard note in his voice, 'Though I cannot compliment you on your good sense.'

He clicked his heels, and walked away.

Ava drained the glass.

Everyone else was smiling and congratulating her. The elderly man with the pince-nez came up and introduced himself. He was Herr Professor

Bruno Kittel, the head of the Berlin Music Conservatory. 'You have potential,' he said. 'If you're interested, perhaps a place could be found for you at the conservatory. Have you ever considered trying to raise your upper registers?' He gave Ava the name of a singing teacher and said that – if she worked hard – perhaps she would qualify for a scholarship to the conservatory when the term began in February.

Ava took his card with trembling fingers. Could it be possible? Could all her dreams be coming true? She looked around for her father, desperate to share the news with him. But Frau Wirth had seized her elbow. 'The Reichsführer wants to speak to you. He is displeased. You must apologise and explain!'

As Ava walked up to the main table, her legs were trembling so much she was afraid they would give way. She steeled herself.

Heinrich Himmler stared at her through his round little glasses. They reflected the light of the candles, making it hard to see his eyes. 'You sang the wrong words,' he said, without any preliminaries.

'I'm sorry,' Ava replied. 'I . . . I was so overwhelmed with the honour of singing in your presence . . .'

'Do not forget again.'

'No, sir.'

Himmler dismissed her with a wave of his hand. Ava turned to go, but Heydrich said softly, 'Fräulein.'

Ava turned back, her heart thumping.

'What is your name?'

'Ava Falkenhorst, sir.'

'There is no need to be overwhelmed in our presence, Fräulein Falkenhorst. Why do you not come and join us for a drink?' He clicked his fingers and a waiter rushed up with a tray of brimming champagne glasses.

'I . . . thank you, sir, but my father is waiting.' Ava turned and walked away, the silver satin cool and supple against her body, very conscious of Heydrich's cold eyes resting on the bare skin of her back.

Her father came to greet her, his face glowing with pride. Ava nodded and smiled, only half-listening to his congratulations, her thoughts in turmoil. Suddenly she put down her glass with a loud click. She made her way through the crowd to where Leo von Löwenstein stood, listening quietly to another conversation.

'Excuse me . . .' Ava's voice failed her. She said it again, with more authority.

Leo turned to face her. A quick flash of surprise was gone as soon as it came, and his face returned to its usual expression of icy composure.

'Fräulein Falkenhorst.' He bowed his head with grave courtesy.

'Tell me, Herr von Löwenstein, was it you who was responsible for me being offered this job tonight?'

He did not answer for a long moment. Ava was surprised to see a faint flush rise in his strong-boned face. Eventually he looked back at her and said, 'I hope you will not think me presumptuous. I heard you sing that day . . . from the window . . . and then . . . well, I knew that your father had resigned from the university and that your family had found itself in straitened circumstances as a result . . .'

'And how did you know that?' she demanded.

'The first time we met I saw your stockings had been darned and your dress had been let down. Your father's coat was shabby, and his collar was frayed. Yet he did not speak like an uneducated man. He was arguing with the Stormtroopers, defending Herr Professor Feidler, saying he had been a war hero and should be treated with more respect. He spoke of his time at the university then.'

Ava was silent. Her skin was hot, and she could not hold his gaze.

He stepped a little lower. 'Your voice could be extraordinary, with training. I . . . I am not the only one who thought so.'

'You mean Herr Professor Kittel. You came in with him. You know him?'

'He is a friend of my mother's.' His eyes were intent on Ava's face.

'So the offer for me to try for a scholarship . . .' Her voice failed her again. She blinked back tears.

'It was your performance that impressed Herr Professor Kittel, not my recommendation. You showed such power, such . . .' he paused, then said with a deepening note, 'such passion.'

Ava was very conscious of his eyes on her face, on her mouth. He stepped closer, bending his head so he could speak even lower. His hand brushed the bare skin at the curve of her spine.

'He was also much struck by your bravado. As was I. Are you afraid of nothing?'

I am afraid of everything, Ava thought but did not say. She did not look at him.

'Leo?' a voice demanded.

He straightened and looked up. The redhead stood before them, her brows drawn together in a look of displeasure. She wore a golden swastika pinned to her black satin dress. Ava felt Leo's fingers stiffen on her bare back, then his hand dropped away. Her skin felt cold.

'Excuse me,' he said. He bowed, very proper and punctilious, clicked his heels again in that arrogant way of his, and went back to the redhead's side. Ava clutched her little silver evening bag, which had once been her mother's. She told herself she was trembling because she was angry. She told herself that she felt nothing for Herr von Löwenstein except dislike and anger.

Even then, Ava knew she was lying to herself.

The Beast's Garden

va walked along the snowy path, her gloved hands shoved deep into her pockets. The sky was plum-bruised. On either side of the path, leafless trees shivered in the twilight cold. The silver columns of birch trees were marked with black and secret runes.

She was so tired that she could scarcely drag herself along. She had spent the morning on her feet selling gloves and hats at the department store, and the afternoon on her feet singing the same handful of notes over and over again. Who would ever have thought singing could be so exhausting? Ava would have given anything to be able to hail a cab, or to have gone to a café for a hot chocolate, but there was no money for that. Every pfennig was needed for her singing lessons. She was determined to win that scholarship to the conservatory.

As usual, Ava was walking the long way home, through the Tiergarten. It was so beautiful that way, and she found that she longed for the peace and emptiness of the snow-filled spaces after her long day. The Falkenhorsts' apartment was always so noisy and chaotic now, with two families living in a space designed for one, and tempers fraying. She breathed in the sharp air deeply, letting it fill her lungs, and gazed out across the snow-carpeted lawns.

Everything so white, pure, clean. Bare branches glistening with icicles. Statues frozen in mid-movement, subdued by soft cloaks of snow. The constant low growl of the city hushed, as if by magic. With her red beret pulled down over her ears, and her coat buttoned up to her chin, the cold and the silence was exhilarating.

Tiergarten. It meant the beast's garden. Usually it was a name for a zoo. There was a zoo, on the far side of the park, but the Tiergarten at the heart of Berlin was not named for it. It was much older than that. Ava's father said it had once been the hunting park for the first king in Prussia, Frederick I, famous for having crowned himself in 1701. It was necessary to make sure that one got the term quite right, Otto always said. Not the first king *of* Prussia. The first king *in* Prussia. The Holy Roman Emperor had been jealous of Frederick's power and his ambition. He would not permit Frederick to be king *of* Prussia. That tiny change of preposition, with all its weighted meaning, would be won by his grandson, Frederick the Great. The young Fritz had, however, never wanted to be great. His father (also called Frederick) had him woken every morning with the firing of cannon. At the age of six Fritz had been given his own regiment of children to drill. Poor Fritz had even been beaten for wearing gloves in winter. Ava shivered and thrust her gloved hands even deeper into her pockets. What father did that to a child? And when poor Fritz was eighteen and had run off with his best friend, what father would arrest him and court-martial him for desertion, then make him watch the decapitation of that best friend?

No wonder Germany was lurching towards war again.

Ava was so cold. She felt as if winter had frozen the very blood in her veins; as if her bones would snap. Her feet were blocks of stone. She could scarcely drag them along.

Then she heard footsteps, coming up fast behind her. Suddenly Ava wished she had walked home along the city streets, blaring with horns and packed with frowning people, but bright with lights. She began to walk faster. So did the footsteps behind her. Ava's heart began to beat in double time. She put on speed.

'Ava!'

She recognised his voice, low and golden as a cello.

She turned to face him.

'What are you doing here?' Leo's voice was stern. 'You shouldn't walk alone in the gardens at dusk. It's not safe.'

'I like the gardens. It's the only time I ever get to be alone.'

He stepped back, his shoulders stiff. 'I intrude. I am sorry.'

Ava inclined her head to him, turned and hurried on. She walked as swiftly as she could without breaking into a run. She was afraid. Darkness was dropping fast.

'Wait! Please.'

She slowed and glanced back at him, her whole body rigid with tension, ready to run.

'You must know it is not safe to walk in the gardens at dusk,' he said, very formal. 'I cannot, in good conscience, allow it.'

'What I do is no business of yours.' Ava kept on walking.

Leo hurried to catch her up. 'No. Of course not. I did not mean . . .' He paused, then said, 'I simply meant that I must see that you get home safely. Would you . . . would you permit me to escort you?'

'Have you been following me?' she demanded.

'I live not far from the park,' he said. 'I saw you from my . . . from the window. I was sure it must be you.'

Ava put up one hand to her red beret. He nodded, but said, smiling crookedly, 'It was the hair, mostly. I've never seen a girl with hair like yours.' He put out one hand and wound a wayward curl about his finger.

Ava flinched. 'Please . . . just leave me be.'

Her voice must have betrayed her fear, for his footsteps checked, then he said, in a different tone of voice, 'Forgive me. I did not mean to frighten you.'

'I'm not frightened,' Ava snapped back, walking faster.

'No. Of course not. I don't think I've ever met a braver girl.'

Ava glanced at him then, in sheer surprise.

'If you would just permit me to see you safe through the gardens . . . I swear on my honour as a German officer that I mean you no harm.'

Ava made a derisive sound.

He caught her arm and turned her to face him. 'You do not believe me?' His voice was sharp. 'I offered you my word of honour.'

She pulled away from his hand. 'Forgive me if I find it hard to trust a man who works for a regime that beats up old men and steals all their money.'

She walked on briskly, and he fell into step beside her. 'You do not agree with the Führer when he says he sees no reason why man should not be as cruel as nature?'

Ava looked straight ahead. 'Oh, the Führer is the fount of all goodness and wisdom, of course.'

Leo was silent. When he spoke, his voice was angry. 'What am I to do? I'm a soldier. My father was a soldier, and his father, and his father's father. Our family lives to serve Germany. For centuries we have served with faithfulness unto death.'

'Are you not the master of your own fate?'

'And the captain of my soul?' he answered at once, surprising her again. Ava had not expected a Nazi officer to be a man who read poetry. Especially English poetry. He went on bitterly, 'When you are born into a family like mine, Fräulein Falkenhorst, you have very little choice in the direction your life takes. It is mapped out for you from the moment you are born.'

'But why? What sort of family were you born into?'

'An old one,' he answered.

Ava laughed. 'All families are old.'

He cast a quick glance at her, then returned his gaze to the dark path slicing through the snow. 'I suppose they are,' he answered after a while. 'But my family *knows* just how old it is. The knowledge of all those ancestors . . . it's a kind of weight on you. All those expectations.'

Ava knew what he meant. She thought of how she liked to sing – joyous and free and full of improvisation and play – and the way her new singing teacher wanted her to sing, as precise and controlled as machinery. 'It can be hard. Keeping everyone happy.'

He nodded, bending his head so she could not see his eyes under his peaked cap. They walked on, side by side. The path led out into the snow-carpeted Floraplatz. The statue of the Amazon on her horse glowed an eerie marsh-light-green. She was surrounded by thorns, and mantled with snow.

'When do you think it is permissible to choose . . . one's own desire . . . over duty?' he asked. Although he stood some distance away from her, his hands in his pockets, his eyes fixed on the statue, Ava felt a jolt of electricity zing between them.

'When your duty is hurting you,' she replied after a while. 'And when . . . your desire . . . is not hurting someone else.'

'Sometimes I feel that everything I do is hurting someone.' His voice was so quiet she could scarcely hear it. He bent and broke off a thorny twig, hung with tiny icicles. 'We are taught to do our Christian duty and be obedient unto death and have faith . . . so what do we do when our faith is shaken? When our duty is in conflict with our conscience?'

Ava thought for a moment Leo was speaking only to himself, but he looked at her with such intensity she realised he meant for her to answer.

'I'm not sure what to say. Surely it's wrong to act against your conscience?'

'Even when we are duty-bound? The Bible tells us we must obey.'

She shrugged. 'It is so much easier for me. I was brought up without religion, and so without all this worry over duty and sin.'

He stared at her. 'Brought up without religion?'

'Father thinks religion is a collective neurosis,' Ava told him, 'and God an infantile delusion.'

His brows contracted. 'So your father thinks believing in God is some kind of madness?'

'Madness is perhaps too strong a word . . . the idea is that religion was born out of the human longing for meaning.'

His frown deepened. 'So humans invented God because they longed for him?'

'Something like that.'

'But then where does the longing come from?'

'Herr Doktor Freud thought it was an Oedipal predicament,' Ava told him. 'Which I think means a childlike pining for a father's love.'

He shook his head. 'I've never met anyone like you before. You seem unafraid to say anything . . .'

'My father thinks it's important to learn to think for ourselves.' Ava smiled in sudden memory of some of the conversations she had had with her father, late at night, after he had read her a bedtime story. He had never failed to answer any of her questions, no matter how many she had asked. They had spoken about death and love and God and why the sky was blue and what happened when a star died.

Leo said, after a long while, 'Do you know that poem by Rilke . . . the one about Orpheus and Eurydice? It has this line. I think it says: "Be ahead of all parting, as if it had already happened."'

'Like winter,' Ava said, 'which even now is passing.'

His eyes flashed to hers. 'You know it!'

She nodded. 'I studied it at school. Rupert and I went to the Musik-gymnasium, you see. Everything we did was about music.'

'Do you remember? It has a line about a winter so endless . . .'

Ava remembered. '"For beneath the winter is a winter so endless, that to survive it at all is a triumph of the heart."'

His face was grim. 'It's about death.'

'It's about rebirth,' she said. 'It tells Eurydice to climb back singing.'

'But she doesn't. Orpheus looks back and she is lost. She's not reborn.'

He was right. Ava shivered and thrust her hands deeper into her pockets.

'Sometimes I feel like Eurydice in that poem. All emptiness inside me.'

She gazed at him, frowning. 'But . . . why?'

'Too much death,' he answered, then shrugged. 'I'm sorry. I'm being morbid. It's the winter. My father died in winter, and I've hated it ever since.' He tried to smile, and passed her the twig with its tiny flowers of ice.

Ava bent her head over it, troubled, not sure what to do with it. She walked on, going down the steps to the Venus Pool. He matched her steps, silent and brooding. Ava stole a glance at his face.

He was not what she had expected at all.

8

Rose in Winter

At the far end of the pool stood the monument to German composers, its cupola bright with gilt. Ava paused on the steps to look down at the pool, glimmering under the darkening sky, frosted with ice along the shoreline. Everything was sharp-edged, as if cut out with a fine-bladed knife. She was very aware of Leo standing next to her, the collar of his greatcoat turned up, his profile strong beneath the peaked cap. She did not know why she stood there beside him, when she should be hurrying home to warmth and safety.

'I do not want to disappoint them,' Leo said at last. 'My mother, I mean, and my grandfather. They have lost so much.'

After a long moment, Ava said, 'I never knew my mother.'

He turned to look at her. 'That's very sad. Do you . . . do you miss her?'

Ava nodded. 'Isn't it strange? To miss someone you never knew. But I miss her every day.'

'It's not strange. I hardly knew my father, yet I miss him. I wish I had known him better.'

'Yes. I feel that too. I know so little about her. If it was not for Tante Thea, I'd know nothing. My sisters never mention her, and Father doesn't very often.'

'Tante Thea . . . that is the Jewess whose house you were running to that night? She is your aunt?'

Ava frowned at the tone in his voice. 'She's only half-Jewish. Her husband is, but they do not practise the faith. And she's not really my aunt. I just call her that. Tante Thea practically raised me. She was a dear friend of my mother, and helped look after me after my mother died. Her son, Rupert . . . he was born the same day as me, so we grew up together.'

'You and this . . . Rupert . . . you are close then?'

Ava nodded, and rather defiantly said, 'Of course.'

He frowned. 'They should not be staying with you.'

'They have nowhere else to go.'

'It'll cause trouble.'

'Why?' Ava demanded. 'Whose business is it if we help out friends who are in trouble? They're trying to sell their apartment . . . but the prices they're being offered are ridiculous.'

'They should take the money and get out as fast as they can,' he answered.

Ava bit back angry words. She wanted to shake her fist and curse the Führer and his cruel race laws. But it would not be wise. This tall man with the nose like an eagle's beak was one of them. He worked for the Abwehr, Hitler's secret intelligence.

Ava took a moment before she answered. 'I'll let them know.'

He hesitated, then said, 'And the little girl? Is she your niece? What is wrong with her?'

'Absolutely nothing,' Ava said at once. 'She is the sweetest little thing imaginable.'

'I'm sure she is,' he answered. 'But you should know . . . your sister should know . . . the Reich is setting up new initiatives in regard to those they feel are burdens on society.'

He was speaking carefully, not looking at her.

Ava was puzzled. 'But . . . do you mean Angelika? She's not a burden! Besides, she's only a baby. Not yet three.'

65

'I just thought you should know. If you love her, be careful.'

'Of course we love her!'

He shrugged. 'Many do not.'

They walked on in silence. Leo was watching Ava with that intent, frowning gaze that made her blood seethe and her stomach twist. What a fool she was! To let him walk with her through that dusk-shadowed garden, confiding in him, telling him about her mother and her friends. He's a Nazi, Ava reminded herself. He's dangerous.

In the distance, the golden statue of Victory gleamed in the last low ray of the sun, so high she seemed about to step onto the delicate tracery of twigs below.

The low growl of traffic on the boulevard sounded to their left. Without a word, they both turned to walk along the woodland path towards the Brandenburg Gate. The path was dark, shadowed by trees. Ava could no longer see his face. He had taken her arm, to keep her steady on the slippery path. She did not draw her arm away, though her heart skittered at his touch.

'So does your family really uphold all that old Junker creed about duty and honour unto death?' she asked. She could not help herself. He was just so unlike what she had expected.

'I am Bavarian, not Prussian,' he answered coldly. Ava guessed she had touched some raw nerve. 'And it is not nonsense. A man's honour is all that is of true worth.'

'An old family from Bavaria,' she mused. 'I suppose you're a Graf or something, with a name like von Löwenstein.'

'There are no titles anymore,' he reminded her quietly. 'They've all been abolished.'

'But once upon a time your family had a title? And a castle too, no doubt.'

'We still have the castle,' he admitted. 'Though it's just about to fall into the moat.'

She could not help but laugh. 'A castle with a moat? How terribly romantic. Please tell me you have a secret passage or two as well.'

'My brother and I spent years searching for one, but to no avail,' he told her. It made her smile, the way he spoke. Like something out of an old novel.

'I didn't know you had a brother. What's his name?'

'Alex. His name was Alex. He's dead now.'

Ava spoke awkwardly. 'I'm sorry. What . . . what happened?'

'He was killed. Street-fighting. It was stupid.'

Street-fighting. That meant he had been caught up in the battles between the Nazis and the Communists when Hitler had first seized power. Ava wondered which side he had been on. A boy from an aristocratic family was unlikely to have been fighting for the Communists, but one never knew.

'How old were you?' she asked.

'I was sixteen. Alex was seventeen.'

After a moment, he went on: 'Alex and I did everything together. When we were kids, we'd make a fort and play Cowboys and Indians, or go canoeing on the moat, or pretend to be spies. We didn't really have anyone else, you see. Our father died from the wounds he received fighting in the Great War. It just broke my grandfather's heart. He was never very well, and he became rather a recluse. He wanted Alex to grow up at the schloss, and so of course Mother and I had to live there too.'

Ava looked up at him, trying to read his face. It was impossible.

'I think my mother found it very lonely,' Leo went on. 'She came to Berlin often – we have a house here – and this is where Alex and I went to school, and then on to the Kriegsakademie. My grandfather, though . . . he has not left the schloss in years.'

'Where is your . . . schloss?'

The sudden flash of his smile. 'It's probably an affectation to call it a "schloss". It used to be a hunting lodge. It's in the Bavarian Alps, so close to Austria that you could walk there if you didn't mind the climb. It's a nice old place. I get back there when I can.'

'And now your brother is dead, you're the heir.'

'Heir to a pile of bad debts,' he answered. 'It's been a long time since the place has made much money.'

'I don't think you're alone there.'

Night had dropped, though she could see the lights of the city through the bare branches of the trees. Three faint stars glimmered amongst the lattice of bare twigs. An owl hooted, and drifted past on pale, muffled wings. Neither spoke. Yet Ava had never been more aware of another human being.

They reached the end of the boulevard. Berlin lay beyond, blazing and awake. The Brandenburg Gate towered against the sky, its thick columns all irradiated with spotlights.

Ava and Leo stood in the shadow of the trees. She looked up at him. He was nothing but a dark shape. 'How . . . how did you know who I was? My name, I mean. Where I lived?'

'It's my job to find things out.' Ava heard faint amusement in his voice.

'But why?'

In answer, he drew her to him, bending his head to kiss her.

Ava had been kissed before, plenty of times. Kissing was like dancing, like singing the blues, like tossing back a gin fizz. Kissing was yet another way to rebel against all the rules.

His kiss was nothing like that. It went through her like a leaping flame. Ava's knees buckled. She had to cling to him with both hands. It was as if the earth beneath her feet had suddenly dropped, and she was left reeling.

At last he dragged his mouth away. If he had let go of her, Ava would have fallen.

'I am so madly in lust with you,' he said against her hair. His arms held her close against him. 'From the very first moment I saw you.'

Ava could not speak.

'Can you . . . will you . . .' he said with difficulty. 'Please . . . come home with me.'

She shook her head. With all her strength, she pushed him away. 'I need to go home. Let me go home.'

His arms fell away. 'I'm sorry. It's just . . . I want you so much. You said . . . that first night . . . it's as if the whole world has run mad. It's how I feel . . . everything is mad and wrong . . .' He stopped abruptly.

Ava pushed past his arm and into the light. 'You . . . you're part of the madness,' she told him, and then she broke into a clumsy run, away from him and towards home.

The next morning, a messenger boy in a pillbox hat brought Ava a rose. A single rose, sweet-scented and gold-hearted with masses of crumpled petals like dark crimson velvet. A rose in full bloom, impossible to find in Berlin in winter.

Leo's card was attached, with a note scrawled on the back. It said: 'Please forgive me. I should not have kissed you, or spoken to you in such a way. I have never felt like this before. I am dizzy in your presence, like Rilke once wrote. Please say we can meet again.' Then he had signed the note with a single swirling L.

Ava knew the poem he quoted. She remembered a few lines. *You who never arrived in my arms, Beloved, who were lost from the start, I don't even know what songs would please you . . . You, Beloved, who are all the gardens I have ever gazed at, longing . . . Who knows? Perhaps the same bird echoed through both of us yesterday, separate, in the evening.*

Her heart was beating far too fast. She took the rose up to her room, and sat on the edge of her bed in the thin winter light, staring down at its dense crimson beauty. Its heavenly scent filled the air. The rose was wrapped in old newspaper. Carefully Ava unwrapped it.

A blaring headline stared up at her. *Make the Jews pay!* it said. A picture of Hitler, mouth contorted, shaking a fist. Her hand jerked uncontrollably. One thorn pierced her fingertip.

Blood welled up, red as a trumpet blast.

Faintness washed over her. Ava felt all the warmth draining from her body, as if her skin was rimed with frost. With shaking hands, she blotted the bead of blood on the newspaper. Her eyes were filled with fizzing lights. She leant forward, resting her head in her hands, trying to catch her breath. It fled away from her in ever-tightening circles of darkness.

When composure at last returned, Ava wrapped the rose in the newspaper, hiding its crimson beauty, then threw the crumpled package into her wastepaper basket. She wrote on the bottom of Leo's note, *I can't. Not ever.* Then she put it into an envelope and scrawled his address on it, ready to post.

Her wounded finger left a faint bloody mark on the white paper.

9

Spring Storm

Through the whirling snowflakes of an early spring storm, German tanks rolled into Prague.

Hitler was driven, standing up in his open car, his hand held high, through the beautiful old streets. German troops were photographed marching through the famous Giants' Gate into the courtyard of Prague Castle.

Ava read the newspaper again and again, unable to believe that Hitler had so shamelessly broken the Munich Agreement, signed only six months earlier. It showed the world that Hitler's word of honour was a sham, a fraud, a mock. She wondered what Leo thought of it all, but then resolutely pushed the thought away. She had to stop thinking about him. He's a Nazi, she reminded herself again. A phrase that had dug a deep groove into her brain.

On the long walk home from the conservatory, the news was broadcast from megaphones on trucks at every street corner, along with militant music that fire-barred the shadowy evening streets. Ava tried not to listen, but it was impossible to escape.

When she let herself into the front hall, she saw the low glow of the fire in the sitting room and heard the loud, excited voice of the radio announcer. She went in, wind-blown and chilled to the core. Her family and friends sat around the room, all their attention fixed on the radio on the sideboard. Monika's face was full of white excitement. Bertha looked tense, her eyes reddened. She held Angelika up against her shoulder. The little girl was crying in a tired sort of way. 'Why he angry?' she wept. 'Why he shout?'

'He's not angry, Angelika,' Bertha said. 'He's happy.'

'I'm glad somebody is,' Rupert responded.

'The Führer has done it!' Monika cried. 'He called their bluff, and they caved again.'

'But what of the Czechs?' Ava asked. 'Do you think they want to be taken over by us? What's going to happen to them?'

'What of them?' Monika answered scornfully. 'They're weak and we're strong. It's the way of the world, Ava, it's survival of the fittest.'

'I don't understand why he did it,' Jutta said. She was sitting on the ground, her arms wrapped around her knees. There were not enough chairs for everyone in the sitting room, so she and Rupert often sprawled on the rug before the fire, or sat with their backs to the sideboard.

'He did it because he could,' Monika said.

'Father, will there be war?' Bertha clutched Angelika close.

'I hope not.' Otto looked grey and careworn.

'Oh, war's coming,' Monika cried. 'And the world will be remade.'

'But will it be remade for the better?' Onkel Franz asked.

There was a long silence. Ava went across and turned the radio off. 'How about some supper?' she said. 'Did anyone have time to get to the butcher?'

The next few days were tense, as the world condemned Germany. Ava was working hard at the department store, taking as many shifts as she could around her lessons at the Berlin Conservatory. Although she had won her scholarship, she still had to earn every pfennig she could. Music sheets cost money, food cost money, and the gas bills had to be paid. The Feidlers were still camping out in the apartment's spare room. Tante Thea had taken over most of the cooking and housework, doing her best to keep the overcrowded apartment in order. Onkel Franz had at last agreed that the family's only option was to try and leave Germany, only to find it was almost impossible to go. There were 56,562 people ahead of them on the waiting list for an American visa, and England had closed her books. Jutta was studying with such dogged determination, it was as if she wished to learn all there was to know in the world.

As for Rupert, Ava hardly saw him anymore. He was angry with her for having taken up the scholarship at the conservatory. Ava knew it was unfair. Rupert had just as much talent as she did, if not more, yet the conservatory was closed to him. He could not even find work as a pianist in a neighbourhood centre, or playing his trumpet in a nightclub. All such routes were closed to him because he was Jewish.

It was more than that, though. Rupert did not think Ava should be studying somewhere that banned Jews. He thought she should have thrown the offer of a scholarship in their faces, and walked away. Yet Ava could not do so. She had respected her father's resignation from the university, but their lives had been very hard since. The family had so little money coming in, and the scholarship was Ava's only chance to make a life of music for herself. She thought sometimes she would die if she could not sing. The thought of spending the rest of her life selling hats filled her with despair.

So Ava had taken up the scholarship, and it took all her time and energy working to keep it. She had no time to go swing-dancing, or to sing jazz in some smoky basement somewhere. Besides, it was getting too dangerous. Swing kids were being arrested, beaten up, interrogated by the Gestapo. Some were even sent to concentration camps.

On the Sunday after the fall of Czechoslovakia, Ava came into the sitting room, her curls tied up in a scarf, an apron tied about her waist, her arms full of brushes and dusters. She tried as much as possible to take on any of the household tasks that did not involve chopping up dead things with sharp knives, and so it was her job to dust, sweep the floors, change the beds and wash the linen.

Jutta was cleaning the rooms upstairs, doing her best to make up for her staunch refusal to do chores from nightfall on Friday to nightfall on Saturday. Ava had to admire her strength of spirit. Both Bertha and

Monika were relentless in their disapproval of Jutta's new-found commitment to her Jewish faith, and her parents were puzzled and apologetic. It would have been much easier for Jutta to just give in, and eat what was put before her, and do a little dusting on a Saturday. Instead, Tante Thea and Ava tried to buy food she would eat and rushed around to tidy the house before Monika got home on a Friday evening.

Rupert lay on the couch, still dressed in his pyjamas and wrapped in a blanket. Ava had not heard him come in. It must have been very late. His long jaw was unshaven, his eyes bloodshot and bleak. He put out one hand and groped for some cigarettes, but he had smoked them all. Ava took one from the box from the mantelpiece, and lit it for Rupert, taking a sneaky drag before she passed it to him.

'You blue, baby?' Ava said, sitting on the edge of the couch.

'So blue,' he answered, after a moment. 'Bluer than I've ever been.'

Ava gave his shoulder a little comforting shake, and took the cigarette from his lips to take another drag. 'What's wrong?'

He shrugged. 'Everything. I can't go anywhere or do anything without being harassed by the Nazi Youths. They're beating up anyone who even looks like a Jew. And Felix . . .'

Ava waited patiently for him to go on. She had wondered what had happened to Felix. Rupert had shown all the signs of being in love again, being out half the night and broody and quiet all day. Yet he did not talk about Felix all the time, nor had Ava seen them together in the street or in the park. Perhaps they were just being careful.

'Felix . . .' she prompted, after the silence stretched on.

'He's disappeared,' Rupert said. 'I can't find him anywhere. Nobody knows where he's gone.'

He reached up and took the cigarette from Ava's hand, sucking on it so hard the tip flared orange.

'Are you afraid . . .' Ava paused, then said gently, 'are you afraid he's thrown you over, or are you afraid he's been arrested?'

Rupert moved restlessly. 'He wouldn't have thrown me over. At least, not unless he was lying through his teeth the whole time.'

A chill spread over her skin. 'So you think he's been arrested?'

'I don't know. I hope not. I don't know what to think.'

'Maybe he's just gone away without telling you. Maybe his letter got lost.'

'Maybe.'

Just then, Ava heard a knock on the front door. Surprised, she got up and went out into the hallway to open it.

Leo stood on the step. He was dressed in a greatcoat, his fair head bare, and he was holding a red rose in his hand. He offered it to her, speaking all in a rush. 'Ava, please, I must speak with you. I can't bear it any longer. Say you'll come and walk with me in the gardens.'

Ava stood frozen, her hands pressed together on her chest.

'I promise, all I want to do is talk.'

'I can't.'

'Please. I have no-one else I can talk to ... no-one else that under-stands.'

Ava shook her head. Her throat was so thick with emotion, she found it hard to speak. 'Please, just leave me alone.'

He gazed down at her, frowning.

Ava tried to shut the door. Leo stopped it with his body. 'Ava, you're not being fair. You see me in my uniform and think that is all that I am. You don't look to see what kind of man I am within.'

She shook her head and tried again to shut the door. But Leo was too strong for her. He took her hand and uncurled her fingers, bending to kiss her palm. Ava jerked back, but he did not let her hand go. He pressed the rose into it, and closed her fingers about it. 'You cannot tell me you do not feel the same,' he said, so close Ava could feel the warmth of his breath upon her skin. 'Ava, please come.'

'Are you deaf? She said she didn't want to go.' Rupert's angry voice sounded behind her. 'So get the hell out of here.'

Ava whipped around, dropping the rose in her agitation. Rupert stood in the sitting-room doorway, his robe hanging open over his pyjamas. He was barefoot, and had a cigarette in one hand.

Leo looked him over coldly. 'Do you intend to try and make me? I will go only if Ava insists.'

'Who are you to call her Ava?' Rupert came out of the doorway, a sneer on his lips, his lean body tense with anger.

Leo made a small mocking bow. 'I am Karl Viktor Graf von Löwenstein, at your service. My friends call me Leo. And you?'

'They call me Hot-Lips,' Rupert answered. 'For obvious reasons.'

'Rupert,' Ava said pleadingly.

'So this is your friend Rupert?' Leo glanced at Ava. 'Still in his pyjamas at this time of day. Très louche.' His French accent was perfect.

'Très chic,' Rupert answered. His French was not nearly so good.

'Please, Leo, just go,' Ava said.

He pressed his lips together, then bowed his head. 'If you wish.' He stepped back, and Ava began to shut the door. Then he put his hand on hers, holding the door open. 'Ava, please, I must see you. I will wait by the lion statue in the Tiergarten. Do you know it? The one with the hurt lioness. I'll wait there till noon. Please come.'

Then he released her hand and stepped back. Ava shut the door in his face, and turned to press her back against it. The rose lay limp and crumpled at her feet. Ava bent and picked it. Its sweet scent rose up all around her.

'You can't go,' Rupert said flatly.

'I'm not going to.'

He was not listening. 'I told you he'd want something in return for getting you that chance at a scholarship! Nazis don't help people for nothing.'

'It wasn't like that,' Ava protested.

'Look at you! You want to go. You're hot for him.'

'You're the one who called him a hot diggedy dog.'

Ava was trying to make Rupert smile, but it did not work. His black look deepened. 'Yeah, well, he may be a hot dog but he's still a Nazi,' he snapped.

She bit her lip. 'He's not like that, Rupert, honestly, he's not. He comes from a military family, he was sent to military school.'

'And that makes it all right? To swagger around as if he owns the place? To think he can just snap his fingers and you'll go running to jump into bed with him?'

'Rupert!'

'You can't go out with him, Ava. You don't know what these Nazis are really like.'

'Yes, I do!' She was beginning to feel angry.

'How could you? It's not reported in any of the newspapers. Did you know that the Nazis ordered the Jews in Vienna to scrub the sidewalks with their toothbrushes? Even sick old ladies were forced to get down on their hands and knees and scrub till their hands bled, while the Nazis stood by and laughed. They murdered a journalist and sent his wife his broken and bloodied spectacles. Can you imagine?'

Ava couldn't bear it. 'Don't,' she begged.

But Rupert went on relentlessly. 'Do you know what they did to Felix's lover? They arrested him and set their German Shepherd on him. The dog tore out his balls. He was only sixteen, Ava. That's what they've trained those dogs to do.'

Ava felt cold and shaky. 'I don't believe you! No-one could do that.'

'They do much worse than that. You've got to stay away from that Nazi, Ava. All he wants is to get into your knickers. He'll break your heart, I can guarantee you that.'

She remembered how Leo had said to her, *I am so madly in lust with you.* Her stomach twisted.

'He's not like that,' Ava said. 'He's not like them.'

Rupert snorted in derision.

She went up the stairs as fast as she could, trying not to let him see how her face was contorted with the effort to hold back tears. She sat on her bed, dashing her hand across her eyes. She still held the rose, and wondered where Leo had found it, so perfect and sweet-scented when snow lay thin and hard on the gardens of the city.

In her head, she was still arguing with Rupert. Ava hated the Nazis, of course. How could anyone who loved peace and kindness and compassion not hate them? She thought of the Stormtroopers striding down the steps of the Feidlers' apartment with truncheons clenched in their hands, of Reinhard Heydrich's cold angry face as he listened to her sing a beautiful old carol, of Hitler, raving and ranting and spraying the crowd with spittle.

Yet Ava was sure Leo was not like that. He had sent her roses in midwinter. He had quoted poetry to her. His brother was dead, and he had let her see the grief shadowing his heart. He had kissed her, and Ava could not see him without wishing he would kiss her again.

She got up restlessly and moved around her room. She put the rose in a little crystal vase by her bed. She took off her apron and headscarf and tossed them into the laundry basket. She tidied the combs and hairbrush on her dressing table. The old book of fairy tales lay on her bedside table. Ava picked it up, and it fell open to her favourite story, the tale of the singing, springing lark. The artist had illustrated the page with a drawing she had always loved. A griffin flew through the sky, a man and a woman riding on its back. The woman had her arms wrapped about the man's neck, and he held her close. They were kissing, half-swooning in their rapture. She had broken the spell and he was a beast no longer.

Ava thought of what Leo had said. *You see me in my uniform and think that is all that I am. You don't look to see what kind of man I am within.* He was right, she realised with a sudden leap of her pulse. She was doing exactly what she hated the Nazis doing. Judging by appearances. Being blinded by prejudice.

Ava stood up. Her breath was coming fast and uneven. She ran out the door and down the stairs. As she flung open the door, she grabbed her red coat and beret from the hall-stand. Rupert came out of the sitting room. 'Ava . . .'

'I'm going!' she cried, and sprang down the steps, slamming the door behind her.

10

Love Is Difficult

Ava ran down the street, drawing on her coat, cramming on her beret. The clock on the telegraph office said it was almost a quarter to twelve. She raced over the bridge, and along the side of the river. It gleamed like pewter in the early spring sunshine. A white swan glided past, followed by a little trail of fluffy, ash-grey cygnets. As she hurried along the Wilhelmstrasse, Ava saw people were unfurling red swastika banners from every balcony. She reached the Unter den Linden, and had to stop to catch her breath.

Church bells began to toll. It was noon.

Ava ran along the plaza and under the shadow of the Brandenburg Gate. The road was busy with cars and buses and bicycles. It took her a while to dodge through, and across to the far side. The Tiergarten lay before her, a tangle of black twigs under the pale blue sky, the ground still frosted with snow under the soaring trunks. Snowdrops unfurled white nodding petals above long green leaves. The air smelt sharp and fresh and new.

Ava ran into the garden, her eyes searching ahead of her. There was the statue of the lions ahead, framed in the arches of bare branches. The bronze lion, stern and strong, was standing over his wounded lioness, stricken at his feet. A tall man in grey stood with his head bent down over his hands, gripping the edge of the pedestal.

'Leo!' she called.

He turned. His face changed. He stepped forward, and she ran into his arms.

Leo bent his mouth to hers. Time folded its wings. Ava was utterly lost to the world, utterly lost in sensation. At last, their mouths parted. They did not let each other go.

'Ava. You came.' His voice was gruff.

She nodded.

'I'm glad.' His fingers twined in her hair.

'Leo,' Ava managed to say, bending her head to rest her forehead against his chest. She could hear his heart hammering away inside the drum of his chest.

'I didn't think you'd come.'

'I . . . I couldn't stay away.'

'Shall we walk?' he asked.

Ava nodded. They fell into pace beside each other, walking deeper into the gardens. Ava had drawn her hand away. Leo reached for it again, turning it over in his, threading his fingers through hers.

'So that was Rupert?' he spoke at last.

'Yes.'

'Your Jewish friends stay with you still?'

'Yes.'

He said no more. Ava stared ahead. Her breath was still uneven. She felt shy and afraid and embarrassed, and yet so happy she wanted to sing. She did not know how to negotiate what she felt. They came to a glade of trees, and he drew her under their shadow, so that he could kiss her again without fear of being seen.

'It's been hell, these last few months,' Leo said.

Ava nodded.

'I didn't want to love you.'

'I didn't want to love you either.'

He looked down at her, his lips softening. 'But do you now, Ava? Do you love me now?'

'I don't know.'

He caught her to him, kissing her again. 'I think you do,' he said, when at last he let her go.

Ava could not speak. 'Is this love, this thing that I feel? It's . . . so hard.'

'Love is difficult,' Leo said, with that quirk of his mouth that was not quite a smile.

'Is that . . . is that Rilke again?' Ava looked up at him in astonishment.

Leo nodded. 'From his *Letters to a Young Poet*. "For one human being to love another human being: that is perhaps the most difficult task that has been entrusted to us."' He smiled a little at the look on Ava's face, and shrugged. 'I once thought I might write poetry.'

'Why did you stop?'

'Oh, my grandfather soon beat that idea out of me.'

'That's terrible.' Ava took his hand and laid it against her face. He turned it so his palm cupped her cheek, then brushed his thumb over her lip. 'Oh, God, Ava, I want you so much.' He drew her closer, kissing her hungrily, and Ava could do nothing but kiss him back. It was as if some cord bound them tightly together. Ava felt the trace of fire on her skin as his fingers slipped inside the collar of her dress. She trembled. He felt it, and drew her even closer, his hand sliding within her brasserie. No boy had ever dared touch her there before. Ava gasped. He pressed her back against the trunk of a tree, his kiss deepening till Ava could feel the earth spinning beneath her. She wrested her mouth away. 'Stop, stop!' she managed to say.

They fell apart, both panting and dishevelled. Ava was unable to look at him. She drew together the neck of her dress. 'You must stop,' she said in a steadier voice.

He cupped her face in his hands, making her look at him. 'I live just down the path from here.'

Ava shook her head. 'No, Leo. I can't.'

He closed his warm mouth over her earlobe. Ava shuddered so violently he put his arm about her, drawing her inside his coat. 'You're cold, and no wonder. It's freezing out here. Let me take you home. It's much, much warmer there.' He kissed the pulse at the base of her throat.

'Leo, please. Don't. This is all too fast. I know nothing about you.' She pushed out from underneath his arm, and walked swiftly away across the grass.

He fell into pace beside her. 'I know everything I need to know about you. I know you are the bravest and truest girl I ever met.'

'I'm not brave,' Ava replied huskily. 'If you only knew how afraid I really am. Sometimes I think I am afraid of everything.'

'But isn't that what being brave is all about? Being afraid, but doing it anyway? The way you went to help your friends, that night of broken glass. The way you sang that Christmas carol, with Himmler and Heydrich sitting right there in front of you.'

'That's not brave, that's just stupid.'

He grinned. 'I certainly thought so. But also . . . so gallant.'

'I . . . I just felt I had to do something!'

'Even if you were risking your own life?'

'Don't you see how wrong that is? That helping old friends is so dangerous?' Ava gazed up at him imploringly.

Leo nodded. His face was stern.

'How can you work for them?' she burst out.

'I am an officer in the German army,' Leo answered sharply. 'In all likelihood, we are headed for war. Do you think I would be permitted to resign my commission, even if I wished to so disgrace my family's name?'

'Would it be such a disgrace?'

He gave a brief nod. 'Especially in the eyes of my grandfather. He would be humiliated. He cannot disinherit me, but he would probably refuse to ever speak to me again. And that would cause my mother much unhappiness.'

Ava sighed. 'Isn't there something you can do?'

'I don't want to,' Leo answered, his voice still edged. 'I am proud of my family's history, proud to follow in my father's footsteps. I am glad that I can work to save Germany from the shame and dishonour of the Treaty of Versailles.'

Ava thrust both her cold hands into her coat pockets. They walked on in silence, keeping to the sunlit side of the path.

'Besides, it would disappoint the Admiral too and he has been so good to me. It would be poor repayment for all his kindness,' Leo added, after a while. His voice had softened, though he did not look at her.

'The Admiral? He is your boss?'

'Yes, and a hard taskmaster he is too. Old Whitehead works twenty hours a day and sees no reason why his staff shouldn't too. He even sleeps in his office most of the time!'

'Isn't he the head of the Abwehr?'

Leo nodded.

'Rupert says that means you're a spy.'

Leo looked faintly amused. 'Not at all. I work in administration. Very boring, really. We've been busy reorganising the place, trying to make it more efficient.'

'But what does the Abwehr do? Isn't it some kind of secret service?'

'We're the Defence Office of the Armed Forces High Command,' he answered. 'We collect information. That's all.'

'Is that what you meant when you said it was your job to find things out?'

He glanced at her then, and one side of his mouth compressed in sudden amusement. He nodded and gave a little shrug. 'Yes, that's what I meant.'

'So how do you find things out?'

'Any way I can.' Leo gave a rueful grin. 'I must say, you're just like the Elephant's Child.'

'The what?' Ava asked.

'"The Elephant's Child." It's a story by an English writer about a baby elephant who is insatiably curious and keeps asking questions, even when he's spanked for doing so. My mother used to read it to us when we were children, doing all the different voices.'

Ava stared at him, then laughed. 'Don't think I haven't noticed that you're trying – not very adroitly – to change the topic of conversation.'

Leo ran his hand through his cropped fair hair. 'I cannot tell you about what we do, Ava. I'm sorry.'

'Don't you trust me?' She felt a prick of anger.

Leo frowned. 'You are rather startlingly frank,' he pointed out. 'I was so afraid of what you'd say when Himmler reprimanded you for singing that Christmas carol.'

She looked away from him. It was no consolation at all that he was right, and she knew she was far too impulsive and outspoken.

'It's as much for your own safety as mine,' Leo added.

Ava did not reply.

Leo hesitated, then drew her under the shadow of a great elm. 'I will tell you one thing. You'd like the Admiral. He feels much the same as you do about certain things, though he is far more discreet.'

'What do you mean?'

'His local pastor was arrested for preaching against the violence of the night of broken glass. Admiral Canaris spoke up for him, and he was released. And he helped Pastor Bonhoeffer get his Jewish brother-in-law across the border into Switzerland. You must not tell anyone this, Ava.'

'I wouldn't,' she cried indignantly.

'I shouldn't have told you such a thing. Your sister works for the Schutzstaffel.' Leo spoke the whole word, not the usual acronym of SS as everyone else did. 'You must promise me you'll never tell her.'

'I promise.'

He gazed down at her searchingly, his brows drawn low over his blue eyes. After a moment, his mouth relaxed. 'All right. It must be my turn to ask questions. Tell me, why are you so different from your sisters? They are so ordinary, so German. You . . . you are like an exotic flower, transplanted from a jungle.'

She laughed ruefully. 'They are only half-sisters. My mother was Spanish.'

'That explains your beautiful wild hair . . .'

Ava gathered up her curls and twisted them back. 'I wish it wasn't so wild. My sister Monika is most disapproving. She likes everything to be neat and orderly.'

'I can't imagine your hair being orderly.'

'Monika says I should just cut it all off but . . . I don't know.'

'It would be a terrible shame.' His eyes were intent on her face.

Ava felt a little breathless. 'Monika used to cut it short when I was a kid. She'd hack it all off, but it just made it wilder and curlier. Once she cut it so short, I looked like a boy. I told her then she'd never cut it again, and she never has, though she used to try and chase me around with the scissors.'

Leo gave that half-smile of his. 'I can just imagine you as a kid, so long-legged and lithe. She'd never have a hope of catching you.'

'No,' Ava agreed. 'I was quite a handful for my poor sisters, I think.'

'And your mother was a singer too, wasn't she?'

Ava nodded. 'She had a low contralto, just like me. My father heard her sing before he ever met her. He says he fell in love with her voice.'

'A siren voice, then, just like you. I heard from Herr Kittel that you won your scholarship. How are you enjoying being at the conservatory?'

As he spoke, he began to walk again and Ava fell into step beside him. 'I don't know . . . my singing teacher asks so much of me. He's never satisfied. I don't think he likes my voice.'

'Impossible,' Leo answered.

Ava glanced at him. He smiled down at her. Her heart accelerated. She looked away. 'He's trying to make me sing higher. He thinks I should try for being a mezzo-soprano so there are more roles for me.'

'What do you want to do?'

'I don't know. I just want to sing. If it means I can get more work . . .'

'You should not change who you are.'

Ava did not answer. She felt troubled and guilty. Leo served Hitler. Ava wanted him to give it all up. To become a poet, or a farmer, or anything else at all. She wanted him to throw it all over, to stand up against Hitler, to renounce the Nazis. She wanted him to change.

11

A Fork in the Path

Men were hoisting swastika banners to hang from every light pole along the Tiergartenstrasse. Other men were erecting barriers.

'The Führer returns from Prague this afternoon,' Leo said. 'They are organising another triumphant parade.' Ava could not look at him. They walked on through the garden, the shadows of trees falling over them like bars. 'He broke his word,' Leo said, after a long silence. 'He promised he had no designs on Czechoslovakia.'

His voice was so troubled, Ava put her hand on his arm. 'It's not the first time he's done so.'

'I know. But somehow this feels worse. He told the whole world, he signed the Munich Agreement. He is our Führer, his word should be able to be trusted.'

'You feel . . . betrayed?'

Leo nodded. 'I knew you would understand. Nobody else seems to care. All my friends are jubilant. They think the Führer has outwitted the English and the French and got his way yet again, without any bloodshed. They think that this will be the end of it all. But I'm afraid it's only the beginning.'

'You think Hitler is leading us into war?'

'Yes.'

Ava looked out at the gardens, a cathedral of dark wood and snow. White blossoms foamed in the branches of a cherry tree. Wood violets sprouted from its tangled roots, and, in the middle of the lawn, a few early daffodils showed a glimpse of yellow petals unfurling. A robin was digging at something under the snow. His breast was red, his eye lively. Children were kicking a ball about, their laughter bright in the air like a handful of flung golden coins. Beyond the bare branches of the elm trees, the domes and spires and clock towers of Berlin floated above a pale blue mist.

'What are you going to do?' she whispered.

'I don't know. What can I do?' His mouth compressed. 'German officers do not break their word of honour, even if their Führer does.'

'If Germany goes to war, will you have to fight, Leo?' She looked up at him as they walked on down the path, her cold hand tucked into the crook of his elbow.

'Of course.' His gaze was distant, troubled. Then he looked down at Ava and drew her closer, one arm about her waist. 'I cannot say the prospect excites me much. Contrary to what you think, not all German officers are war-mongering hawks with blood on their claws.'

'I'm sorry.' She looked away.

'I met him once, you know. The Führer.'

Ava did not speak.

'We had to wait for hours for him to come. We were all in our Hitler Youth uniforms. It was so hot in the sun. And when he came, he spoke all about our shame, our dishonour. How it was not our fault that we had lost the Great War, that we'd been tricked and stabbed in the back. I . . . I cannot tell you what a relief this was. My father fought in the war, you know. He was badly wounded. He lived for years in pain and humiliation. I think he was glad to die at last. He never recovered from the disgrace of it.'

'That's so awful.' Ava thought about her own father. He had fought in the Great War too. He had always said that war leaves a country with three armies – an army of cripples, an army of mourners and an army of thieves. He had taught Ava to fear the very idea of war.

Leo fell silent, his gaze turned inwards. 'Then the Führer told us how he could save us, how he could save Germany. He said all we had to do was trust him. I can't describe to you the feeling . . . we were all caught up in it. I remember my brother Alex . . . his eyes were shining. We shouted till our throats were hoarse, we stretched out our hands as high as we could. Here was our hope, here was our salvation! We could not sleep that night, we sat by our campfire talking about him all night long. It was . . . it was exhilarating.'

They had come to a fork in the path. Ava paused, not knowing which way to go, not knowing what to say.

'I have to trust the Führer, Ava. I have to stay loyal. He made us a promise – to save us from the humiliation of our defeat, to restore to us our honour – and in that he has not failed us. We always knew the struggle would be bloody and hard. Now is not the time to lose faith.'

Ava felt cold, and drew her coat more closely about her. They had been walking a long time. The sun was sliding down behind the trees and the wind had risen. It blew from the east, from the icy Russian steppes, making the trees shake in their boots of snow. In the distance she could see the burnt-out hulk of the Reichstag and, standing tall before it, the Victory column. The golden angel gleamed in the sunset light, soaring far above the trees, holding aloft a crown of laurel.

'I heard that the Führer threatened to bomb Prague into rubble if the Czech President didn't grant the German army free passage. Is that true?'

Leo nodded. 'I believe so.'

'I heard the Führer kept the poor old man waiting till after one o'clock in the morning before he deigned to meet with him. Then, when he heard the threats, the Czech President suffered a heart attack but Hitler would not let him rest till he signed the terms of the surrender.'

'I . . . I don't know if that is true. It sounds callous, I know, but . . .'

'It's more than callous, it's cruel!'

'It may not be true.'

Ava gestured violently. 'He's driving us towards war. Can't you see he must be stopped?'

He caught her hand. 'Ava, please . . . I don't want another war . . . no-one I know does . . . except perhaps my grandfather. But can't you see? The Führer has done so much already . . . he's restored our national pride, he's given us back all our lost lands . . .'

'Through murder and lies and robbery.' Ava knew she was speaking wildly.

'I . . . I cannot like the thuggery, the violence, the breaking of his word of honour . . . oh, but Ava, can't you see . . . I swore a sacred oath of obedience to the Führer. I swore to defend him with my life.'

A grey feeling of hopelessness came over her. Ava saw in that moment that there was no chance of changing him. She either had to accept Leo as he was, an officer in the service of the Third Reich and a loyal follower of the Führer, or she had to never see him again.

'I think . . . I think I should go home.'

Leo stopped and turned to face her, gripping her shoulders with his strong, hard hands. 'Please, Ava. Don't. Stay with me.'

She hesitated, her feelings in turmoil. Tears dampened her eyes, and she dashed them away with her fingers.

'Ava, please don't cry.' Leo kissed her, and she turned her face away, the tears coming faster. He tried to make her look at him, and she resisted.

He held her fast. 'Ava, I . . . I think I'm in love with you. I think . . . you're the only beautiful, true thing left in a world of ugliness and lies.' He spoke quickly. 'I tried to keep away from you, I tried to forget you. But it's impossible. You're in my blood now. I'm sick with longing for you, I can't sleep for wanting you. I can't bear it. I have to have you!'

Ava broke away from him. She ran blindly along the dusk-shadowed path, her breath coming in rags. She heard his footsteps behind her. She was within sight of the road when he caught her.

'Ava, stop! What is it? What's wrong?'

A procession of Brownshirts marched along the road to the Reichstag, flaming torches in their hands. Ava could hear faint snatches of their song. Crowds lined the road, cheering. Searchlights probed the sky. She could see a procession of cars crawling along the road, headlights blazing.

Hitler would be in one of them, waving to the crowd, accepting their jubilant cheers. He had dismembered a democratically elected government, a land that had once been full of hope for the future. Czechoslovakia no longer existed. It was now a vassal state. How much further would Hitler go? How many other countries would be ground under his boot?

'You Nazis think you can have anything you want,' she cried. 'Well, I am not yours for the taking!'

Leo's hands gripped her painfully. He spoke, very low. 'I want you in my life. I want you in my bed. Ava, I need you. We can find some way to make this work. Say you'll see me again.'

Ava shook her head.

For a moment, Leo was utterly still. Then he cried, in a voice of such anger it frightened her. 'Why not? Ava . . .'

'I can't. I won't.'

'But . . . why?'

Ava wrenched herself free. She pointed one shaking hand at the procession of flaming torches, at the sleek black cars sliding between the screaming crowds.

'You're one of them . . .'

There was a long silence. When he spoke, Leo's voice was bleak. 'It's what I do, Ava, what I've been brought up to do.'

'What you're doing is not right.'

There was a long silence.

Beyond the dark forest of the Tiergarten, Berlin was a fairy-tale land of lights. People were singing. Fireworks began to pierce the sky above the Reichstag.

'Is it because of him?' Leo's voice had changed.

'Him?' Ava said stupidly.

'The Jewish boy. Rupert. Are you in love with him?'

She shook her head, bewildered. 'No!'

'He's in love with you.'

Ava opened her mouth to tell him that Rupert was not interested in girls. He had never been interested in girls. As long as Ava had known him, it had always been a good-looking boy that had caught his attention. But she could not speak. She knew what the Nazis thought about boys who loved boys. She could not betray Rupert so.

Leo felt her hesitation. 'Are you lovers?' he demanded.

'No!' Ava cried. But her voice did not ring true, shaken by all she could not say. She heard the false note in it, and so did he.

'I'll kill him!' Leo cried. He seized Ava again, bruising her with the hardness of his grip. 'I cannot bear it. You're mine.'

Ava struggled to be free. 'I'm not yours! I belong to myself.'

He let her go. 'Don't you understand what they'll do to you if they find out? They'll shave off all your beautiful hair. They'll parade you through the city with a notice reading "whore" about your neck. They'll castrate him and sterilise you. They'll . . .'

She fled away down the road, pushing her way through the cheering crowd. She was blind with tears. She heard Leo call, 'Ava! Ava! Stop!'

But she did not stop.

That night, Ava was woken by the sound of fists hammering at the door. She tumbled out of bed. She could hear her father's surprised voice calling out, and the sound of someone shouting, 'Open up! Gestapo!'

When Otto opened the front door, he was pushed roughly back into the apartment by a troop of men in the sinister black uniforms of the SS. There was another man, in a long leather coat, who all the soldiers deferred to.

They dragged Rupert away with them. He barely had time to throw on some clothes or slip his feet into shoes.

'But why?' Tante Thea wept. 'He's only a boy. He's done nothing.'

'Subversive activities,' the Gestapo man said. Then, chillingly, he flicked a look at Ava, in her nightgown, barefoot, her hair falling out of its plait. She felt his look like a punch in the stomach. Her legs folded. She sat down on the step, not knowing how she got there.

Then Rupert was gone, dragged out into the cold wind of the dawn.

Beech Forest

Ava had her head between her knees, her hands over her eyes.

'It was you! You did it!' Jutta shouted.

Ava hunched her shoulders.

'How could you do such a thing! If you didn't want us here, why not just ask us to go?' Jutta's voice broke.

'You stupid fool,' Monika responded sharply. 'You think I want the Gestapo knocking on my door in the middle of the night? You think I want our name associated with dirty Jews?'

'Monika! Don't you speak that way!' Ava's father was angry. He was so rarely angry.

'You work for the SS. You love the Nazis. You never wanted us here.' Jutta hurled her accusations at Monika.

Ava tried to focus. She was so cold. She gripped the balustrade and waited till the dancing lights in her eyes had cleared. Jutta stood in the hallway below, facing Monika. Ava's sister looked cool and composed. Not a hair out of place.

'Oh God, oh God, what will they do to him? What will they do to my boy?' Tante Thea had turned to Onkel Franz, and buried her face in his chest. He held her, his arms stiff, his eyes blank with horror.

'How can you accuse Monika so?' Bertha cried. 'We took you in when no-one else would – you've lived under our roof for months, we've fed you and put up with you, and now you have the cheek to accuse Monika this way!' She sobbed, strands of blonde hair clinging to her round, flushed face. Her large breasts heaved under her flannel night-gown. Unlike Monika, she had not taken the time to put on her slippers and robe. Lying curled on the floor, Angelika whimpered, her toy lamb in her hand.

'If it was not you, then, who was it?' Jutta demanded. 'Someone knew he was here, someone denounced him. Was it your fat old housekeeper? She never wanted us here.'

'And now you accuse poor old Frau Günther,' Monika said bitingly. 'Whose only crime was to cook you meals you refused to eat. What makes you think it was one of *us*? Your brother was always hanging out with a wild crowd, all those dirty jazz-loving Jews! Maybe it was one of *them*.'

Onkel Franz straightened his shoulders. 'Us, them. Now we know what you really think. Jutta, Thea, get your things. We leave this house now.'

'But, Franz, it's five o'clock in the morning,' Ava's father protested. 'There's no need for you to go.'

'I will not stay in this house another moment,' Onkel Franz said. 'I thank you for your hospitality, Otto. But we should never have accepted it. We need to find a place amongst our own people now.'

'Franz,' Father said pleadingly. 'Monika did not mean . . .'

'Yes, she did,' Onkel Franz answered. He put his arm around his wife. 'I'm sorry, Thea. I was obstinate. I wouldn't listen. I couldn't believe that the Germany we loved could so turn against us. We should have left long ago. Then perhaps Rupert . . .' His voice broke on his son's name.

'We'll find him, Father,' Jutta said.

Onkel Franz nodded his head. 'Yes. We'll find him and we'll get him out of there, no matter what it costs.'

Ava's frozen brain realised what was happening. She stumbled down the stairs, her hands held out like a sleepwalker. 'No. No. Don't go. Please. We're sorry. Let us help.'

'I think you've done enough,' Jutta cried. 'Rupert told me how you went out with that Nazi. How could you? When you know the things they've done!'

Ava shrank back. 'I'm sorry. I didn't mean . . . I didn't know . . .'

'Ava's done nothing except try to help you all,' her father cried.

'Get your things,' Onkel Franz said to his wife and daughter.

Tante Thea moved like an old woman, as if every step hurt her. Jutta, however, was in a frenzy, gathering up armfuls of things and throwing them into boxes and bags. They had all been living out of suitcases for months now. It did not take long before they were ready to go.

'Please don't go,' Ava wept. 'I'm so sorry.'

'Ava, be quiet,' Monika said. 'It's better that they go.'

As the Feidlers went out the front door, Otto caught his old friend's arm. 'Franz, we had nothing to do with it. None of my daughters would do such a thing. You must believe me.'

Onkel Franz went out without saying a word. Tante Thea followed silently behind.

'Jutta!' Ava called. Jutta looked back at her. 'I must know where you go! Please! Let me know. There must be something I can do to help.'

Jutta hesitated, then nodded.

Ava could not get warm. She crept into the sitting room, and lay down on the couch where Rupert had been sleeping only half an hour earlier. She drew his blanket over her and lay staring into the fire, sunk down into ashes. It stared back at her with two dozen slitted fiery eyes.

She did not think it possible that she could sleep. Her thoughts spun around and around like a scratched record. Not Leo. He couldn't do such a thing. Could he? Not Monika. She had called Rupert a dirty Jew, she admired Hitler and all he had done, but could Monika betray a boy she had known all her life? Not Bertha. No, surely not. Though Bertha hated disorder, she hated her routines to be upset. It must have been Frau Günther! If so, then it was all her fault. Ava had been the one to get the housekeeper sacked. Perhaps it had been Felix . . . if he had been arrested . . . if he had told them about his affair with Rupert . . . but Rupert had been arrested on the very night she had broken with Leo. It must have been Leo. She had been a fool, a stupid impulsive fool. She had fallen for a Nazi, she had brought him to their doorstep, and look what had happened.

No, no, her sore heart cried. It can't have been Leo. He wouldn't, he couldn't do such a thing. It must have been someone else. And once again her thoughts whirred around.

Ava had the strange sensation of her body growing heavier and heavier, sinking down into the soft cushions while her mind seemed to be drawn upwards, growing smaller and smaller and lighter and lighter. Just before the tiny spark of her was snuffed out and obliterated, she bent her will to her body again, feeling a kind of wild dumb panic. Her body was falling. With a wrench, she tried to find a centre of gravity, some sense of where she was. She opened her eyes, groping out with her hands. She was standing on a staircase. It went down into darkness. Ava crept down the steps. Her heartbeat drummed in her ears. She saw dimly, at the bottom of the stairs, an iron door, bolted and barred. She struggled to unbolt it. Her body was too weak. She exerted all her strength. With a rusty scream, the door opened. Shakily Ava stepped forward. She saw a cell with barred windows. A man was tied to a chair. He was naked. His head fell forward on to his chest. A pool of blood seeped across the floor. A red and bloody tide, spreading, quickening. Ava opened her mouth to scream, but her vocal cords were strangled. She could not scream. She could make no sound at all.

Ava woke with a jerk. For a moment she could not breathe, or make sense of where she was. Then she realised she lay tangled and sweating in blankets, on the couch in the sitting room. The fire was dead. Grey light leaked around the edges of the curtains. Grey as the music of funeral marches and fugues.

Ava got up and dressed. Her fingers were clumsy. She found it hard to tie her bootlaces and do up the buttons of her cardigan. She could not bear to wear her red coat and beret. Instead she drew on an old brown coat of Monika's with a rather squashed and shapeless brown hat.

She followed Monika through the busy morning streets. Her sister was immaculate as always in a tight black suit and high heels, her cropped blonde bob swinging under an elegant black hat that she wore tilted over one eyebrow. Monika did not look back. She crossed the River Spree, then headed straight down the Friedrichstrasse.

Ava had begged her sister for help, but Monika had been adamant. 'Don't be an idiot,' she had said crisply. 'Going to the Gestapo offices will do nothing but draw attention to you, and put Rupert in more danger. Aryan girls are not meant to fraternise with Jewish boys. You're lucky you were not arrested too.'

Ava could not stay at home and do nothing, however. She knew, from what Monika had once said, that the Gestapo headquarters were next door to the offices of the SS, where her sister worked. She knew that they were on Prinz-Albrecht-Strasse which was near the Philharmonie where Ava went for her music studies. She did not know how to get there, though, and so she followed her sister through the chilly grey morning. Ava kept her head down, tucking her chin into her scarf, finding it hard to meet anyone's eyes. Buses blasted their horns, bicycle bells dinged, car engines roared, trams rattled along. All the sounds were too loud, all the colours too bright. It was a cacophony of atonality, like coloured paints splattered against a wall by a drunk.

And all the time Ava's thoughts whirred around and around. Not Leo. Not Leo. But who?

At last Monika turned off the crowded main road, and went down a wide avenue with big, gracious mansions and hotels set in manicured gardens. Monika went into one grand building, her heels clacking on the stone steps. Ava waited for a while in the street, her hands pushed deep into her coat pockets, watching young men in uniforms come up and down the stairs, saluting each other, and young women in neat suits hurry about, carrying heavy folders. She asked one which was the Gestapo head-quarters, and the young woman pointed her to a stately old building with rows of high arched windows and an ornate pediment topped with huge stone urns. It looked like a luxurious hotel, or a museum. It did not look anything like what Ava had imagined. Emboldened, she went in.

A large and airy vestibule lay within, with a beautiful arched ceiling and a broad marble staircase leading upwards. Long wooden benches were set against the walls, crowded with anxious-faced people. Some had shopping baskets on their knees, or folded coats and blankets. Others held sheafs of paper.

A long queue of people stood before a desk where a harassed-looking older man sat with a telephone at his elbow, and great piles of folders. One old woman was trying hard not to weep, her crumpled handkerchief pressed to her mouth. A thin woman held a baby against her shoulder, a toddler gripping her skirt. As groups of men hurried past, she would call to them, 'Please help me, please.' Her voice was hoarse and hopeless.

Onkel Franz sat on a bench nearby, twisting his hat between his hands. He was dressed in a long dark coat, and his bearded face was bewildered. Jutta sat bolt upright beside him, her feet set neatly side by side, her dark hair shoved behind her ears. Her black eyes were brilliant with anger.

Ava went to join them, trying to smile in greeting, but finding her mouth too stiff with tension to move.

'What are you doing here?' Jutta said without preamble.

'I had to come. I had to find out if Rupert was all right.'

'He's not your brother.'

Ava fell back a step in her surprise. 'I . . . I know. I'm sorry.' She gazed at Jutta in consternation, realising for the first time how Rupert's little sister must have felt all those years, being locked out of his room while he and Ava had played records and sang and danced.

'Jutta,' Onkel Franz said warningly. 'Ava did not need to come. And perhaps she can help.' He looked up at her, his face creased with worry. 'We have been here more than an hour already, and have got nowhere. They have given us a number, but there are hundreds ahead of us. Perhaps they will talk to you.'

'I can try,' Ava said. She looked around, wondering who she could ask.

'Why did you wear that horrible old hat?' Jutta demanded. She jumped up and dragged it off Ava's head. 'Take off your coat too. Can you loosen your hair? Why have you got it all screwed up like that?'

Ava stood dumbfounded as Jutta unpinned her hair and shook it down onto her shoulders, then unbuttoned the top few buttons of her cardigan. 'What is the point of being beautiful if you don't use it?' Jutta scolded her. 'Go and smile at that young officer over there.' She pushed Ava roughly.

Ava made her way across the vestibule to where a young man in uniform stood on guard before a set of heavy double doors. She smiled at him, though her pulse was racing along far too fast, and looked up at him beseechingly. He smiled back at her.

'I do hope you can help me,' Ava said.

'So do I, Fräulein,' he answered admiringly.

'An old school friend of mine was arrested last night. His family is beside themselves, and no-one seems to know where he is or what has happened to him.'

'Oh, he would have been taken down to the cellars.' The guard indicated the doors beside him. 'Do you know why he was arrested?'

'Subversive activities.' Ava could barely manage to say the words.

The guard frowned. 'Is he a Jew?'

'Yes.'

The guard's expression changed. His eyes became hard and cold. 'And he is your friend, you say?'

Ava felt her face beginning to burn. 'An old friend. From childhood.'

'Best not to have friends like that, Fräulein.'

'If I could just let his parents know what has happened to him.'

The guard shrugged. 'Most likely he'll be sent to a labour camp.'

'But . . . what has he been charged with? Shouldn't there be a trial?'

The guard gave a brief bark of laughter. 'A trial? Oh, no. He'll have signed a Form D-11, asking for protective custody. The Reich will grant him his wish and send him off to a camp. For his own safety.'

Ava could not make sense of what he said. 'But . . . why would Rupert sign such a form? He hasn't done anything!'

'The police can be very persuasive,' the guard answered.

At that moment, a thickset man in a leather coat came through the vestibule. He had the face and hands of a thug. Broken nose, cauliflower ears, scarred and reddened knuckles. Every uniformed man leapt to prompt attention, their hands flying up, the clicking of their heels like a swift shower of hail. 'Heil Hitler!' they shouted. The thickset man ignored them. He came straight to the double doors. The guard Ava had been speaking to was now standing stiff as a ramrod. He opened the doors. A strange, unpleasant smell rolled out, and strange, unpleasant sounds. Thwacks like a leather belt into the palm of a hand, low cries and moans, a shrill squealing like a piglet being dragged into an abattoir. The thickset man ran his eyes over Ava. 'What is she doing here?' he asked.

'Nothing,' the guard responded, in a stiff voice. 'Enquiring after the powder room, sir.'

'Don't let me catch you fraternising with prisoners' next of kin,' the thickset man warned. Then he pushed through the doors. They swung shut behind him, cutting off all sound.

'The powder room is over there,' the guard said, pointing the way. In a lower voice, he added, 'You'd best go, Fräulein. There's nothing you can do for your friend. And you do not want the police to start looking at you.'

Ava went to the powder room. She drank some water. She could not seem to fill her lungs with enough air. She washed her face, then went to tell Jutta and her father what she had learnt. They all sat on the hard wooden bench, staring at each other, not knowing what to do.

Then Onkel Franz roused himself. 'Go on home, Ava. Thank your father for his hospitality these last few months. I shall send you our address when we have one.'

Ava nodded and rose to her feet. She put her coat back on. Jutta sat, staring down at her clasped hands. The nails were bitten down to the bloody quick.

'Jutta . . .'

Rupert's sister looked up.

'I'm so sorry,' Ava said.

Jutta jerked her head in acknowledgement.

Ava went home. A red rose had been delivered for her, with a letter from Leo. She did not read the letter. She tore it up into the tiniest pieces she could manage and threw them on the fire. She tore the crimson petals from the rose's thorny stem, and threw them on the fire too. Then she sat down at the table and wrote a note to him.

It said: *I never want to see you again.*

Part II

Lion by Day
July – December 1939

Now the beast was an enchanted prince. By day he was a lion,
but by night he was a man.

'The Singing, Springing Lark', the Brothers Grimm

13

The English Sisters

The train whistle screamed. Clouds of smoke fumed up as the big wheels began to turn. Ava sat back in her seat, folding her white gloved hands on her lap. Her suitcase was in the rack above her head, her shabby hand-me-down handbag beside her.

'Isn't it hot?' The plump lady sitting opposite was perspiring profusely, dark crescents of sweat under her arms. She dabbed at her face with a handkerchief.

'Yes.' Ava smiled mechanically, then took out a magazine from her handbag and pretended to read it so that she did not have to make conversation. She did not really see the words, though. All her thoughts were taken up with what lay before her.

Ava was on her way to Bayreuth. Richard Wagner had once made his home there, and built an opera house where his immense works could be properly staged. In late July and early August, the town was taken over by a month-long music festival celebrating Wagner's work. Ava was to spend the summer there, singing in the chorus.

She should have been thrilled. It was a great coup for her to be invited to Bayreuth. All the other students in her music classes were envious. Yet Ava could muster no enthusiasm. Sometimes it seemed that her ability to feel anything at all had been cauterised on the night Rupert had been arrested. In the four months since, Ava had moved through life like an automaton. Obeying every directive of her teachers, she sang with as much precision and as much soul as a clockwork angel. They had been pleased, and rewarded her with this invitation to sing at Bayreuth.

Ava did not want to go. Hitler would be there. Wagner was his favourite composer, and Hitler had not missed a festival in Bayreuth since he had become the Führer. The whole town would be filled with his bodyguards and his sycophants. She would be forced to be a part of it. The very thought of it made her feel nauseous.

The train rattled out of the city, through a flat landscape of meadows and fields and towns with tall church spires. Ava stared out the window, her pale face superimposed over the racing landscape. Gradually the view changed. Low dark hills began to shoulder out of the plains. Fields gave way to houses, and then to apartments and industrial plants. The hills grew steeper and more rugged, and then the train clattered into the city of Jena. A multitude of silver train tracks ran side by side through dark blocks of buildings. The train stopped with a great hiss of steam.

Passengers hurried to disembark, while others struggled on with suitcases and packages. Ava saw a group of laughing young men in field-grey uniforms getting on with bulging packs. She pressed herself back in her corner, and raised the magazine. The train huffed its way out of the station, and then out of the city. Ava began to feel an unbearable restlessness. She walked up and down the passageway. To the west, a long flank of mountain lifted from the valley, dark with pine trees. Ava stared at it. Somewhere out there was the labour camp they called Buchenwald. That was where Rupert had been sent.

Ava went to visit the Feidlers whenever she could. They were living in a tiny, dank apartment in the Scheunenviertel slums, scraping a living any way they could. Onkel Franz was working in a factory that made paint for submarines and jet fighters. Tante Thea took in sewing when she could, while Jutta sorted old clothes and shoes at the Jewish charity. One day,

Jutta had met her in high excitement, saying they had received a letter from Rupert.

'It does not sound much like him at all,' Jutta had said with a perplexed frown. 'Though Father says any letters are probably read by the guards, and so Rupert is just being careful.'

She had given Ava the letter to read. *I am as well as can be expected. The work is hard, but at least I am doing my duty serving the Reich. Buchenwald means beech forest. Sometimes I see the trees waving their green hands above the walls. It brings me comfort. There is an oak tree in the centre of the camp. Goethe is said to have composed the Walpurgis Night sections of his Faust here. I can understand why. Tell Father I feel like his old friend Josef K.*

The letter had been written on a camp letterhead, printed with the rules of contact. Rupert's details were printed on the top. He was Prisoner No. 24161, in Block 22.

'A camp in a beech forest doesn't sound too bad, does it?' Tante Thea had said, a shawl wrapped around her thin, stooped shoulders. 'Surely the country air will be good for him?'

'I hope so,' Ava managed to say.

'Father says Josef K is a character in a book,' Jutta asked. 'Someone who is arrested and put on trial, but never told what his crime is.'

'Yes,' Ava answered. 'It's a book by Franz Kafka. Your father gave it to us to read when the Nazis first got in.'

'But what does he mean about the oak tree?'

Ava had glanced at Tante Thea, gazing down at the letter with eyes full of hope. In a low voice, Ava told Jutta, 'Walpurgis Night is when the witches meet to celebrate their satanic rites. In Goethe's story, Faust is taken there to encounter evil in all its forms. It's like a descent into hell.'

Jutta had stared at her in shocked understanding.

Remembering, Ava leant forward until her forehead was pressed against the glass. The train rocked sickeningly from side to side. She closed her eyes and tried not to think.

In the early evening, the train drew in to the station at Bayreuth. Although the sun had dropped from view, the air was still balmy and filled with the scents of summer. Many others got off at the station too, some carrying instrument cases. Ava was met by a pretty young woman with blonde plaits wound neatly about her head, dressed in an old-fashioned dirndl over a white blouse with puffed sleeves, just like the ones Bertha liked to dress Angelika in.

'God greet you,' she said with a beaming smile.

'Hopefully not too soon,' Ava answered, in the usual sardonic way of a Berliner.

The young woman's smile died away in puzzlement, then leapt up again as she got the joke. 'Yes, yes, hopefully not soon. You are Fräulein Ava Falkenhorst, yes? I am Britta Hummel. You are lodging with us.'

She took Ava's bag and led her out to where a pony and cart was waiting, keeping up a steady stream of cheerful small talk that made it unnecessary for Ava to do more than murmur an occasional response. The pony clopped through cobblestoned streets lined with elegant houses and shops, and past a church with a charming pepper-pot spire. Ava could not help but look about her and exclaim with pleasure, and Britta looked pleased. On the hill stood the Festival Theatre, a majestic red building with columns and a heavy triangular pediment. Ava did not think much of the architecture. Britta pulled out a handkerchief and offered it to her. Ava looked at her enquiringly.

'You do not weep,' Britta said in surprise. 'Most people who come cry when they see the Festival Theatre.'

'Oh. Not me, sorry.' Ava tried to smile.

Britta looked puzzled and put her handkerchief away.

The pony trap pulled up outside a small house in a row of houses, all exactly the same. A boy ran out to take the pony and cart, and Britta led Ava inside the house. It was clean and comfortable enough, presided over by Britta's stout mother, Frau Hummel. Ava was plied with food, which she could not eat, and was then shown to her room. It was small and neat and impersonal. Ava sat on the edge of the bed, feeling lonelier than she ever had.

Rupert, she thought. *My dearest almost-twin. I hope all the rumours I hear about these camps are untrue. I hope you are safe and well. I wish . . .* She could not find the words to frame the thought. Tears needled her eyes. *I wish I had never met him . . .*

Steel tools clattered on hard granite.

Grunts. Groans. Shouts of anger. A terrible cacophony. Rupert lifted a heavy rock and did his best to carry it up the hill. His arms trembled. His feet slipped in the mud. A hard blow across the back of the head. 'Hurry! Hurry!' He stumbled to the top of the slope. Dropped the rock. Ran down the hill. Struck on all sides by truncheons. 'Dirty pigs! Hurry! Hurry!'

Rupert ducked his head. Tried to protect his face. Reached the bottom of the hill. Heaved up another rock.

At last, too dark to see. Marched back to the camp. The camp brass band stood within the gates, playing a martial tune. Meant to make the prisoners march faster. The musicians were mostly gypsies, and had been dressed as circus performers. Red shirts with sweeping dolman sleeves, tight black jodhpurs, tall black boots. The prisoners did not look at the musicians, and the musicians did not look at the prisoners.

Lined up in rows on the Appellplatz. The SS like perfectly straight columns. Must stand to attention. Look straight ahead. Thumbs lined up with seams of trousers.

'Caps off!'

Every one of the ten thousand men in the camp whipped off their striped caps.

'Caps on!'

Rupert slapped his cap back on to his shaven head.

'Caps off!'

Everyone obeyed at once. The guards repeated the command a dozen times or more, till everyone was obeying with sufficient robotic precision. 'Caps on! Caps off! Caps on! Caps off!'

Rupert tried only to obey quickly enough.

At last they were allowed to stand down. Everyone queued up for food. Most tied their metal bowls to their waists, so they did not have to waste time fetching them. A ladle of thin scummy soup. A slice of black bread full of sawdust.

Rupert was too tired to eat.

'You must keep your strength up,' a voice said. The block elder of Block 22 stood beside him, frowning. 'If you don't eat, you'll die.'

Rupert was too sick at heart and weary to even shrug. The block elder lifted his own bowl to Rupert's mouth. 'Here. Drink up.'

Rupert swallowed obediently. It tasted foul.

'Don't give up hope,' the block elder said. 'They let many prisoners go after the Night of Broken Glass. They might let you go too.'

Rupert did not bother answering. He was so tired, his neck felt too weak for the weight of his head. The lights wavered strangely.

'Don't faint,' the block elder warned him. 'You'll only be beaten. Keep your feet, whatever happens.' He slid one arm around Rupert's shoulders and helped him walk back towards the barracks. The shock of the human tenderness was electrifying. Rupert had felt nothing but blows and kicks for months. 'You're not strong enough for quarry duty,' the block elder said. 'I will see if I can get you kitchen duty for a while.'

'Why . . .?' Rupert managed to ask.

The block elder grinned, a flash of teeth in a thin, dirty face. 'You have a Berlin accent. I'm a Berliner too. We need to stick together. My name is Rudi Arndt. What's yours?'

When Rupert told him, he realised he had not heard his name spoken in months. His throat closed over.

'Steady now,' Rudi said. 'Almost there.'

They made it back to the barracks. Layers of wooden bunk beds down either wall. Thin mattresses stuffed with straw. Rudi helped Rupert climb up to one of the top bunks, near a window. 'The secret to surviving in this place is to keep your strength up, stay invisible, and never stop hoping,' Rudi told him. 'I know. I've been in one prison camp or another for more than six years now.'

Rupert did not answer. He was glad to lie down. The straw rustled with lice. He was too exhausted to even scratch.

Rudi stood by the bunk beds, frowning, hands on bony hips. He wore only a sack-like set of striped pyjamas. A yellow triangle on his chest was overlaid with a red triangle, showing he was both a Jew and a Communist.

'Here.' Rudi gave Rupert a pen, much chewed at the end, and a creased piece of paper. 'Write it down. Else you'll just give up. Give up, and you let the bastards win.'

Rupert took the pen and paper, and hid them under his body. The barracks were full of men. Most lay down, exhausted, but a few played some kind of game with knucklebones. Rupert rested in silence. Waves of blackness lifted him and rolled him down again. Other men clambered into the bed beside him, till they were wedged in like sardines, heads to feet.

'Lights out,' Rudi called. The bare bulbs went dark, only a fiery filament within still burning for a few scant seconds. Men moaned, snored, belched, scratched. The straw rustled. Rupert thought the noise would drive him mad.

As the searchlight swept past, a hollow knot in the wooden wall of the hut allowed a feeble light to pass over him. Rupert sat up, taking care not to disturb the men who lay on either side. He crouched next to the tiny hole, pressing the paper up against the wall. He wrote, in a hand so weak it barely made a mark upon the paper, 'All names are lost, only numbers.'

The searchlight passed by. Rupert waited in the darkness, counting silently in his head. As each wave of light washed over him again, he wrote: 'All memories gone, all grace . . . all hope vanished, all honour . . . nothing left but fragments . . .'

He had filled up his scrap of paper. Rupert folded it very small and thrust it into the crack in the wood. It blocked out the light. He lay down. Somehow he slept.

The next day, Britta showed Ava the way to the theatre. The streets were thronged with people, strolling along, enjoying the sunshine. Britta pointed out everyone they passed. A tall elegant-looking blonde was identified as Germaine Lubin, the famous Parisian soprano and the first French woman to ever sing at Bayreuth. A small man with dark, intense eyes and a pronounced widow's peak was named as Victor de Sabata, the man who was to conduct Madame Lubin in *Tristan and Isolde*. 'He's half-Jewish, you know,' Britta said. 'We are all amazed that the Führer will permit him to be here. The Führer wanted Herr Toscanini, of course, but he would not come. Maybe he'd heard we all call him Toscanono . . . Because all he ever does is shout, "No, no!"' She laughed.

Ava was about to pass on the rumour that Toscanini had refused to return to Bayreuth in protest at Hitler's rule, but then thought better of it and did not speak.

The lawn was crowded with people lining the road. Then Ava heard a burst of cheering. Britta's face lit up. 'The Führer!' she cried. 'I'd heard he was in town.' She raced towards the road, and Ava had to follow after her or lose her guide.

The crowd surged forward. Men in black uniforms held the masses of people back. Everyone had their right hands held up in the rigid Hitler salute. They were all shouting 'Heil, Hitler! Heil, Hitler!' Many of the women looked faint with excitement.

A large black Mercedes drove slowly past. The Führer sat in the back, smiling and waving at the crowds. The sight of him made Ava's stomach lurch. Britta nudged her, and Ava realised she was the only one whose right hand had not sprung into the air. She raised it, hating herself as she did so.

Two blonde women sat on either side of the Führer. Ava was surprised to see that both wore red lipstick painted on their mouths in a cupid's bow. It had been so long since she had seen a girl wearing make-up. And they wore it while sitting right next to Hitler!

'Who are they?' Ava whispered in Britta's ear, lowering her arm with relief.

'Some English ladies,' she answered. 'The Führer calls the younger one his Valkyrie. Her sister is said to be the most beautiful woman in England . . . and the most hated.'

'Why?' Ava asked, gazing at the two women with interest. Certainly one of them was very beautiful, with perfectly groomed blonde hair cut in soft waves just under her ears, and a classical profile. Her skin was pale and very fine, and her eyes so pale a blue as to be almost transparent. She was dressed in an elegant wool suit with pearls. Her sister was dressed all in black, an odd choice for such a hot day. She wore a golden swastika badge prominently on her collar. She was pretty enough, but next to her sister faded into insignificance.

'Her name is Lady Mosley,' Britta said. 'She caused a great scandal by leaving her husband and sons for another man, and then marrying him in secret, here in Germany, at Herr Goebbels' house. His wife had only just died. They kept their marriage hidden till she had his baby, and then they had to tell everyone.'

Britta led Ava up the slope towards the theatre, still chatting away. 'The other sister is Miss Unity Mitford. She is meant to be madly in love with the Führer. She follows him around just like a little lapdog. Wherever he goes, she pops up soon after. Of course, everyone's a little in love with the Führer. Have you heard the tale of women eating gravel that he has stepped on?'

The Mercedes had drawn up outside the theatre. People crowded around the Führer. Ava was surprised by how short he was, and how neat his hair. She had only ever seen Hitler on newsreels before, pounding the podium, punching the air, his hair falling in his eyes and being flicked back. He had seemed so huge and angry. Now he seemed so mild, almost like an ordinary man. The SS officers kept the crowd back, as Hitler passed through into the theatre. The two English sisters followed him. Britta proudly pushed her way after them, showing the bodyguards her performer's pass. Ava did the same. It was much cooler and quieter in the vestibule. The Führer was being greeted by Victor de Sabata, who was surrounded by his own entourage of fawning subordinates.

Herr de Sabata smiled and nodded at the beautiful Lady Mosley, but it was her younger, more awkward sister that he greeted most effusively. Two bunches of flowers were pressed into her arms. 'Welcome to Bayreuth,' he cried.

Lady Mosley frowned and looked displeased at the attention lavished upon her younger sister.

'Oh, Honks, don't look so frightfully cross,' the younger sister said, in English. Her voice was clear and carrying, and sounded just like the newsreaders on BBC Radio. 'I can't help it if they adore me. They think I've got the Führer's ear.'

'Poor sweets, they will be disappointed,' the elder answered.

'Oh you're always so mean. I do have his ear, I do!'

'Well, then, I wish you'd bend it on our behalf, Bobo,' Lady Mosley replied. 'Poor Oswald is having a terrible time with money at the moment. You know how much trouble he's having with his little radio project. It'd make all the difference in the world if we could get some more funding from the Führer.'

The younger one said loudly, 'I think the Führer has quite enough on his mind at present.'

Hitler, catching the sound of his title, turned and smiled at her. 'Come join us, my child.'

She tossed back her blonde curls, gave her sister a triumphant smile, and went bounding across to join the Führer. He beckoned to her sister as well. 'Lady Mosley, my dear Miss Mitford, I'd like to introduce you to Herr Lorenz, our famous tenor . . .'

Ava, following Britta away towards the rehearsal rooms, heard no more. But she could not help thinking about the English sisters all afternoon. They had been so astonishingly frank. Was it just because they had not expected anyone in the crowd to speak English? Surely not. Many of the singers and musicians in Bayreuth worked on the international circuit. Germaine Lubin had sung in London earlier that year. Perhaps they just did not care if anyone overheard them. This seemed incredible. Ava thought of the way her fellow Germans all guarded their very thoughts now, for fear they should show some trace of expression on their faces. She felt a pang of sharp envy for those self-assured English sisters.

How Ava wished that she was not afraid.

14

Shun the Ring

Ava found the next few days very difficult.

It was not just that she was expected to stand and sing all day long in a hot and airless wooden theatre. It was because of the music. Ava was singing in the chorus of *Tristan and Isolde*, a tragic tale of love gone awry. It cut her to the heart. On the night of the first performance, when Ava heard Germaine Lubin sing Isolde's famous 'Liebestod', her last song over the dead body of her lover, her throat muscles cramped with grief. When Isolde sang, 'drowned . . . engulfed . . . unconscious . . . in utter bliss', Ava could scarcely stand it. That was how she had felt when Leo had kissed her. And now it was all gone to dust and ashes.

The Führer came backstage after the opening performance and took Germaine Lubin's hands in his. With tears in his eyes, he said, 'Never in my life have I heard such an Isolde.'

A hot flush of rage flamed over Ava's skin. How could a man that wept at the beauty of a love song be the same man who ordered old women to scrub pavements with their toothbrushes and sent laughing young men to concentration camps? Ava could not stay. She went out into the evening, and bent her head down into her arms.

A soft voice spoke behind her. 'Are you all right? Do you need a glass of water?'

Ava shook her head.

The woman leant closer. 'You must be careful. Many saw how you ran out when the Führer came in. They will not be pleased.'

Ava stood up. 'I . . . I was so moved by the music . . .'

The woman nodded. 'That is better. You need to speak with more conviction, though. Remember, when you play a role, you must throw yourself into it heart and soul.'

Ava recognised her. Plump and pretty, she was the Jewish wife of Max Lorenz, the great Wagner tenor who ruled here at Bayreuth. Ava had heard all the gossip. He was a homosexual who had been caught having sex with a young singer in a urinal a few years earlier. He had been put on trial, and Hitler had told Winifred Wagner that he was no longer permitted to sing at Bayreuth. Winifred had said she would have to shut the festival down, as it was impossible to hold it without Max. Hitler had capitulated. Max had been set free, and his Jewish wife went unmolested.

Ava tried to remember her name.

She smiled. 'I'm Lotte Lorenz. And you?'

'I'm Ava Falkenhorst.'

'I saw how you lost your composure in the "Liebestod". Just remember that when you speak of how the music moved you. Let the conviction of it shine through.'

Lotte began to usher Ava back into the theatre, but Ava stopped her. 'How can you bear it?' she cried.

Lotte did not misunderstand her. 'What other choice do I have?' she answered softly. 'We cannot flee Germany. As long as Max is wanted by the Nazis, we must stay. We'd both be arrested if we tried to leave, and my poor old mother too. So we both play a part. Max is the larger-than-life artist, the heart and soul of any party, and I am his faithful drudge of a wife.' For a moment she was silent, then her shoulders squared and she lifted her face to smile at me. 'And there is always the music, my dear. Never forget the music.'

*

Rupert was kept late in the kitchens, scrubbing the enormous vats in which the prisoners' soup was boiled. He and the other kitchen hands called it mockingly 'Universal Political Prisoner Soup'. It was made from old potatoes, green turnip tops, putrid onions, mouldy lentils and the occasional old bone. Rupert was able to snatch the occasional extra ladle, however, or hide a limp carrot in his shoe to share with Rudi later. It was hard and dirty work, but infinitely better than the quarry. The Nazi cook was fat and dirty and indolent. As long as Rupert did what he was told, he was rarely beaten anymore.

At last Rupert was free to return to the barracks. He crept out of the kitchen, past the huge old oak where Goethe was meant to have written *Faust*. The oak leaves susurrated in the warm evening breeze. Rupert took a moment to lay his hand on the warm, rough bark. The oak tree was the only green, living thing inside the camp. Even grass and weeds struggled to grow in the cracks between the pavers on the Appellplatz.

It was growing dark, the sky above the camp beginning to prickle with stars. The air was thick and heavy, stinking with the foul odours of the latrines and the barracks. Rupert kept a sharp lookout for patrols of SS guards with their half-starved dogs. Even though he had permission to miss rollcall, thanks to his kitchen duty, the guards always struck out first, and asked for explanations last. He made it safely to his barrack.

As Rupert opened the door, he froze, mid-step. Music lilted into the foetid air. Rough hands dragged him in, and shut the door behind him. 'Sssh,' Rudi whispered.

Two tables had been pushed together to make a stage. Four gaunt and filthy prisoners sat playing Mozart in the dim glower of the hanging light-bulbs. Two had violins tucked under their chins. Another played a viola, and the fourth held a cello beneath his knees. The instruments were old, battered and slightly out of tune, but the sound was full of lightness, joy, possibility.

Rupert could not look away. The four musicians were haloed in light. Every man in the barracks, exhausted and hollow-eyed, marked with bruises, watched in the same breathless silence. Some conducted with little swoops of their thin hands. One or two wept. Some laughed out loud.

The music came to an end. 'Mozart's little serenade,' Rupert breathed.

Rudi turned and glanced to him. 'You know the tune?'

Rupert nodded. 'Serenade No. 13 for Strings in G Major, written by Mozart in 1787 but not published until after his death.'

'You're a musician?'

'I was.' Rupert looked down at his hands, red and raw with filthy broken nails.

Rudi clapped him on the shoulder. 'Then we shall have to find you an instrument too.'

'But how . . .? It's like a miracle.'

'I found one of the violins abandoned in the clothing depot, and bribed the guards to find the other. The cello belonged to a Czech musician who died. The viola took me a while. One of the doctors in the infirmary has a taste for fine music. He got it for me if we promised to play for him.' Rudi's dark eyes were bright with satisfaction.

'But is it allowed?'

'Of course not. Isn't that part of the joy of it? We shall have to find good hiding places for the instruments, else a SS brute will put his boot through them.'

The four men had begun to play a slow, dark, moody piece. Rupert recognised Mozart's Quartet No. 19 in C Major. He listened, his heart swelling with painful joy. He tried to remember the last time he had heard it played. His lover Felix, busking on a corner at Christmas time with some friends, whisking off his cap to pass it around the listening crowd. It had been cold. The trees silhouetted black against a sunset sky. Afterwards, Felix had put his cold hands in Rupert's coat pockets. They had leant together against a wall, the white smoke of their mouths mingling. He had felt the fiery ice of Felix's fingers through the cloth of his trousers.

The memory was too much to bear. Rupert climbed up into the shadows of his bunk. He lay there, his back turned to the musicians, as they began to play Mendelssohn's No. 6 Quartet in F Minor, written after the death of his sister. The musicians were stiff-fingered, unpractised, and many a note was scraped out of tune. Yet the music was still full of fire, longing, sorrow. Tears dampened Rupert's eyelashes. He thought of his own sister, Jutta, and his almost-twin Ava, and his parents. He had tried his best to forget that other world existed outside the barbed-wire boundaries of this world, but the music made it impossible.

Rupert sat up. He took down an old sardine tin hidden above the rafter. It was full of tiny scraps of paper. He took out the chewed fountain pen, spread a scrap of paper out against the rafter, and laboriously wrote, 'music – a key to open the locked chamber of my heart – a needle sewing back my tattered soul.'

'Of course he's sleeping with her,' one of the violinists said. 'What man can resist a pretty young woman throwing herself at his head?'

'Not the Führer!' cried a fat soprano. 'He's above such earthly concerns.'

The violinist made a rude noise.

Ava listened with interest. She had not heard people speak with such frankness in a long time. The singers and musicians of Bayreuth felt themselves protected from the usual fears and suspicions, and so – amongst themselves – they gossiped as freely as the schnapps flowed.

'Rubbish,' Max Lorenz said at once. 'The Führer has no interest in silly English girls. He has an eye for a handsome young Stormtrooper, that's all I'll say.'

'But he has a mistress already,' Lotte argued. 'A big-eyed, baby-faced girl just like this Unity. He keeps her at his mountain retreat at the Berchtesgaden.'

'Camouflage,' Max said briefly before moving away to refill his glass and flirt with a handsome young tenor.

'Eva Braun, her name is,' a giggling flautist said. 'I heard she tried to kill herself when the Valkyrie came on the scene.'

'You know that's really her name,' a drunken baritone added. 'Valkyrie, I mean. Unity Valkyrie Mitford. It's what her parents named her.'

'Poor girl. No wonder she's so unbalanced,' Lotte said.

'She says she was conceived in a town called Swastika,' the soprano said. 'Surely not!'

'Well, that explains why she feels fated to be with the Führer,' another said. 'I heard she used to go every day to the restaurant where the Führer had lunch and sit and wait, hoping he would notice her.'

'I heard *she's* the one with the taste for a Stormtrooper,' someone else said. 'Apparently she's as debauched as all those English girls. She likes them to do it to her with their boots on and the "Horst-Wessel-Lied" playing in the background.'

It seemed impossible to believe. Unity Mitford had such a round innocent face, such baby-blue eyes. She gazed at the Führer with such naked adoration, it was embarrassing to see. He treated her like a pretty but rather silly child, patting her on the head and allowing her to call him Herr Wolf. Ava saw that she annoyed Winifred Wagner, who wanted Hitler all to herself, and her sister, who did not like sharing the limelight.

Lotte did not approve of them. 'They are intoxicated with power, like so many young fools today,' she said to Ava one afternoon. 'I heard Unity dined with friends in Berlin one night, and one of the guests spoke out against the Führer. He and his wife were arrested forty-eight hours later, and sent to a concentration camp.'

Ava found it hard to breathe. She wanted to defend Unity. *Perhaps she did not mean for that to happen. Perhaps it was a mistake.* But she could not say a word.

Ava still did not know who had denounced Rupert. But because she so desperately hoped it was not Leo, she felt sure it must be him. And if it was Leo who was responsible for Rupert's arrest, then it was all Ava's fault. It did not matter how many times she told herself, *I did not mean for it to happen.* She still had to carry the burden of her guilt.

Ava tried to throw herself into her music, and forget. It was easier in Bayreuth than in Berlin, for the outside world seemed very far away. Nonetheless, a few shadows disturbed the long golden days. Lotte told Ava that an ocean liner carrying almost a thousand Jewish refugees had been refused permission to land in America, after having already been turned away from Cuba. The Americans had even fired a shot at them. 'Where are they meant to go?' she asked Ava. 'Poor souls, nobody wants them.'

Then Sir Nevile Henderson, the British ambassador, came to Bayreuth in an attempt to beg Hitler not to invade Poland. Winifred Wagner was English; she beseeched Hitler to speak to him. The Führer refused, and said that if she brought Sir Nevile to the Wagner box at the theatre he would get up and leave and not come back. She gave in. The opera that day was *The Valkyrie*, with its magnificent – and militant – 'Ride of the Valkyries'. Hitler listened to it raptly, his fingers beating time on his knee, a faint smile on his thin lips.

Ava felt the strain of it. Would there be war? Surely Hitler would not defy the world and invade Poland too?

The very next day Madame Lubin unexpectedly left Bayreuth, leaving everyone in the lurch. Lotte said that she had been afraid of war breaking out, and finding herself interned on German soil. Other performers left as well, and Herr Tietjen, the artistic director, was thrown into a tailspin.

Lotte came in search of Ava. 'Do you know how to sing "Erda's Warning"?' she asked in an urgent voice.

Ava nodded. It was the only song for a contralto in the whole of Wagner's repertoire. Tante Thea had made Ava practise it again and again.

Lotte seized her hand. 'Then come with me. Hurry!'

And so Ava found herself singing one of the lead roles in a Wagnerian opera at the famous Bayreuth festival. As her reward, she was offered two free tickets to the final performances and she sent them to her father at once, rejoicing in the thought that she would see him for the first time in almost a month.

On the evening her father arrived from Berlin, Ava went to meet him at the train station. To her surprise, Monika climbed down from the train too, looking very chic in a pale grey suit with a silk camellia on the lapel. Ava had hardly seen her sister in the last few months, as Monika had been given a promotion at work and, as a result, had moved out of home and into an apartment closer to the SS offices on

Prinz-Albrecht-Strasse. She had said, rather coyly, that her boss, the Ober-führer, needed her at all times of day or night.

Ava's father looked more rumpled than ever, with pipe ash smeared on his jacket and his white hair sticking up from his bald spot. Ava ran and threw her arms around him, and he hugged her tightly. 'Eh, how's my girl then?' he asked.

'I'm fine,' Ava told him. 'Rather tired. They keep us standing and singing for hours on end. I don't know what hurts more sometimes, my feet or my voice.'

'We're looking forward to seeing you tonight.'

'You'll have to hire some opera glasses, and even then you might have trouble spotting me. I come up through a hole in the ground, and I have to wear an awful green wig.'

'It's got to look better than your usual golliwog look,' Monika said.

Ava twisted back her curls. 'Whatever are you doing here? I thought you hated opera.'

'Oh, I do,' Monika answered. 'But I've heard Bayreuth is absolute-ly heaving with handsome officers at this time of year. I thought that sounded like fun.'

'The mood is rather tense at the moment,' Ava told her. 'Everyone's afraid war's about to break out.'

'Well, maybe they'll be looking for some distraction,' she answered with a meaningful lift of her eyebrows. 'What about you, Ava? Picked up any handsome young men?'

Ava shook her head and turned away, leading the way down the platform.

When Otto saw the Festival Theatre on its hill, his eyes misted over. 'To think my little girl is singing here. At Bayreuth! Where Herr Wagner himself once lived.' He pulled a handkerchief out of his pocket and blew his nose with a trumpeting noise. Ava had to smile, thinking of Britta and her handkerchief, and gave his arm a little squeeze.

That night, as Ava waited in the shadows for her cue, she thought over the role she had to play. Erda was the Earth Goddess in Wagner's

Ring Cycle. She only sang the one song in this opera, but it was a key dramatic moment.

The first thrilling chords rang out. Ava was raised up through a hatch in the floor to the stage. The lighting was all green and dark and ominous.

'Yield, Wotan, yield!' she sang with all her strength. 'Escape from the ring's curse.'

Ava had sung these words many times before, but never before had she truly felt their electrifying danger. The song is a prophetic warning of death and darkness to come. Erda sings to Wotan, the lord of the gods, to prepare him for the consequences of his greed and lust for power. The ring he has stolen is cursed.

'I know whatever was; whatever is; whatever shall be . . .' Ava stretched out her hand towards the Führer, who sat in the shadows in the Wagners' private box with the Mitford sisters on either side. She invested her voice with all the power and pleading she possessed.

'Hear me! Hear me! Hear me! All that is shall come to an end. A dark day dawns for the gods: I charge you, shun the ring!'

15

Herr Wolf

'The Master understood psychology,' Otto said on the walk home after the final performance of *Twilight of the Gods*. His eyes were red and he had to keep blowing his nose on his very crumpled handkerchief. 'What an insight into the human soul he had.' Monika cleared her voice but did not speak. Ava noticed her nose was a little pink.

Ava had been unspeakably moved herself. She had heard *Twilight of the Gods* sung numerous times before, and had spent the last few weeks rehearsing every note until her dreams were haunted by the music. She had never heard anything like that final performance, though. The mood of impending doom had rolled out into the audience, till the air quivered with tension. No-one coughed or stirred. The spectators edged forward, listening, as the drum beat out its low, threatening thud and Siegfried's dead body was carried away. When Brünnhilde flung herself upon his flaming funeral pyre, a ripple of distress ran through the whole crowd. Even Hitler had wept, holding hands with Winifred Wagner, as Valhalla had collapsed into ruins.

The month at Bayreuth, with the intense focus of the rehearsals and the passion and intensity of the performances, had shaken something loose in Ava. Her frozen inner landscape had thawed. She had made new friends in Lotte and Max Lorenz, after thinking she could never again be friends with anyone. And she had regained in some small measure her courage and inner conviction as she had pleaded, through the words of 'Erda's Warning', for Hitler to choose peace over war. Ava felt wrung out, yet also exultant. She did not sleep that night, but went out walking on the hills under the stars, feeling the music still thrum through her in all its fiery beauty.

The next day, Ava was invited to a farewell lunch at Wahnfried House. It was another summery day, the sun beating on her shoulders through the thin cotton of her frock. She walked there with Lotte and Max, but could not, of course, sit with them. They were seated at Hitler's table, along with the Mitford sisters, Winifred Wagner and her sons, and Herr Doktor Goebbels and his wife, Magda. The Goebbels were an odd couple. He was small and dark and crooked and intense. She was tall and fair and coolly remote. They did not ever touch, or look at each other and smile. They had a whole tribe of flaxen-haired children who felt free to cluster around the Führer, clamouring to be taken upon his knees, and calling him Uncle Wolfie. Watching the Führer smile and pat their silken curls, it was hard to believe that this was a man who had ordered the murder of so many people.

After lunch, everyone strolled around the gardens, listening to the very fine quartet playing. Some began to dance on the close-clipped lawn.

Ava was chatting with some of the tenors when she saw Unity Mitford hurry up to the Führer and clasp his arm with both hands. Her face was distressed. They spoke in low tones, then he turned and accompanied her away from the crowd.

Ava rose to her feet and quietly followed after them. She hardly understood the impulse that drove her. She had been fascinated with the Mitford sisters since first seeing them, especially with Unity. She just could not understand why the young English woman was so wildly and stupidly infatuated with the Führer. Ava wanted to know the truth of their relationship. It was also in her mind that some evidence Hitler was having an affair with a young English woman might, perhaps, cause a scandal big enough to break the power the Führer had over the people of Germany. Ava remembered the headlines after Hitler's niece Geli had killed herself, in Hitler's apartment, with Hitler's gun. All sorts of nasty rumours had flown about then.

Besides, Ava knew that no other opportunity might ever present itself. In Bayreuth, at the private home of his friends the Wagners, Hitler was not surrounded by bodyguards at every step. He had moved through the crowd quite freely, stopping to chat with whomever he pleased. Ava had to seize the chance while she could.

Diana Mosley was waiting for the Führer and her sister at the edge of the lawn. Hitler bowed and kissed her hand, and – with one of the sisters on either side of him – walked down the steps to the shady grove in which Wagner's grave lay, shrouded in ivy.

Ava slipped around to another path that led down through the shrubbery. She could see Hitler and the two sisters standing by the grave, but not hear. Greatly daring, she slipped closer, hiding in the shadow of an oak tree.

Diana spoke, cool and aristocratic. 'You do understand, don't you, my Führer? It simply wouldn't be cricket for us to stay on here when you've turned away our ambassador. People back home wouldn't like it.'

'I don't want to go!' Unity cried. 'Oh, Wolfie, say I can stay with you?'

There was a discernible pause, then the Führer answered, 'I am afraid it may be a while before I can see you again, child. It seems England is determined on war. It would be best if you went back home now.'

'Oh, no!' Unity's voice was shrill. 'Oh, no, no, no. I couldn't bear it. You mustn't fight them, Wolfie, you mustn't.'

Unity sounded like a child. Yet Ava knew she was in her mid-twenties. Ava wondered how much of Unity's naïve manner and high-pitched childish voice were merely affected mannerisms she put on to please the Führer, or if she spoke like that at home as well.

'I'm afraid war is inevitable now,' Hitler replied. He had a trick of rolling his r's as if to give his words greater emphasis. It made the word 'war' seem as threatening as the sound of the horns in Siegfried's funeral march.

'I cannot bear it,' Unity said. 'I swear I shall kill myself if war breaks out!'

Ava heard Diana draw in a sharp breath. 'Don't be silly, Bobo!'

'I shall! I shall shoot myself, Honks, I swear.'

'You must come home with me, Bobo. We'll leave tomorrow.'

'I won't! I won't leave Germany. I love it too much.' There was a hysterical edge to Unity's voice. 'Herr Wolf, you don't want me to go, do you?'

'You must,' he said impatiently.

'Well, I won't. There's no need for me to go. London only has about three aircraft guns anyway. You'll beat them in no time.'

'Bobo!' her sister said in a shocked tone of voice. 'You must not speak so.' She then raised her voice to speak over the top of Unity's angry protestations. 'Don't listen to her, my Führer. She is such a poor dear silly, she knows nothing about it. I must get home, of course. Oswald will need me. I promise you that he will continue to campaign for peace as long as he is permitted to do so.'

'Thank you, Lady Mosley, but there is no need. We are not afraid of war.'

Ava heard Diana's heels tapping away on the stone paving, then her imperious voice calling, 'Coming, Bobo?'

'No, I'm not,' Unity answered. 'I need to speak to Herr Wolf alone.'

Ava tried to breathe quietly, hidden in the shade of the tree. Her pulse thudded in her fingertips.

'What is it, child?' Hitler asked, with a tone of barely controlled impatience in his voice.

'You don't want me to go away, do you, Wolfie?' Unity asked in a wheedling voice. 'You'd like me to stay with you, wouldn't you?'

'Of course, child, but it cannot be. Once we are at war, I shall be very busy.'

'But why does there have to be a war?' She gave a little stamp of her foot.

'I want there to be a war,' Hitler answered, like a parent explaining something difficult to a particularly stupid child. 'Germany needs more land, she needs more workers, she needs more resources. War is the only way to get what Germany needs if she is going to be a great nation again. And we will be great again, I promise you that, if I have to crush every country that stands in my way.'

'But . . . but . . .' Unity stammered.

His voice dropped. 'In just a few weeks, Poland will be ours. We plan to hit them hard and fast, and take them completely by surprise. We'll annihilate them! Of course I hope that England and France will not interfere, but I cannot be seen consorting with you, an English girl, when at risk of being at war with your country. I have given you fair warning so you have time to get home safely. I know I can trust you not to divulge my plans to your government.'

'But Wolfie . . . my Führer . . . I can't bear to leave you! Can't I stay here with you? I don't have to be English anymore. I could be German. You could marry me! Then you wouldn't need to send me away. Oh, please!' Unity was crying.

'Don't be a fool! I cannot marry you, or anyone for that matter. I am married to the destiny of Germany! What would people think if I was to marry a silly English girl only a few weeks before starting a war?'

'But I . . .' She was gasping with sobs now. 'I can't go home. I'm . . . I'm going to have a baby!'

Ava could not help a sharp intake of breath. She pressed both hands to her mouth, hoping desperately she had not been heard.

Hitler's voice was cold and hard. 'I cannot help you. You must do whatever you think best.'

Then Ava heard the brisk tattoo of his boot heels as he walked away, and the muffled sound of Unity crying. Then the English woman ran back towards the house.

Ava leant against the tree, unable to stop her legs from trembling. She fumbled in her bag for a cigarette, and found one at last, rather crumpled. She did not, however, have a light. She straightened and turned to go back to the house.

A tall young man in a black SS uniform was standing on the slope above her. Ava's heart began to slam against her ribs.

'What are you doing here?' the soldier snapped. His uniform collar bore the skeleton-key design that showed he was one of Hitler's personal bodyguards.

'I . . . I just came out for a cigarette,' Ava replied. 'I didn't want anyone to see me. Bad for my voice, you know. But now the festival is over . . .'

The bodyguard grinned. 'Lucky the Führer did not see you. He was just here a moment ago. He hates to see women smoking.' He came down the path towards Ava, pulling a silver lighter out of his jacket pocket. Ava let him light her cigarette. His lighter was engraved with the double SS rune. Ava took a quick drag, then smiled up at him and thanked him.

'Wish I could have one with you, Fräulein,' he said. 'But the Führer would have my head if I came in smelling of cigarette smoke.'

He bowed, clicked his heels, and went on his way. Ava stayed in the shadow of the tree, and smoked the cigarette down to its very last ember. Hitler's words rang through her brain. *I want there to be a war . . . if I have to crush every country that stands in my way . . . We plan to hit them hard and fast . . . we'll annihilate them!*

And poor Unity Mitford. *I'm going to have a baby,* she had said. Ava wondered if the baby's was the Führer's. They had not spoken like lovers, but the look in her eyes when she gazed at him was one of utter adoration. She loved him, of that Ava was certain. So if it was not the Führer's, whose was it? Were the rumours that she slept with Stormtroopers true? Ava found it hard to believe, but then Ava had seen other sweet-faced girls who seemed to have few morals. Jutta's old school friend, Stella, for example, had been sleeping round with boys since she was fourteen.

When Ava felt safe again, she slipped away from the garden. Her steps quickened as soon as she went through the gate. Soon she was half-running, half-stumbling along. She forced herself to slow. No-one must guess Ava had been eavesdropping on the Führer. No-one must know what she had heard. At last she made it back to their lodgings, and went at once to find her father. He had been enjoying an afternoon nap, but was now sitting writing in one of his little notebooks. He looked up, startled, as Ava burst in upon him.

'Ava? What is it? What's wrong?'

She was unable to catch her breath. Otto sat her down and gave her some water to drink. At last she was calm enough to tell him what she had heard. He listened closely, occasionally saying, 'My God,' and shaking his head in horror.

Ava was not sure what had upset her more. The coming ruin of Poland, or the ruin of the English girl, only a few years older than she was. Ava wondered if there was the same shame and stigma attached to unmarried mothers in England as there was in Germany. Under the National Socialists, all birth control clinics had been shut down and abortions were banned. Illegitimate children of SS men were adopted out, to ensure the survival of their pure Aryan genes. No-one ever spoke about what happened to the unwanted babies that were not of Aryan blood.

'Did anyone see you?' her father asked urgently.

Ava shook her head. 'No. I don't think so.'

'That is good. We will go home on the first train tomorrow. It is best you do not see anyone, your face will give you away. You can write a note to your friends and tell them you were taken ill.'

'But what are we going to do? We have to warn Poland, we have to let them know what he plans.'

'I will write to some friends,' her father said. 'Herr Doktor Freud is in London, he has many friends in high places. I will write to him, and to Herr Doktor Wertheim in America, and Herr Doktor Neumann in Tel Aviv, and yes, to everyone I know in Warsaw.'

'But it's so dangerous.' Ava clasped her shaking hands together.

'Yes.' Otto's face was pale and deeply graven with lines. 'But we cannot sit by and do nothing. I will write as carefully as I can, and we will post the letters from as many different postboxes as we can.'

Ava swallowed a lump like uncooked potato. 'I'll post them for you.'

'We will begin tonight. No need to tell Monika. It'd be best if as few as possible know what we plan.'

Engulfed

Ava walked all over Berlin to post those letters, feeling as if every stranger she bumped into, every soldier she saw, could see the secret burning on her face. Ava tried to remember what Lotte had said about playing a role, both onstage and off. *Throw yourself into it heart and soul*, she had said. So Ava imagined she was just a normal German girl, posting letters to a friend.

One week passed, then two weeks, and they heard no reply. Ava kept thinking about Unity Mitford. Ava had come so close to succumbing to Leo. She too could be pregnant and frightened now. Ava wondered about Unity's parents. She had said she could not go home. Ava could not imagine her father throwing her out if she had gone to him in trouble. But then her father was an atheist. He thought sin was an interesting manifestation of the internalisation of the super-ego. Or something like that.

Ava also worried about Poland, and tried to think of other ways to warn the Poles. Every night she had a series of little nightmares, waking with her body drenched in sweat, her heart pounding, her chest constricted. In many of them Ava dreamt she was in some way paralysed. Sometimes she woke, feeling sure someone was in the dark room with her, staring at her.

Ava tried to comfort herself. Their letters had got through, and people were talking to other people in high places. Plans were being laid. Warnings were being issued. It meant nothing that no-one had replied. They all knew it was too dangerous.

Her father was worried too. The bags under his eyes were bigger, the smell of pipe smoke stronger. He missed his nightly chess games with Onkel Franz, Ava could tell. He often sat there, staring at the chessboard, not moving a single piece, drinking his schnapps too fast. The apartment seemed so big and echoing now, with the Feidlers gone, and Monika moved out, and no Frau Günther humming tunelessly as she rolled out dough in the kitchen. Bertha was more tense and unhappy than ever, and Ava found most of the work of the house fell on her. She swept and dusted and scrubbed the dirty sheets with soap and put them through the wringer on her own, and did her best not to scorch them with the heavy irons, heated on the kitchen fire. It was the cooking that troubled her the most. Ava had always hated the sight and smell of raw meat, and the shining blades of those knives. It was easier just to boil up some red cabbage and potatoes, and fry a few sausages, and hope for the best.

Then the news broke that Germany and the Soviet Union had signed some kind of peace treaty. Everyone was stunned; they had thought Russia the enemy. The papers were full of it; so too, the newsreels in the cinema. One American cartoon showed Poland as Little Red Cap startled to find a wolf (Germany) in bed with a huge bear (Russia).

It was so hot that night Ava could not sleep. She tossed and turned, kicking off her sheets, turning over her pillow to try and find a cool spot. In the end she dragged off her damp nightgown and flung it on the floor. Naked, in the dark, Ava could not help her thoughts turning to Leo. She was plagued by memories of his kisses, and by restlessness she could not ease. At last she sank into sleep.

Ava was woken much later by a pounding on the door. She sat up. Her heart beat staccato. She groped for some clothes. Her hands were shaking so much she couldn't clip her stockings on. Footsteps ran down the hall. The pounding at the door grew louder. Ava pulled on her shoes. Ran out.

Gestapo men in the hallway. More in Father's study. Going through papers. Knocking books off the shelves. Smashing his Venetian glass collection. Putting a boot through his beloved Kandinsky.

Otto was hurried down the hallway. His shirt was buttoned up wrong. Ava remembered Rupert. She leant against the wall to stop herself falling. Angelika was screaming. Bertha tried in vain to calm her.

One of the Gestapo men said to another, 'A defective.'

'Useless eater,' the other said. 'Should have been smothered at birth.'

'You need to register her with the Reich Committee for Congenital Illnesses,' the officer said to Bertha. 'They know what to do with cretins like her.'

They took Otto away into the night. With him went his precious book, pages and pages of Ava's hard-won typing. She could see the words scorched against her eyelids. Eroticised homicidal maniac. Fear of castration.

Bertha was shocked and silent, standing with Father's broken pipe clenched in her hands. 'He'll want his pipe,' she kept saying.

At last Ava steadied herself. She rose and went to the bathroom, washing her face carefully. She unplaited her hair and let it hang down her back in a mass of ringlets, and powdered her face with an old compact of Monika's. She found her red beret buried in the bottom of her cupboard, and pulled it on. As Ava came down the stairs, Bertha looked up at her dully. 'Where are you going?' her sister asked.

Ava could hardly frame the word. 'Leo.'

Ava reached the Tiergarten in the first delicate flush of dawn. Birds sang, and the sun struck through the columns of trees in broad shafts of golden light. Ava walked up and down, up and down, along the Tiergartenstrasse. She cursed herself. If only she had gone home with Leo when he had asked. She would now know where he lived.

A thunder of hooves. Ava turned and looked, not really expecting to see him. But there he was, on a huge golden horse, galloping along the path. Ava scarcely noticed that two others rode with him. The white-haired Admiral, looking dishevelled in a shabby old coat. Reinhard Heydrich, cool and contemptuous in a crisp military overcoat. They rode past her. Heedless of the horses' hooves, Ava leapt out in front of the golden stallion, hands held out in entreaty.

Leo drew his horse up to a rearing stop, and leapt from the stallion's back. 'Ava?' he said incredulously.

Ava could not speak. She held out her hands to him. Leo came to her swiftly, leaving his horse to crop the grass. The sun was brightening over the city. It showed the tension in his face and his shoulders. His eyes were as pale as the dawn sky. He seized her shoulders.

'What is it? What's wrong?' he cried.

'Father,' Ava whispered.

He was silent a long moment. Ava realised he was looking over her shoulder to make sure the other men had ridden on, and could not hear. Then he asked, in a low urgent voice, 'When?'

'Just now. A few hours ago.'

'Gestapo?'

Ava jerked her head up and down.

'Why?'

Her voice was just a croak. 'Letters.'

He shook her roughly. 'Ava, what have you done? How can you be so reckless?'

She blazed up. 'We had to do something! Your beloved Führer is driving us all to war. You might be able to justify all the evil he is doing, but I cannot!' Then she put her hands up to cover her face, for it struck home to her then that he was right. This was all her fault. Her gentle father was in the hands of the Gestapo, because she simply could not learn to keep her head down and her mouth shut. Her body shuddered with the force of her sobs.

Leo pulled her into his arms. 'Don't cry, little love, please don't cry.' His arm was strong about her, his hand gentle on her hair. 'It's all right, it'll all be all right.'

She shook her head. 'How? How can it be all right?'

He drew her closer. 'I'll work something out. I don't know how. It'll not be easy.'

'I'll do anything,' Ava said. 'Anything. Please help him.' She looked up into his face imploringly.

For a moment, he gazed down at her. Ava could feel the intensity of his regard like a burn on her skin. Then he stepped away, turning so she could not see his face. 'I'll try.' For a moment he was remote. Then his attention returned to her. 'You're trembling. Let me take you home.'

Ava nodded, and then found she could not stop. Leo put his arm around her, catching up his stallion's reins in his other hand. The huge golden horse ambled behind him, as mild as a lamb. Stiff-legged, cold-skinned, Ava stumbled along as meekly.

They walked through the Tiergarten, all clothed in green and gold, and across the Tiergartenstrasse to a house set on the corner of a street lined with grand-looking villas. Leo unlocked a gate in the wall, and led her through. Ava saw a long garden, with a multitude of crimson roses above some plant with pale blue bells and silvery leaves. The panes of a glasshouse in the corner reflected the sun in a blinding flash, and a pear tree grew against an old shed. Leo shut the gate and tied his horse to it, then led Ava towards a pretty old house, two storeys high, with stone lions crouched at the end of a wide set of curving steps. She breathed in short, sharp gasps, her chest hurting. 'Sssh,' he said. 'All will be well.'

Leo unlocked a door and led her into a sunny kitchen. A primrose-yellow gas range took up most of one wall, with two pale cream dressers on either side. They were stacked neatly with green plates and bowls and cups. A deep ceramic sink near the window had a small towel folded neatly and hung with mathematical precision in the exact centre of the rack.

A fusillade of barking, a clatter of claws on the stone floor, then a huge slavering beast leapt upon them. 'Down, Zeus!' Leo cried. The beast sat down, tail wagging. Ava saw it was an immense brindled Great Dane, all silvered around the jaws.

Leo led Ava through to a small room hung with golden silk, sat her down on a couch by the fireplace, took off her shoes, and tucked her up with a soft blanket. She sat hunched, shivering as violently as if she had a fever. He brought her hot coffee with lots of sugar and told her sternly to drink it all.

'Stay here,' Leo said. 'Don't go back to the apartment. If they have tortured your father, he may implicate you. You'll be safer here.'

She did not speak, but her eyes must have shown her horror, for his face softened and he bent and laid one hand against her face. 'I'm glad you came to me. I'm sure I can help him somehow.'

Ava nodded, gripping the coffee cup so tightly her knuckles were white.

'Zeus, mind her for me,' he said. The Great Dane wagged his tail, then settled down on the floor next to the couch.

Then Leo left Ava alone.

Ava used the telephone on the desk to ring Bertha and tell her that Leo had gone to see what he could do to help. Bertha's voice was so thick with tears it was hard to understand her. Then Ava rang Monika. She was just about to go to work. Her primary concern was for her own position at the Schutzstaffel. 'I must go and see the Oberführer at once!' she cried. 'He must know I had nothing to do with any of this.'

'Perhaps he can help?' Ava asked.

'I would not ask it of him!' Monika responded sharply, and rang off.

The conversation upset Ava so much that she had to sit and cry for a while. Zeus was distressed, and pushed his big square head onto her lap. She mopped her eyes and stroked his silky ears, and tried to calm herself.

The morning passed. The house was peaceful and quiet. The only sound was the soft ticking of the clock on the mantelpiece. Ava could not rest. She walked around the room, taking books off the shelves, then putting them back. Leo liked detective novels. He had rows of them, many of them in English and French. He had them arranged alphabetically. She took down a battered old spy novel to read, but could not concentrate. Ava was on a mental rack, each minute turning the screw.

With the old Great Dane following along behind her, she explored the rest of the house. A central hallway with an antique tapestry hanging on the wall, and a fine old oak chair, a pale blue sitting room with white garlands on the ceiling and a white grand piano, a dining room next to the kitchen with a long oak table so old it looked like it must have come from a monastery. Everything was neat and in place. Not a speck of dust to be seen.

Under the stairs was a locked doorway. Ava turned the handle a few times, then kept on exploring. A scullery off the kitchen, spotlessly clean, and a door down into a coal cellar. She hesitated, then went upstairs.

Four bedrooms and two bathrooms. One room was clearly Leo's. His bed was neatly made with a tawny brocade coverlet, his uniforms all hanging side by side in a dressing-room, his boots and shoes polished to a high sheen and laid neatly in a row. Ava did not think she had ever seen such a tidy house. Feeling restless and uneasy, she went back downstairs and out into the garden. The quietness was almost unbearable. Ava tried hard not to think, not to imagine what might be happening, but it was impossible.

The sun poured down on the garden. The red roses nodded their heavy heads. Bees hummed amongst the blue flower spires. Ava could see nothing beyond the wall but green hedges and trees moving restlessly in the wind. How was it possible that the world could be so full of beauty when such evil was being done?

Ava went to sit in the shade of the pear tree. Zeus sat with her, his head on her knee. Ava shut her eyes, her hands clenched together. If she had believed in God, she would have been praying. As it was, she wished with all of her strength that Leo could save her father.

Leo came back much later. He was dressed once more in his field-grey uniform. It made his eyes seem grey too. His face was set and hard. 'I've found your father. I'm afraid he's in rather bad shape.'

Her limbs jerked. Ava stilled them with an effort.

'But we've got him out. The Admiral arranged all the papers he needs. We can put him on a train to Switzerland tonight. We've said he has tuberculosis. It'll mean no-one will examine him too closely.'

Ava tried to say 'thank you', but she could not get a word out.

'Someone will have to accompany him.' Leo's voice was cool and distant. 'He needs a nurse. We have the necessary papers for her too.'

For a moment, Ava imagined herself dressed in a crisp white uniform, holding her father's hand as he slept. She imagined the train rushing through the night, kilometres opening up between her and Berlin and this devilish regime. Dawn would break, pale pink and golden, over the snowy heights of the Alps. She and her father would be free.

Then Ava remembered Bertha's bloodless face, contorted with fear, as she clutched her little girl as close as she could against the cold stare of the Gestapo. Ava thought of her little niece's starry eyes and soft, pale ringlets, and the police officer who had called her a useless eater. And she thought of the debt she owed this man.

Ava stood up. His hand steadied her. 'Could my sister go with him? You remember she has a little girl who is . . .? The Gestapo man called her a cretin . . . could she go too? Can you get them both out?'

For a moment his eyes had that distant look, as if he was making silent, lightning-fast calculations. 'No problem. We can manage that. They must be ready to catch that train tonight, though.'

'Thank you,' Ava managed.

'I cannot get you all out,' he said. 'I'm sorry.'

She laid her hand on his arm. The muscles were rigid under her fingers. 'You've done so much. I don't know how to thank you.'

Leo moved away a step, not looking at her. 'What will you do now?'

Ava suddenly felt desolate. 'I don't know. I won't be able to stay at the apartment. It's much too big for one, and besides, how could I afford the rent? I'll have to sell the furniture, I suppose, to send some money to Father so he and Bertha have something to live on . . .' She took a deep breath and squared her shoulders. 'I'll find a room somewhere, I suppose. I'll be fine.'

Leo frowned. He began to say something, then stopped himself.

Ava moved closer to him. He did not look at her. 'Thank you,' she whispered. Then she rose up on tiptoe, and kissed him.

Ava had meant to kiss him on the cheek, but he had turned to look at her at the last moment and so her kiss fell awry. Her lips touched the corner of his. She felt the jolt of it down to her heels. His breath caught. They stood motionless. Then Leo made a deep guttural noise in his throat and seized her in his arms, his mouth devouring hers. Ava let herself be drowned. Engulfed.

17

A Good Nazi Wife

Ava lay still on the soft grass, in the dappled shadow of the pear tree, Leo's arm flung over her waist, trying to steady her breathing. She felt as if she had been unravelled and then knitted anew. Nothing would ever be the same.

Ava slowly eased free from the weight of his arm. It tightened about her. His eyes opened. 'Don't go,' he whispered.

'I have to. My father . . .'

For a moment he was still, then he nodded and sat up, pulling up his trousers, buttoning his shirt. 'I'll take you.'

'Thank you.' Her voice was low. Without looking at him, she pulled her dress towards her. Blood marked the pale cotton. At the sight of it she stilled, hardly breathing. She felt light-headed, heavy-limbed.

'Ava . . .'

She did not look up.

'Ava, I didn't know. I'm sorry.'

Ava understood him. She had heard the halt of his breath when he had broken her maidenhead. Ava shook her head and shrugged, not looking at him. She drew the dress on over her head.

'I thought . . . we had been told . . .'

'What?' she asked, after a long pause.

'It doesn't matter.'

'Tell me.'

He gave a little twisted smile. 'We were told that girls who listened to jazz were . . . rather free with their favours. To put it politely.'

Ava stared at him in astonishment.

'I believed it. I misjudged you from the start. I'm sorry.'

Ava shrugged, pretending she did not care. 'Just another lie from the propaganda desk of Herr Doktor Joseph Goebbels.'

'I shouldn't have slept with you, Ava. It was wrong of me. It's just . . . you've driven me half-crazy.'

She looked away, her jaw set. 'I didn't mean to.'

'I need to make it right. I think we should be married. As soon as possible.'

'Because you think you have dishonoured me?' Colour rushed to her cheeks.

'Because it's the right thing to do. Because I cannot think how else to keep you safe. Heydrich will have recognised you this morning. He never forgets a face, particularly one as beautiful as yours. He will hear how we got your father out, and he will know why. Ava, I cannot bear to think of you in the hands of the Gestapo. But Heydrich will hesitate to move against you if you are my wife. He and the Admiral are friends, and he needs the Abwehr.'

Ava looked down at her interlocked hands. Something was fluttering madly in the pit of her stomach. Leo bent and drew her to her feet, putting his arm around her. He kissed her.

'We can be married tomorrow. We'll need a special dispensation. That shouldn't be a problem. I'll arrange it in the morning, and then we can be married in the afternoon. Shall we say four?'

She leant into his strength, trying to think. But the world was whirling around her.

'Ava?'

She rested her forehead on his chest, hearing the steady beat of his heart. 'All right.'

Otto lay on a stretcher, his eyes shut, the blanket tucked tight under his white beard. He had a surgical mask tied on over his mouth. It was spotted with blood. One of his eyes looked shadowed with bruises. Both his hands were hidden.

Ava bit her lip. 'Is he all right?' she asked Leo. It was late, and the train station was crowded with people carrying suitcases, coats folded over their arms. The train hissed quietly as it stood at the platform, clouds of black smoke drifting past.

Leo looked down at her, hesitating. 'He will be.' He gave Bertha a bottle of medicine to slip into her bag, giving her instructions in a low voice. Bertha was dressed in a starched nurse's uniform, a neat white cap hiding her fair braids. She looked frightened, but determined. Angelika lay sleeping in her old pram, her tattered lamb under her cheek. Bertha had given her a sleeping draught to make the journey easier. A single brown suitcase stood at Bertha's feet. It was all that she could manage to carry.

It was time for them to go. Ava bent to kiss Angelika, then her father's bearded cheek. One of her tears fell on his face. He cracked open his swollen eyelids, saying in surprise, 'Why, Ava, what's wrong? Don't cry.' He tried to lift his hand, but found it trapped under the blanket. Ava freed it, then bit back a cry. His fingertips were swollen and black. All his fingernails had been torn out.

'Everything's all right now, Father, you're safe,' Ava whispered. He tried to smile and lifted his hand to pat her face. Then his eyes closed and he was wheeled onto the train.

Rupert trudged through the camp, carrying a heavy tray laden with delicious food. Potatoes mashed yellow with butter. White bread spread with honey. Great slabs of sizzling-hot steak glistening with fat.

It was the cruellest kind of torture. Every prisoner in the compound turned and stared at Rupert. He could see the tension in their thin bodies, the maddened glint in their eyes. A few slipped hands into their pockets to finger the crude weapons they fashioned from sticks and stones. Rupert's arms shook. He wanted to cram the food into his own mouth. He knew he would be beaten to death if he even tried. Two block elders marched on either side of him, guarding his every movement. They were big brutes of men, with shaven heads and hands like sledgehammers. Green triangles on their chest showed they were not political prisoners, but imprisoned for crimes such as theft, arson, murder. Both had their striped sleeves rolled up high, showing thick forearms corded with muscles. One had a crude blue tattoo that took up most of his inner arm. It depicted a sword locked in chains.

The block elders led him to the zoo built just outside the camp gates. The Commandant had built it for the amusement of his young family. As the prisoners trudged about their vast concrete pen, they could hear the shrieks of monkeys, the bellow of bears, the lonely howling of a wolf.

Rupert made his rounds, feeding the meat and bread and honey to the bears, the mashed potato to the monkeys. Whenever he could, he tore off a tiny piece of food and stuffed it into his pockets, to eat later when he was not so closely observed.

Childish laughter. Rupert's stomach flipped. He backed against the wall, dropping his eyes. A woman walked past, plump legs encased in silk stockings and white, high-heeled shoes. She wore a tight dress, the top four buttons undone to show her deep cleavage. Her flame-red hair was arranged in stiff waves. She carried a small baby, and a little boy trotted by her side. He was dressed in a white linen romper suit, and had soft curls of the palest gold.

The woman was Ilse Koch, the wife of the Commandant. She was called the Beast of Buchenwald for her viciousness. Her children had been born at Buchenwald, but they were rarely seen. To Rupert's relief, they ignored him. Frau Koch lifted up the little boy so he could see the monkeys. He laughed and pointed. Rupert edged slowly away. The bowls on his tray clattered. Frau Koch glanced his way in irritation. 'Get out of my sight, you dirty swine,' she said.

The block elders rushed up. The tattooed one gave Rupert a quick blow across the back of the head. 'Stupid dog.'

'You! Come here.' Frau Koch was smiling and beckoning forward the block elder. 'What a fine hunk of a man you are. What's your number?'

He told her, and she scribbled it down with a gold pen she kept in her handbag.

'Well, don't keep hanging around,' she snapped. 'You think I want my children to have to look at you?'

Rupert and the two block elders beat a hasty retreat. The tattooed one boasted all the way back to the kitchens. 'Everyone knows she's a lusty piece. I've heard she's screwed half the officers! She'll be my ticket out of here, I promise you that.'

Later, at the evening rollcall, the block elder's number was announced. He was to report to the infirmary. The blood drained from his face. He trudged off, as ordered. He did not come back. Rupert told Rudi all about the strange encounter, as they surreptitiously shared the bread and honey he had stolen from the bears.

'He was tattooed, you say?' Rudi's face was creased with revulsion. 'Then it was not his body the witch wanted. It was his skin.'

'His skin?'

'Yes. She collects tattoos.'

'Collects? How can you collect tattoos?'

'You kill the man who has them, then peel off his skin and tan it, just like you would the hide of an animal.'

Rupert stared at him in utter disbelief.

Rudi shrugged. 'I work in the infirmary. I've seen the tanned skins. One of the doctors there did his dissertation on tattoos and the criminal mind. He got the Commandant's wife all interested in the subject too, and now she collects any that she sees and likes.'

'So . . . so they've killed the block elder for his tattoo?'

'That's my guess. I've heard she has books bound in human skin, and even a lampshade. I wouldn't be surprised.'

Rupert felt nauseated. Bile rose in his throat, but he choked it back down. Rudi put a gentle hand on his shoulder. 'It may not be true. All we have to eat in this camp is rumours and gossip. I'm sure you'll see your block elder guard again later.'

But he did not.

That night Rupert wrote on a tiny scrap of paper torn from a medical form: 'My soul gutters, my wick is burnt out. Nothing but skin to shield my fragile flame. Nothing but bones to hold the seeping oil.'

Leo and Ava were married the next day. Ava wore the most beautiful dress she had ever owned. Simply cut in white silk, it was tightly fitted with lace sleeves. Leo had, that morning, sent around a great bunch of crimson roses and a note, saying, 'You must need a dress. More than one! Put what you need on my account at Wertheims. See you at the city hall at sixteen hundred hours. Don't fail me.'

It had given Ava a great deal of pleasure, she had to admit, to walk back into the department store where she had worked for most of the past year, modelling clothes she thought she could never afford, and sweep out again a few hours later, laden down with hat-boxes and elegant white bags.

They were married in the Red City Hall, near Alexanderplatz. Ava did not know how Leo could have managed to organise it so fast. Monika was one of her witnesses, and Admiral Canaris the other. He bowed over Ava's hand and wished her luck in a deep, rather gravelly voice. He had a gift for her. A bottle of fine champagne.

The registrar gave her a copy of *Mein Kampf*, and told her the Führer would be pleased and that she must try to have many sons for the Fatherland. Ava nodded and smiled, but dropped the heavy red book as soon as she could. The golden ring on her finger felt strange.

As they signed the register, Ava realised she did not even know how old Leo was. She watched him fill in the forms, and so discovered he had been born on the 7th August 1916. That meant he had only just turned twenty-three. She wondered how much more she did not know about her husband.

'My favourite colour's green. What's yours?' she asked.

'Blue,' he answered with a wry twist of his mouth. 'Cats or dogs?'

'Dogs,' Ava answered.

'That's a relief.'

'I like cats too,' Ava told him.

'Zeus doesn't,' he replied.

Ava smiled, laying the pen down. There it was done. She was married. Monika popped the champagne, and Leo and Ava drank out of the customary bridal cup, taking care not to spill a drop. The Admiral toasted them solemnly, then left to go back to the office.

'I must go too,' Monika said, pulling on her gloves. She had taken the news of Ava's marriage with surprising calmness, after asking a few sharp questions about Leo's family and background. When she had learnt of his name, and his position as adjutant for Admiral Canaris of the Abwehr, and the possession of a fine house in the Tiergartenstrasse and an old castle in Bavaria, she had shown a begrudging admiration. 'Good catch,' she had said. 'I hadn't thought you quite so smart, Ava.'

She kissed Ava goodbye, her cheek smooth and cool against Ava's hot skin. 'I'll arrange an auction for all the furniture,' she said. 'You must come and help me clean out the apartment.'

'When we get back from our honeymoon,' Leo said.

Ava glanced at him in surprise.

'I've been given a few days off,' Leo said. 'I thought I'd take Ava to meet my mother. I wrote to her last night. She knows we've been married.'

Her heart sank. Ava did not feel ready to meet his mother. She was glad she had bought herself a few new dresses and a new hat.

'Well, have fun,' Monika said, heading out the door. 'When you're back, ring and let me know.'

Ava nodded, surprised by a prickling of tears in her eyes. Just like that, her old life had been severed from her. She looked at her husband, so tall and straight and severe in his grey uniform. He drew her closer, as if sensing some of her feelings, and together they went out into the evening. Ava held a little suitcase, packed with a few clothes and records and her father's battered book of fairy tales, while Leo carried her mother's chest. That was all that was left of her old life. The thought thrilled her almost as much as it frightened her.

Leo hailed a taxi. 'Let's go home to bed,' he whispered in her ear. 'It's been torture, thinking about you all day. I can't wait to make love to you properly.'

Ava felt a wrench in the pit of her stomach. She did not know if it was desire. Or fear.

Ava lay naked in a tangle of sheets, watching her husband pull on his shirt. He was all lean muscle, with only a dusting of gold hairs on his pale skin. Leo felt her gaze, and looked up.

'Good morning.' He came over and bent to kiss her, drawing the sheet away so he could lower his mouth to her shoulder. Ava let her eyes close. She felt the now familiar clench of desire in her groin. It was natural for her to want her husband, she told herself. Any woman would. And it was dangerous to deny the natural sexual energies. It led to all sorts of tensions and disturbances in the psyche.

Leo's natural sexual energies did not seem to have been dissipated by the activities of the night at all. By the time he collapsed into the bed beside her, Ava felt as if all her bones had been turned to molten gold. He lay for a while with his eyes closed, then sighed and looked at her, toying with one of her curls again. 'I wish we could stay in bed all day,' he murmured. 'But I promised my mother we would be at the schloss for dinner. We have to go, Ava.'

She nodded and got out of bed, taking the sheet with her. She went into the dressing-room and chose one of her new dresses to wear. It was an elegant pale green linen that brought out the unusual colour of her eyes.

Leo's housekeeper was busy downstairs, scrubbing the kitchen floor. She was a thin, wiry woman with a flowered scarf tied up over her grey braids. Her eyes were bright with curiosity as Leo introduced Ava as his wife, but she only bobbed her head and said, 'Pleased to meet you, Frau Gräfin von Löwenstein.'

'Frau Klein, will you look after Zeus for me? I cannot take him with me this time.'

'Of course,' she answered. 'When will you be back?'

'In a week. Can you water my roses for me too?'

'Yes, Herr Graf von Löwenstein.' She went back to her work.

Leo picked up the bags, but to Ava's surprise he did not carry them out the front door, but through the kitchen and out onto the terrace. He led the way to the small shed at the back of the garden.

'I think now might be the time to confess I have another woman in my life,' Leo said.

Ava stopped in her tracks.

He laughed, and opened a door to what proved to be a small garage. 'Perhaps I'd better introduce you. Ava, meet Gilda.'

He stood back to show her the most beautiful car Ava had ever seen. Slung low to the ground, it was pale gold in colour with a long elegant bonnet and a steeply slanted rear. The car's fenders rose and swooped in a graceful arc over pale cream tyres. Two huge round headlamps at the front gave it the look of a wide-eyed doll. Its leather roof was folded back, showing two low seats tucked in behind the windshield. Leo opened the passenger door for Ava, giving her a little bow.

'You call it Gilda?' Ava asked. The car was so low, Ava had to hitch up her skirt to slide in. She was very conscious of Leo's eyes on her legs. She smoothed down her skirt as soon as she could.

'You must always call her a "she". She'd be very insulted to be called an "it". The name Gilda comes from *Rigoletto*, of course. It means she's a beautiful girl.' Leo swung the garage door open, then came round to the driver's seat and slid in, disposing his long legs below the steering wheel. Ava folded her hands in her lap, tucking her elbows close against her side. It made little difference. Leo's hand on the gear stick brushed against her knee as he changed gears. It was like a feather-stroke of fire. Ava jumped, and tucked her knees to the other side as the car started with a throaty roar.

'You might want to tie that scarf over your hair,' he told her, as the car rolled out into the Tiergartenstrasse.

'Why?'

'Else your hair will get in a real tangle.' As Leo spoke, he put his foot down hard on the accelerator and the car leapt forward. Ava's hair whipped around her face. She tried to catch it, and Leo laughed. Ava untied the scarf from about her neck, and quickly knotted it over her hair.

As they sped along, people turned to stare at the car. 'She is beautiful,' Ava said.

'Independent suspension, hydraulic brakes and a supercharged engine,' Leo said, negotiating his way through the crowded traffic on Potsdamer Platz.

'I'm guessing that's good?'

'Very good,' he averred. 'I tell myself I need all that power so that the drive home is not such a drag.'

'How long does it take you to get home?'

'In Gilda, only six hours,' he answered. 'It means I can do it in one run. I don't get home very often anymore, though.' His lips compressed into a thin line.

'Why not?'

He looked at her and shrugged. 'I don't get much time off work. I'm amazed the Admiral has given me a week. Usually I'm lucky to get a weekend. I'm afraid I won't be a very attentive husband, Ava. Whither the Admiral goest, there goest I.'

'That's all right,' she said. Ava was surprised that she felt disappointment, rather than relief, and warned herself once again to guard her heart. Nothing's changed, she told herself. He is still a Nazi. Even if he did not denounce Rupert, there are many ugly things he must do in the Reich's service. And she had not forgotten Leo's anger when he had thought Rupert was her lover. He's dangerous, she told herself. Be careful.

Once they reached the countryside, Leo changed gears and the car sprang forward. Ava was glad to leave Berlin behind. It was full of marching men and snapping swastika banners, and clusters of nervous people reading notices pinned to every wall. Ava's gaze was drawn to her husband's stern profile, his nose shaped like the beak of some bird of prey, his strong jaw stubbled with gold. The wind flattened his shirt against his body, so Ava could see the planes of his chest, the bunched muscles of his arm. He must have felt her eyes upon him, for he glanced at her. 'You're being quiet?'

'I'm a little tired.'

'I'm not surprised.' He grinned. For a moment, Ava felt hope flare. Maybe, just maybe, all would be well between them.

Then a shadow fell on his face again, and he looked back to the road. 'We have a long way to go. Try and get some sleep.'

Ava was too aware of him to rest. Every time he changed gears, his hand would brush against her knee and Ava would feel that thrill of nerves deep in her abdomen.

Her body ached in strange places, her limbs felt boneless and her lips tender. Whenever she remembered what they had done in the darkness of the night, her stomach lurched and she needed to clench her knees together. She stared out at the changing landscape – the svelte brown fields with great rolls of hay, stands of trees with blowing green leaves, little villages with timber-framed houses, and churches with spires the colour of gooseberries – and tried not to shiver as he put his hand on her thigh, his fingers gently caressing the soft inner curve of her knee.

Around noon, Leo drew the car up under a tree by a deep green lake and laid down a rug on the ground, in the shadow of a bent pine tree. He unpacked a basket of food that his housekeeper had prepared for him, as Ava sat on the rug, tucking her knees beneath her. He poured her a glass of cool white wine, and served her golden-skinned chicken and potato salad. As they ate and drank, Leo asked Ava questions about her childhood, and what she liked to read, and her favourite music. He was serious and intent.

Ava found it hard. Every anecdote of her childhood, everything Ava loved, was entwined with memories of Rupert. And Ava could not talk of Rupert with her husband. The only way she could move forward in this new life of hers was if she locked her dearest friend away in the most secret and sombre part of her mind, just as he was imprisoned behind high walls and barbed wire in real life. She had to put a padlock on her tongue and a shield over her heart. She had to learn to be a good Nazi wife.

Witches, Bitches and Britches

Leo and Ava drove on into the afternoon. Gradually the landscape changed. Mountains piled like whipped-cream clouds. Green meadows, iced with clover. Lakes as blue as gentians. It was like a scene out of a fairy tale.

Ava wondered what it would be like to grow up surrounded by such loveliness. Surely it must make you a better person? But then Ava remembered that Hitler had been born not far from here, in upper Austria, said to be one of the most beautiful places on earth. And Mahatma Gandhi had been born in western India, which everyone said was a hot and dirty desert. It troubled her. Ava had always thought that people could make the world a better place by seeking out beauty, by creating it with their hands and minds and voices. But perhaps it was not enough.

Ava sighed. Leo glanced at her. 'All right?'

'What have you told them about me?' she asked.

He understood what she meant. 'I told them that we met a few months ago, and decided to be married as soon as possible in case war broke out.'

Ava bit her lip.

'They'll be surprised, of course,' he said. 'But you needn't worry. My mother will love you for my sake.'

This did not really comfort her, but Ava smiled and lifted her chin. 'Tell me about her. I know nothing at all. Does she look like you?'

'Maybe . . . apart from the nose.' He grinned at her. 'Seriously, I have her colouring, I think. Her hair is very fair, like mine. She's half-Dutch, but she was raised in Austria and educated in France.'

'What's her name?'

He laughed in surprise. 'My God, I keep forgetting how little we know about each other. Her name is Isabelle.'

'What about your grandfather?'

He sobered. 'He is called Viktor, which is my middle name. But you should address him formally to begin with, not forgetting the title. He's very old-fashioned, very stiff-backed. You might find him . . . difficult.'

Ava absorbed this for a moment.

'He's stern with us all. He's not well.'

'What's wrong with him?'

Leo shrugged. 'Gout. Old age. Sadness. Mother says he never recovered from the death of my father.'

'He died soon after the end of the war, didn't he?'

'Yes.'

His voice was so grim, Ava asked no more questions. They drove on in silence. The road rose higher and higher towards the mountains, veiled in lavender mists.

'I'll need to go into Rosenheim,' Leo said. 'We should buy some wine and some flowers for my mother.'

The road snaked down towards a wide river, with a ruined castle on a hill above a sprawling township. The most striking feature of the town was two churches side by side, each with a green onion-shaped spire that did not quite match the other. Ava thought it utterly enchanting. Leo parked Gilda and disappeared into the marketplace, and Ava sat and watched the crowd, smiling at the sight of an old woman in a dirndl, with grey plaits wound over her ears, carrying a giant wheel of cheese in red wax. Leo soon returned with a bottle of wine, and a bunch of pink lilies wrapped in pale blue paper. He passed Ava the flowers, and then tried to find space for the bottle in Gilda's tiny luggage compartment.

As Gilda nosed her way through the crowds, a stout woman with flaming red hair recognised the car and began to wave at Leo. He raised a laconic hand and waved back, and then accelerated rather dangerously to get away.

'Who was that?' Ava asked curiously.

'Just a neighbour,' he answered.

They drove up a long, winding road, with a deep valley below them filled with the shining waters of the lake, and the steep flanks of the mountains above, streaked white with snow. At last the car turned into a driveway flanked by two dilapidated stone lions on high pillars, and an iron gateway that stood ajar crookedly.

Ahead was a cluster of mismatched cupolas and turrets, reflected in blurred streaks in a wide moat dappled here and there with lily pads. Leo parked Gilda before the steps, which led up to a tall arched door of oak banded with intricate iron filigree. He turned to Ava and caught her hand. 'I just want to say . . . he's an old man, my grandfather, and very conservative. Perhaps it'd be better not to . . . well, you know . . .'

'Argue with him about politics? Or sing jazz to him?'

Leo grinned. 'Neither of those things!' He jumped out and came around to open her door. As he drew her out of the car, he bent his head and kissed her, taking her breath away. 'We only need to stay a night or two. We can go out all day tomorrow, if you like. I can show you the countryside.'

Leo did not seem to wish to spend much time with his family now that they were here, Ava thought.

A slender, pale-haired woman came down the steps to welcome them. 'Leo! You're here at last. We've been looking for you for at least an hour.' She had a faint, attractive accent, and her eyes were the same extraordinary pale blue as her son's.

'We stopped in Rosenheim.' Leo put down the bags so he could give her a hug. 'Mother, this is Ava.'

She turned and held out her hand. Ava shook it, then showed her the lilies. 'These are for you, Frau Gräfin von Löwenstein.'

She took the lilies, smiling with genuine warmth for the first time. 'My favourite flowers! These are just like the ones that I carried at my wedding. So lovely of you. But please, you must call me Isabelle. And may I call you Ava? I do hope we can be friends. Please, won't you come in? You must be chilled to the bone, if you've driven all the way from Berlin in that ridiculous car of Leo's.'

'Gilda is not ridiculous,' Leo responded at once. 'Ava loves her. Don't you, Ava?'

'I do,' Ava agreed, even as she dragged off her scarf and tried to bring some order to her wind-blown hair.

The front hall was a vast, shadowy room with a high arched ceiling, furnished with fine oak antiques that gleamed with polish. Ava saw a tall grandfather clock, beautifully carved with a glass door that revealed the brass inner workings, and a hand-painted chest that looked very old. An immense faded tapestry took up all of one wall. Ava could just make out the shapes of knights on horses, racing through a dark tangled forest after a leaping white hart.

Isabelle led the way into a pleasant, old-fashioned room, lit by a few lamps set on low tables. An old man sat in a stiff-backed chair by the fireplace, one foot propped up on a padded footstool. He had a rather magnificent white moustache, as if to compensate for thinning white hair, and piercing blue eyes. A huge portrait of Hitler hung on the wall above the fireplace.

'Grandfather, this is my wife, Ava.'

'How do you do, Herr Graf?' Ava said.

The old man frowned. 'She's pretty enough, I suppose. Though very dark. What's your blood, girl?'

'My mother was Spanish,' Ava explained. 'I'm said to look like her.'

'She must've been very beautiful,' Isabelle said, with a faint, apologetic smile. 'Come, sit here by the fire. Let me pour you some mulled wine. I thought you might be a little chilled, not being used to our mountain climate.'

Ava was indeed rather cold, and gladly held her hands to the blaze.

'Thank you so much for coming all this way to see us,' Leo's mother was saying, as she gracefully sat down, her back as straight as a ruler. 'I'm sure it is not how you'd wish to spend your honeymoon.'

'Not at all,' Ava answered. 'I was eager to meet you all.'

'So tell me all about it. Where were you married? What did you wear?'

Ava answered carefully, while Leo's grandfather began to interrogate him about his work. 'What are you doing with the Abwehr? I've heard Admiral Canaris is a fool. You should be with the Schutzstaffel. That's where all the up-and-coming men are.'

'The Admiral's a good man. And much cleverer than people give him credit for.' Leo turned to his mother. 'You must hear Ava sing. I know you'd love her voice.'

'Really?' Isabelle's smile thawed even more.

Ava did her best to charm both Leo's mother and his grandfather during dinner, though occasionally she caught an echo of herself being delightful and childish, as Unity Mitford had tried to be in front of Hitler. Ava pushed the memory away, and pretended she was a sweet innocent new bride, with no opinion on politics or religion. It was hard. Ava was a Berliner, and used to making a quick and cynical rejoinder to almost any comment. And Viktor von Löwenstein was almost unbearable. He was a fierce supporter of the Nazi Party. 'The Führer is the best thing to happen to Germany. He brought us back from the brink of despair!' he declared.

Except all those locked up in concentration camps! Ava thought but did not say.

Ava told herself he was an old man, set in his ways. He lived out in the country, far from the nerve centre of Berlin. He could have no way of knowing how Hitler's Stormtroopers terrorised the population. He couldn't have seen the bonfire of books, the smashing of glass, the beating of old men. Yet, even as Ava tried to calm herself, the rage boiled in her blood and she had to clench her jaw shut to keep the angry words in.

Leo sensed her tension. He tried to change the topic, but his grand-father would not be distracted. Enraged, his rant turned to a tirade against Leo.

'Your father would be so disappointed,' the old man said, splashing himself another goblet of wine. 'Why did we pay all that money to send you to the Kriegsakademie if you are to waste your time at the Abwehr? You should be one of the Führer's best men! Does our name mean nothing now? There's war coming . . .. You should be on the front line . . .'

'Enough!' Isabelle pushed back her chair and stood up. She took a moment to compose herself, then said, 'We are celebrating Leo and Ava's wedding, Viktor! This is no time to talk about war.' She turned to Ava. 'Won't you sing something for us? Music is one of my great joys.'

'It would be my pleasure,' Ava replied, and went with her into the drawing room. A beautiful grand piano was set in an alcove near the window, with a shelf full of music sheets nearby. Ava found a few songs that she knew, and sat down to play Schubert's 'Das Lindenbaum'. It was hard not to think of Rupert. He had been made to play this tune for her so many times. Ava's voice shook a little, and she bent her head, hiding her face.

When she had finished, there was that small space of silence that meant she had sung well. Isabelle clapped her hands. 'Why, Ava, you have the voice of an angel!'

Viktor hurrumphed, blowing his nose into his silk handkerchief. 'Her voice is too deep. What are her teachers thinking? They should be opening her voice up. Who wants to hear a woman sing like a man?'

Some measure of her control snapped. She turned on the piano stool and smiled at the old man. 'You'd be surprised, Herr Graf.' She made her voice as husky and seductive as she could. 'Many people love a woman with a low voice. And it means I get all the most interesting roles to play.' Ava let her smile widen. 'You know. All the witches, bitches and britches.'

Isabelle's eyes widened. Leo stared at her in consternation. But his grandfather slapped his knee and hooted with laughter. 'My God! She's right. Witches, bitches and britches!'

Everyone else laughed too, in surprise and relief. The old man kept repeating the line to himself, 'witches, bitches and britches', and Leo's face was alive with amusement and admiration for Ava's boldness. Viktor bade her sing again, but Leo stood up and said firmly, 'No, poor Ava has sung enough. It's been a long day. I think we need to get to bed.'

Ava saw his heavy-lidded look, the tension in his body, and felt her own body begin to thrum in response. He caught her hand and drew her to her feet.

'Of course.' Isabelle stood up. 'I have prepared the master bedroom for you, Leo. I didn't think you should take your bride into your old room. It's far too small.'

She led the way up a fine sweeping staircase to the upper floor, and along a wide hallway furnished with heavy old antiques and gloomy paintings in ornate tarnished frames. The carpet was worn almost to the threads. She opened a panelled oak door and led Leo and Ava into a vast bedchamber. It was lit only by candles, and a small fire on the hearth. A four-poster bed hung with a swathe of faded green curtains stood on a stage, with a quaint set of steps leading up to it. A vase of flowers was set by the bed, filling the air with fragrance.

'I do hope you like it,' Isabelle said, making a little gesture with her hands.

'I do. Thank you so much.'

'Sleep well, my dear.' She kissed Ava on the cheek. 'Welcome to the family. Good night, my boy. Sweet dreams.' Then she went out, closing the door behind her.

'You're a wonder.' Leo put his hands on Ava's narrow waist, drawing her closer to him. 'A marvel. I've never known anyone to make my grandfather laugh.'

'I'm guessing no-one ever answers back to him,' Ava said.

'He used to thrash us if we ever spoke out of turn.'

'That's terrible,' she cried.

He looked at her in surprise. 'It's just the way things were. We were always being thrashed for one thing or another . . . breaking a window with our ball or not eating every mouthful on our plate.'

Ava gazed at him, troubled at this glimpse into his childhood.

Leo gave her his rueful half-smile. 'Let's not waste time talking about my grandfather.' He slowly walked Ava backwards until she was stopped by the bed. It was so high he had to lift her so that she could sit on the edge. He knelt before her, sliding up her skirt, finding the top of her stocking so he could unsnap it from her garter belt. He rolled down her stocking slowly, following the track of his fingers with gentle kisses. 'I have a much better idea of what we can do with our mouths.'

After Leo fell asleep, his naked body pressed close behind her, Ava lay awake staring into the darkness. She had never known she could feel such things. She pressed her hands to her eyes, and then to her mouth.

Ava was so afraid she had fallen in love with her husband.

19

His Brother's Ghost

The ghost of Leo's brother walked beside them the next day, so omnipresent he was almost visible.

'Alex and I used to play hide-and-seek all through the schloss in winter, when it was too cold to go outside,' Leo said, leading Ava along endless corridors. 'Once I searched for him for hours and hours and couldn't find him. He had just told me this terrible story about how a bride had gone missing on her wedding day, and her skeleton had been found years later – still all dressed in her white silk and tulle – in the bottom of a huge old chest. I was terrified, thinking the same thing had happened to him. My mother helped me look in every chest in the house, but he wasn't in any of them.'

'Did you find him in the end? Where was he?'

'Lying on his bed, reading.'

'You must've been furious!'

Leo grinned. 'Oh, no, I was just so happy to find him alive.'

Then the familiar shadow fell on his face again, and he walked on in silence. Ava's heart ached for him, but she did not know how to comfort him. She was beginning to understand why he came home to the schloss so rarely.

It was a vast place, going to rack and ruin for lack of care. Many rooms stood empty or draped in dustsheets. Darker patches on the walls showed where paintings and tapestries had been taken down, presumably to be sold. Damp stained the walls nearest the moat, and cobwebs hung in the eaves. In one room, the delicate silk wallpaper was stained black down one wall from rain pouring in through a broken roof tile. It seemed such a shame.

'I send money home for Mother, but this house is just too much for her,' Leo said. 'It's hard to know what to do. Grandfather should sell it and move somewhere much smaller and easier, but he utterly refuses to do so. The schloss has been in the family for generations. Mother wants me to sell the house in Berlin and come home to manage the estate, but I couldn't live under the same roof as Grandfather. Besides, my salary is the only thing keeping the old place afloat.'

'Couldn't you do up some of the rooms and take in a few paying guests?' Ava suggested. 'The main reception rooms are all so beautiful, and the schloss itself is wildly romantic. I'm sure people would love to come and stay here.'

'My grandfather won't hear of it,' Leo answered. 'Mother would like that, I think. It's very lonely here for her, and she cannot afford anyone to help her. She does all the work herself.'

'She cooked that delicious meal last night?' Ava asked, surprised.

Leo nodded. 'Mother does all the work in the house and the garden as well. All of what we ate last night would have been grown by her, or raised by her.'

'She's a redoubtable woman.'

Leo nodded. 'I wish I could make life easier for her. I know she'd like it if I moved back here ... if *we* moved ...' A quick grin flashed over his face. 'I still can't quite get used to being married,' he told her.

'Me either.'

'I guess we'll soon be like any old married couple,' Leo said. 'Sitting by the fire in our slippers. I'll be smoking a pipe and you'll be sewing baby clothes.'

Quick panic flashed over her. 'I can't sew. Or cook.'

'I thought all good German girls were taught to cook and sew.'

'Not me!' Ava changed the subject quickly. 'Show me where you used to sleep when you were a boy.'

Leo took her up a narrow wooden staircase to a long room that had obviously once been a kind of schoolroom. There was a large globe on a stand, a blackboard with faint chalk marks, an old upright piano, and bookcases laden with paperbacks. At either end of the room were small bedrooms with sloping roofs. They were furnished simply with white iron beds, covered with faded patchwork quilts. She went across to the bookshelf. There were books she recognised, like *Emil and the Detectives*, and many she did not know. Some were in English. Ava picked them up and read the titles. *Kim. The Thirty-Nine Steps. A Study in Scarlet.*

'Spy novels,' Leo said. 'Playing spies was our favourite game.'

He stood looking out the dormer window. It was so dirty, the light seemed greenish and gloomy. He picked up a tin soldier from the bookcase and tried to set it upright. The soldier had lost a leg, though, and fell down again.

Leo moved restlessly. 'Let's go outside.'

But his brother's ghost was in every corner of the huge, overgrown garden too. 'Alex and I built a fort in that tree,' Leo told her, 'and for one whole summer we played Cowboys and Indians. Alex got into such trouble for making his headdress out of Mother's best ostrich fan.'

The kitchen garden near the house was in good order, with winter crops of broccoli, cabbage, cauliflower and beans all laid out in neat rows. Parsley had gone to seed in lacy green parasols, and late pumpkins romped all over the paths. Leo and Ava passed Isabelle in a pair of old muddy men's trousers and a battered straw hat, digging up beetroots. 'I hope you like beetroot soup,' she called.

Beyond the vegetable patch, though, the garden had been left mostly to itself. The hedges grew wildly, shooting in all directions, and the lawn was tall enough to wade through. A marble statue lay broken and overgrown with ivy. Leo took Ava through an archway so criss-crossed with tangled climbing roses that she had to practically crawl to get through, wincing away from the sharp thorns. Beyond was an overgrown rose garden, surrounding a long oblong pool in which a marble goddess smiled at herself in the murky waters. Here and there a heavy crimson rose hung in late overblown beauty, or small pink fairy roses cascaded, but most of the bent roses were wound about and strangled by weeds and dark creepers.

'This was my grandmother's rose garden,' Leo told her. 'It was her favourite place to be. I remember her working here almost to the day of her death. I spent a lot of time with her here. She planted the garden at the Tiergartenstrasse as well.'

'Was it your grandmother who taught you how to grow roses in winter?' Ava asked.

Leo smiled at her. 'In the glasshouse.' He drew her close and kissed her. 'Did you like them?'

Ava nodded, looking up at him. 'It seemed so impossible . . . Full-blown roses in the snow . . .'

'Impossible as falling in love at first sight.' He kissed her again.

They crept through the overgrown yew hedge, Leo holding back the branches so they would not scratch her, and explored the rest of the garden, and the tangled forest beyond. The shadows had gone from Leo's face. He laughed and teased Ava, and caught her close to kiss her. But then their wandering feet brought them out near the gateway, where two stone lions guarded the entrance. His eyes darkened. 'This was where we left secret messages for each other,' he told her. Leo climbed up and thrust his hand between the fangs of one snarling lion's mouth, drawing out a grubby candle stub and an old box of matches. 'See? Alex gouged out quite a deep hole there. We used to leave notes for each other there, written in invisible ink. We needed to hold them above the candle flame to read them.'

He looked down at the dusty relics in his hand and then shoved them back into the lion's mouth. 'Let's get out of here.'

Ava ran to get her coat and scarf, and then they drove around the countryside. The grimness in Leo's face did not lessen, though, and all her eager questions and comments did not bring him ease. At last Ava said, on a whim, 'Would you teach me to drive?'

He hesitated a moment. She frowned and crossed her arms. 'Don't tell me you think girls shouldn't drive, for then I'll think you're as old fashioned as your grandfather!'

He laughed at that and pulled the car over to the verge. 'Very well, let's swap. But please be careful! Gilda's rather easily bruised.'

The next hour or so passed in laughter and mock-terror and not-so-mock-exasperation, but finally Ava got the hang of the clutch and the brake and the steering wheel, and Gilda began to run a little more smoothly. And the white tension was gone from Leo's face.

The Commandant dragged his twelve-year-old son along by the wrist.

Frau Koch stood near the camp gates, smiling, her own young son perched on her hip. She was dressed in a fine silk dress, and high-heeled shoes, her hair tied back with a bright blue bow.

The gates opened, and the Commandant marched in, towing along the elder boy. He was screaming and fighting. His father hit him hard across the face. 'What you need, my boy, is discipline.'

The boy turned and screamed at Frau Koch, 'I hate you! I hate you!'

'I'll teach you to be impudent to your stepmother!'

The boy was struck so hard, he fell to the ground. His father hauled him up and marched his sobbing son in through the iron doors of the Bunker, the prison within the prison. Within were the solitary confinement cells, where prisoners were taken to be beaten or tortured before execution. The screams from within were intolerable.

The Commandant came out alone ten minutes later, straightening his jacket and smoothing back his hair. He ignored the crowds of prisoners busy about their work, and went out to his wife and young son. Frau Koch kissed him as openly as if they did not have an audience of several hundred prisoners and guards, and they strolled off together into the warm sunshine.

Rupert waited till they were out of sight, and then hurried back to the kitchen, head lowered. The Kochs were having a party that day, and Rupert and the other kitchen hands were called upon to prepare the food. Dozens of fat pink hams had to be baked in red wine and brown sugar, eggs stuffed, pork sausages and cheese sliced, and onions chopped by the dozens for the little tarts Frau Koch loved so much. The Commandant funded his monthly parties by forcing the entire camp to go without food for a whole day, so everyone hated the announcement that a party was to be held. Rupert had grown adept at slipping small slithers of food into his mouth, his pockets, his shoes, the cuffs of his sleeves. He was sure that these extra secret rations had helped save his life, and always tried to smuggle something out for Rudi.

After the noon meal, where he nervously served the SS guards in their mess hall, Rupert slipped across to the Bunker. It was not long after midday, and the sun beat down mercilessly on the camp. Any prisoner on his lunch break would sit or stand in the shade of one of the huts, but no-one dared shelter in the deep shadow cast by the Bunker. Rupert moved slowly along the heavy concrete wall, hearing the moans and prayers of those unfortunates locked inside. When he could hear a child sobbing, he drew a tiny handmade whistle out of his pocket. He began to play a lilting tune.

The sobbing eased. Soon a small, tear-stained face appeared at the barred window. The boy would have to be standing on tiptoe on a chair to look out.

'Who . . . who are you?' the boy whispered.

'I'm . . . My name is Rupert.'

'I'm Manfred. What are you playing?'

'It's just a little whistle. I made it from a stick. It makes quite a pretty tune, though.' Rupert blew a few notes. 'I play it when things seem really bad. It helps somehow.'

'Play some more,' the boy commanded.

Rupert looked quickly around. No-one was paying him any attention. The day was too hot, the shadow of the Bunker too heavy. He played an old folk tune.

'I like that,' Manfred said. 'I wish I could play like that.'

'Here, have it.' Rupert reached up and passed the wooden whistle in through the bars of the window. 'Hide it where no-one can see it. Then, when you're alone, try and play a tune. It's fun working out how.' The boy smiled and took the whistle. 'I have to go. I'll be in trouble if they catch me.' Rupert began to move away.

'Wait!' the boy cried. 'What did you do, to be locked up in here?'

'What did *you* do?'

A sullen expression settled down over the boy's face. 'Nothing.'

'Neither did I.'

'That's so unfair!'

'I know. But you'll be let out soon, I'm sure, and maybe I will be too.' Rupert moved away. He felt a little flutter with him. *Hope . . . butterfly-winged . . . storm-blown . . . but valiant . . .*

Childhood Friend

Proudly Ava drove Gilda back to the schloss. Coming a little too fast down the drive, she saw a big black car drawn up before the steps. A stout middle-aged lady with improbably red hair was being helped out by a uniformed chauffeur. Ava had to brake rather hard and brought Gilda in to a clumsy swerving halt.

Leo's hand was white-knuckled on the door handle.

'Sorry,' Ava said but then realised that he was staring at the other car. The middle-aged woman turned to wave as the chauffeur helped a younger woman out. Ava recognised her at once. She was the haughty redhead who had spoken to Leo at the Christmas concert. Her hair was set artfully in a series of stiff curls across her brow, and over her ears, and she had darkened her lashes and brows with a careful and subtle hand. A dozen gold chains hung from her throat to her belt, and she wore a golden swastika brooch.

'Oh God,' Leo said in a strangled voice. He got slowly out of the car and came round to open Ava's door. Ava got out, trying to smooth down her hair and dress. Leo said in a quick undertone, 'Ava, I'm sorry. I didn't know she was here . . .'

There was no time to say more, for the stout woman was hurrying towards them, hands held out. 'My dear Leo! So lovely to see you home. And look who is here! Such a surprise!'

'Good afternoon, Frau Breiter, Gertrud. I did not know we were expecting you.' Leo's voice was cool.

Frau Breiter kissed him exuberantly on both cheeks, then stood back to allow the redhead to do the same. She stepped very close to Leo to do so, and her kisses seemed to linger. Ava felt herself stiffen.

Leo stepped away. Gertrud linked her arm through his, smiling. 'Oh, there's no need for old friends like us to stand on ceremony! Mother said she saw you in town and so we thought we'd pop by and say hello. It has been such an age since we saw you.' There was a note of reproof in her voice.

'I thought you were in Berlin still,' he answered.

Gertrud laughed again, as if he had said something highly amusing. 'Oh, I was. I should really still be there. We are so busy! But it looks as if we are only going to get busier, and so I thought I'd pop home for a few days and see the Mater.'

Leo's brows constricted. The stern look had settled down on his face again. He tried to extricate his arm, but Gertrud pressed it closer. 'But who is this pretty child?' she asked, turning to Ava. 'Has Isabelle got a little friend come to stay? How nice.'

Leo yanked his arm free and came to stand beside Ava. She could feel the stiffness in his body. 'Ava, let me introduce you to some old friends of my mother's. This is Frau Breiter. She and her husband live just down the road from us. This is her daughter Gertrud. She works with the Schutzstaffel in Berlin. Gertrud, this is my wife, Ava.'

Gertrud gasped. The colour drained from her face. 'Your wife? You're married?'

Her mother was gabbling in amazement. 'But Leo! Oh my God! How can you be married? We had no idea! When did this happen?'

'Ava and I were married two days ago in Berlin,' Leo said. 'But we have known each other for quite a few months now.'

The colour had come rushing back into Gertrud's face. She flicked a look at Ava. 'I've seen you before, haven't I? That's right. You're some kind of singer.' She made it sound as if being a singer was little better than being a street walker.

'Ava is studying at the conservatory. She's already done a season at Bayreuth,' Leo replied frostily.

'Really? You seem far too young. I wonder your parents would permit it. I've heard all sorts of stories about what goes on backstage there.'

'Have you really?' Ava answered sweetly. 'For the Führer himself seemed to find nothing amiss with our parties. He joined us nearly every night.'

Frau Breiter clasped her pudgy hands together. 'The Führer? You met the Führer?'

'Of course,' Ava answered. 'He said our performance of *Tristan and Isolde* was the best he had ever seen.'

Gertrud pressed her lips together. She did not dare say anything more, for then it would have seemed as if she was criticising Hitler.

At that moment, Isabelle came down the front stairs. 'Ursula, Gertrud, what a lovely surprise. Come in. Can I offer you some coffee? I suppose you've heard the news?'

'I can hardly credit it's true,' Frau Breiter responded. 'Leo, married! To a girl we've never heard of!'

'Yes, isn't it romantic?' Isabelle smiled and held out her hand. Ava took it and she led her up the stairs. Frau Breiter followed, talking loudly. But Leo did not follow. He was frowning down at Gertrud, who had stepped close to him, one long-nailed hand on his arm. Ava strained to hear what they were saying.

'I'm sorry you had to find out this way.' Leo's voice was so low Ava could barely hear his words. 'I was planning to write. It all happened so fast.'

'Is she pregnant?' Gertrud demanded. 'Is that why you've married her?'

'No!'

'Then why? I thought we had kissed and made up!' Gertrud slid her hand up his arm.

Leo's mother led Ava gently but firmly inside the house. She and Frau Breiter were still talking. Ava did not hear a word. Her ears were hissing with rage and jealousy and anguish. Somehow she managed to concentrate enough to answer some of the questions being fired at her by Frau Breiter. Although the stout woman smiled and pretended to be genial, Ava could tell she was seething with anger. Her fingers clicked the clasp of her handbag open and shut again and again, and two spots of colour burned on her flabby cheeks.

'So, you're a Berliner? Where does your family live?' When Ava told her, Frau Breiter's voice grew sharper. 'Is that not near the synagogue? Are you Jewish?'

'No,' Ava answered, her voice growing sharper too.

'So what does your father do?'

'My father was a professor of psychology at Berlin University,' Ava replied. 'He has retired now, and is living in Berne with my sister.'

'So how did you and Leo meet?' she demanded.

Ava did not know how to answer her. Her whole body felt hot. Just then Leo came into the room. He walked straight to Ava, and perched on the arm of her chair. Ava sat stiffly, not relaxing into the curve of his arm.

'We literally bumped into each other,' Leo said. 'It was love at first sight.'

Ava looked up at him then, and he looked down at her. Something leapt between them. He bent and kissed her temple, brushing away one of her curls. Gertrud came in and saw his kiss. She set her jaw. Ava let her body relax against Leo's arm, and looked back at Frau Breiter.

'I had to hunt her down, though,' Leo went on. 'I had no idea what her name was or where she lived. I spent all my free time haunting the streets near where we'd met. Then I heard her singing, and so I found her. She was standing in the window, and I saw all her hair hanging down her back and knew her at once.' He smiled and coiled one of her ringlets around his fingers.

'How sweet,' Gertrud said. 'It's like something from a storybook.'

'Isn't it?' Isabelle said. 'It's the most romantic story I've ever heard.'

Isabelle went to fetch coffee and cakes, and everyone was very polite to each other. Leo stayed close beside Ava. She was grateful, for the looks from Frau Breiter and her daughter could have stripped flesh from bones.

After their coffee was drunk, Frau Breiter turned to Leo and said, with what was no doubt meant to be a winning pout, 'Leo, my dear, I do wish you would take a look at our car. It is making a most unpleasant knocking sound, and our chauffeur is utterly useless.'

Leo rose to his feet. 'Of course.'

Gertrud turned to Ava. 'Leo's an absolute wizard with cars, aren't you, darling? Oh, but I suppose you must know that.' Her tone of voice made it clear she supposed no such thing.

As Leo went out with Frau Breiter, Isabelle said, smiling, 'Indeed, yes. When he was a boy, Ava, Leo built a motorbike from spare parts and was off zooming around the countryside all day long. I was sure he'd be brought home on a stretcher.'

'Except in the end it was Alex's body brought home, not Leo's,' Gertrud said. She was being deliberately cruel, Ava was sure of it.

Isabelle's smile died. She rose. 'Excuse me a moment, please . . .' With swift, uneven steps, she went from the room.

Gertrud turned to Ava at once. Her smile had disappeared. 'So, you think you've got your hooks into him. Wanted to be a Gräfin, did you? Was it a shock to come here and see the place half in ruin? It'll take a pretty pfennig to put it in order, and he knows I've got the cash. He'll soon tire of you, and remember his duty by his family. And then he'll come back to me. He always comes back to me. And, trust me, a misalliance like this is easily broken. The Führer does not like his men to marry tainted blood . . . and I can tell by looking at you that yours is tainted.'

'How can you say such a thing?' Ava managed to stammer. She was so taken aback by Gertrud's vitriol that she could scarcely speak.

'There'll be some rattling skeleton in your background that'll hurt him if it's found out, and so I'll find it out, don't you fear. You don't get hair like yours and a mouth like yours with pure Aryan blood. Schutzstaffel officers are only permitted to marry those who are racially pure . . .'

'Leo is not in the Schutzstaffel.' Ava cut across her, hands clenched into fists.

'He will be. He's just being stubborn. Leo knows he has to make his mark, and the Schutzstaffel is the way to do it. And he'll soon realise that a dirty slut like you will only hold him back.'

Ava's face flamed.

'And then I'll get him back. I promise you.' Gertrud rose, patted her rigid curls to make sure not a hair was out of place, and sailed out of the room. Ava sat, her nails cutting into her palms, trying to get her breathing back in order.

Hearing Isabelle's heels clicking across the floor, Ava jumped to her feet and went out through the French windows and into the garden. She could hear an engine being turned over, and the sound of voices nearby. She went away from the sound, stumbling, wiping her eyes. Her way was blocked by the moat. Green and opaque, floating with water lilies, it stretched between her and escape. Ava could not go back. So she sat down on the stone edging, took off her sandals, and dangled her feet in the water. A shock of cold. Ava leant her head against the sun-warmed stone of the old house, and shut her eyes. Tears slid down her face.

A little while later, Ava heard footsteps behind her. She bent and scooped up some water, then pressed her cold, wet hands against her face.

Leo sat down beside her, unlaced his shoes and put his bare feet into the water. 'Thank God they've gone at last.'

Ava did not answer.

'I've been looking for you. I could not think where you might have gone.'

Still Ava did not answer.

'I suppose I should have told you about Gertrud,' he said. 'I didn't think she'd turn up here, though. Her mother must've rung Gertrud as soon as she saw us in Rosenheim. It's the only way she could've got here so fast.'

He waited a moment, but Ava still made no response.

'Did she say something to you? What did she say?' His voice was angry.

Ava put up one hand and wiped her eyes as surreptitiously as she could.

Leo sighed. 'I suppose she told you we were lovers. It's true ... we were ... but I don't love her, Ava.'

When Ava did not answer, he went on. 'I've known her all my life. She only lived down the road. When we were kids, we were back and forth on our bikes all the time. Her father was something important in the National Socialist Party ... she joined the Band of German Maidens even before the Führer was made Chancellor. It was Gertrud who made us join the Hitler Youth. She used to tease us and call us lily-livered cowards ...' His voice trailed away.

There was a long silence. Ava looked down at her bare feet, green-hued, swirling the water about in heavy frills of foam.

After a while, he went on, his voice constricted. 'Alex was in love with her. He tried so hard to impress her. Everyone thought they'd marry. Grandfather said she'd make a perfect Gräfin ... and they have money, you know. It would've saved the schloss. But Gertrud wanted him to prove himself to her ... that's why Alex went into Munich that night. It was stupid. So stupid ... I rode my motorbike all the way to Munich, looking for him. They beat him to death ... I tried to stop them.'

Ava turned to face him.

'I couldn't be bothered with anything after Alex died. I didn't go to the Hitler Youth meetings, I didn't go anywhere. Gertrud came. She made me go. She said I owed it to Alex to honour his memory. One night she ...'

He fell silent. Ava swished her feet in the moat. She could just imagine.

'I was only sixteen. My brother was dead. I thought she loved me. I tried ... I tried so hard. But she said I was only a boy. She began going out with one of the Hitler Youth leaders. They used to laugh at me because ... well, just because.'

Ava smoothed her dress over her knees.

'I went back to school. There was nothing else to do. Afterwards ... well, they offered me a job in the SS but I wanted nothing to do with them. She was there by then, you see. So I went to the Abwehr instead. I had friends there.'

The sun was sinking. The moat glittered as if with golden fish scales. Ava's bare feet were numb.

'That was when I met you. You wanted nothing to do with me. I felt . . . nothing was any use. She was there that night, when you sang at the Christmas concert. She made it clear she'd like to get back with me . . .' Ava felt him slant a look at her.

'So you slept with her.' Ava did not mean for her words to sound so accusatory, but the force of her emotions was too much for her.

He nodded. 'Yes. I slept with her. A few times. I thought it might help.' He shrugged. 'It didn't. I only wanted you.'

Ava did not know what to say. She was hurt, angry, jealous, all those things, and yet she was pierced with love and pity too. She longed to believe him. She thought: *he married me. He's mine now. I'll not let anyone else have him.*

And so she told him what Gertrud had said to her. His eyes darkened, and his jaw tensed. 'She always was a little cat,' he muttered. Then he took her hand, raising it to his mouth so he could kiss her palm. 'I'm sorry, Ava. I should never have slept with her again. It's just I felt . . . I felt as if the whole world was going to blazes, so what did it matter? We don't need to see her again. She's got some SS man on a string, she'll soon forget about us.'

Remembering the look of malice on Gertrud's face, Ava was not so sure.

21

War Fever

War Fever in Poland! Polish Forces Mobilise!

Ava read the newspaper again and again, as if trying to squeeze more juice from a lemon.

'I should go back.' Leo moved restlessly from the empty fireplace to the window and back.

'You were given a week, weren't you?' Isabelle said, her face bloodless. 'You're on your honeymoon.'

'It doesn't matter. The Admiral will need me. I must get back.'

Ava went to pack her bag.

Isabelle knocked on the door, then came in. Her face was strained and lined. 'Ava, I have something for you.' Carefully she opened a blue velvet box. Inside lay a necklace made of double strands of pearls, flowing from a huge, slightly misshapen pearl surrounded by sparkling diamonds. Below it was a matching bracelet. Ava caught her breath. She had never seen anything so lovely.

'These are the Von Löwenstein pearls. They were given to me when I married Leo's father and now I give them to you.'

'But . . . I can't take them! They must be priceless.'

'I'm far too old to wear them now,' Isabelle said. 'Besides, where do I ever go anymore? No, no. You are in Berlin, you will need to go to many functions. Take them, my dear, wear them with pride.' She shut the box reverently and passed it to Ava.

'Thank you. Are you sure? I'll be terrified each time I wear them.'

'You'll look beautiful in them.' Isabelle kissed Ava's cheek. 'Look after my boy for me, Ava. He so deserves to be loved. Please look after him.'

'I'll try,' Ava promised.

As they drove into Berlin that evening, Ava saw chains of people filling hessian bags with sand and piling them against the bases of buildings. Workmen were painting the kerbs with phosphorescent paint.

Otherwise, the streets were deserted. Only a few people trudged along the pavement, carrying bulging shopping bags. The trams clanked past, empty of passengers, and the only cars were army jeeps, carrying grim-faced men in uniforms. When they reached the Tiergartenstrasse, Leo locked Gilda safely away and hurried back to the house. Ava sat on the bed and watched as he stripped off his shirt and trousers, and re-dressed himself in his uniform. His flared-hip breeches with the scarlet stripe. His field-grey jacket with its scarlet lapels and golden eagle and swastika, buttoned up to the throat. The grey cap with its golden braid and badges, fitted down over his frowning eyes. His shiny black boots. Before her very eyes, Leo was transformed back into the Nazi officer she had first met and feared.

'Don't wait up for me,' he instructed, before he kissed her brusquely and strode off into the dusk.

Berlin failed to light up against the night sky. All was eerily dark. Leaflets had been left in the letterbox from the block warden, with strict instructions on what had to be done to each house to make it ready for war. Ava walked about the house, drawing all the curtains, realising all were too thin. Zeus followed close at her heels, his tail slunk low. Ava was hungry, and made herself a rough meal of cheese and crackers. She then sat in the dimness of a single candle, Zeus's head resting against her knee, trying to read. When Ava went to put the Great Dane out for the night, he whined and gazed up at her imploringly. Ava relented and took him upstairs with her. He lay down beside the bed, and the thought of him was a comfort of sorts.

Sometime later, a strange wailing noise filled the night. Up and down, up and down, like the howling of some mechanical wolf. Zeus whined and cowered on the floor. Ava sat up in bed, not knowing what to do. It must be an air-raid warning, she realised. She jumped up and ran down to the coal cellar, Zeus at her heels. Ava sat there in her nightgown on the filthy floor, her arms about the dog's neck. At last the wailing died away and Ava crept back to bed, but it was a long time before she slept again.

Leo came home very late. She only realised when she woke drowsily at the tipping of the mattress under his weight, and felt his body press close against her. They made love in total silence. When Ava woke the next morning, he was gone again. He had taken his suitcase with him. A note on his pillow read: 'I have to go to Poland with the Admiral. God willing, I'll be home soon.' It was signed only with a cross.

Ava listened to the radio feverishly all morning. It said Poland had attacked Germany, and the Third Reich had simply retaliated. Hitler shouted that bombs would be met with bombs, poison gas with poison gas. Ava heard that German forces were advancing all along the line, and the Poles were in disarray. Danzig was in German hands, and so too Teschen. Ava could not believe it. She hesitated, then took the radio down into the coal cellar, turning the dial to the BBC. It was there Ava heard that Warsaw was being bombed to rubble.

Gripped with a feeling of doom, Ava turned the radio off, unable to bear hearing anymore. She had no classes that day, for she was meant to be preparing for her exams. But she could not settle to study or singing practice, and there was little food in the house, Frau Klein not having expected them home so soon. Ava took some notes from the jar of housekeeping money in the pantry and went out to get some groceries. Everyone she passed looked hunched and afraid. In the butcher shop, when Hitler's voice began to scream once more from the radio, there was only silence. It was the first time that Ava had not heard his voice being met with shouts of 'Heil Hitler!'.

She bought everything she could find that was exempt from rationing, and piled the tins and cans in the pantry, just in case.

The block warden came around that afternoon with a clipboard, angry that the house had not been fully prepared for war, according to instructions. Herr Nadel was a thin man with a receding hairline and peering eyes magnified by the thick spectacles he wore. With his thin, knock-kneed legs and stooped shoulders, he looked rather comical in his perfectly pressed brown uniform and long socks, but he had such an unpleasant manner that Ava dared not smile.

Ava had to shovel sand into hessian bags all by herself, and cut black paper to fit the windows, accompanied everywhere by an anxious-faced Great Dane who gazed at her with imploring eyes, whining for his master to come home. Ava set up a camp bed and some blankets in the cellar, so that she would not need to sit on the filthy ground next time there was an air-raid, and brought down a hurricane lamp and some matches.

When Ava went to bed that evening, tired and aching all over, she felt small and alone in Leo's big bed.

On Sunday, she went to help Monika clean out their father's apartment. It was hard, dirty work, and Ava did not know what to do with her old books and film-star posters. In the end, she threw out nearly everything, keeping only her old bicycle which she thought might come in useful. By the end of the day, the apartment was in order and ready for new tenants, with a large number of boxes and suitcases to be sent to Otto or given to charity.

'I suppose I had better take Muschi,' Monika said with a sigh. She bent and picked up the huge old cat, which had been fed by a neighbour since Otto's arrest. Monika pressed her face down into his fur and took a rather shaky breath. Ava looked at her in surprise, never having thought she cared much about the cat. Monika had always called him 'fish-breath' and 'moth-eaten furball'.

'What?' Monika demanded, straightening up. 'You don't want him, do you?'

'I think Leo's dog would think him a tasty mouthful,' Ava answered.

Monika snorted. 'Well, then. I guess it's up to me to look after him. As usual.' She gave a long-suffering sigh, and hefted the immense cat higher. Ava could hear his rusty purr from where she stood. Monika rubbed his ears, and then pretended to be checking for fleas.

'Monika . . .' Ava said hesitantly.

'What?'

'Do you know . . . how to stop a baby happening?' Ava was so embarrassed she could not look at her sister.

Monika stared at her. 'You don't still fall apart at the sight of blood, do you?'

Ava flushed. 'I just don't want to bring a baby into a world that is at war,' she answered in a suffocated voice.

'Or lose your figure,' Monika said cynically.

'Is there anything I can do?'

'Try not to sleep with your husband in the middle of your cycle,' Monika said. 'But if you can't stop him, give yourself a good wash out with disinfectant afterwards.'

Ava made a face.

'Or vinegar if you can't get hold of disinfectant.'

Ava stopped by the shops on her way home and bought a large bottle of disinfectant and a large bottle of vinegar, just to be certain.

The next day, after her singing exam had finished, Ava went to visit the Feidlers. She had been postponing the visit, not wanting to have to tell them about her father's arrest and subsequent flight to Switzerland. Ava felt guiltily that they must wonder how it was she had managed to get her father out, but not her oldest friend. She did not know how she could possibly explain.

Onkel Franz was still at work, but Tante Thea huddled in bed, her iron-grey hair in a loose plait. She was knitting a sock for Rupert from wool she had unravelled from one of her jerseys. The sock was now almost as long as one of Ava's stockings, but Tante Thea did not seem able to stop. Jutta was studying at the table, pushed under the only window so that she did not need to switch on the electricity. The tiny apartment was stiflingly hot, and smelt of onions and sewage.

Jutta greeted her cordially enough, and was pleased when Ava showed her the basket full of food she had brought.

'What a feast,' she cried. 'Did you carry that heavy basket all the way here?'

'No, I . . . I caught a bus.' Ava felt her cheeks warming.

Jutta raised her eyebrows. 'Flush with funds all of a sudden, are we?'

'I . . . yes . . . it's hard to explain. So much has happened in the last few weeks.'

Jutta had paused in her unpacking of the basket. 'You'd better sit down and tell us. I'll make us some coffee, since you've been so kind to bring us some.'

Ava sat down at the table. 'I couldn't ring you or write to you . . . it just wasn't safe . . .'

'What wasn't safe?' Tante Thea asked, clutching the sock to her thin chest. 'Ava, what's wrong? You're frightening us.'

'There's no easy way to tell you.'

Jutta brought in three tiny cups of coffee, and sat down opposite her. 'Spit it out. What have you done? Eloped with a millionaire?'

'Sort of,' Ava answered, laughing a little wildly.

'Are you joking?' Jutta demanded. 'Though I must say you are looking far too swish for Scheunenviertel. Wherever did you get that hat?'

Ava put her hand to her hat self-consciously. She unpinned it and lay it on the table.

'I . . . oh, Tante Thea. It was so awful. Father was arrested. By the Gestapo. He and I had written some letters . . .'

Tante Thea gasped and put one thin hand to her chest.

'That's why I couldn't ring you . . . they might have tapped our phone.'

'Is he all right? Did they hurt him? Have they sent him to a concentration camp?' Jutta's questions came thick and fast.

'No. I mean, yes, they hurt him . . . badly, I think. But . . . we managed to get him out. He and Bertha caught the night train to Berne last week.' Ava was conscious she was gripping her hands together too tightly, and tried to relax her fingers.

'But . . . how did you get him out? And what has that got to do with having a new hat?' Jutta's frown had deepened.

'I . . . do you remember the officer who helped you the night of broken glass? I went to him. He got passports for Father and Bertha and Angelika. He helped get them out.' Ava's cheeks were fiery red. 'I . . . I was left all alone, and Leo . . . the officer . . . he was afraid the Gestapo might arrest me too. Because of the letters, you see. So I . . .'

'You married him? You married a Nazi?'

Ava nodded.

Jutta stood up and went out to the kitchen. She stood for a moment, her hands clenched on the edge of the sink, her back turned towards Ava.

Tante Thea was dismayed, but did her best to hide it. 'I'm sure he's a good man, if he helped save Otto. Is he a good man, Ava?'

'He is. I'm sure he is.' How Ava hoped he was.

'Is he in the SS?' Jutta asked, not turning around.

'No. He works for the Abwehr. He speaks a lot of languages. French, Dutch, English, Italian, and a little Russian too.' Ava tried not to remember their wedding night when Leo had seduced her with murmured phrases of one language or another.

'What about Rupert?' Jutta spun around. 'Can your husband help him?'

Ava shrank back. 'I'm sorry. I can't . . . he can't . . .'

'Because Rupert is a Jew, I suppose.' Jutta's shoulders drooped.

Ava did not speak.

'Well, it was good of you to come and tell us. I guess we shall not be seeing so much of you anymore.' Jutta came and gathered up the coffee cups, and took them into the kitchen to wash.

Ava picked up her hat but did not leave. 'I'll be able to help you more now,' she burst out. 'Leo's not a millionaire by any means, but he has more money than any of us ever did. He's given me an allowance, on top of the housekeeping money. I'll be able to bring you food and some warm blankets. Anything you need, just let me know.'

'We don't need charity,' Jutta responded.

Ava could have wept. 'It's not charity when it's from friends! Tante Thea, you practically raised me. Please, please, let me help you now.'

'Of course.' Tante Thea held up her arms and Ava bent to embrace her. 'It's very kind of you, and I must admit it'll be a help. Poor Franz is wearing himself out working in the factory all day. It's not what he's used to.' She looked unhappily around the tiny room, with damp stains on the ceiling and a fire-escape right outside the window.

'So where are you living now? Somewhere swish, I suppose.' Jutta's fierce look had not softened.

'We live near the Tiergarten,' Ava admitted. 'It's so close to the conservatory, I don't have far to walk for my lessons anymore. Leo's not home. He's gone to Poland with the Admiral, his boss. We had only a few days together before the war broke out.'

'Who does he work for again?' Jutta asked.

'Admiral Canaris. He's the head of the Abwehr.'

'Isn't that like . . . spies or something?'

'The Abwehr is the military intelligence arm of the Wehrmacht.'

Thoughtfully Jutta tapped her finger against her mouth. 'That could be useful,' she murmured. Coming to some kind of decision, she beckoned Ava into the kitchen. Ava noticed that there were two of every pot, pan and utensil, each handle marked with either red or blue paint.

Jutta spoke in a low voice. 'Ava, if your husband works for military intelligence, it's likely that he'll be privy to all sorts of top-secret information, won't he? Like new laws to be passed, or new attacks on the Jews.'

'I suppose so,' Ava replied warily.

'Do you suppose you could keep your eyes and ears open? And if you hear anything useful, let me know?'

'Why? What would you do with it?'

'I don't know. Warn people. Try and prepare them for what's coming. I've been working at the Jewish Community office, Ava. You can have no idea of the misery.'

Ava squeezed her hand. 'I'm so sorry. What can I do to help?'

'Well, food and clothes and blankets and things are always useful. But information is even better.'

Ava drew away from her. 'But . . . I don't want to spy on Leo. It doesn't feel right.'

'Not even to help Rupert?'

'How will spying on Leo help Rupert?'

'The only way to get Rupert out of that awful place is to overthrow Hitler! And the only way to overthrow Hitler is to do everything we can to stand against him. We can try and make the German people realise how wrong this war is, and we can try and help those who are being victimised.'

Ava thought of her father, and the cost he had paid for sending a few letters. 'I'll do anything I can,' she answered, even as fear knotted her stomach.

Broken Toy

One morning, as Ava sat at the kitchen table with her coffee and sweet roll, she opened the newspaper only to find screaming headlines proclaiming that Unity Mitford had shot herself in the head. She had survived, but was in hospital in Munich, thought to be so brain-damaged she would never recover. She was just twenty-five. Ava could only stare at the newsprint, choked with grief, and wondering if the young English woman had known she had tried to commit suicide in the exact same manner as Hitler's niece so long ago.

Ava was unable to eat another mouthful. She folded up her newspaper, hiding the photograph of Unity's face, and gave the rest of her roll to Zeus. She went to her classes at the conservatory, but found the tissues of her throat were so thick she could scarcely make a sound. She told her teacher she was sick, and went home to bed. She lay curled under the coverlet for the rest of the day, dry-eyed but with a pressure on her chest that would not ease. Frau Klein brought her a cup of soup, but she could not drink it. Ava wondered what Unity Mitford had been thinking as she put the pistol to her temple and pulled the trigger. She wondered what Hitler felt. Guilty? Remorseful? Or did the Führer love the death drive so much that her action would please him, even arouse him? It was an unpleasant thought.

The following Sunday, Ava had arranged to meet Jutta at the Jewish Community office, to bring some old clothes and blankets she no longer needed. It was a clear, bright day and the sunshine seemed too bright for Ava's eyes.

The suitcases were heavy, and Ava was glad she could afford the bus fare now. Having some money in her purse did make life so much easier. She sat and stared out at the busy streets of Berlin, crowded with buses, cars, bicycles and the occasional horse-drawn cart. Heavy guns were being installed on the roofs of buildings along the Unter den Linden. Tanks rolled along the street, followed by jeeps jammed full of soldiers.

Jutta was waiting for her outside the New Synagogue, just across the road from her old home. The gilded Moorish domes gleamed brightly in the sunshine. The ornate windows had been repaired, but there was still a large scorch mark on the pavement where the Stormtroopers had lit their fire on the night of the broken glass. Jutta was pleased to see the heavy suitcases, and took one from Ava.

'The Jewish Community offices are just next door,' she told Ava.

Queues of people stood patiently outside, waiting for help with their emigration visas or for aid. A soup kitchen had been set up, handing out bowls of thin broth to hungry-looking young mothers with wailing children clutching their skirts. A group of men in tall hats and long black coats stood talking on the doorstep, waving their hands around with great animation. Their forelocks were long and set in tight ringlets.

As Ava walked down the corridor, she glanced in through the doors and saw young men with skull caps bending their heads over books, or rows of girls sitting, patiently running cloth through sewing machines. Another room was full of children playing, looked after by a thin, dark-eyed girl with a scarf tied over her hair.

'So this is where you work? What exactly do you do?' Ava asked, swapping the heavy suitcase to her other hand.

'Jews aren't allowed to live in Aryan apartment blocks anymore, so we try and find places for them to live. We also help Jews that need food, or clothes, or money, as much as we can, and help them fill in forms, or find lost papers. We also do what we can to help train people so they can find a job once they emigrate.'

From another classroom, Ava heard the chanting of Hebrew and, somewhere distant, the playing of a piano and the sound of singing. Jutta smiled at the sound. 'I go to Hebrew classes here too, and I've been teaching a kindergarten class so that the children's mothers can go out and work. I'd very much like to go to one of the agricultural schools in the country, but I cannot leave Mama and so I do what I can here.'

Jutta took Ava to a long room where women in neat white aprons and caps were sorting through great piles of clothes and shoes. 'I work here every week,' Jutta said. 'Lots of people who are emigrating can only take a small suitcase with them, so they donate their clothes to the Winter Aid program. We give them to people who are too poor to buy their own clothes, or who are emigrating themselves and need some smarter clothes for when they apply for jobs overseas.'

Ava recognised some of the girls in the row. There was Irmgard Zarden, a small, dark-eyed girl whose father had once been some bigwig in the Weimar Republic government. She used to come to the Hot Club sometimes, along with the blonde girl standing next to her, Stella Goldschlag, who liked to think she looked like Jean Harlow. She had her white cap pulled on at a rakish angle, and her lips were far too red to be natural. She recognised Ava at once and came over to say hello, helping her and Jutta unpack the suitcases.

'I remember you! Still singing hot jazz?'

'Not really,' Ava answered. 'I'm at the conservatory studying opera now.'

Stella made a face. 'What a bore! You poor thing. No hot boys at the conservatory.'

'I'm married now,' Ava told her.

Stella opened her baby-blue eyes wide. 'Married! You?'

'I have the certificate to prove it,' Ava retorted with a smile.

Irmgard smiled at her. 'Congratulations, Ava! That's wonderful. When did all this happen?'

'Not even two weeks ago.' Ava felt herself beginning to colour.

'Honeymooners!' Stella gave her a wink. 'How are you enjoying married life? Is he hot in bed?'

'Very,' Ava answered at once, and she laughed.

Just then, the door swung open and in walked one of the most beautiful and glamorous women Ava had ever seen. She was in her mid-twenties, slim but curvaceous, with wheaten hair cut in soft waves about her ears and luminous blue eyes. She was dressed simply but elegantly in a pale blue dress with a white belt. Her gloves and shoes were white, and her hat was a charming confection of pale blue silk flowers and white tulle. In one hand she lugged a heavy suitcase.

'Irmgard!' she called. 'I'm here, as promised.'

'Frau Gräfin!' Irmgard looked up with a delighted smile. 'Thank you so much. It's very kind of you.'

'Please, just call me Libertas,' the blonde woman replied with a smile. 'You know the title means nothing anymore. Besides, I'm married now and just an ordinary, everyday hausfrau.'

'What an unusual name,' Ava said. 'Is Libertas not the Roman goddess of freedom?'

'She is!' Libertas cried. 'Well done. Not many people know that. I was named for the heroine of one of my grandfather's books, though. He wrote poems and songs and various fairy-tale collections, including one called "The Tale of the Freedom" in which my namesake starred.'

'Libertas's grandfather was Philipp Fürst zu Eulenburg,' Irmgard said, clearly impressed by the princely title.

'For his sins,' Libertas rejoined, and heaved the suitcase up on the table. 'I went around and asked all Mother's friends for their cast-offs as well, so we have quite a haul for you.' She opened the suitcase and began taking out piles of clothes. The young women all clustered around, exclaiming over the beautiful garments that tumbled out. There was a heavy winter coat with a fur collar, some elegant day dresses, several well-cut tweed suits, and one pair of pale blue gauntlet gloves in the finest lambskin, the cuff decorated with a most striking design of fretwork.

Stella held one of the silk day dresses against her. Then she picked up the blue gloves and rubbed the soft leather, her face envious. 'I've never seen clothes like these before.'

'The Gräfin . . . I mean Libertas . . . her father is Otto Haas-Heye, the fashion designer and head of the fashion department at the Museum of Decorative Arts,' Irmgard explained. 'She always has the most beautiful clothes.'

'I'm very happy to give them away to someone who needs them more,' Libertas said. 'I do hope I brought the right sort of thing, Irmgard? I didn't think you'd need evening gowns or lingerie.'

'They're perfect,' Irmgard replied.

'Particularly the winter coat,' Jutta said. 'We'll need a lot of those.'

'Then I'll bring you some more.' Libertas smiled.

'Let me introduce you all.' Irmgard made a little sweeping gesture with her hand. 'This is Libertas Schulze-Boysen. I've known her for years. Her mother is the Gräfin zu Eulenberg-Hertefeld, who grew up at the court of the Kaiser.'

'Poor thing,' Libertas said. 'It marked her for life.'

Ava smiled, and Libertas cast her a laughing look.

Irmgard went on: 'This is Jutta Feidler, who looks after much of the work of the Winter Aid, and this is Stella Goldschlag, who badly wants to emigrate to America so she can become a Hollywood star.'

'Really?' Libertas looked at Stella in sudden interest. 'I work for MGM's Berlin office. Maybe I could help you get some kind of work there.'

Stella's face was sullen. 'I'm Jewish. They won't give me a job.'

'Oh. Of course. I'm sorry.' Libertas gave her an apologetic smile. 'I guess you'll have to go to America.'

'You think I haven't tried?' Stella turned away, beginning to unpack the rest of the suitcase with abrupt movements.

Libertas looked at Irmgard, who shrugged and gave a rueful smile, before turning to Ava. 'Libertas, this is Ava . . .' She hesitated and then said, 'I'm sorry, Ava, I don't know your new name.'

'Ava von Löwenstein,' she replied.

Libertas raised her finely arched eyebrows. 'No relation to Leo von Löwenstein, by any chance?'

'He's my husband.'

She exclaimed in surprise. 'The devil! Why wasn't I invited to the wedding?'

'It was very small,' Ava answered. 'Just Leo and me and two witnesses.'

'I can't believe it!' Libertas looked Ava over with interest. 'Did you marry in the synagogue, or just a civil service?'

'Oh no,' Ava said. 'Just a civil service. I don't go to church or the synagogue.'

Jutta explained quickly, 'Ava's not Jewish. She's brought us some old clothes and blankets too.'

'Good for you!' Libertas cried warmly. She took Ava's hand and pressed it between both of her own. 'I do wish more Berliners would do something to help. Everyone seems to want to stick their heads in the sand like ostriches.'

'Ava's promised to help in any way she can,' Jutta said with a meaningful look.

'I say, are you living at the von Löwensteins' house near the Tiergarten?' Libertas said. 'I live in the Westend, only ten minutes from there. Do you want to walk home together? We could stop for coffee and cake. I do so want to hear more about this wedding of yours. Leo said nothing about it to me when I saw him a few weeks ago at a reception at the Dutch embassy.'

Ava assented eagerly, and said her farewells to Jutta and the other girls. Then the two young women walked out on to the busy street, deep in conversation. 'I've known Leo since he was a boy,' Libertas said. 'I knew his brother, Alex, a little better, he was only one year younger than me. They used to come and spend the summers at my grandfather's schloss at Lienbenberg. They were always tremendous fun.'

'I never knew his brother. Leo and I only met a few months ago.'

'That was a quick romance! Was it love at first sight?'

'Something like that,' Ava admitted.

Libertas sighed. 'I fell in love with my husband the instant I saw him too. I love stories like that! Tell me all about it.'

Ava obeyed. Libertas was so full of warm interest and sympathy it was not long before Ava found herself confessing her hurt over the things Gertrud had said, and the knowledge Leo had had an affair with her so close to their wedding.

Libertas frowned. 'I wouldn't worry. Leo would not have married you if he didn't love you.'

Ava could not tell her that her husband had not spoken one word of love to her since they had been married.

The next day, Libertas and Ava went together to the movies, and a few days later, met for coffee and cake.

Ava felt she had known the elegant young woman for ever. Her friendship helped ease some of the loneliness Ava had suffered ever since Rupert had been arrested. Although she had made an effort to see Jutta several times since her marriage, Ava could not go to the movies with her, or walk in the park or play a game of tennis, or even be seen talking to her on the street. Besides, Ava's feelings about the Feidlers were so twisted with guilt and remorse, it was difficult to be entirely natural with them. There was no such restraint with Libertas, who loved music and art and films and books just as much as Ava did.

Soon the two young women were meeting nearly every afternoon, after Ava's singing lessons. One day they went to the movies together again, but were so upset by the newsreels that preceded the feature, they both caught up their coats and hats and fled to walk together in the Tiergarten.

'The English and the French have declared war. Why don't they do anything to stop Hitler!' Libertas exclaimed. 'At this rate, nothing will be left of Poland.'

'How is it possible they have got so far so fast?' Ava wondered. 'Do you think Warsaw will really fall so quickly?'

'By the looks of those newsreels, there's not much left to fall,' Libertas sighed. She looked pale and edgy. 'Oh, Ava, I wish we didn't have to live in such a world! What is it with men and guns?'

'Is your husband . . .' Ava hesitated.

Libertas looked away, her face tensing even more. 'He works for the Ministry of Aviation. At least he's not actually dropping bombs on people. I couldn't bear that.'

As dusk fell, Ava walked home through the park. The leaves were beginning to colour, golden and tawny as a cello suite by Bach. The Neuer See reflected the grey sky with the sheen of steel. She was glad of her new green coat.

As she came in through the gate into the garden, Zeus went mad at the sight of her, leaping up stiffly and whining. His whole body seemed to undulate with the force of his wagging tail. She patted him, saying, 'What is it, boy? You hungry?'

As she unlocked the back door, the Great Dane pushed past her and bounded through the house, his claws clattering on the stone floor. Ava put her keys down on the kitchen table and followed him.

The door to Leo's study stood half open. Ava pushed open the door and stepped through. It was the first time she had ever been inside his study, but she took no notice of the book-lined shelves and thick Persian rug. Leo sat at his desk, his head bowed down into his hands. Zeus sat beside him, pawing at him, trying to push his great head onto Leo's lap. Leo did not respond. Ava called his name and he lifted his head. Ava cried out in dismay. His face was chalk-grey, his eyes red with exhaustion.

'Leo, what is it?' Ava went to him swiftly.

He put his arms around her, burying his face against her stomach. Ava could feel his shoulders shaking. 'What's happened?' she asked.

'Warsaw . . . has fallen. They . . . they've slaughtered . . . so many people . . . women, children . . . they bombed the hospitals! Schools! The whole heart of the city has been bombed to rubble. And they shot people, just dragged them out into the street and shot them. In Bedzin, they set fire to the synagogue . . . and the whole Jewish congregation were locked inside. We could hear them screaming as they were burned to death. I saw them do it, Ava, I saw them do it.'

Leo's hands were trembling, but his jaw was locked so tight he could scarcely get the words out. Zeus whined and pawed him again.

'Who? Who did it?'

'The SS. They have special task forces whose only job is to kill people. Old people. Young people. Children. It didn't seem to matter.'

'Couldn't you stop them?' Ava's legs felt like jelly.

'We . . . we tried. We were told we'd be court-martialled. The Admiral even went to see Hitler. He could not believe the Führer could be a part of it. He was told to mind his own business. Ava, they've rounded up thousands and thousands of people and shipped them out, we don't know where.'

'How can you keep on working for them?' Ava cried.

'What choice do I have? We are at war. I cannot resign my commission without being court-martialled and shot.' He looked up at her, his face agonised. 'I'd have to desert. My grandfather would never forgive me. And what would happen to you? To my mother? Oh God, what am I to do?'

Leo pressed his face against her. Ava could feel tears dampening her dress. She could only hold him and stroke his head as if he was just a boy with a broken toy.

Totentanz

In early November, someone tried to murder Hitler.

It happened in Munich, at the traditional anniversary of the failed Beer Hall Putsch. Hitler usually ranted at the party faithful for hours and hours and hours. But that night, fog closed the Munich airport. Hitler and his thugs left early to catch the night train back to Berlin. Thirteen minutes later, the bomb went off.

The newsreels lingered on the piles of rubble, the collapsed ceiling and broken rafters, the injured in hospital with bandages wrapped about them. Sixty people had been wounded. Eight were dead. But not Hitler.

Then Ava heard on the radio that the bomber had been caught trying to sneak over the border into Switzerland. His name was Georg Elser. Some said he was in the pay of the British, others that he was a Russian spy. It seemed he had spent long careful months building his bomb and concealing it in a pillar of the beer hall. Months of preparation and he had missed the Führer by thirteen minutes.

Ava would never have believed that she could be sorry a bomb missed its target. *This war is turning me into a beast, just like them*, she thought.

'What do you think?' she asked Leo over breakfast the next morning, as he read the newspaper with frowning concentration. 'The butcher's wife insists it's a sign that the Führer is under some kind of divine protection.'

'Perhaps he is,' Leo said, only half-listening as he scrutinised the newsprint. Then he looked up and flashed a wry grin to her. 'Or satanic.' He rose, folded his newspaper, and bent to kiss her goodbye before pulling on his cap and striding from the room.

These were the first words that Leo had spoken to Ava about Hitler and the war since returning from Poland. It was as if he was ashamed of his breakdown before her. Ava had asked him once or twice for news, both for her own interest and so she could tell Jutta, but her husband was closemouthed. Instead, he seemed intent on a whirl of parties and dinners and diplomatic functions. Ava and Leo were out nearly every night, dining and dancing with numerous tall young men with square shoulders, stern faces, straight spines, sleek hair, and heels that clicked together in the haughtiest manner. They all had names like Axel Freiherr von dem Bussche-Streithorst and Ewald-Heinrich von Kleist-Schmenzin. Many of them served together in Infantry Regiment 9 which was, Leo had told her, nicknamed Graf Nine for the number of noblemen that served in it.

Ava barely had a chance to catch her breath, as she was whirled from the arms of one young officer to another. Laughing, joking, Leo's friends seemed to take nothing seriously. Yet Ava knew that their laughter was volatilised with dread. She and Leo and his friends were dancing with death, like the medieval woodcuts of skeletons leading popes and kings and peasants in a merry jig to the grave. *La danse macabre*, it was called in French. *Totentanz*, in German.

The night after the failed assassination, Leo and Ava and some of his friends went out to dinner at Roma's, an Italian restaurant that was very popular at that time, pasta being free of rationing restrictions. Ava asked what they thought of Hitler's close escape, but they only replied, with stiff faces, 'Thank the Lord the Führer was not injured,' and then turned the talk back to Ava.

'So you are singing at the Linden Opera?' Axel asked. 'It is a performance of *Mona Lisa*, yes?'

'Yes,' Ava agreed. 'And what a tale of madness and death it is!'

He smiled at her. He was an open-faced young man, much the same age as Ava, with thick dark blond hair that did not quite conform to the neatness required of the Wehrmacht.

'And what part do you sing, Frau Gräfin von Löwenstein?' Axel, like Leo and all his friends, was very polite and very formal.

'I'm the courtesan, Ginevra,' Ava flashed him a smile. 'My memorable refrain is "Sin is the salt of all delight."'

'I'm sure you must utterly enchant the audience,' he answered. 'We must all try and see the performance before we are posted back to the front.'

'You were in Poland, weren't you?' Ava asked. 'Is it true that the fleeing refugees were strafed by the Luftwaffe?'

All traces of humour fled from Axel's face. 'That is not something I can speak of,' he said. Ava noticed the looks of unease on the faces of the other young men at the table.

Leo stood up, saying politely but with absolute authority, 'Do please forgive us. I must get my wife home to bed.'

'Perfectly understandable,' Ewald-Heinrich said. 'If I had such a beautiful bride, I don't think I'd ever go out at all.'

The officers all stood, bowed, kissed her hand, and bid her goodnight. Once she and Leo were alone and speeding home through the night, he said to her, in a very calm and reasonable tone of voice, 'You must not go asking such questions, Ava. They cannot answer, and yet it goes against the grain for any of them to be rude to a woman.'

'But . . . I just want to know what's going on. You can't trust the newsreels, it's all propaganda.'

'You need to restrain your insatiable curiosity, Best Beloved,' he replied. His eyes were steady on the dark road, marked only by the occasional stripes of phosphorescence. 'It's not wise to ask so many questions in a time of war.'

'But the war seems to be over,' Ava said. 'Poland has fallen, and no-one has attacked us. Are the English and French just going to let Hitler get away with it?'

'No,' Leo answered her. 'I don't think so. They're both building tanks and fighter planes at a most extraordinary rate. But don't tell anyone else what I've said, Ava, for the love of Christ. And please, please, don't ask questions or let your feelings show so clearly in public. It is not safe.'

They made up, as always, in the dark and privacy of their bedroom, but Ava could not help feeling as if she was being shut out of Leo's real life. As he lay beside her, one arm flung over her bare waist, she wondered – not for the first time – what he really felt and thought and feared and dreamed. He was a mystery to her.

The next morning, Leo rose early as usual to go out for his ride in the park. He hired his mount from a riding stable near the Bendlerblock, where the Abwehr offices were located. Most mornings, he rode with the Admiral. That morning, Reinhard Heydrich joined them, as he often did. Ava watched them ride past from the window of her bedroom, which looked out across the Tiergarten. She could not understand how her husband could ride in the beauty of the dawn with a man like Heydrich, the head of the Gestapo. How could he smile, and listen politely, and even laugh? She put her hand down to fondle Zeus's ears, muttering, 'And they call you a beast,' then dressed herself and took the Great Dane out for his early morning walk.

It was only later – at the breakfast table – that she read the newspaper. It reported the SS guards at Buchenwald had rounded up twenty-one Jews and shot them in retaliation for the assassination attempt against Hitler. Ava stared at the newsprint, cold spreading through her body. *Not Rupert, please, not Rupert*, she thought. Then she was ashamed. All those twenty-one dead men were someone's son, someone's friend.

'I'll be late home tonight,' Leo said. 'Don't wait up for me.'

Ava must have murmured something, for he came and kissed her goodbye. She read the newspaper again. Then, for the first time, she did not go to her singing rehearsal. She went out and hailed a taxi, and used nearly all her housekeeping money for the week to get to the Feidlers' apartment as fast as possible.

There was no consolation in their damp and freezing set of rooms. Tante Thea sat hunched in her bed like an old woman, her coat on over her nightgown, her face all furrowed with bewilderment. Her knitting needles lay idle beside her. Jutta was white-faced, her eyes swollen with tears. She said, as soon as Ava rushed in, 'We don't know. There's no way to know.'

'If he's died they'll send us a death certificate,' Onkel Franz said. 'Won't they?'

Tante Thea began to weep quietly. 'If only we knew!'

It was awful to see Tante Thea so old and broken. Ava stayed as long as she could bear it, then almost ran out into the gloom of the day. The ground was frozen black, the swollen clouds promising snow. She felt the east wind cut at her face like razor blades. *Rupert, Rupert*, she thought but could not say.

'Stupid swine! Filthy pigs! Run! Run!'

Rupert stood in rigid formation, staring straight ahead, as a procession of bewildered-looking men were forced to run the gauntlet through a passage of laughing SS guards wielding whips, sticks, rubber hoses and heavy boots. Guard dogs snapped and snarled, lunging at the end of their leashes. One man stumbled and fell, and a dog tore at his arm. He screamed, and managed to roll away, blood spurting between his fingers.

'Quick! Run! Sub-human filth!'

The deportees were all still dressed in civilian clothes, though these were dirty and disordered. All had yellow stars sewn to their coats. Rupert felt a sick lurch of pity. The Jews were the bottom of the dung heap in the camp. The SS would make these poor panicking men realise that fast. One guard caught a man by his necktie and twisted it cruelly, choking him half to death. 'Jewish filth!' he screamed. Another guard seized an old man by his long beard and dragged him along by it.

Then two lines of block elders threw buckets of freezing water over the bruised and bloodied men. They gasped in shock. It was bitterly cold. Snow lay in muddy piles under the bunkers and coated the roofs in white. 'Strip! Quick, quick!'

Slowly, hesitantly, the men began to take off their damp coats. 'Faster! Faster!' The Jews tried to obey, but they were exhausted and in shock. One old man fell, and was kicked and thrashed mercilessly. 'Faster!'

When the men were naked, more water was thrown on them and the block elders began to roughly shave and disinfect them. Shivering with cold, dazed with shock, the newly arrived prisoners looked around. Long rows of wooden huts. High concrete walls. Coils of barbed wire. Machine-gunners in watchtowers. Endless rows of hollow-eyed prisoners in striped uniforms. And, by the wall, a heap of dead naked men, stiff as driftwood, stacked in a neat pile, head to feet like sardines in a can. They had been chosen, at random, from the Jewish barracks and shot. No-one knew why.

A guard turned to the ranks of silent prisoners. 'Sing the Jew song!' he ordered. The band at once struck up the tune. Rupert and his fellow Jews began to sing as ordered:

'For centuries we deceived the people.
No swindle was too large or too bad.'

'Dance, Jew!' the guards ordered the naked prisoners. 'Dance!'

Nobody obeyed at first. Then, as the blows and kicks rained down on their exhausted bodies, one by one they began to dance.

'We have lied, cheated and swindled.
Now the paradise has come to a sudden end.'

'Quick! Quick!' the SS guards bellowed. 'Dance!'

The wild movements of the naked men quickened. They capered and spun, barefoot in the snow. The Commandant and his red-haired wife watched, laughing, from the gatehouse. Anyone who danced too slowly was whipped along. More buckets of icy water were flung on them. 'Dance!'

'If there's a race that is still more base,
Then it is surely related to us.'

The sun set, and the band played on. The prisoners were forced to keep on dancing in the freezing night air. If they fell, they were forced to waltz on their knees. If they fainted, they were beaten in time to the music.

The music only ended when all of the new prisoners lay on the ground, unable to rise. The Commandant made an announcement. 'Welcome to Buchenwald. Anyone who wishes to hang themselves should place a piece of paper with his prisoner number in his mouth so that his identity can be quickly established.'

Released from the Appellplatz, Rupert stumbled towards his barracks. He could not get the sight of the capering naked men out of his mind. He wrote, in tiny letters spiralling round on the cardboard cut from the bottom of a paper cup: 'Dancing in snow, thin-legged scarecrows, to the beat of bitter blows, eyes and tongue food for crows.'

A Grim Christmas

It was the grimmest winter Berliners had seen in more than a hundred years. The cold was relentless. The River Spree was frozen over, and the coal barges were unable to make their way to the capital. Intrepid children ice-skated on the ponds and lakes, or built slopes to slide down on their toboggans. Every street corner had a snowman with pebbles for eyes and sticks for hands. Not one snowman wore a hat or scarf; no-one had any warm clothes to spare. Giant placards were posted on every notice-board, reading: 'Nobody shall hunger or freeze.' Ava hoped they were right, huddling with Zeus before the porcelain stove in the kitchen, dressed in her coat and beret and gloves indoors.

One night she woke from a deep sleep to find the bed beside her empty. She sat up, and heard a murmur of voices from below. She slipped out of the warmth of her eiderdown, and pulled on her robe and slippers. She crept slowly down the stairs. As she reached the landing, she saw a thin ray of light shining out, and realised that there was a gap in the joints of the study's ceiling. It was an old house, with many cracks and chinks through which the sharp wind stabbed in winter. Ava sat on the step, bent low, and put her eye to the gap.

She was looking down into Leo's study. It was lit only by a low fire on the hearth. Leo stood on the rug, dressed in his uniform. The jacket was unbuttoned and his head was bare. Another man in uniform sat in one of the chairs by the fire. Ava could see his boots stretched out to the warmth. Then, as the man leant forward to speak, she saw a high forehead, grey hair neatly combed back, a beaky nose. He had a great many medals hanging on his breast and collar, and his ribbon bar was long and bright with many different colours. He must be a General or something important, Ava thought.

'I need your help,' the General said. 'I fear I am being watched . . .'

Leo said something. His voice was so low Ava could not hear what.

The General said something about the Admiral, and loyalty, and then Ava heard the word 'Venlo'. She had heard that word before and racked her brains trying to think where. Then she remembered. After the Munich bomb attack, two British spies had been snatched from a town named Venlo in the Netherlands and brought to Germany. The radio reports sounded like something out of one of Leo's spy novels. One man had been shot dead and his body dragged across the border into Germany. The British agents had been accused of being part of the plot to kill Hitler. Ava shuddered to think what might have happened to them in the Gestapo cellars.

'Hitler will use it as an excuse,' the General said, then added something else Ava could not make out.

She wished she could hear better. On an impulse, she tiptoed back up the stairs and grabbed the glass of water from her bedside table. She drank it straight down. The water was so cold, it made her teeth ache. Then she crept back down the stairs, avoiding the one that creaked. She lifted the glass and set it against the wall, and then put her ear to it.

The officer was speaking. 'The Admiral tells me your mother is Dutch . . . I need you to speak to the Dutch ambassador. I have warned them again and again that Hitler intends to invade . . . but of course they mistrust me. They think I am feeding them false information . . .'

'Are you sure?' Leo asked. 'The Netherlands are neutral.'

'Of course I'm sure,' the older man snapped back. 'If it was not for this blasted snow, the Führer would have launched his campaign already and they would have seen my information is good!'

Then he lowered his voice and all Ava heard was '. . . if the Gestapo discover that it was an Abwehr agent who had been in contact with the British . . .'

Ava could not help a little jerk of surprise. Her glass tinged against the wall. At once the voices in the study stopped. She retreated back upstairs. It seemed as if her steps, her shallow breaths, the very beat of her heart, must be heard.

Ava heard the handle of the study door being turned, then the rap of boot heels walking down the corridor. A low murmur of voices, then the sound of the kitchen door being eased open. Ava felt the blast of cold air and heard the faint crunch of footsteps walking away over the snow. She crept back into the warmth of her bed. Her feet were freezing and she wrapped them up in the flannel of her nightgown. Leo must not come to bed and find her with cold feet.

He came quietly upstairs a few minutes later. Ava lay still, pretending to be asleep. He undressed and slid into bed beside her. But it was a long time before his breathing deepened. Husband and wife lay beside each other in silence for hours.

Ava wondered a lot about what she had overheard, and scoured the newspapers for any other mention of the Netherlands. There was nothing. She even tentatively asked Leo whether he thought the Dutch were in any danger.

'The Netherlands is a neutral power,' he answered. 'It would be against the Geneva Convention to invade them.'

And that, she thought, was no answer at all.

Ava had never known such a tense and anxious time. It was strange. The whole city was prepared for war, but nothing happened. There were no more air-raid sirens, and no more battles. Yet the grocery stores were all empty, with no extra rations for Christmas, and it was hard to find anything to give for gifts. Ava bought Father a new pipe but could not find any tobacco, and she chose a new book of fairy tales for Angelika. That was easy to find, for Hitler had decreed every household should have a copy of the Grimm brothers' tales. For her sisters, all Ava could think of were new hats, since they were the only article of clothes not being rationed. She did not know what to get Leo. She felt, at times, as if she hardly knew him. She saw many things she would have liked to have given Rupert. A new jazz record, bought on the black market. An umbrella with a hooked handle. A monocle.

But Ava did not know what to buy her husband.

In the end, she selected an expensive hardback edition of Rilke's poems, using nearly all of her month's allowance to pay for it.

Leo had a beautifully wrapped box for Ava. She opened it eagerly on Christmas Eve, sitting with her husband by the fire, the air sweet-scented from the little fir tree that sparkled with baubles and candles near the window.

Inside was a guidebook for SS wives, written by the leader of the Women's Nazi League. It had instructions on how to cook and clean, as well as rules on how to behave as a perfect Nazi wife. Ava stared at it blankly, then looked at Leo.

His grin slowly faded. 'It's a joke, Ava. I thought you'd find it funny.'

'Jokes are always an expression of the joker's repressed desires,' she told him.

All the humour was gone from his face. 'Ava, sometimes a joke is just a joke.'

She did not answer. Tears were thick in her throat. Leo came and knelt before her. 'I'm so sorry. I didn't mean to hurt you. I honestly thought you'd find it funny.'

'I'm sorry I'm not the perfect Nazi wife,' Ava managed to say. 'You should have married Gertrud when you had the chance.'

'I never wanted to marry Gertrud! You know that.'

Ava lifted the SS Wives Guidebook in mute display.

Leo sighed. 'Don't worry about Gertrud. She's found herself bigger fish to fry. Some camp commander in Bavaria. She's gone to work there with him.'

Ava did not answer. She could not help wondering how he knew where Gertrud was, and what she was doing.

'You're the perfect wife for me.' Leo drew Ava into his arms. 'I don't want anyone else, I promise you.'

Ava wiped her eyes and tried to smile. 'I'm sorry. I think you may have hit a raw nerve.' She picked up the SS Wives Guidebook. 'I mean . . . really?'

'I'll take you shopping and buy you something you really want,' he promised her. 'What would you like? A new hat? A necklace?'

'A camera,' Ava told him.

Leo was surprised, but swore he'd buy her the very best camera he could find as soon as the shops opened again. Ava smiled and tossed the guidebook into the wood basket. 'At least now I have something to burn when the nights grow too cold.'

'A-ha! A joke. Is that an expression of your repressed desires?' he asked, and swooped in for a kiss. 'Surely it's my job to keep you warm in winter?'

Ava could not help saying, 'Whenever you happen to be home.'

He sat back and regarded her with frowning eyes. 'It's the war, Ava,' he said at last with difficulty.

'I know. I'm sorry.'

Leo sat in silence for a while, playing with her fingers, then said in a burst, 'Ava, it's Christmas Eve. I know you don't believe but . . . I'd like to go to church. To the midnight service. It's just down the road.' There was a pause, then he said, 'We always went as boys.'

'All right,' Ava said after a moment.

'Wrap up,' he said. 'It'll be cold, and the churches have been forbidden to light coal braziers this year.'

Ava pulled on her heaviest coat and her red beret. Together they walked out into the cold winter night. The snow was deep on the ground, and every tree in the street was mantled with white. She gazed upwards in amazement. She had never seen so many stars. They glittered in the night sky, so bright the whole sky seemed to glow.

'Aren't they beautiful!' she cried.

'It's because of the blackout,' Leo answered, lifting her over the snow-heaped gutter. 'It lets the stars shine through.'

'It almost makes the blackout worthwhile,' Ava said. 'Almost.'

Leo pressed her close to his side, and she was glad of his warmth and his strength. She felt her discomfort ease. They were a family now, she reminded herself. They had to honour each other's traditions, and make new ones.

The church was a black shape at the end of the lane, its pointed spire cutting out the stars. As Ava and Leo walked up the street, the church bells began to ring out. Leo opened the heavy arched door and Ava tiptoed in. The nave was lit only by candles. Their flames shivered in the blast of cold air, sending spectral shadows dancing over the walls. People sat or knelt quietly. An old man in a long white surcoat was lighting two branches of candles on either side of a simple wooden cross.

'The Grimm brothers used to worship in this church,' Leo whispered as they gathered up hymn books.

Ava turned to him in delight. 'Really? Here?'

'Yes. They used to live just down the road. It is said they used to walk in the Tiergarten whenever they could, even in the rain or the snow.'

A thrill ran through her at his words. Ava could not believe she was in the same church where Jacob and Wilhelm Grimm once sat. Perhaps she was sitting on the very spot! Ava ran her hand reverently over the back of the old wooden seat, wondering if the fingers which had written down those wonderful old stories had ever rested here, where her fingers now touched. The thought gave her goose bumps.

An organ began to play mournfully. A procession of doddery old men in church vestments over thick sweaters walked up the aisle, followed by a stout and serious-faced young man wearing round wire-framed spectacles. Leo stiffened and leant forward.

'Who's that?' Ava whispered.

'That's Dietrich Bonhoeffer,' he whispered back. 'You must have heard of him. He fled to America, but I heard a rumour that he had come back.'

Ava had heard of him. Dietrich Bonhoeffer was the son of Karl Bonhoeffer, a Berlin psychiatrist. When Hitler had first been installed as Chancellor, Dietrich had famously preached against the Nazis on the radio. He had been cut off the air in the middle of a sentence. Later, in protest against the Church's collusion with the Nazis, he and another pastor named Martin Niemöller had set up a new church that steadfastly preached against Hitler and all his doings. Niemöller had since been sent to a concentration camp, and so too would Bonhoeffer if he was caught in Berlin. His twin sister had married a Jew, and Leo had once told Ava how Canaris had helped them escape Germany.

A little stir of surprise and nervous excitement ran over the small group of worshippers in the church. Leo said in an undertone, 'Look, the whole Bonhoeffer clan is here. That is his father with the white hair and moustache, and those are his brothers Karl and Klaus. Those women must be his sisters. One of them is married to Hans von Dohnányi, who works at the Abwehr with me. I know the families are very close; one of Dietrich's brothers married a von Dohnányi girl too.'

He could say no more, for Dietrich Bonhoeffer had come to stand in the pulpit. The pastor began by saying that he had only just managed to return to Germany in time, catching the last steamer from New York before war was declared. 'I felt I had to suffer through this time of trials with my fellow Germans,' he told the congregation.

He had a beautiful, deep, musical voice that reached every corner of the church with seemingly little effort. It was the dark toffee colour of a double bass, and spun a spell on all who listened. His heavy-jawed face was set with determination, his eyes behind his spectacles alight with passion.

'All of us Germans face a terrible dilemma in this time of war,' he said. 'We either hope for the victory of our nation, in the full knowledge that this may mean the destruction of civilisation as we know it, or we hope for the defeat of our beloved country in order that Christian civilisation may survive. I know what choice I must make. Do you?'

He then spoke for some time on a verse from Revelations, which read: *Behold, I stand at the door and knock.* 'Christ is knocking on your door, in the form of a beggar, in the form of a ruined human being in torn clothing, in the form of little children being quietly murdered by those who should protect them, in the form of those thousands of poor souls suffering unspeakably in the prisons and labour camps of this country. He confronts you in every person that you meet. Christ is walking on the earth right now, calling to you. Will you keep the door locked or open it to him?'

Everyone in the church was utterly still and silent. No-one coughed, or fidgeted, or rustled the pages of their hymn books. All were riveted by the words of that stout and plain young man. Dietrich ended by saying, 'Silence in the face of evil is itself evil: God will not hold us guiltless. Not to speak is to speak. Not to act is to act.'

Leo was very quiet after the sermon, his brows compressed. Ava too was silent, her spirit in tumult. Pastor Bonhoeffer was right, she thought. *Somehow I must speak out, somehow I must act . . .*

Ava crept through the chilly darkness, her heart beating like a timpani.

Ahead of her, Jutta was just a fleeting shadow among the shadows. Her torch flashed up onto a propaganda poster stuck to a wall. It showed a blond, Aryan-looking soldier chatting to a friend over glasses of beer. Nearby, an evil-looking man leant close, eavesdropping. The caption read: 'Take care with conversations, for WHO is listening?'

Ava drew out her fountain pen, crossed out the WHO and scrawled quickly above: THE GESTAPO.

As soon as Ava had written the last letter, Jutta turned off her flashlight. The two young women ran away as silently as they could through the pitch darkness of the blacked-out city. Ava did not stop till they were several streets away. Then she drew Jutta into the shelter of a doorway. Both tried to catch their breaths. Ava could not hear any signs of pursuit, and gradually her heartbeat slowed.

'I can't come tomorrow,' she whispered. 'Leo will be home. I'll leave you a message to let you know when I'm free again.'

She and Jutta had set up a system of coded messages for each other, using the monuments in the Tiergarten, for both feared to send letters or postcards, or use the telephone, which everyone knew was tapped by the Gestapo. So three times a week, Ava went to a different monument in the Tiergarten, hiding or finding notes written in code in the nooks and crannies of marble robes and beards and fists.

'I'll look out for some more posters tomorrow,' she whispered to Jutta. 'I think we should stay away from here for a while. We've been lucky.'

'All right,' Jutta whispered back. 'Let's leave one last message before we go.'

She clicked on her torch and flashed it onto the wall beside her. Ava pulled out some chalk and wrote, in huge, thick letters: 'DOWN WITH HITLER!'

Part III

Torn to Pieces
June 1940 – December 1942

Her family was overjoyed when she came home for her sister's wedding. All had believed she had been torn to pieces by the lion.

'The Singing, Springing Lark', the Brothers Grimm

Dominoes

Swastika banners snapped in the hot wind. Church bells clanged. People cheered hoarsely, waving streamers from balconies. Megaphones on every street corner blared martial music.

Ava stood, watching. She dared do nothing else. The block warden, Herr Nadel, was keeping a close eye on her. He was angry because she had not hung a swastika flag out of her windows like she was supposed to. Ava had explained Leo was away in Paris, and so Herr Nadel had come to do it himself. Now he stood nearby, waving a huge flag, his thick glasses fogging up with emotion as the Führer's parade passed through the Brandenburg Gate.

A sudden roar. A long black Mercedes convertible drove slowly down the Unter den Linden. Hitler stood in the back, arm held up stiffly. His face was full of satisfaction. Girls in brown uniforms screamed and threw flowers. 'Sieg Heil! Sieg Heil!'

Ava took photos of the shouting crowd, the children waving tiny swastika pennons, the young women weeping and half-fainting. It was as if this awful, astonishing day would only become real to Ava if she pinned it down with her swift-winged shutter.

Paris had fallen. It seemed impossible. In just six weeks, one of the mightiest countries in the world had fallen to its knees. *Blitzkrieg*, they called it. Lightning war.

The whole world seemed to be going down like dominoes, and Germany had gone mad with joy.

Not Ava.

Her father had taught her to fear war.

She had asked him once what it was like. He had answered, 'War shatters the soul beyond all hope of repair.'

'But you fought in the war,' Ava had said.

'Yes,' he had answered.

Ava often thought of that conversation with her father.

'Ava!' a voice called.

She looked around. Libertas was waving from the top of the Lions' Statue. She sat sideways on the great bronze lion, dressed in a navy blue polka-dot dress with a red scarf knotted around her throat. Ava wondered uneasily if she realised she was wearing French colours, then realised that she did so on purpose. Libertas always dressed with great care. Ava waved back. With a quick backwards glance at Herr Nadel to make sure he was not watching, she fought her way through the crowd to her friend's side.

'Come on up!' Libertas waved a champagne bottle so wildly, liquid splashed on the heads of those below. Ava smiled, and climbed to join her.

'Drink!' Libertas commanded.

Ava took the bottle and swallowed a mouthful. It fizzed down her throat like joy. 'What was that?' she cried.

'The very best French champagne,' Libertas shouted back. Her cheeks were flushed, her eyes glittered like silver bullets. 'Have some more.'

Ava obeyed.

'What are you doing here?' Libertas asked, taking back the bottle.

Ava lifted up the camera Leo had given her for Christmas. 'Bearing witness,' she said in a low voice.

Libertas nodded. 'I know what you mean. I couldn't bear to stay in. I had to come and see. Isn't it just so frightful?'

Ava looked about at once, to make sure no-one was listening. A tall man in a Luftwaffe uniform was standing right below them. Ava caught her breath. He turned and looked up with cold, frowning eyes. 'Quiet, Libs,' he hissed. 'Not here.'

Libertas leant down and wound her arm about his neck, kissing him on the mouth. 'Sorry, Harro,' she said contritely. 'It's just I'm so, so sad.'

'I know, darling,' he whispered back. 'But you must be careful. Won't you please take off the scarf? It'll be like a red flag to any Hitler Youth that marches by.'

'All right, darling, if you insist.' She took off the red scarf and tied it in a neat bow about the bronze lion's tail.

Libertas sloshed down another mouthful, then passed the bottle to Ava. 'I was born in Paris. I cannot believe it's fallen. Did you see the awful photos of Hitler posing under the Eiffel Tower, and the Wehrmacht marching through the Arc de Triomphe?' She spoke the last few words with a flawless French accent. 'It made me want to vomit!'

'We'd better get her home,' an older woman said. She was fair and earnest, and sensibly dressed in a skirt and jacket and lace-up leather shoes. 'This is not the time or place to be talking like that!'

'Come on, Libs, let's get you home,' the man in the Luftwaffe uniform said.

'Only if Ava comes too!' Libertas cried. 'I want her to meet you all. Ava, this is my beautiful, beautiful husband, Harro.' She leant over to him and kissed him again, and he held her steady so she did not slide right off the lion's back. 'Harro, do you know Leo von Löwenstein? This is his wife.'

Harro Schulze-Boysen greeted Ava with a polite bow and a rather unsteady click of his heels. He was a handsome man, around thirty years old, with fair hair combed straight back from his high forehead. He was clearly besotted with Libertas, keeping his hand on her thigh even as she twisted around to point at her other friends.

The serious-faced woman in the lace-up shoes was introduced as Mildred Harnack. She spoke with an American accent. Her husband was Arvid Harnack, and he looked like a bespectacled schoolmaster.

He worked at the Reich Economics Ministry, 'doing something awfully serious', Libertas said.

Another couple were introduced as Adam and Greta Kuckhoff. 'Adam is ever so clever,' she explained. 'He's written a book that absolutely eviscerates war, but the stupid Nazis are too dumb to see it and have let it be published.'

'For heaven's sake, Libertas!' Arvid Harnack remonstrated. 'Keep your voice down.'

'What's the point?' she cried. 'Paris has fallen! My beautiful Paris.'

To Ava's dismay, Libertas's face contorted with tears, like a child's. She took another defiant gulp of champagne. Mildred passed her up a handkerchief and said anxiously, 'I know how much you loved Paris, Libs, but indeed you must be careful. A single overheard word!'

'Oh, God damn it!' Libertas answered. 'I can't stand it anymore. Let's get out of here. There's more champagne at home. Let's go drink it.'

They all caught the bus back to the Schulze-Boysens' spacious apartment in Charlottenburg. The living room was a fascinating mixture of fine French antiques, silver Moroccan lamps, little inlaid tables, gold silk cushions and modern paintings. A red leather chaise-longue with rolled arms took up most of the space. The kitchen looked more like a cocktail bar, with rows of bottles in every shape and colour, a bowl of lemons, and a cocktail shaker. Ava could see no sign of any food, apart from cans of pâté and boxes of crackers.

'I'm a shocking cook,' Libertas confessed, as she opened the refrigerator to get another bottle of champagne. 'Harro and I eat out most nights. It's been an absolute horror since rationing came in.'

The kitchen bar was mobbed by people mixing cocktails, slicing lemon and grabbing ashtrays. Libertas lifted out two dewy bottles with necks wrapped in gold foil. 'Does anyone have a sabre?' she shouted. 'Let's open them with style.'

Harro took one of the bottles from her and popped the cork into the crowd. Everyone roared their approval, and he popped the other one. 'Not a good idea to swing a sabre around in here, darling,' he said. 'We'll cut someone's head off by mistake.'

'Shame we can't cut off Hitler's head,' she said.

'He'd be like one of those Greek monsters, darling. Cut off his head and he'd grow two more,' Harro said, sloshing absinthe and champagne into a glass together.

Libertas poured foaming champagne into a row of glasses, then grabbed one for herself and Ava. 'Come and meet the Schumachers. You'll adore them. Kurt's a sculptor. Even Göring has some of his work, and you know how he loves to collect masterpieces. And Elisabeth is a photographer like you.' She introduced Ava to a bohemian-looking couple. He was dressed in a shabby tweed jacket and a soft flowing tie, and his hair had not seen scissors or soap for quite a long time. Elisabeth was dressed in the most beautiful orange tea gown, with geometric patterns at the hem and collar, and had thick lustrous honey-brown hair coiled low on her neck and a long Jewish nose.

'Ava's a singer, she's got the most gorgeous voice,' Libertas said, then plunged off into the crowd in search of more absinthe. Kurt Schumacher nodded and smiled, and wandered away to examine one of the paintings on the wall.

'So what do you sing?' Elisabeth asked. 'Opera?'

'Sometimes,' Ava answered. 'My voice is too deep for most operas here. I sometimes get roles as a mezzo-soprano, but only if they can't find someone to fill the part. I'm still a student really. I'm at the conservatory.'

'You do have a beautiful deep speaking voice,' Elisabeth said. 'And a most interesting face. The combination of all that dark hair and those green eyes is very striking.'

Ava pushed back her hair self-consciously. In the heat of the day, a great many curls had fallen from their pins and twisted around her face.

Elisabeth lifted her hands and made a square frame with her fingers. 'I'd quite like to photograph you one day. With a black shawl and a rose. And maybe a guitar. Do you play?'

Ava nodded. 'I can. I mostly play piano, though.'

'Not nearly as visually interesting.'

'Nor as easy to drag around. I had a friend who used to play guitar sometimes. It had the most beautiful rich, blue tone.'

She bit her lip, not wanting to think about Rupert. It hurt too much.

Libertas came to sit on the arm of Ava's chair, pouring her more champagne. 'Do you want to see a photo of me in Paris? Wasn't I adorable? Look at that hat! I was a style icon even then.'

'Libertas's father was a fashion designer,' Elisabeth explained, as Ava bent over the photograph of a bright-eyed little girl in a huge hat decorated with a white spray of feathers, standing in the shadow of the Eiffel Tower.

'My father used to teach at the Museum of Decorative Arts on Prinz-Albrecht-Strasse. When I was little, I played there all the time. Now it's the Gestapo offices. Isn't it awful? Look, here's one of me in Zurich. I went to finishing school there. I tell Harro that's why I'm so useless. Can't cook, can't sew, can't change a car tyre. I do, however, dance beautifully. Oh, and this is me in London. I bobbed my hair there, and my mother was scandalised.'

'I'd love to have travelled as much as you,' Ava said. 'I've hardly been out of Berlin.'

'Oh well, once this wretched war is over, I'm sure you'll have your chance to see the world,' Libertas said. 'If we're not all taken out by the bloody Gestapo first.'

'Libs!' Mildred Harnack cried, turning and shaking an admonishing finger. She was a sober figure in her dark skirt and jersey and sensible shoes, and seemed much older and plainer than Libertas and her friends. Libertas seemed to love her, though. She flung her arms around the slight American woman, and cried, 'Why? I'm in my own home now. No listening ears here.'

'How do you know?' Arvid Harnack asked seriously. 'Libertas, you must be more careful.'

Libertas jumped to her feet. 'I don't want to be careful! I want to live life as fully as I can! I want to love and laugh and dance and say what I think. Why do we have to live in these hateful times?'

'We cannot choose the time we are born in.' Elisabeth looked desolate.

'But we can try and change the times, can't we?' Libertas cried.

'What's the use?' Greta sighed. 'What's the use of anything? Nothing will stop the Nazis now. They're taking over the whole world.'

'Enough moping!' Libertas ordered. 'Let's play some music. Ava, do you dance? I bet you do! Come on. Let's mourn the fall of France properly – with song and dance and drink!'

Putting a swing record on the gramophone, Libertas kicked off her shoes and began to dance. She was utterly unself-conscious, her slim figure undulating sensuously, her blonde hair flowing like sunlit water. Ava had never seen a woman so aware of her own beauty and sexuality. Harro leapt up to take her in his arms, and the Schumachers joined them on the floor. Ava stood, tapping her foot.

'Would you care to dance?' a dark-haired young man asked.

Ava took his hand with a smile, and did a deft spin.

Libertas cheered. 'See! I told you,' she called to Mildred. 'No swing baby could be a Gestapo spy.'

Ava saw the look that flashed between Arvid and Mildred, but nobody said anything. Ava smiled at Libertas, and threw herself into the music. She had not danced swing since Rupert had been arrested, and it made her feel both happy and sad at once. She gulped down a full glass of champagne, to try and tilt herself towards the joyous end of the spectrum of her emotions.

Libertas put on a slower song by Zarah Leander which Ava knew and loved. Harro was smoking a cigarette. He passed it to Libertas who took a deep drag, then blew three perfect smoke rings over his head. At once Ava wanted one too. She had not smoked since Bayreuth. Her teachers were most disapproving of the effects on her voice.

'Would you like one?' The young man offered his battered silver cigarette case. Ava took one a little guiltily. He lit it for her, and then one for himself. 'I'm Helmut Roloff. You're an old friend of Libertas's?'

'I've known her about nine months, I suppose. She's amazing, isn't she? So beautiful.'

'She will need to learn to be more careful what she says,' he answered soberly.

'It's hard,' Ava said. 'I think I've learnt to guard my tongue, then one day my temper gets the better of me, and I say something I regret.'

'That's only human.'

'Perhaps, but the Gestapo are not known for their forgiveness,' Ava answered dryly.

'You surprise me. I thought they were models of mercy and compassion.'

Ava laughed.

As the afternoon faded into evening and empty bottles piled up, the talk began to flow even more freely. Ava listened to a tense discussion of how the Nazis had established some kind of ghetto in Poland, where hundreds of thousands of Jews had been crammed into only a few blocks, with no running water and no sewage system.

'How can they possibly survive?' Libertas asked.

'Surely they cannot mean to leave them like that?' Mildred asked. 'It must be temporary.'

'It's just like the Roman Empire,' Harro said. 'The Nazis have conquered so much so fast, they don't know how to control it all. Their empire's got too big, and so it shall certainly fall soon.'

'Not that we want that,' Arvid said, with a warning glance to Harro.

'No. Of course not,' Harro answered stiffly.

Quite some time later, Ava went to the kitchen to refill her glass, and heard Kurt Schumacher say angrily, to Arvid, 'But we aren't *doing* anything! Surely it's time to take action? Else that madman will take over the whole world.'

'We must be careful,' Arvid said in response. 'I am doing my best to build bridges with both America and Russia. But they suspect my motives. After all, I work for the Economics Ministry.' His voice was dry.

'I want action,' Kurt said with a restless movement. 'We've helped people escape before. Can't we do so again?'

Arvid saw Ava nearby and said sharply, 'Enough! We'll talk more later.'

Ava felt a fizz of excitement in her stomach. Could these friends of Libertas's be involved in some kind of resistance against the Third Reich? The idea thrilled her. She hoped that they would trust her and let her help.

For months, she and Jutta had crept out into the city in the midnight hours, scrawling their anti-Nazi graffiti on walls, and defacing Nazi propaganda posters in subways and bus-stops. It was no longer enough.

Ava wanted to do something bigger. Something that would really make a difference.

Rudi was dead.

He had been shot in the quarry. The guards said he had been trying to escape. Rupert knew he had just given up all hope. What hope was there, when Hitler ruled and the whole world was a concentration camp?

So many people died at Buchenwald, they had built a giant brick chimney. Its hungry orange maw was fed all day and all night. Black smoke streamed out into the sky. Tiny snowflakes of ashes could be caught on the end of your finger. Each mouthful of air was a mouthful of smoke. When they burned Rudi, Rupert breathed in deep. He took the smoke and ashes into his own body. He felt the burn of his friend deep in his lungs. For a long time, he could not write. The birds stopped singing. The sky was always a furnace.

But one day he saw a screwed-up shopping list thrown in the kitchen bin. He folded it up small and hid it in his shoe. All day, as he dragged his bony carcass about the camp, he composed lines in his head.

'Grey smoke in grey skies . . . all blown away . . . grey ash in grey grates . . . all blown out . . . my life a fire shut up in stone . . . just a glimmer.'

Subversive Activities

The air-raid sirens screamed into the night.

Ava woke with a jerk. 'Not again!' Bleary-eyed, she shook Leo awake. 'Wake up. We have to go to the cellar.'

He groaned and rolled over. 'What?'

'Bombers heading our way. Come on, get up.'

Zeus was howling downstairs. He hated the discordant sound of the siren. Everyone did. It came from all directions, high, low, far, close. It cut through Ava's nerves like a rusty saw.

Barefoot, dressed only in her nightgown, Ava ran about in the darkness, folding back the shutters and opening the windows wide. 'Leo, you need to turn the mains off.'

Leo pulled on his trousers and a shirt, and went downstairs. In the last month, he had been to Spain and Finland with the Admiral, and so had not yet suffered through an air raid. It was a comfort having him home. Ava pulled on some clothes and ran downstairs, grabbing her coat and suitcase from where they stood ready in the hall. Leo came in from the side alley, his torch casting a pencil-thin ray of light before him. Zeus came in with him, tail slunk between his legs.

'Leave the door open,' Ava commanded. 'Leo, you should unlock your study too. They say all doors and windows must be left open.'

He frowned. 'I have sensitive documents in there. I cannot leave them unattended.'

'You're meant to take important documents with you,' Ava said. She lifted the suitcase in her hand. 'See? I've got all my papers and ration cards in here, plus anything else I don't want bombed.' Her book of fairy tales. The von Löwenstein pearls.

Leo looked troubled. 'I can't unlock my study. The Admiral trusts me to keep my papers secure. I've heard how thieves sneak about during the air raids and rob people's houses. It's too big a risk.'

'Oh well, as long as you are prepared to explain to our dear block warden when he comes to check. Herr Nadel does like the rules to be kept.'

'I'll take the keys with me.' Leo unlocked the little drawer in the hall cabinet where he kept his keys securely locked away. Ava could hear the drone of planes approaching. Closer and closer they came. 'Leo! Hurry!'

Then the flak guns began to stutter. White flashes of light rimmed the blackout cards. *Tat-tat-tat-tat-tat-tat! Tat-tat-tat-tat-tat-tat!*

'Leo!' Ava caught his arm. 'Come on!'

He ran down to the cellar with her, his keys in his hand. Ava lit some candles, then they sat together on the camp bed, huddling under the blankets. Zeus sat as close as he could get, his head pressed against Leo.

The airplanes sounded as if they were right above. Then Ava heard a high-pitched, whistling sound. She closed her eyes and pressed herself against Leo. A massive thump. *Boom!* The whole house shook. Windows rattled. Dust and debris rained down upon their heads.

'That was close,' Leo said.

The whistling sound came again, even closer. Ava braced herself. Another great thump and boom. Cans on the shelves rattled. Some fell.

'Even closer,' Ava said. She and Leo sat in tense silence, listening. The hum of the airplanes slowly faded away.

'They've gone. Can we go back to bed?'

'They haven't sounded the all-clear yet,' Ava told him. 'We need to stay in the cellar till they do.'

He groaned. 'I'm so tired. Why do they have to come in the middle of the night?'

Ava did not bother answering him. He shifted his weight till he was lying back on the pillows, her head resting on the hollow of his shoulder. 'I'm sorry I wasn't here for you,' he whispered. 'Were you frightened, here all by yourself?'

'Yes,' Ava told him truthfully. 'I hate it when you're away.'

He drew her closer, kissing her forehead. 'That's good.'

They lay together in silence, and gradually his breathing slowed and deepened. Soon Leo was fast asleep.

Ava could not rest. The night was still filled with the rumble of enemy airplanes, the whine of falling shrapnel, and the distant *rat-tat-tat* of the flak guns. But it was not that which kept her awake. It was the keys which Leo had tucked into his trouser pockets. He kept them locked away at all times. This might be her only chance to take them and look inside his study.

Ava badly wanted to strike some blow against the Third Reich, but months had gone past and no opportunity had presented itself. Harro and Arvid were polite enough to her, but she knew they mistrusted her because she was married to a man employed by the Abwehr. Libertas believed in her, but she adored her husband and would not disobey him. Ava had to find some way to prove her usefulness to Harro.

Ava slowly slid out from under the warmth of Leo's arm, till she stood in the dimness cast by the candles on the floor and the table. Leo slept peacefully, his face eased of its tension. For a moment, she baulked. Ava did not want to go sneaking into his study, searching through his secret papers. She did not want to steal his keys. But resolutely she put aside her qualms and slid her hand into his trouser pocket. Folding her fingers about the keys, she slowly eased them free. Leo stirred and shifted his weight. Ava froze till he was still again. Then she picked up one of the candles and climbed the steps out of the cellar. Zeus looked up at her and thumped his tail, but did not leave his master's side.

Her candle cast a wavering light through the kitchen and down the hall. Ava unlocked the study door. The click seemed very loud to her, even over the thrum of the planes flying overhead and the distant clack of the anti-aircraft guns. She tiptoed in, holding her candle high.

Leo's study was neat and tidy. Her husband had an orderly mind, Ava knew. She put down her candle and began to carefully ease open drawers and look through folders. She hardly knew what she was looking for. What would be of most use? What would prove her commitment to resisting Hitler? She found lists of raw materials needed for the armaments industry, and accounts of the effect of the British blockade, but they were simply facts and figures. Nothing that seemed clandestine or forbidden.

Then Ava found a folder marked Top Secret. She opened it with shaking hands. Key phrases jumped out at her: *Our Eastern territories will be occupied by stronger military effectives in the next four weeks . . . must not give Russia the impression we intend to attack . . . able at any moment and with strong forces defend our interests . . .*

Another piece of paper was tucked inside the envelope. Scrawled across it, in Leo's handwriting, were a few sentences. They read: *H. planning invasion of SU? Luftwaffe to attack Kiev first. War of extermination – aim to crush Bolshevism.*

Ava heard the creak of the camp bed in the cellar below. Panic thrilled through her blood. She could not let Leo find her rifling through his papers. Yet she felt sure they were important. Glancing about, Ava saw a small Oriental dish on the bookshelf. Quickly, she poured some hot wax from her candle into the dish, blowing on it to help cool it faster. She then took the study key, pressed it deep into the warm wax, and rubbed away any wax that had adhered to the steel. Ava then dropped the wax impression into her coat pocket, snatched up her candle and the keys, and went out into the hall, quietly locking the door behind her. She hurried back down the cellar stairs. Leo lay asleep on the camp bed, one arm bent above his head. There were shadows under his cheekbones and jawbone. She bent and tried to ease his keys back into his pocket. He stirred and turned towards her. His eyes opened. 'Ava?' he murmured.

She bent to kiss him. 'It's just I haven't seen you for so long. And there's no room for both of us in this camp bed. Unless, of course . . .'

She hitched up her nightgown, straddling his hips. His keys fell with a rattle to the floor. But Leo did not notice.

With the Great Dane trotting at her heels, Ava went out into the golden afternoon.

She walked down the road and then crossed over into the Tiergarten. Zeus put his nose to the ground and followed some invisible trail across the grass. Birds sang, and a red squirrel scampered up a tree. Some boys were kicking a ball around. Ava took a deep breath and felt the knots of tension in her shoulders ease a little. The tranquillity of the Tiergarten never failed to soothe her. Like the Grimm brothers, Ava had formed the habit of walking in the gardens every day. Today the forest was a cathedral of green shot through with gold. Soon, it would be amber and persimmon and flame, and then the leaves would fall, and all would be black and white and grey, the colours of death.

Ava shivered. How much longer could this war go on? Was Hitler hungry enough to eat the whole world?

Would it help stop the war if Ava shared the information she had found in Leo's study? Would it help save lives? Ava was sure it would, but still her conscience was troubled. She had not liked spying on her husband, and she did not like the idea of betraying her country.

Ava was also afraid of the Gestapo. Everyone knew they watched suspects for months, waiting for them to betray themselves. Ava's best friend and her father had both been arrested. She had married Leo to try and keep herself safe. What was she doing, passing along confidential information? Was she putting herself, and Leo, in danger?

Ava walked and walked, but in the end she knew she had to do it. Hitler had to be stopped.

She caught the bus to Charlottenburg.

Libertas was having coffee with Mildred Harnack. Ava told them what she had found. 'I cannot believe it,' Libertas said. 'The Soviet Union is an ally of Germany's. They carved up Poland between them. Are you sure, Ava?'

Ava nodded. Libertas and Mildred looked at each other.

'I'll tell Harro,' Libertas said. 'He'll investigate it, see if it's true. If it is, we'll have to try and warn them somehow.'

'Arvid knows someone in the Russian embassy,' Mildred said in her soft American voice. 'We can try to pass the news along to him. And Donald Heath will want to know. If Hitler really plans to invade the Soviet Union, it will change everything for the Allies.'

'Donald Heath is the American First Secretary,' Libertas explained. 'Mildred is friends with his wife, Louise.'

Mildred nodded. 'I could let her know. I'm sure she'll pass the information on to her husband.'

'Could you take a photo of the memos, Ava?' Libertas asked. 'If we had concrete proof . . .'

'I could try,' Ava said. 'I've taken a wax impression of his key, but I don't know how to get it made.'

'Ask your friend at the Jewish Aid,' Libertas said after a moment's thought. 'She will know someone who can help you. Those poor Jews can only survive if they know someone who can do such things.'

Ava told her how she and Jutta left messages for each other at different statues through the garden, so that they did not need to risk being overheard by anyone.

'It's a good idea,' Libertas said. 'Let's do the same. We'll choose different monuments, though, to make sure we don't get our messages muddled.'

'Jutta and I leave messages at all the musical memorials,' Ava said.

'Then let us choose statues of women,' Libertas said. 'The Amazon!'

'And the Flora,' Mildred suggested.

'There's the statue of the Folk Singers too.' Ava looked from one bright eager face to the other. Swiftly they made arrangements, and then parted company. Ava walked the long way home, her blood seething with excitement. She felt she was striking a real blow against the Nazis, at last!

*

Ava bent and felt under the lyre on the statue of Wagner in the Tiergarten. A small wad of paper was wedged beneath. She slipped the wad of paper up her sleeve, then walked deeper into the park. When she was sure she had not been observed, Ava sat down on a park bench and carefully unfolded the note.

It was the one she had left for Jutta earlier in the week. Jutta had never collected it.

Ava sat, biting at her nail. What could have happened to her? Why had she not come to check if Ava had left her a message?

She got to her feet and began to walk across the lawn, heading east. As she walked, she surreptitiously tore the note she had written to Jutta into tiny pieces. Stealthily she threw the scraps of paper away, then hurried from the park and through the busy evening crowds towards the Jewish quarter in the Scheunenviertel. She could not go home without finding out what was wrong.

She went a circuitous route through the narrow maze of streets and courtyards. A long queue of women stood outside a bakery, scarves tied over their heads, baskets on their arms. Ava squeezed past, and crept at last up the many flights of steps to the Feidlers' apartment. She could smell cabbage cooking, and hear children squabbling.

Ava knocked on the Feidlers' door. She heard a slow shuffle of footsteps, then the door opened a crack.

'Ava!' Tante Thea opened the door and let her in. She was dressed in an old, baggy dress, a cardigan that was unravelling at the elbows, and down-at-heel carpet slippers. Her face was gaunt, and her nose was red and inflamed. It was impossible to believe she had once been a glamorous opera star, dressed in velvets and jewels, singing an aria in the spotlight to a thunderous burst of applause.

Before she shut the door, Tante Thea looked up and down the hall to make sure no-one was watching. 'You should not be here! You know we could all get into trouble.'

'I was worried. I haven't heard from Jutta in days.'

'She's been sick, Ava. We all have. All the dust in the air after the bombings . . .'

'I'm so sorry, Tante Thea! Have you called in a doctor?'

'We haven't the money for a doctor. And no doctor would come into the Jewish quarter, anyway. She's all right now. You can go in and talk to her. A visit might cheer her up – she's been feeling very low.'

Tante Thea opened the door into a tiny room with a sloping roof. It had no window, so the only light came from a small electric lamp set on the floor next to the bed. Jutta lay there, reading.

'Ava! What are you doing here?'

Sitting cross-legged on the floor, Ava explained. 'If I can get a key made, it means I can get in whenever I like. Jutta, I've already found out some important information. Can you help me get a key cut?'

Jutta nodded. 'I think so.'

Ava slipped her the wax impression, and she hid it under her pillow.

Dusk was closing over the crooked headstones of the Weissensee cemetery. Mist hung in the autumn-brown trees, and cobwebs in the ivy were beaded with moisture. Candles were set in a row, their wavering flames causing strange hunch-backed shadows to dance over the crumbling walls of the mausoleum.

Jutta stood under a dripping tree, her hands shoved into her pockets. She was hungry, and doing her best to ignore it. It seemed she was always hungry.

The old Jewish cemetery stretched away as far as Jutta could see, crooked tombstones inscribed with Hebrew all overgrown with trees and vines. A long avenue of flaming golden trees led towards the entrance gate, but otherwise all seemed old and forgotten in the falling night. An owl hooted, making Jutta jump.

An old man stood nearby, holding a tin box of ashes. His long black coat hung from angular shoulder blades. The left lapel had been sliced apart. A group of young people stood near him, holding flickering candles and talking in low voices. Like Jutta, they were all skinny and shabby and nervous. It felt dangerous to be here.

Lotte Jastrow, a friend from the Jewish Community offices, came to greet her. A thin-faced young woman with endearingly crooked teeth and lustrous black ringlets, she was a year older than Jutta, at nineteen.

'I'm glad you could come,' Lotte said. 'It's very sad. His son Rudi spent twelve years in prison or a camp, for nothing more than speaking out against the Nazis. Then they shot him, for helping people in the camp.'

'He was a good friend to my brother,' Jutta said. 'In Buchenwald. Rupert often mentioned him in his letters.'

Lotte nodded. 'You must tell Herr Arndt. It'll be some comfort.'

She led Jutta up to the group, and introduced her. A gaunt young man with intense black eyes was introduced as Herbert Baum. Jutta knew him by reputation. He had invented a leaflet bomb that could be left in a public space, tucked behind a statue. Half an hour later, the bomb would explode, showering the square with anti-Nazi leaflets.

His wife, Marianne, was a pretty, anxious-eyed young woman who had worked as a kindergarten teacher, while an older woman with a limp was introduced as Lotti Paech, a nurse. There were a few other friends from the Jewish Community offices, including sweet-faced Hanni Meyer who was only sixteen, and a group of serious-faced young men.

Jutta had seen one of them before. Heinz Rotholz was tall and gangly with a bony face and dark brilliant eyes. His hands seemed too large for his skinny wrists, which protruded several inches from the sleeves of his coat. He had a thick mop of dark hair, tucked under a cap which he wore tilted over one eye.

He smiled at Jutta. 'Thanks for coming today. We have to do anything we can to show our solidarity. Lotte says your brother is in Buchenwald?'

'Yes. He's been there almost eighteen months now. My mother dreads him coming home in a tin box like that.' She jerked her head towards the box Herr Arndt clutched to his chest.

'I'm so sorry. It must be very hard for your parents.'

'My father blames himself. My mother wanted us all to emigrate years ago, and he refused. He thought of himself as German, you see.'

'My father was the same. He fought for Germany in the Great War and suffered a lot. He could not believe that all that struggle and sacrifice would count for so little.'

'My father was a university professor! And now he spends all day working in a paint factory, doing the most menial of tasks. It just doesn't make sense.'

'They like to give the well-educated Jews the worst jobs. Cleaning out sewers and collecting garbage. It's to humiliate them, you know.'

Jutta nodded in agreement.

'I could have gone,' Heinz said. 'I had a chance to go to Palestine. They want strong young men there.' He grinned and made a fist, pretending that he was muscular. 'But I wanted to stand and fight. Somebody has to try and save Germany from the Nazis!'

Jutta gazed at him in wonder, a flush of warmth all through her body. 'That's just how I feel.' Her voice was low and choked, and he had to lean in close to hear it. When he caught her meaning, he smiled. Jutta could not smile back. She had to look away.

Just then Lotte called for silence. Herr Arndt wished to speak. In a trembling voice, the old man told them that his son Rudi had done what he could to help others in the camp. Rudi had hidden sick men in the infirmary and smuggled them food and medicine. But he had been betrayed and had paid for it with his life. Now he would never see his son again.

Then an earnest-eyed young woman named Ilse spoke about Rudi's work as a young Communist in the early days of Hitler, and how – as a concentration camp veteran – he had helped so many others endure. 'We feel we must follow in his footsteps, and work together to reach his goal,' she said simply. Jutta found herself unbearably moved.

Prayers were recited, then everyone stepped forward one by one and laid a pebble in a small cairn on a wall. Afterwards, everyone blew out their candle and walked towards the cemetery gate. Jutta caught Heinz's sleeve. 'Can you introduce me to Herbert Baum?'

'If you like. Why?'

'I . . . I've heard that he's useful to know.'

His face lit up. 'He is. We all are. Come and meet him.'

The cemetery stretched away on either side, a tangle of pale tombstones and dark leaves. Heinz caught her arm so she would not stumble on the uneven paving stones. They hurried to catch up with Herbert and Marianne, and Heinz introduced her, keeping his voice low.

'I'm wondering if you can help me.' Jutta hesitated, twisting her fingers together. 'I need to find someone who can make a key for me. Quietly.'

Herbert glanced at her. In the swiftly gathering darkness, it was hard to see his face. 'Your brother is in Buchenwald?'

'Yes.'

'Why?'

'Subversive activities,' Jutta said. 'Why else?'

'What do you need the key for?'

'Subversive activities,' Jutta said again. 'Why else?'

His teeth flashed in a quick smile.

'All right. It'll cost quite a bit.'

'That's no problem.' Jutta thought of the money Ava had slipped her for this exact purpose.

He raised his brows. 'You're the first Jewish girl I've ever met for whom money is not a problem.'

'I have friends. Good friends.'

'Good friends always come in handy.'

Jutta nodded.

Herbert seemed to come to some decision. 'All right. I'll get this key made for you. It might take a few days. How will I get it back to you?'

'You could come and join one of our meetings,' Heinz said quickly, looking at Jutta, then away. 'If you want.'

Jutta felt a wave of colour scorch up her face. She lifted her chin, and looked him in the eyes. 'I'd like that,' she answered.

'Good,' Herbert said. 'We're always happy to make friends with someone who is not afraid of subversive activities.'

Fulcrum

A va turned twenty-one at the end of September.

A birthday package arrived the day before from Switzerland, with letters from her father and sister, a drawing from Angelika, and a block of Swiss chocolate which Ava ate all at once, till she felt sick with the richness of it.

She went to the conservatory as usual, had a quick lunch with her sister Monika at noon, then spent the afternoon studying and practising. She felt restless. It was her birthday, and Rupert's. Once they would have celebrated together.

But this birthday Ava was all alone.

She did not expect Leo any time soon. The war was revving up. Göring's Luftwaffe had been pounding the British cities into rubble, while the RAF had responded in kind. Berlin had been bombed again and again, the air-raid sirens wailing nearly every night.

Ava put down her books, and sat for a while, staring into space. Zeus whined, putting his heavy paw on her lap. She let him out into the garden, then made herself a pink fizz. Ava drank it down fast, made herself another one, and then lit an illicit cigarette. The smoke hit the back of her throat like a blow. Ava went into the sitting room. It was dusk, and the room was filled with shadows. She made sure all the windows were shut tight, then she put 'Summertime' on to the gramophone.

As the familiar notes of the trumpet rang out, Ava lifted her glass and said, aloud, 'Happy birthday, Rupert-twin. I hope you're alive. I hope you're well. I wish you were here.'

Billie began to sing, and Ava sang with her, dancing by herself with her glass in one hand and the cigarette in the other. The trumpet and clarinet began their duet. Ava took a swig of gin, then a deep drag of her cigarette, swaying her hips. She spun on one foot, lifting her arms. Leo stood in the doorway, a sheaf of red roses in one hand.

His face changed as he saw the tears on her face.

'Ava! What's wrong? Why are you crying?'

Ava wiped her tears away. 'It's nothing! Just this song. It always makes me cry.'

He put down the roses. 'But . . . why?'

Ava turned away, stubbing out her cigarette. 'It's such a sad song.'

Leo came and put his arms about her. He kissed the back of her neck. 'Ava, tell me what's wrong.'

'Nothing's wrong,' Ava lied.

He stroked away the curls that had tumbled out of her loose bun. 'Tell me.'

Ava remembered another time she had stood in his arms in the shadows, and spoken the truth to him. Somehow she could lie to him no longer. 'It's Rupert's birthday too. We were born on the same day. I can't help it, Leo. I miss him! I miss him terribly.'

Billie had begun to sing again: 'One of these mornings you're gonna rise up singing, and you'll spread your wings and you'll take to the sky.'

Her tears quickened. Leo sat down, drawing her onto his lap. 'I don't understand. If you miss him so much, why don't you just go and see him?'

The record had come to its scratchy end. The room was silent.

Ava stared at him. 'But . . . how can I? They don't let visitors in.'

His look of puzzlement deepened. 'Who don't?'

'The camps.' Ava saw his expression change, and was pierced with a terrible, beautiful doubt. 'Rupert's in a camp. Buchenwald. He's been there for the last eighteen months. I . . . I thought you knew . . .'

He shook his head.

'My God.' Ava could only stare at him.

For eighteen months, she had tried to convince herself that Leo could have had nothing to do with Rupert's arrest. She had pointed the finger of blame at everyone else it could possibly have been, even her own sister. But now, as she saw the dawning comprehension on his face, she realised – with a sudden joyous spring of her heart – that he was indeed guiltless.

She flung her arms about his neck. 'You didn't know? You really didn't know?'

He pushed her away from him. 'You thought I had something to do with it?'

'No!' she cried. 'Oh, but . . . Leo, you have to try to understand. Rupert was arrested the very night . . . the very night I met you in the Tiergarten. I wanted so badly for it *not* to be you who had denounced him . . . but the more I told myself it couldn't be you the more afraid I was . . . it's been torture . . . wondering . . . worrying . . . all the time . . .'

'You thought *I* had denounced him?' Leo stood up, took a few long strides away, then turned back. 'You thought I denounced your best friend and yet you still married me?'

Ava bent her head. 'I didn't know . . . I told myself you couldn't do such a thing.'

'How could you?' His voice was raw.

Ava lifted one hand to him, then let it drop. When she spoke, her voice was low and hopeless. 'I was in love with you.'

He stared at her. 'What?'

'I was . . . I am . . . in love with you. I tried not to be, I really did. But I couldn't help it. I love you madly.'

For a moment, Ava's life rocked on a fulcrum. Then Leo seized her in his arms, kissing her eyes, her mouth, her throat. 'I love you too, Ava. I love you so much.'

She kissed him back with all her might. 'I'm sorry,' she sobbed. 'I loved you so much but I thought . . . I was afraid . . .'

'Damn this war! Damn these times!'

'I love you,' Ava cried again. His hands were urgent on her body, dragging away the silk slip. 'Oh, Leo, I love you so much!'

It was such a relief to finally say it.

When Rupert's number was called, he thought life was at an end. He walked numbly through the ranks of prisoners to the front of the Appellplatz. *They found out about the stolen food*, he thought. *They know about the wooden whistle I gave the boy. My poems! They found my poems.*

Instead he was given a brown paper package. It had been roughly torn open, then the paper tucked back into place. The package was addressed to him, in his sister's handwriting.

Rupert had to hold the package against his sunken chest to stop himself from dropping it. He waited till all the prisoners marched off to their work details, then opened the torn paper.

Wrapped inside was his trumpet.

A short note was enclosed, written in his sister's usual messy scrawl. *Dear Rupert, we have been told you are now permitted to receive packages. I packed up everything I thought you would like. I hope the food and the cigarettes are a comfort to you, and that you can buy anything you need with the money. I've thought you might like your trumpet too. We are all well, though life is hard. Ava helps us as much as she can. Happy birthday! Love, Jutta.*

There was nothing in the package but the trumpet. No food, no money, no cigarettes. But Rupert hardly cared. He ran one hand over its gleaming golden curves.

He felt as if he had been punched in the solar plexus. In his mind he could hear the notes flowing up and away like sunset banners. Songs of glory and triumph.

His cheeks were aching strangely. Rupert realised he was smiling.

*

It was one thing for Ava to admit she loved her husband. It was quite another thing to trust him.

So Ava did not tell Leo that she now had a secret key to his study. Her life became one of constant subterfuge, rifling through his papers and giving anything of interest to Libertas or to Jutta.

Her biggest challenge was getting enough film. It was, of course, rationed. Leo could occasionally get her some from the Abwehr stock, but she had no way of explaining to him why she needed new film all the time. Jutta had contacts on the black market, but it was incredibly expensive and Leo expected Ava to keep neat household accounts, with every pfennig accounted for. Sometimes, when Leo was away, she half-starved herself so she could swap food coupons for illicit film.

Ava found the strain of the double life difficult to bear. She had always found it hard to mind her tongue, and her face was naturally expressive. Sometimes, before she went out to dinner with Leo and his officer friends, or to another diplomatic party, she would sit in front of the mirror and think of Gertrud, that perfect Nazi woman. She imagined Gertrud's look of utter confidence, her faint sneer towards anyone she thought to be of lesser blood, her ingratiating deference to anyone she thought could be of use to her.

One day, in late winter, Ava was sitting reading by the fire, her stockinged feet resting on the sleeping Great Dane, when Leo came home. Snow dusted his shoulders and his peaked hat. Ava jumped up to kiss him. As she pressed her body against his, she heard a faint crackle of paper in the pocket of his exquisitely tailored uniform jacket. 'Frau Klein has worked a miracle,' she told him. 'Roast pig's knuckle! With potato dumplings and slow cooked red cabbage.'

'Sounds delicious,' he answered, in a preoccupied voice. 'I'll just go and get changed. My feet are soaked.'

'I'll get the dumplings on,' Ava said. 'Frau Klein has managed at last to teach me how not to overcook them. I have to stand there, and watch them boil till they float. Then I have to get them out fast.'

Leo gave an absentminded grunt, and turned away. Then his hand went to his pocket. He pulled out a note, tossed it on the fire, and left the room. Ava hesitated just a moment, then darted forward and pulled the note from the hot coals with the fire tongs. The paper was singed and half-burnt away already, but she was able to see a few words, in a strong, old-fashioned hand. '. . . at the Lions' Bridge at dawn . . .'

Ava tossed the note back on the fire and went to boil the dumplings, her mind alive with curiosity. Who did Leo plan to meet at the Lions' Bridge at dawn? It was a cold and uncomfortable place for a rendezvous. It had to be a clandestine meeting, at such a place and such a time. Somehow Ava had to get there first, and listen in. She was so engrossed in wondering how she was going to manage this that she let the water boil dry and burnt the dumplings. Leo was so lost in thought, he did not even notice.

Ava was roused in the early dawn by her husband quietly rising and dressing in his riding clothes. She lay, tense and alert, hearing every soft step and rustle. As soon as Leo had gone, she jumped up and dressed herself warmly. She heard the click of the back door, and went to the window, watching the dark shape of her husband stride down the cul-de-sac towards the church. The riding stables were only five minutes' walk away. Ava had to hurry.

She sped downstairs, pulled on her coat and a dark knitted hat, and ran through the garden. The dangling rosehips were all frosted with snow, and a wren sat in the thorns, feathers ruffled against the cold. Ava got her bicycle out of the garage, and pedalled as fast as she could along the Tiergartenstrasse. Her breath plumed away from her mouth. All the way, she listened for the sound of galloping hooves behind her.

Tyres skidding on the icy black path, she rode the long winding way along the lake. As Ava approached the Lions' Bridge, she slowed down, peering ahead. It was only just light, and birds were beginning to twitter. Stashing her bike under a bush, she crept down a winding snowy path that led through a dark shadowy glade. Tall trunks soared away through an awning of evergreen yew. Ahead, a narrow wooden structure spanned the half-frozen stream. Two great cast-iron lions on either side of the path held the ends of the linked handrail in their mouths. Mist drifted overhead.

Ava's hands were like lumps of ice in their gloves, and the skin of her face felt numb. She crept through the yew bushes, until she was pressed up against the cold stone of one of the pedestals, half-hidden by the span of the footbridge.

Dead leaves rustled. She heard footsteps on the bridge above her head. She shrank down, pressing her face in her gloves, trying to hide the white smoke of her breath. The clop-clop of horses' hooves, then the sound of boots hitting the ground.

'Good morning, Admiral,' a man's voice said. 'Is it cold enough for you?'

'I hate the cold!' the Admiral said. 'Evil times, when an old man cannot stay in bed on a day like this. Have you meet my adjutant, Leo von Löwenstein? His mother was Dutch, and he speaks the language fluently. You may speak freely before him.'

'Come out on to the bridge,' Leo said. 'To make sure we can't be overheard.'

'Who but fools like us would be out on such a morning?' the stranger said.

'Better safe than sorry,' Leo replied tersely.

'A man with a suspicious mind,' the stranger replied. 'I like it. Men with suspicious minds survive.'

Boot-heels rapped on the wooden planks overhead, as the men walked out into the middle of the bridge. They began to speak in low voices. Ava strained her ears. She could catch only a few words. '. . . they've started arresting the Jews . . . there's been pitched battles on the streets of Amsterdam . . . they've cordoned off the streets and made a ghetto in the old Jewish quarter . . . the police have arrested more than four hundred Jews and locked them up . . . sent to Buchenwald . . .'

Ava jerked. The leaves rustled, and a bird flew up with a loud clap of wings. She crouched lower, hardly daring to breathe. Ava heard the sound of quick footsteps as someone looked around. When the conversation resumed, the stranger's voice was even lower.

'. . . on strike to protest . . . police violence . . . only the beginning . . .'

Then Leo's voice sounded. 'What do you want us to do?'

'. . . get them out . . . they have to pay . . . transportation . . .'

'We'll need a good excuse to send away so many Jews,' the Admiral said, then something about foreign currency. Ava felt her chest tighten with frustration. She was very cold and very uncomfortable, and all she could hear were snatches.

Then the stranger said words of thanks and farewell, and strode off towards the other end of the bridge. Admiral Canaris and Leo walked back, deep in conversation.

'You will need to go to Amsterdam,' the Admiral said. 'I can't trust anyone else with so much money. Be careful. It'll be dangerous.'

A jingle of bridles and the sound of men settling into saddles. Ava waited till she could not hear their hooves clopping any longer, then scrambled back onto the path. Her woollen stockings were wet and filthy, her coat was muddy and covered in decaying leaves, and her boots were thick with clay. She brushed herself off quickly, then ran back to her bicycle. She had to get home before Leo.

It was hard to know how to decipher the conversation she had overheard. Were Leo and the Admiral conspiring to save Jews in Amsterdam, or planning to help deport the Dutch Jews to concentration camps? What had the stranger meant when he said: they must pay? Ava puzzled over it all the way home.

She was stripping off her clothes when she heard the back door open, and Leo come in. She just had time to shove her wet and muddy clothes under the bed, and crawl under the eiderdown. She pulled the covers up to her chin, and closed her eyes, pretending to be asleep. Leo came in, and sat at the end of the bed. 'Ava?'

'Mmmm-hmmm?'

'I need to go to Vienna. Important business for the Admiral. I'll be home in a few days.'

'All right,' she murmured. Leo bent to kiss her forehead, then went to pack his suitcase. Ava sat up, frowning. He had lied to her without any hesitation whatsoever. She wondered what else he hid from her.

28

Rose Thorns

Jutta sat cross-legged on the threadbare rug, holding a lukewarm cup of chicory coffee in her hands.

The Baums' small sitting room was so crowded with people there were not enough chairs for them. Heinz Rotholz sat on the ground beside her, his long legs stretched out. His brother Sigi sat on a wooden chair nearby, Lotte leaning her back against his legs. Every now and again, Sigi would caress her neck gently and Lotte would flash a smile at him over her shoulder. Marianne Prager, Alice Hersch and Sala Kochmann sat side by side on a sagging couch, while Hanni Meyer perched on an old three-legged stool. Sala's husband, Martin, sat in one shabby armchair, and Marianne's boyfriend, Heinz Joachim, in the other.

Herbert Baum stood before the empty fireplace, speaking with his usual passion and fire, while his young wife, another Marianne, sat at his feet, gazing up at him in adoration.

'If we want a better world, we must never cease to think about what kind of world we want . . . and we must not be afraid to do whatever it takes to make the world the way it should be. It is not enough just to talk. We must act! And there's only one way to make the world a better place, and that is to bring down Hitler's Reich!'

'Hear, hear!' his audience cheered.

'But how?' Martin Kochman asked, when the tumult had calmed down. Herbert looked troubled. 'Any way we can, my friend. Any way we can.'

When Leo returned, he was given a rare free Sunday. He took the chance to wake Ava from her sleep, and tenderly make love to her. Afterwards, he drew her into the crook of his body, his hand slowly stroking her stomach. Ava tensed, afraid he was going to make some comment about why she had not yet conceived. They had been married for almost two years.

'You're so thin.' Leo ran his hand up the bony jut of her hip. 'Are you eating properly while I'm away?'

'Frau Klein makes me some soup. It's just so hard to get supplies these days. The shops are all empty. You can queue up for hours to get no more than a few old turnips, or a sausage.'

'Are you giving any of your food coupons to your Jewish friends?'

Ava looked at him quickly. 'No,' she lied.

He gazed at her, searching her face, then rolled over and got up. 'Well, I'm going to cook you a good breakfast.'

'There's no food in the house,' she told him. 'Unless you want sardines on crackers.'

He rose and dressed, and went out. A long time later, he came back with no more than a loaf of dusty-looking bread and two eggs. 'A feast!' Ava teased him, as he boiled the eggs and tried to cut the bread into slices without it falling to pieces.

It was a fresh spring day, and they wrapped up well to eat their breakfast on the terrace. The roses were a tangle of thorns and rosehips, and the bare branches of the pear tree were just beginning to bud. White narcissus nodded their dainty heads around the base of the mossy old sundial.

Leo spoke little over their meal, his gaze abstracted. As Ava washed up, he changed into his oldest and most disreputable pair of trousers, went back out into the garden, and began to dig up his roses.

Ava threw on her coat and rushed out. 'But Leo, your roses . . . what are you doing?'

'You can't eat roses,' Leo replied. 'It's wrong to lavish so much care on them when I should be growing cabbages and potatoes.'

'But they're your grandmother's roses!'

He shrugged. 'We need the room to grow vegetables, Ava, and get some chickens. You're so thin and pale, you're not getting enough fresh food to eat. If I dig up the roses, we'll have room enough to grow food for an army.'

Ava thought at once of Jutta and her parents, and did not protest anymore. But she went down the steps and put her arms around her husband, holding him tightly. After a moment, he returned the embrace. They stood silently in the pale spring light, leaning into each other.

'Can't you save them somehow?' Ava whispered at last. 'For when the war is over?'

Leo was silent. She knew he was wondering if the war would ever stop.

'I tell you what, let's harvest the rosehips,' he said. 'We'll keep the seeds, and one day we'll plant them and grow the most beautiful rose garden again.'

Leo put down his spade, and went to the garage to get some secateurs. When he walked towards her, holding the gleaming blades, Ava looked away. She had never liked scissors, not since Monika used to chase her around threatening to chop off all her hair. Ava did not like any sharp-pointed things, not even knitting needles or pencils. The thought of her skin being pierced and blood welling out was enough to make her feel faint.

Leo did not notice how pale she had grown. He was efficiently cutting sprays of little scarlet hips from the spindly stems. Suddenly he exclaimed, and drew his hand away. He pulled off his glove, to show a bead of blood on his hand. 'Those thorns are sharp!' He sucked his finger.

Ava felt the all-too-familiar wave of giddiness and nausea pass over. She sat down abruptly.

'Rilke died after pricking his finger on a rose thorn,' Leo said. 'It's odd, when you consider how many poems he wrote about roses. Even his own epitaph was a rose poem.'

He glanced over at Ava, then dropped his gloves and came swiftly to kneel at her side. 'Ava, what is it?'

'I don't like blood,' she told him, through the high whine in her ears. 'I don't like thinking of you dying.'

He drew her hands away from her face. 'I won't die from a thorn prick, my love. Rilke had leukaemia, that's why it killed him.'

'It might not be a thorn prick. It might be a bomb falling on our heads. It might be a bullet.'

Leo sat back on his heels. It was a long moment before he spoke. 'It might be. None of us can ever know the time and means of our death, even if we were lucky enough to live in peacetime. But remember what you said to me, the first time we met? How we have to stand up for what we believed in? You said we'd probably die anyway, but it'd be a death without honour. I've been thinking over those words of yours so much lately . . . trying to think of the best thing to do. And I've come to realise that it works both ways. You have to live with honour . . . you have to have courage . . .' He compressed one side of his mouth into a half-smile, more rueful than bitter. 'You of all people know that, my brave Ava.'

She shook her head. 'I'm so not brave.' She gulped a breath, then looked at him defiantly. 'I . . . I don't like blood. It makes me sick. Even the thought of blood makes me sick.'

His half-smile deepened. 'Ava, the bravest girl in the world, is scared of blood?'

'It's not my fault. I see blood, and I get all faint and dizzy.'

'Lots of people faint at the sight of blood. It's nothing to be ashamed of. But you cannot pick a rose without first braving the thorns, you know that.' Leo drew Ava to her feet. 'Come on. You can cut the rest of the roses, so that we've gathered the hips together. I'll show you how to avoid the thorns.'

Slowly Ava stepped down to his side. She did not want to admit how frightened she was at the idea. He drew her into the circle of his arms, and showed her where to cut to avoid being pricked by the thorns. His big hands were gentle on hers. Ava took a deep breath, and squeezed the blades of the secateurs together. The stem parted, and the rosehip dropped. Leo caught it, and added it to the others. Ava let out her breath in a long sigh, and cut another thorny stem.

Soon they had a whole bowl of rosehips, all fat with seeds that one day could be planted in the earth to grow a new garden. It made Ava happy to think of it.

At last, rollcall was over.

With a small group of other men, Rupert was marched out of the gates, and towards the private riding hall Commandant Koch had built for his wife. It took up most of an acre and was covered with a steeply pitched slate roof set with huge skylights so the thin spring sunshine filtered down upon the arena.

Rupert had been conscripted into the camp band. He had to wear tall black boots and a flamboyant red jacket like a circus ringmaster, a black hat tilted on his head. The band had a new leader, a Czech Communist named Jiri Zak. He insisted on regular rehearsals, and proper tuning of the instruments. As one of the band, Rupert was released from the more arduous of his kitchen duties. He played whilst the other prisoners marched and worked and were beaten.

Standing on a raised platform at one end of the hall, the prisoners lifted their instruments and began to play. Rupert thought of nothing but the music he was making. He did not look as Frau Koch rode in on her white horse, her flaming red hair hanging loose on her shoulders. She wore a black shirt and skin-tight jodhpurs, which showed off every bulge of her figure. In one hand she clenched a long riding crop, which she used mercilessly on the smooth flanks of her gelding. She cantered around and around, while the small band of men played the modern jazzy tunes she liked.

Frau Koch had had another baby that year. Another fair-haired little girl. She and the Commandant had gone away on a skiing holiday, and left the baby at Buchenwald. The air was foul with smoke and noxious fumes, and there had been outbreaks of typhus, in the camp and in the village. Rumour had it the Nazi doctors in the infirmary were injecting prisoners with the bacteria on purpose. The little girl had sickened and died. Her parents had been too busy enjoying their holiday to return.

Rupert kept his gaze fixed resolutely away from her. One of the other musicians was not so careful. Frau Koch suddenly screamed. 'He's looking at me!' She galloped up to the platform, raised her crop and slashed the musician across the face. At once the SS guards dragged him off the platform, and beat him viciously with their clubs. As the beaten man fell to the ground, Frau Koch whipped her horse into a gallop. The SS guards jumped out of her way, and she rode her horse straight over his limp body. Blood spread out across the sawdust.

Rupert and the other musicians played on. He poured all his horror and loathing into the music. Ava had always said a trumpet's notes were red.

Red as blood.

Red as slaughter.

Red as a danger signal.

Panzer Tank

'I have a joke for you!' Libertas perched on the arm of the chair, a cup of chicory coffee in her hand. The Schulze-Boysens' apartment was full of people talking and laughing, and the air was blue with cigarette smoke. Outside the big picture windows, the larch trees were all clothed in summer green, the same colour as the absinthe Harro was pouring into rows of little cocktail glasses.

'What?' Ava asked, smiling up at her.

'A Berlin man has grown so desperate of life that he tries to hang himself. The rope is not a real rope, though, it's an ersatz-rope made of nettles and so it breaks. So the man tries to drown himself, but his suit is an ersatz-suit made of wood and so he floats. He decides dying is all too hard and gives up, but he has nothing to live on but his ration cards, and it's not long before he dies of starvation.'

Ava grinned ruefully. Like all jokes, it worked because it was so close to the truth.

Like everyone else in Berlin, Ava spent hours every day queuing up for food. Nothing was real; everything was pretend. Ersatz-bread was made from potato starch and sawdust. Ersatz-coffee was made from roasted chicory. Ersatz-meat was made from who knew what. New shoes were

241

particularly hard to come by, and everyone was wearing shoes that had been patched and re-patched. The truly poor were wearing wooden clogs like medieval peasants.

'I think I'd give anything for a proper cup of coffee,' Libertas said. 'And proper soap!'

'You know what I call this?' Ava lifted her cup of ersatz-coffee. 'Mucke-fuck. From the French term *mocca faux*.'

Libertas shouted with laughter. Her husband, Harro, looked up, and smiled. After a moment, he came to stand behind Libertas, his hands gently massaging her shoulders. She leant her head back, and he bent and kissed her. He was wearing a loose shirt, unbuttoned at the throat, and a pair of loose flannel trousers. Ava liked him much better out of his Luftwaffe uniform.

He sat down next to Ava and spoke in a low voice. 'I just wanted to let you know that your information about Russia was good. The Luftwaffe has been given orders to fly over Soviet territory, and mark the positions of railroad junctions, electric power stations, factories, things like that.'

Ava bit her lip. 'Can you do anything about it?'

'Arvid and I have passed the information on to the American ambassador, and a contact of ours in the Soviet embassy. He's going to give us a radio so we can send messages to Moscow.'

Ava's stomach twisted. 'That sounds dangerous.'

He nodded. 'Yes. Arvid doesn't like it. But at least then we know anything we find out is getting through.' He stood up. 'We will need to hide the radio. Can we count on you?'

Ava nodded.

A week later, Libertas left a note for Ava hidden under the left knee of the Amazon statue in the Tiergarten. It told her, in code, that the meeting had been set with the Russian spy. Greta Kuckhoff was to meet with him, and they wanted Ava to trail along behind and make sure she was not being followed.

Ava did as she was instructed. She understood why Greta was chosen to meet the Russian, and not one of the men who might well have been under observation. Greta looked just like an ordinary *hausfrau*, with smooth hair she wore in a neat bun and a thin, rather serious face.

It was a grey, drizzly day, and Greta wore a new yellow raincoat over her usual skirt and jersey. She had thought it would make her look less suspicious, but all Ava could think was that it made Greta very easy to follow. Ava walked along behind her, carrying a black umbrella, a scarf tied demurely over her bundled-up hair.

Greta made her way to the Tiergarten S-Bahn station and stood there, uncertainly, looking around. A tall, thin, saturnine-faced man in a shabby raincoat stopped beside her. His jaw was dark with stubble, which made Ava feel nervous. SS men were checking people's papers nearby, and they were always quick to harass anyone who looked dirty, scruffy or down at heel. The Russian spy spoke to Greta in an undertone, eyeing the SS men. Then the two of them walked down the street a little way, pretending to stare at the new construction of a massive flak tower at the zoo.

A loud crash of some masonry made the Russian spy visibly jump. He dropped the bag he carried. It fell so heavily, it made a distinct clank as it hit the ground. The SS men looked around. The Russian spy walked away hurriedly, leaving the bag behind. Greta bent and picked it up, and rushed away too, her face betraying her tension. It looked heavy, and she carried it with difficulty. Ava looked around anxiously, but the SS men had gone back to their task of checking papers and did not seem to have noticed the awkward little scene. With her heart thudding so loudly it made her feel sick, Ava followed Greta back to the Kuckhoffs' apartment, a few blocks away from the Tiergarten. Libertas and Mildred were waiting there. The four women sat in a circle and stared at the bag.

'Does anyone know how to operate a long-wave radio?' Mildred said at last. Everyone shook their heads.

'What are we to do with the thing?' Libertas cried.

'He dropped it,' Greta said. 'I have a dreadful feeling he broke it.'

'I guess we'll soon find out,' Ava said.

'He told me to hide it in my air-raid bag,' Greta said. 'I don't want to have to carry it into my air-raid shelter. Our block warden is always so suspicious.'

The radio did not seem to work very well. Arvid spent hours translating messages into code and transmitting them, only to receive a note a few weeks later asking why he wasn't using the radio. The Russian also demanded evidence of the German plans to invade the Soviet Union. Greta said crossly, 'How do they expect us to get that? We're not the kind of people who can crack safes and steal documents.'

At the end of June, Germany invaded Russia. Despite all their efforts to warn the Soviets, Stalin was taken completely by surprise. Divisions of the German army penetrated fifty miles inside Russian borders in just the first day. The streets were filled with tanks and army jeeps and marching soldiers, and Ava felt blank with despair.

'Arvid asked the Russian spy what else we could do. He suggested we strew nails on the roads leading east from Berlin to stop any military vehicles heading east,' Libertas said, a note of hysterical laughter in her voice. 'Can you just imagine it? You and me standing on the road, throwing nails in front of a Panzer tank? It's no use at all. Nothing is of any use.'

Jutta paused to wipe her arm across her perspiring forehead. She could not afford to let sweat run down into her eyes.

Stretching on either side of her were long rows of women dressed in filthy overalls, standing up at wooden benches, their heads tied up in scarves. It was dim and smoky in the long room, and the air rang with the clangour of the machinery. Steel bobbins spun at high speed, winding enamelled wire. It was tiring and monotonous work, but the women's hands moved swiftly and automatically. A heavy-set overseer stood on a platform nearby, a truncheon in her meaty hand. She had no compunction in striking anyone she felt was working too slowly.

Other SS guards patrolled the rows of women, always on the lookout for sabotage. Even though being caught meant a beating and deportation to a concentration camp, the young Jewish women did whatever they could to slow production down. Sometimes a sprinkle of sugar into the machinery, sometimes a quick loosening of a bolt so the bobbins rattled and did not spin true. Because the wire they were spinning was for the motors of the new Messerschmitt fighters.

Jutta felt dizzy, and put her hand down on the table to steady herself. Stella Goldschlag, who worked beside her, whispered, 'Take care, Jutta. She's watching you.'

Jutta opened her eyes and at once began to work at top speed again. 'Thanks,' she muttered.

Jutta had gone to school with Stella, who had been the prettiest girl in their year. She had once wanted to go to Hollywood to be a movie star. No Hollywood producer would look at her now, in her greasy boiler suit and wooden clogs.

At last, their shift came to an end. Jutta's feet were so swollen from standing on them all day she could barely walk. 'Here, lean on me a little,' Stella whispered. 'You look worn out. When did you last eat?'

'A little bread this morning,' Jutta whispered back. 'I only had a bite or two. My mother is not well, I wanted her to have it.'

'Wait till we are away from here, and then I'll give you what I have.'

Jutta hobbled away from the factory. It was right near the railway lines, and the roar and rattle of trains passing by was almost constant. They found a kerb to sit down on, and Stella dragged off her scarf and used it to wipe some of the dirt off her face and hands. Then she drew a small white roll out of her overall pocket, and pressed it into Jutta's hand.

Jutta stared at in amazement. She had not seen such soft white bread for a long time. 'The supervisor gave it to me,' Stella explained. 'He thinks I'm far too pretty to be Jewish, and is always giving me little presents.'

Jutta stared at her. 'You'll get in such trouble if you're caught.'

Stella tossed her blonde curls. 'I'll be fine. Herr Schwab won't let anything happen to me. Eat it fast, before anyone sees.'

'I can't take it all,' Jutta protested.

'Here, I'll break it in half.' Stella tore the bread in two, and gave the smaller piece to Jutta. Both devoured their portion hungrily.

'One day,' Jutta said, 'when the war is over, I'm going to eat nothing but the softest white bread.'

'You need to dream bigger!' Stella chided her. 'I'm going to go to the nicest café in Berlin and I'm going to order every sweet pastry on the menu. Then I'm going to go to the most expensive department store and I'm going to buy a pink satin dress and a fur coat, and one of those dinky little hats with a feather in it. And then I'll go to a nightclub and drink champagne and dance all night with every man there.'

'One day, when the war is over, I'm going to take a sledgehammer to that machine in there,' Jutta said through her teeth.

'And then what?' Stella asked.

Jutta shrugged. She could not think beyond that.

In the heat of a July noon, Ava put on her best hat and walked through the noisy streets to the SS offices on Prinz-Albrecht-Strasse.

It was Monika's birthday and the sisters planned to have lunch. Ava had not seen Monika in months, even though the SS offices were only five minutes' walk away from the Philharmonie where Ava spent most of her days. Ava was busy, it was true. She was in her second year of studies at the conservatory, and had started Italian lessons as well as voice coaching and music history.

That was not the reason Ava did not see her sister, though. Even if Monika had not denounced Rupert – and Ava was almost sure it had been her – she could not bear the way Monika spoke about the war and the Führer and the Jews. It was almost impossible for Ava to keep a still tongue when in her sister's company. After an hour, Ava's jaw would be rigid with tension.

The Schutzstaffel office, where Monika worked, was situated in a grand former hotel, with wide steps and elegantly proportioned rooms. Yet Ava felt as if the walls were closing in on her. Men in well-tailored black uniforms and shiny black boots strode up and down the stairs. Men in leather coats lounged against the walls, listening as obsequious civilians bowed and wrung their hands and made promises.

How can Monika bear having to work here? Ava thought.

Ava asked one of the secretaries to take a message to Monika, and waited on a seat by the wall for a very long time. Just as Ava stood up and decided to go to lunch by herself, she heard the *clack-clack-clack* of high heels coming down the marble stairs. Ava turned, sure she would know Monika's impatient step anywhere. Her sister hurried towards her, dressed in black with heavy pearls about her neck, drawing on a pair of white gauntlets. She looked very thin and very chic.

'Ava, I'm sorry. We are just so very busy, and the Oberführer cannot manage without me.'

'What are you so busy with?' Ava asked.

Monika slanted her a look. 'You should know better than to ask that. Remember, the enemy is listening!'

'So have you heard from Bertha?'

'Oh, yes. Of course. All the time. Some fat old businessman is courting her, she's never been happier.'

Ava felt a stab of hurt. It had been a long time since she had heard from Bertha. Ava's father wrote every few weeks, but she would have liked to have heard from Bertha too.

'So how are you?' Monika asked, in the manner of someone making polite conversation. 'Still caterwauling?'

Ava nodded. 'I've been getting quite a few small roles. I sang in the chorus of *Tristan and Isolde* at the Linden Opera in March.'

'I really don't see why you keep it up, Ava. Surely that husband of yours would prefer to have you at home rather than yowling on a stage somewhere every night.'

As she spoke, Monika headed out into the street. Ava had to walk quickly to keep up with her, despite her longer legs. Monika always walked as if she was on important business.

'I'm still only a student,' Ava replied. 'I go to classes during the day, when Leo is at work, and get the occasional evening role. It's not like I'm a full-time performer. Besides, he knows how much I love to sing.'

Monika gave a harsh laugh. 'Oh, yes, I remember you as a kid. Always singing and dancing and trying to grab the limelight. Nothing's changed.'

Unexpected tears prickled Ava's eyes. She blinked them away, wondering how it was Monika always managed to find a way to hurt her.

'I'll have to be quick,' Monika said. 'Come, let's go in here. The Oberführer has an account.'

Monika led the way into an elegant café, with tables set with white linen, silver cutlery and fresh flowers in vases. Men in black uniforms sat at nearly every table, accompanied by women in elegant dresses and high heels, their hair set in stiff, ornate curves over their foreheads. Waiters bowed, and poured a cascade of champagne into crystal glasses, and somewhere music was playing softly. Ava thought of the meal she had eaten with the Feidlers just a few days earlier. She had had to pass long lines of scruffy Jews in wooden clogs and ragged clothes, queuing in silent humiliation for bowls of clear broth with a few shreds of cabbage floating in it.

Anger scalded her skin.

'What will you have? Lobster consommé? Caviar? Waiter! Champagne!' Monika clapped her hands.

She talked almost without stopping for the next half an hour. Ava heard a great deal about the Oberführer, and the importance of his work, and how indispensable Monika was to him, and how he insisted on rewarding her with fine clothes and jewels and rare wine. 'Look! My shoes! Handmade in Milan. I don't know how he knew my shoe size.'

Ava listened quietly. It had been in her mind to refuse the champagne and the twice-baked crab soufflés, but Ava had not seen food like this in years. If she ever had.

As Ava ate hungrily, Monika only toyed with her food. All her movements were sharp, and she kept straightening her cutlery and making sure her glass was at the exact right angle to her plate. If a crumb fell on the table, she brushed it away as if it was a cockroach. When she was not keeping the table in order, she kept twisting her huge pearls about till it seemed as if she might strangle herself. The bottle of champagne disappeared quickly, and Monika at once looked around to order another. She seemed ready to scream with impatience when a waiter did not appear at her elbow at once. Although he came in what seemed like only a few seconds, she frowned and told him that the Oberführer would not be pleased. The waiter was pale faced and nervous. He filled the glasses to the very brim, till the champagne slopped over.

Ava only sipped at her glass. Monika drained hers in a gulp, then snapped her fingers for more. Then she smoked, in jerky motions. Ava saw her nails – usually so perfectly shaped and polished – were bitten down to the quick.

'I wasn't the one who denounced Rupert,' Monika said suddenly. 'I want you to know that.'

Ava stared at her. Monika could not meet her eyes. She dragged deeply at her cigarette. 'Do you ever see them? The Feidlers?'

'Sometimes,' Ava answered cautiously.

'Tell them to get out. Tell them to get out now.'

Madness

'Where are we meant to go?' Jutta said. 'No-one in the world wants us. Besides, it's no use. Mama will not leave without Rupert, and Father will not leave without Mama, and I will not leave without either of them.'

Jutta wore a grey boiler suit, stained heavily with grease and soot. Her hair was tied up in an old rag. Her eyes, usually so brilliant and full of fire, were dull and sunken. A yellow star, emblazoned with the word 'Jew', was sewn to the front and the back of her overalls.

Jutta was working ten hours a day at the armaments factory, and it took an hour to travel each way. To see her, Ava had got up before dawn to catch the U-Bahn. They stood side by side, each clinging to a pole, the train swaying as it raced through the tunnel.

'I have some food for you,' Ava whispered. Quickly she slipped Jutta a rather knobbly packet. 'Give your parents my love.'

Jutta nodded, as the train drew into the station. 'Thanks. See you soon.' She raised a red-raw hand in a gesture of farewell, then was lost in the crowd as the train carriage emptied. Ava subsided back onto one of the seats. She felt as if an abyss was opening up between her and the Feidlers.

It was harder than ever to see them. Any Aryan caught even talking to a Jew could be arrested. It was madness.

Jutta made her way through the crowd into the synagogue, under an inscription emblazoned in Hebrew: 'O house of Jacob, come ye, and let us walk in the light of the Lord.'

It gave Jutta fierce satisfaction that she could read it.

She had changed out of her boiler suit into one of her few dresses, and tied a long white scarf over her head. It was Yom Kippur, and Jutta was determined to celebrate it as well as she could.

Lotte beckoned her, smiling. She was sitting in a row with many of the other women in their group – the Hirsch sisters, Marianne Baum, Hanni Meyer, Sala Kochmann and Marianne Prager, who had only a few weeks earlier married Rupert's old school friend, Heinz Joachim. He sat with the other men downstairs.

Jutta had not eaten since the day before. Her temples throbbed. The muscles in her legs ached all the way up to her thighs. The congregation chanted the final prayers of repentance, their voices rising and falling in song-like cadences. Jutta had a curious sensation, as if she was floating on the waves of the prayer. She closed her eyes, keeping herself steady with two hands on the back of the pew. 'Hear, O Israel,' the cantor sang.

As the last notes were chanted and the shofar horn was blown, a palpable sense of joy filled the hall. Jutta looked around at her friends, and felt a sense of belonging she had never experienced before. It was as if she had, somehow, been made new.

'Now we can go and get something to eat!' Sala cried. 'You'll come back to our apartment, won't you, Jutta? Martin and I have prepared a break-the-fast feast!'

'That sounds good,' Jutta replied. 'I'm starving.'

'We're meeting the boys on the steps.' Marianne looked eagerly for her husband.

Talking animatedly, the young women pulled on their coats and went through the grand portico and into the street. But then their laughter and chatter died away. Rows of SS officers stood outside, hands on their weapons. A man in a heavy leather coat menaced Rabbi Baeck, his legs set wide, his hands on his belt.

'Hand over the keys to the synagogue,' the Gestapo officer commanded. 'That's the last service you'll be holding.'

'What do you mean?' Rabbi Baeck cried. He was a kindly-faced bespectacled old man who was also the leader of the Reich Organisation of Jews.

'Your synagogue is being taken over. We have another use for it now,' the Gestapo man replied. 'Give me the keys.'

The rabbi hesitated, looking back at the synagogue. Light streamed out of its open doors, illuminating the crowds of shabby Jews in their white shawls and wooden clogs, all huddled together in fear at the sight of the soldiers.

'What are your intentions?' the rabbi asked, holding fast to the keys in his hand.

'Come with me to Gestapo headquarters and I'll tell you,' the policeman responded, snatching the keys out of the old man's hand. Then the SS guards all marched inside the synagogue, pushing their way roughly through the crowd.

Jutta and her friends slipped away into the night, drawing off their white scarves and prayer shawls, and trying to arrange their bags to cover the hated *Judenstern*, so large and yellow on their coats. All the joy and comradeship of the evening was gone. Everyone felt anxious and afraid.

'What do you think it means?' Jutta asked Heinz.

'Nothing good,' he answered.

The next day, Jutta heard that the synagogue had been turned into a transit camp. The Jews of Berlin were to be deported.

Lotte came by and begged Jutta to come and help. Her father, Herr Jastrow, worked for the Jewish Community offices and they were all run off their feet. Jutta did not hesitate, even though she had worked all day at the armaments factory. Carrying piles of pillows and blankets, the two girls hurried through the crowded evening streets.

The synagogue was now little more than a bare hall. The elegant wooden pews and the lectern had been ripped out. Hessian sacks filled with straw were lined up in rows. Children screamed, their mothers doing their best to comfort them. One old lady rocked back and forth, muttering to herself. Harried-looking women passed out cups of thin soup, or helped the sick and the elderly. Lotte and Jutta did what they could to help, but could not stay. It was a long walk back home, and it was very easy for SS patrols to know if a Jew was running late, now that all wore the yellow star on their coats.

Two days later, the synagogue was emptied. It was Saturday, so Jutta did not have to work. She had gone to help Lotte make up packages of bread and cheese for the deportees. It was pouring with rain, and the long lines of men and women and children trudged through the streets of Berlin, carrying their suitcases towards the train station at Grunewald. People stopped to stare in curiosity. Some were smiling and pointing. Others looked troubled and afraid.

'There's a thousand of them going,' Lotte said, standing with Jutta under an umbrella. 'No-one knows where. My father thinks they're going to Poland, probably to a labour camp. One of the SS men said they were being sent somewhere where they'd finally be taught the meaning of hard work.'

Jutta shivered. 'Will it be us next?'

'Father says anyone working in the factories will probably be safe.'

The following week, another thousand Jews were shipped away. Another thousand followed a week later. Jutta did what she could to help, but everyone was uncertain and afraid. One day, a woman who lived on the floor above the Feidlers flung herself from her apartment window. She lay like a broken china doll on the pavement, a pool of blood slowly spreading out around her. In her hand she clutched her deportation notice.

Jutta had to walk past the dead woman to go to work. She felt cold through and through. 'Where are they taking them? What is happening?'

she asked Stella that day, trying hard to stop her hands from shaking so she could wind the bobbins of gleaming steel. Stella had no answer.

That Saturday, Jutta went to the Jewish Community offices to help the Winter Aid, which was organised by Lotte's mother. Warm clothes and blankets were needed more urgently than ever before, for all Jews had been ordered to surrender their electric heaters and the cold weather was closing in. Many of her friends were there to help – Hanni Meyer and Lotte and the two Mariannes and Sala Kochmann and Stella Goldschlag, who seemed most interested in looking through the parcels donated by rich Jewish families. Somehow Stella always managed to have nice clothes and proper shoes, unlike most of the girls who had to clack around in wooden clogs.

'I got threatened with being deported today,' Hanni said, looking very white. 'An SS guard tugged at my star, and some of the threads tore loose. He said I had to sew it on properly or else I'd be shipped off too. I have to go and show it to him at the SS headquarters tomorrow.'

'He just wants to paw at your breast,' Stella said. 'I'll teach you a nifty trick. Sew your star onto a pocket instead, then tack the pocket on to your coat. They test the star, not the pocket. Then, as soon as you're out of sight, you can tear the pocket off and stuff it in your pocket. Then no-one knows you're a Jew, and you can go around just as you please, and catch the tram, or get a hot chocolate in a café. It's blissful.'

The others all stared at her. 'It's fine for you,' Lotte said at last. 'You're blonde and blue-eyed. No-one would ever expect you to be Jewish. We all look Jewish.'

'Well, that's not my fault,' Stella said. 'I was lucky enough to be born this way.'

Jutta felt the familiar burn of impotent rage flash across her skin. She turned away from Stella, and went to the far end of the long room, where piles of dirty old clothes remained to be sorted. They were all so filthy that no-one had wanted to touch them. Lotte came to join her.

'These clothes are coming back on the same trains they took the deportees on,' Lotte said. 'Isn't that strange? I wonder why.'

Screwing up their noses, the two girls began to sort the clothes into piles. 'They'll all have to be washed,' Lotte said. 'They stink!'

'Someone's peed in their pants,' Jutta said, holding the trousers away from her, covering her nose with her other hand.

'Someone's done more than that!' Lotte tossed a dress that was stained dark all down the back into the laundry pile.

'Maybe they belong to tramps?' Jutta asked. 'Though the quality of the cloth seems too good . . .' She did not want to touch the next coat, which was stiff with ordure, so she gingerly lifted it by its hem. Suddenly her face changed. She felt all along the hem, then drew a pair of scissors towards her. She unpicked the stitches carefully. A wedding ring rolled into her hand. 'But . . . tramps wouldn't hide jewellery in their hem. Would they?'

Lotte began to examine the hems of all the dirty, mud-encrusted coats heaped before them. She found some money sewn into the lining of one, and a small diamond ring in another. Jutta copied her. In one long black coat, she felt the rustle of paper within the lining. When she cut the coat open, she found old-looking parchment. It was inscribed with passages in Hebrew. She showed them to her friend.

'Passages from the Torah!' Lotte looked at her in utter dismay. 'Jutta, these aren't the clothes of tramps. They're the clothes of the Jews that have been transported. But . . . why don't they need their clothes anymore?'

'What's happened to them?' Jutta asked, faint with horror. 'Where are they all?'

Leo had been home only a few days when he had to fly out again. To Prague this time.

Ava sat on the bed as he packed a small bag.

'But why do you have to go away again? I never see you.'

'I'm sorry, Ava. I wish I could stay. But you know I can't.' Leo took three clean white shirts from a drawer and laid them in his bag.

'Then why can't I come with you? I've always wanted to go to Prague.'

He looked at her, frowning. 'You wouldn't want to go to Prague now. Hitler's named Heydrich the new Reich Protector there. He had a hundred people shot within his first seventy-two hours in Prague, and thousands more rounded up and sent to concentration camps. They're calling him the Blond Beast.'

'So how can you go there, knowing that? How can you help him?'

'I'm not going to help Heydrich!' Leo exploded. 'He's arrested Paul Thümmel, the head of the Abwehr in Prague. We have to get Thümmel out of the hands of the Gestapo. That's why I'm going to Prague, not on some tourist jaunt!'

'But why was he arrested?' Ava asked.

'Heydrich suspects him of helping the Czech resistance,' Leo said, putting socks and underwear into his suitcase. 'It's really a ruse, though. Heydrich wants to take over the Abwehr and so he's trying to discredit the Admiral.'

'But why?'

'Heydrich thinks the Admiral is squeamish because he's protested against the atrocities in Poland and Russia. They're shooting all the prisoners of war, Ava, and massacring civilians! It's against the Geneva Convention. The Admiral sent Hitler a memo protesting, and now Heydrich is using it to try and get rid of the Admiral.'

Ava opened her mouth to ask more questions, but Leo held up his hand. 'I can't talk about it. Not even to you. I have to go. I'll be back before Christmas, I promise.'

After a long while, Ava got up listlessly and went down to the kitchen. Frau Klein had left some soup for her to reheat. Zeus followed her downstairs and lay on the kitchen floor, his ears drooping. He knew as well as Ava what it meant when his master packed a bag.

Ava was stirring the soup on the stove when she heard a frantic tapping on the glass. Zeus looked up and wagged his tail. She went to the back door and opened it, peering out into the darkness.

Jutta stood outside. It was a wet, wild night, and her dark hair was plastered to her face. Her skin was chalk-white, her eyes haunted and staring. 'Ava,' she whispered. 'You've got to help me.'

Ava drew her inside the kitchen and shut the door fast. 'What's wrong! It's after curfew. What are you doing out? Did you walk the whole way here? You're shaking!'

Jutta's clothes were wet. She dripped onto the linoleum. Ava grabbed a towel, and flung it around her. 'Is it Tante Thea? Your father? What's wrong?'

'You know they've been deporting us? Train-loads of Jews, heading east. But . . . oh, Ava . . . the trains are coming back full of their clothes.'

Jutta stopped, unable to go on. Ava took her hand. It was icy cold. 'Ava. Their clothes are all soiled. And we've found things hidden in the hems. Rings and coins and small jewels. I think, surely they wouldn't let go of those willingly? And . . . oh, Ava . . .'

'What?'

'We found a scroll . . .' Jutta could not go on. She was gripping Ava's hand so tightly it hurt. 'Verses from the Torah . . . no Jew would let go of such a thing. They're sacred. Ava! What's happening to them all?'

'I don't know,' Ava said slowly. 'Surely you don't mean . . .'

'I don't know what I mean. I'm so frightened. I thought things could not get worse . . . but they say they want Berlin Jew-free! The world Jew-free!'

'But . . . how? That's impossible.' Ava stared at her in utter disbelief.

'They've emptied all the Jewish nursing homes and hospitals.' Jutta tore at her thumbnail with her teeth. 'The Gestapo come with their deportation orders and say, *hurry, hurry, hurry* . . . but then leave everyone sitting in a railway station with no food or water or latrines for days on end. It makes no sense! Why? Why? What do they intend? What are their plans?'

'I don't know.' Ava squeezed her hand.

Jutta's eyes were wild. 'You must find out! I got you that key. Can't you search your husband's offices? Surely he must know? The Abwehr know everything! Ava, I need to know. Are they killing them all? Are they all dead?'

Liquidation

Carefully Ava unlocked Leo's study door and slipped inside.

She had fed Jutta soup and tucked her up in bed. The girl was too exhausted to walk home again, and besides, it was well after curfew. She would have to leave first thing in the morning.

The wind swept around the house, rattling all the windows and shaking the chimneys. The rain came, loud on the slate tiles.

Leo's desk was neat and tidy, as always. A pile of cardboard folders were set to one side, each clearly labelled. Ava went through them methodically. Lots of details about troop movements and armament production. Payments to people in places with exotic names. Bucharest. Istanbul. Madrid. Helsinki.

At the very bottom was a file. It was labelled 'Report on Riga deportation'. Within was an efficiently typed official report, outlining the outcome of a deportation of one thousand and fifty-three Jews from Berlin to Riga in Latvia on 27 November 1941. On arrival two days later in Riga, no accommodation had been ready for the deportees, so they had been kept in the cattle trucks overnight. The following morning, all one thousand and fifty-three Jews had been marched straight from the station to the nearby forest of Rumbula, where – the report stated – they were lined up on the edge of freshly dug pits and shot. Thirty-eight were children under ten years of age. The liquidation had been successfully concluded before 9 am.

The nearby ghetto of Riga had been emptied at 4 am, and the inhabitants marched to the forest in columns of a thousand apiece, the report went on. Arriving at the pits soon after 9 am, the sub-humans were disrobed and their luggage confiscated, before they too were shot. The shooting continued all day, until there was no more light to see by. In total, the estimate of people shot that day was thirteen thousand.

Ava had to read the report over and over again before she could make sense of it. When she was finished, she sat still. She hardly had the strength to draw a breath. Her blood was as cold as iced water. When she lifted her camera to take photographs of each page, her hands shook as if she had delirium tremens.

When it was done, Ava put everything back as neatly as she had found it, went out, locked the door, and crawled into bed. She lay curled in a ball, under a heap of eiderdowns, and still she could not get warm.

Why did Leo have such a report? Was he a party to the massacre? Or was he collecting such information in order to protest and condemn? Ava did not know. She had no way of knowing. Only her desperate heart protested – again and again – that Leo could not condone such a thing. He could not. He could not.

Ava did not weep. She did not sleep. She lay, hardly breathing, keeping herself as still as she could.

In the early dawn, Ava rose, went downstairs and developed the film in the darkness of the coal cellar. She made two sets of prints. One for Jutta. One for Libertas. Then she destroyed the film. She woke Jutta and fed her. It was very hard to show her the photographs of the reports. Ava had to steel herself. She tried to explain why her husband would have such a report. 'It's his job . . . the Abwehr . . .' she said lamely. Jutta did not gasp or cry. Her thin face just set harder and whiter as her eyes scanned the terrible statistics, till it seemed carved from marble. 'I knew it,' she said at last, in a hoarse voice that sounded nothing like her usual tones. When she rose to her feet, Jutta swayed and had to put a hand on the table to steady herself. 'We have to do something,' she whispered. 'We have to stop it.'

'I'll see what else I can find out,' Ava said, feeling such raw grief and shame she could not meet Jutta's eyes. Her friend nodded and left without another word.

Ava sat for a while, stroking the Great Dane's soft ears, before forcing herself to rise and go in search of Libertas.

Her friend had changed jobs and now worked at Goebbels's Propaganda Ministry, in the hope of getting access to better inside information. With Harro working with Hermann Göring at the Luftwaffe, and Arvid at the Reich Economics Ministry working with Walther Funk, it was hoped they could each gather as much sensitive information as possible. Harro called the odd assortment of fellow resisters the Zirkel, which meant a pair of compasses, to try and describe how they all worked independently of each other, yet were connected like a series of overlapping circles.

The strain of working so closely with Goebbels was showing in Libertas's face. She was too thin, her eyes too bright, her voice too shrill.

Ava told her what she had found.

Libertas went white. 'But . . . but why? How? How is it possible to murder so many people?'

Ava did not answer.

Trying not to weep, Libertas locked the photographs away in her filing cabinet. She had filled the cabinet with newspaper clippings, letters, snapshots and reports of eyewitnesses. She and Harro used the collection to convince people of the horrors of the Nazi regime, and hoped it would one day help convict them.

'What can we do?' Libertas spoke in such a low and broken voice her words were almost inaudible.

'We need to do more.' Ava moved restlessly.

Libertas took her hand, squeezing it tight. 'We are doing all we can, Ava. We've been back in contact with the Russians. They've sent a man to meet us. We've given them as much information as we can. Maybe it'll help stop this madness!'

Ava did not know what to say. She shrugged helplessly and said her goodbyes. She could not go home. Ava walked the streets, her hat pulled down over her eyes so she did not have to look anyone in the face. It was frosty, and her hands burned inside her gloves. Then she saw soldiers in black uniforms, banging on doors and shouting. People were huddled together on the street corner, carrying suitcases. Their coats were all marked with a yellow star. The soldiers were rough with them, haranguing them, hitting them with rifle butts if they were too slow.

Ava followed them to the train station, taking hurried photographs when she could.

Hundreds were herded into the train station, and brutally sorted into groups. It was a terrible sight. Families were being torn apart, children dragged away from their parents, husbands separated from their wives. Anyone who tried to protest was beaten. Ava saw suitcases wrested from people's hands and the contents ransacked.

No-one tried to hide what they were doing. Some of the guards even posed for her. Ava did her best to smile and pretend to flirt with them. 'But you're going away,' she pouted. 'Where are you going?'

'Lodz,' one told her. 'But we won't be gone for long. We'll dump this trash, and then we'll be back. We could get together for a drink then.'

'That'd be nice,' Ava answered. 'So what happens to them all once they get to Lodz?'

The guard shrugged. 'Better not to know.'

Ava took a photo of him, grinning and holding high his rifle, while behind him an old man was clubbed to the ground.

'Hey, you!' a woman guard shouted. 'What are you doing?'

'Just taking a goodbye shot of my boyfriend,' Ava called back, and reached up to give the guard a kiss. The woman guard was not appeased, though. She began to struggle through the crowd, saying, 'No photos!'

Ava slipped away. As soon as she was out of sight, she quickly took the film out of her camera and rolled it up inside her heavy bun, securing it with her leather barrette. Ava just had time to insert a new film inside, before the guard chased after her, took her camera and dragged out the film, exposing it to the light.

'I was just taking a few snapshots,' Ava protested.

'Don't do it again,' the guard warned her, giving back her camera. Ava nodded and walked away. Her hair hung heavy on her neck.

Rupert blew with all his strength into his trumpet. The band had to play loud to cover the sounds of the shots.

Each day, trainloads of Soviet prisoners of war were brought to Buchenwald. They were taken straight to the riding hall. Part of it had been portioned off and made to look like an infirmary. One by one, the prisoners were undressed and led to stand on a contraption that looked like a complicated weighing machine. Smiling doctors in white coats adjusted the machine, so that the back of the prisoner's neck was in line with a small round hole in the wall. Then an SS guard shot a pistol through the hole. The prisoner fell, and was neatly trundled out one door while the next prisoner was led through the other.

The bodies were piled high onto a lorry and driven down to the crematorium to be burnt. Other prisoners were kept busy shovelling rock salt onto the road to soak up all the dripping blood.

Rupert's throat was hoarse and his hands shook but he dared not stop blowing his trumpet. Snatches of a poem danced in his head. *My tongue is numb, I cannot blow, my tongue is dumb, I cannot scream, my tongue is dead at the root . . .*

The Blond Beast

The loudspeakers crackled. An excited voice announced: 'Havoc wrought as Japanese attack Pearl Harbor, the US Navy's island bastion. The Japanese struck first and declared war afterwards! Extensive damage and losses.'

Rupert put down his trumpet and listened. It was no use playing over the noise of the newscast. The SS guards all cheered and grinned. The prisoners stood with hunched shoulders and grim faces. The war just kept escalating, and all it meant was more hunger, more cruelty, more death.

It was early morning in winter, and the sun had not yet risen. The prisoners shivered in their thin uniforms. Many wore only wooden clogs, or sandals made of a strip of canvas nailed to a thin leather sole. Frostbite blackened their bare heels and toes, their ears, their fingers. The mind-numbing routine went on. The on, off, on, off of the caps. The counting and recounting of heads. The calling of numbers.

Quite a few rows of prisoners propped up the lolling corpses of those who had died in the night. The dead as well as the living must be counted. Others had their arms about the sick, the fevered, the faint, trying to keep them upright long enough to survive the rollcall.

They waited for the order to march off to their work details. For many of them, that meant some kind of warmth and shelter. But the order did not come.

The sun rose, a conflagration of crimson behind the ever-smoking chimney. The frost silvering the dirt began to melt. Far away, the hoot of a train. Still the order did not come. All morning the prisoners stood, waiting, knees locked to stop themselves from falling. Many did. Those who were dead were dragged away and stacked neatly against the wall, a fire pile of bones and skulls. Those who were still breathing were strung up with rope, their arms bent backwards behind their heads.

The sun crawled across the vast sky. Those still standing had no choice but to relieve themselves where they stood. Piles of excrement steamed faintly in the freezing air. Puddles of urine froze, faintly gleaming in the ruts of mud. They stood. They fell. They died.

The sun slid down into darkness.

Still the order did not come. It was a battle of endurance. Fall and die. Stand and live.

Rupert stood. Rupert lived.

On Christmas Eve, Leo and Ava drove through a whirling snowstorm to Admiral Canaris's house. The streets were pitch-black. Snow spun in the pencil-thin ray of light from Gilda's shaded headlamps. The Mercedes's tyres slid on the black ice of the roads.

'I'm lucky they didn't requisition Gilda,' Leo said. 'If I wasn't the Admiral's messenger boy, they would have for sure.'

'How did your meetings in Prague go?' Ava asked. Leo had arrived home only that afternoon, and there had been no time to talk.

'As well as can be expected,' he answered after a moment. 'Honestly, I was surprised. Sometimes I think the Admiral must have something on Heydrich.'

'Like what?'

Leo shrugged. 'Nothing. I shouldn't have said anything.' He was silent for a moment, then said, 'Perhaps Heydrich did not want to bring down an old friend. He and the Admiral are neighbours, you know.'

'Will he be there?'

'Perhaps. He may have come back to Berlin for Christmas.' Ava was silent. Leo glanced at her. 'If he is there, Ava, keep away from him. You do not want to catch his eye. He has a reputation for being ruthless with women. And it's most probable that he will remember you from the time you sang "Silent Night".'

'I'll gladly keep away from him!'

Admiral Canaris and his family lived out beyond the Grunewald, in the leafy suburb of Schlachtensee. It took a long time to get there. At last Leo pulled up in front of a long, low building with high-pitched eaves set amongst high mounds of snow. Heavy curtains shielded the windows, but Ava could hear music, the clinking of glasses and a low hum of conversation.

The rooms within were crowded with men in uniform, drinking and smoking. Solid modern pieces furnished the house, with many artefacts from foreign countries – Moroccan rugs, carved wooden masks, brightly painted Italian bowls, red Turkish glasses in silver filigree. Bookshelves lined the walls, and Ava saw many were not in German. She remembered Leo telling her that Admiral Canaris could speak six languages fluently.

Leo led her through the crowd, waving to people he knew and calling out greetings. Here and there were clusters of older women in long gowns and fur stoles, drinking heavy pewter mugs of steaming mulled wine.

'I will get you some glühwein,' Leo said, and went to the long bar in one corner of the room where a smiling waitress in a snowy white apron was serving the hot spiced wine from a big oaken barrel. When he brought a cup to her, Ava drank it gratefully, for she was chilled from the long drive.

'I must find the Admiral and let him know we are here,' Leo said.

Just then, a tall, angular woman with a bitter, compressed mouth approached them. 'Leo, you've arrived at last. The Admiral wants you. In his study.'

'Of course. I'll go at once. Frau Canaris, this is my wife, Ava . . .'

'Pleased to meet you,' Frau Canaris responded, not looking very pleased at all. Her face was tired and strained. 'If you'd excuse me . . .' She strode away, lifting her long skirt with one tightly clenched hand.

Leo said, 'I had better go and see what the Admiral wants. Things are rather tense, what with the Americans entering the war and Rommel retreating from Tobruk.'

'What should I do? Should I come?' Ava asked.

Leo hesitated. 'Come and say hello to the Admiral. Then, if he wants to talk to me in private, you can come out again.'

He led the way down a hallway towards the back of the house, then knocked on a door.

'Who is it?' a gruff voice called.

'It's Leo, sir.'

'Come in.'

Leo and Ava walked in, and the men within all rose to their feet. The small room was hot and surprisingly crowded. The Admiral's face was flushed with the heat, and his mop of white hair was dishevelled. Of the other men, two were in civilian dress and four in uniform. Their faces were grave, and one – a man with a square jaw and a shock of dark hair – looked angry.

'Welcome, Leo, dear boy. How are you?' Admiral Canaris asked. 'Glad to be home?'

'Indeed. Prague was a little too hot for me,' he answered, then drew Ava forward. 'You will remember my wife, Ava.'

'Of course. How could I forget such a beautiful bride?' The Admiral smiled kindly, showing teeth yellowed with nicotine, and his two dachshunds sniffed her ankles with interest. 'Tell me, how are you enjoying married life?'

'As much as is possible with a husband I never see,' Ava answered, smiling to show she was only teasing.

'Ah, yes. My poor wife is always complaining she never sees me too. Busy times, I'm afraid. Busy times.'

The Admiral then introduced the other men. General-Major Hans Oster, the deputy head of the Abwehr, was around fifty years old, and had sparse grey hair brushed neatly backwards, and a great many medals on his uniform. His eyes were tired but shrewd. Ava recognised him at once. He was the man she had once overheard talking to Leo about the Netherlands. He had been right, Ava thought. Germany had invaded.

An older man with frowning eyes and deeply marked lines bracketing his mouth was introduced as General Ludwig Beck, the former Chief of Staff. The third man was introduced as Fabian von Schlabrendorff, the adjutant and cousin by marriage to General-Major Henning von Tresckow. He had a pronounced widow's peak, and his eyes behind his round glasses were red-rimmed with exhaustion. Sitting beside him was a stern-looking man with heavy eyebrows speckled with grey and small, round glasses. He wore an Iron Cross at his collar. He was introduced as General Friedrich Olbricht. He bowed over Ava's hand and clicked his heels together smartly, but it was clear that he was filled with consternation at her presence.

The square-jawed man with the shock of dark hair was Herr Carl Goerdeler, the former mayor of Leipzig. Ava had heard of him. He had resigned as mayor after the Nazis had insisted on taking down a statue of Felix Mendelssohn, the famous German-Jewish composer.

Finally Ava was introduced to a younger man in a well-cut dark suit and sober tie. He looked as if he was in his mid-thirties, and had a long, narrow, sensitive face and dark, receding hair that had left him with a pale and prominent forehead. His name was Helmuth James Graf von Moltke.

'The Graf is an expert in international law,' Admiral Canaris said, 'and has recently come to work with us at the Abwehr. We need all the help we can get, don't we, Herr Graf?'

The Graf smiled and said, in a beautifully modulated voice, 'I'm afraid my wife sees very little of me these days either, Frau Gräfin von Löwenstein. I am based in Berlin now, while she has stayed on our estates at Kreisau with our children. I think it is safer for them there.'

'Berlin is not the place for children now,' the Admiral agreed. 'I am trying to convince my wife and daughters to relocate to the countryside, but they just laugh at me and ask what on earth they would do there.'

He continued, with a vague and amiable smile, 'Talking about my daughters, Eva and Brigitte are out the back playing music and dancing with the other young things. I'm sure they'll look after you, Ava, if you'll excuse us for a moment. I have some business I wish to discuss with your husband.'

It was a dismissal. Ava smiled, inclined her head and left the room.

She stood outside the door, hesitating, casting a quick glance around her. The hallway was only dimly lit, and the shadows pooled most thickly near where she stood. She could hear the faint murmur of voices through the study door. She could also hear the roar of the party at the far end of the hallway, and see a group of men standing near the fire, glasses in their hands. No-one was looking her way. Ava sat down in the chair by the study door, and bent, pretending to fiddle with her shoe but actually inclining her head as close as possible to the keyhole.

'Surely now is the time to seize our chance? It's madness to keep on hurling men and tanks at Moscow in the middle of winter! The generals must see that as clearly as we do, particularly now the swine has sacked them all and declared himself Commander-in-Chief of the whole army!'

Carl Goerdeler's angry voice carried clearly. Ava caught her breath, shocked to hear someone calling the *Führer* a swine.

'We've lost a hundred and fifty thousand men, and many of our tanks, in just the past three weeks.' There was agony in the voice of the man who spoke next. Ava thought it was Fabian von Schlabrendorff. 'Our men have no winter clothes or boots. They're dying of frostbite as much as from Russian bullets. We must do something!'

'We've tried smuggling information to the British, to the Pope, to the Americans, but no-one trusts us. They think we're feeding them false information . . .' Ava's pulse jumped as she heard Leo's voice.

'The Führer must be made to see that there is no chance of conquering the Soviet Union now.'

'He will never admit it. He believes his own propaganda!'

'But surely now that the Americans have entered the war ... surely he does not think he can win against Great Britain, Russia and America?'

'He's a madman! He must be stopped.'

'He's a dangerous madman. We must be very careful.'

Ava could not tell who was speaking. She heard a burst of laughter from the party down the hall, and then the tapping of a woman's footsteps, coming towards her. Ava rose and moved quickly away from the study door, just as Frau Canaris turned the corner and came towards her.

'Ah, I was just looking for you, Frau Gräfin von Löwenstein. Aren't those men tiresome? Always talking business, even on Christmas Eve. Come and meet my daughters, they are only a few years younger than you.'

'That would be lovely,' Ava responded, following her hostess back into the party. She kept her face serene even though her thoughts were in turmoil. It was not surprising to find the Admiral closeted away with the General-Major and the Count, when they were both employed with the Abwehr, but the presence of Carl Goerdeler was startling. He was a former politician, a businessman and a well-known opponent of Hitler. Since his resignation over the Mendelssohn statue, he had not been much in the news but it was clear from the words Ava had just overheard that his disapproval of Nazism had deepened into overt resistance, if not rebellion. It was also interesting that General Beck and General Olbricht had been present, as well as the adjutant of General von Tresckow. If there was some kind of conspiracy going on, it involved some of the most important officers in the Wehrmacht.

Ava found that her hands were damp with perspiration. She had to stop herself from wiping them on the thin satin of her gown. Smiling, she took another glass of mulled wine, though she was not cold anymore. She was as hot as if she had a fever.

What did it all mean? Ava had not realised that the war in Russia was in such a sorry state. The newspapers and newsreels were full of stories of German advances and victories. Ava had known that the Führer had named himself Commander-in-Chief, of course, but she had thought that was because the head general had fallen ill. If the invasion of the Soviet Union had failed, did that mean the Russians would be striking back at Germany? And was the Admiral – the head of the German secret service – plotting against the Führer? What did they plan? To overthrow him? To kill him?

Ava's mouth was dry, and she felt light-headed. She drank down her wine, trying to ease the churning knots of tension in her stomach. Terrors whirred their frantic black wings through the shadows of her mind.

The bell rang, and Frau Canaris hurried to open the door. Reinhard Heydrich stood on the doorstep, a violin case tucked under one arm. A strong-boned woman was beside him, carrying a sleepy little girl in a frilly white dress. A small boy in brown knickerbockers followed close behind.

Frau Canaris exclaimed in surprise. 'Reinhard! Lina! We were not expecting you. I thought you were in Prague.'

'We thought we'd surprise you,' Lina Heydrich replied, smiling. She was dressed in a loose blue dress, and held one hand curved protectively over her abdomen. 'You see . . . we have news!'

Frau Canaris's eyes widened. 'Already?'

'Silke is two and a half years old already. We thought it was time, didn't we, Reinhard, dear?'

Her husband gave a smile that did not reach his eyes, murmured something and walked away. As a waiter hurried to give him a glass of wine, Heydrich's steel-blue eyes swept the crowd. His brows contracted. He walked to stand at the entrance to the hallway, looking towards the Admiral's study.

Ava's heart thumped once, hard, then seemed to stop. If Heydrich went to the study in search of the Admiral, he would see all the conspirators meeting there. He may even overhear their words, as Ava had done. He would be sure to be suspicious.

She walked straight across the room, eyes fixed in what she hoped was an adoring gaze on Heydrich's face.

He was a man who came close to being startlingly handsome. His sleek fair hair, his straight aquiline nose and his hard, lithe, athletic form should all have added up to an ideal of masculine beauty. Yet, somehow, his looks were repellent. His mouth was thin and cruel, his eyes too close set, and his jaw seemed to recede away from his prominent forehead. The part in his hair was so straight, it was as if he used a ruler.

Ava found it hard to walk naturally. 'Good evening, Herr Obergruppen-führer,' she said in a clear, carrying voice. 'What an unexpected pleasure to see you back in Berlin. I do hope that you will give us the very great privilege of playing your violin for us tonight? I have heard you are an absolute virtuoso.' Ava smiled up at him.

Heydrich had snapped his frowning gaze to her face as she first spoke, but then gave a thin smile and a faint incline of his head. 'Frau von Löwenstein, is it not? I shall play my violin for you if you will sing for me.'

A chill ran through her. He knew her name. Leo had been right. He had not forgotten who she was.

Ava stiffened her knees, and smiled up at him. 'It would be an honour, sir!'

He stepped closer, lowering his head so he could whisper in her ear. 'Oh, I'm happy to honour you . . . or dishonour you . . . in any way you wish, Frau von Löwenstein.'

She felt his finger stroke her spine through the thin satin of her dress. Colour scorched her face. Ava dropped her eyes, not knowing what to say.

'Reinhard! Merry Christmas! What an unexpected pleasure.' The Admiral had come out of his study, smiling jovially. His dachshunds trotted at his heels. 'I thought you were in Prague still.'

Behind him, Leo had shut the study door and followed close behind, his eyes like chips of ice in his stern face.

Ava stepped away from Heydrich. Then Leo was beside her. She put a hand on his arm, trying to steady herself. His muscles were rigid with tension.

No-one else had come out of the study. Amidst all her whirling thoughts, Ava wondered if they did not want Heydrich to see them there. Canaris was trying to draw Heydrich away, but he only smiled and would not budge. 'No, no, my dear Wilhelm. Frau von Löwenstein has promised to sing for me. That is a treat I cannot miss.'

'It would be a pleasure, sir.' Ava left the safety of her husband's arm to smile at the Blond Beast and lead him away to the piano. 'Will you turn the pages for me?'

Ava sang a host of songs, keeping Heydrich's attention all on her. He stood behind her, his gaze slithering down the curves of the satin gown, probing the gap of her cleavage. As he leant forward to turn a page of the songbook, he lightly rested his free hand on Ava's shoulder.

From the corner of her eye, she saw the other men slip away, one by one, through the crowd and out the door. Ava let no sign of her relief show in her face or body. She was aware of Lina Heydrich's simmering anger, and Leo's cold displeasure, but she smiled and sang and bent forward so that Heydrich would have a better view down the front of her dress. Only when the last conspirator was long gone did Ava allow herself to stop. Admiral Canaris was by her side in a moment, helping her stand up from the piano stool, giving her a fresh cup of hot mulled wine. Ava thought he understood what she had done.

Then Heydrich picked up his violin. He played Chopin's Nocturne No. 20, Frau Canaris accompanying him on the piano. Ava had never heard anything so exquisite. Shivers ran over her skin. All the hairs on her arms were erect. She watched Heydrich's long, insistent fingers on the strings, his bow smoothly stroking. Ava thought: *how awful that he plays Chopin, a Polish composer's memories of his homeland, while all of Poland lies in smoking ruins. Does he do it on purpose? Is he mocking us? Is he so cruel?*

Yet Ava was moved against her will. She had to press her fingers against her eyes to force back tears. Heydrich should not be able to play so. Surely only someone with a good soul could coax such beauty into life?

Sometimes Ava did not understand the world at all.

The Mercedes skidded on the black ice. Leo gripped the wheel with white-knuckled hands, straightening the car, then putting his foot to the floor once more. Ava clenched every muscle in her body, holding herself still and silent. Outside, the landscape flashed past. Black sky. Black branches. Swirling snow.

As they drove into Berlin, the car slowed. It was too dangerous to speed in the blackout. But still he did not speak. He waited till they were alone, in bed, in darkness.

'Ava, Ava,' he muttered against her hair. 'The way he looked at you! The thought of him touching you! I cannot bear it.'

She held him close. 'I'm sorry. I couldn't think what else to do.'

He gripped her tighter. 'You know?'

Ava shook her head. 'I . . . suspected . . . I hoped.'

'We can't do anything else. How can we stand by and watch while such evil is being done? Ava, you don't know . . . you can't know . . .'

'I know a little,' she whispered against his bare shoulder.

'It's treason, what we're trying to do,' he said. 'If we're caught . . .'

'Does he . . . does Heydrich know?'

'I'm afraid he suspects.'

'Oh Leo, be careful!'

'It's gone beyond being careful now,' Leo said grimly. 'I can't say anymore, Ava. The less you know, the better. If you should fall into the hands of the Gestapo, the only thing that will save you is innocence.'

Ava thought of the photographs she had taken, the food she had smuggled to those in need, the leaflets she had spread around the city. She thought of the Russian spy, and her courage quailed. Germany was at war with Russia. Would Leo understand? Would he forgive her? She badly wanted to confide in him, but she had been silent for so long. It was as if all the muscles of her jaw and tongue could no longer work together to speak of her secrets.

She did not speak. She lifted her mouth to his, and tried to let her hands and her body say what she could not.

33

Tainted Blood

The car screeched to a halt, half on the pavement. Two men got out. They were dressed in long leather coats. Ava stopped in her tracks, her heart thumping unpleasantly. Zeus growled, all the hair on his spine lifting.

'Frau von Löwenstein?'

'Yes?'

'We need you to come with us.'

'Why?'

'The Obergruppenführer wants to see you.'

Reinhard Heydrich.

Ava caught her breath and tried to smile. 'I'm sorry, I'm afraid it's not convenient right now.' She lifted the hand that held Zeus's lead. 'I'm sure the Obergruppenführer does not want me bringing my dog into his office.'

'We will wait while you put the dog away.'

Ava put Zeus inside the house, then got into the car with the two Gestapo men. 'Will I be long? My dog will begin to whine if he's left alone too long.'

'It'll be as long as it needs to be,' one answered.

They drove the rest of the way in silence.

The car pulled up outside the palatial building that housed the Schutz-staffel. Ava was taken upstairs, which was a relief. Everyone knew the torture chambers were in the cellars. Heydrich sat behind a huge, highly polished wooden desk. He was writing and did not look up as Ava was shown in. She looked around, noting the priceless tapestry, the marble head of Hitler. A photograph of his smiling wife and children sat nearby. At last Heydrich looked up. 'Frau von Löwenstein, what a pleasure to see you. You look as fetching as ever. Please, sit down. Will you have coffee? No? You're not chilled after your long walk in the Tiergarten?'

Ava sat down on the edge of the seat, telling herself it was a cheap trick to intimidate her. She walked Zeus in the park every morning.

'You wished to see me?' Ava was proud at the steadiness of her voice.

'Of course. What man would not?'

The sound of her pulse in her ears was suffocating her. 'How can I help you?'

He got up and walked around the desk, coming to stand behind her. He took off her hat and set it on the table. He put his hand on her shoulder. 'May I take your coat?'

Ava's impulse was to shake his hand off and tell him there was no need, she was not staying. But she did not dare. She stood up, and let him slide her coat off her shoulders. Ava had dressed that morning for warmth and comfort, but still she wished her red woollen dress was thicker and did not hug her curves quite so lovingly. His eyes on her body felt like a trail of slug slime. Ava sat down again and folded her hands in her lap. Heydrich sat on the edge of the desk. Far too close.

'Cigarette?'

'No, thank you.' She did not want him to see how much her hands were shaking.

He lit one, and blew a blue plume of smoke. 'I have had complaints about you.'

Ava stiffened. 'What kind of complaints?'

'I've heard that your background may be somewhat suspect.'

Her thoughts flew at once to Gertrud. Had the complaints come from her? Had she denounced Ava?

She lifted her chin. 'I find such insinuations offensive.'

He laughed. 'I'm sure you do. Your father was German, I know, although his . . . philosophies, shall I say? His philosophies were most unwise. Your mother, though. What was she?'

'She was Spanish.'

'From what part of Spain did she come?'

'Seville. I . . . I don't know much about her. She died when I was a baby, and my father rarely spoke of her.'

'I've heard rumours she was a Gypsy.'

Ava was startled. She had been looking steadfastly ahead, but now her eyes flew up to meet his. He was smiling, but his eyes were icy cold.

Monika, Ava thought.

'My mother was an opera singer,' she said. 'She once danced the role of a Gypsy in *La Traviata*. That was how my father met her. My sisters liked to tease me, saying I was a wild Gypsy girl, but it was just a joke.'

'I can imagine just how wild you could be.' He leant forward and lifted one of Ava's curls. His fingers brushed against her bare skin. She flinched. He twirled the ringlet about his fingers, then tucked it behind her ear, his hand lingering on her neck.

'Why are you not a member of the Party?' he whispered in her ear.

Ava jumped. 'I . . . I . . . I was always too busy with my singing to go to Party functions.'

'You must join.' He stroked her throat, then slid his hand under her curls to cup the back of her neck. 'Herr Doktor Goebbels needs singers for his Reich Culture Chamber. We must keep the morale of the troops up. A beautiful girl like you, with such a beautiful voice . . . you are just what Herr Goebbels wants.'

Ava could not speak. His other hand gripped her chin, forcing her to look up at him.

'But you will need to prove that your mother was not a filthy Gypsy. Her baptism records are not enough. You must trace your lineage back to 1800 and beyond. Else I shall be forced to conclude that you are of Gypsy blood, and you will be deported to the camps. Which would be such a shame.'

'She was Spanish,' Ava gabbled.

'I'm glad to hear that.' He half-dragged her out of the chair and crushed her mouth with his. Ava tasted the metallic tang of her own blood. He pressed one knee between her legs, forcing her back into her chair. She tried to wrench herself free, but he was far too strong for her. When Ava would not open her mouth, he forced her jaw open so hard she feared it would break. Then he thrust his tongue inside. She gagged.

He lifted his mouth, still holding her chin so tightly she whimpered in pain. 'Because if you were of Gypsy blood, you'd be a sub-human and you would have just defiled me. And that is not something I would forgive easily.'

He let her go. Ava pressed the back of her hand against her mouth.

'I leave for Prague this afternoon, but I'll be back soon. I'll send for you. Make sure you have your certificate of Aryan blood. And wear something a little more revealing. I look forward to you proving your loyalty to the National Socialists to me.'

Ava could not tell Leo.

Yet her neck was bruised. Her lip was swollen and bleeding. How could she hide the marks from him?

As Ava walked home, she kept bending and snatching up handfuls of snow, holding it against her mouth and throat till her skin burned with cold. She could only hope it would ease the swelling. It was dusk, and the city lay dark and silent, every crack of light papered over. An electric blue spray of sparks from the S-Bahn seemed shockingly bright in the gloom.

Ava let herself into the lightless house. Zeus pranced and reared, beside himself with anxious joy to have her safely home. She poured herself some brandy and drank it down, trying to ease the trembling that would not stop. Then she went down to the cellar, where she had stowed her mother's old chest. Ava opened it and looked quickly through. Her mother's beautiful old dresses and fur coat were still there, folded neatly in tissue paper. The black velvet pouch of twigs and charms was there too. She sat back on her heels, wondering. Had her mother really been a Gypsy? Was this bag of charms some kind of Gypsy magic? Or was it just some kind of old Spanish superstition? Ava had no way of knowing.

She should have burnt the bag of charms, but she could not bear to. It was one of the few things left of her mother. She took it up to bed with her, spreading out the charms on the coverlet. A bunch of twigs tied together with green thread. An acorn. A shell with a hole through it. A white feather. What did they all mean?

She heard Leo's quiet footsteps coming up the stairs and quickly swept the charms back into the bag and tucked it underneath the mattress. She pulled the sheet up to her chin.

Leo tiptoed in. The room was lit only by his bedside lamp. He sat down on the edge of the bed and began to undo his collar. 'Ava,' he whispered. 'Are you awake?'

'Mmmm-mmm.'

'I'm sorry, sweetheart, but I need to go to Prague.'

Ava stiffened all over.

'There's a new crisis,' he whispered. 'Heydrich's men have arrested Paul Thümmel again. You remember? He's the head of the Abwehr in Prague. He tried to warn a Czech spy that the Gestapo was closing in on him, but was caught. The Czech spy shot down half-a-dozen Gestapo men before using his last bullet on himself.'

He sat in silence for a moment. 'It's going to be hard to save Thümmel this time.'

Ava understood, without him needing to explain. Any evidence that an Abwehr operative was working with the Czech resistance against the Nazis was enough to bring the whole Abwehr down, and the Admiral and Leo with it. She sat up. She switched on the bedside lamp. 'There's something you need to know.'

He caught his breath at the sight of her. 'What happened?' he said through his teeth.

'Heydrich called me into his office.'

Leo seized her in his arms. 'Did he . . .' He could not finish the sentence.

Ava shook her head. 'He mauled me about a bit but . . . I'm fine. He told me I had been denounced as having tainted blood.'

Leo's hands balled into fists. 'Gertrud!'

'Maybe. Though someone's been talking to my sister as well. He said that I had to get a certificate of Aryan blood, or he'd have me sent to a concentration camp!'

'I'd never let that happen!'

Ava gazed up at him. 'What am I going to do? Spain is in ruins after the civil war!'

'The Admiral has many contacts in Spain,' Leo said. 'I will speak to him. Don't you worry, my love. I will not let that swine Heydrich hurt you!'

Ava put her hand on his arm. It was rigid with tension. 'Leo, I'm afraid . . . I think he means to use all this against you. He'll try and upset you, anger you. If he says anything . . . Leo, please, just ignore it.'

Leo traced the bruises on her throat, then laid one finger against her torn lip. 'You think I can ignore another man touching my wife in this way? You are very much mistaken.' Very gently he kissed her, then got up and began throwing things into his suitcase.

'Leo, please . . . promise me!'

'I promise you he'll be sorry,' Leo answered, and slammed his suitcase closed.

A violin sobbed into the evening dusk. Ava had never heard such a melancholy sound.

Clutching her bag close, she walked through the maze of ornately carved wooden caravans. Thin dogs barked at her from beneath dilapidated carts. Big-eyed children stared at her from the openings of tents made from filthy canvas flung over branches. Many of the children were barefoot, despite the cold, their legs begrimed with mud. A boy in a ragged coat and a black hat shouted something at her in a language she did not understand.

'Anyone from Spain?' she asked him, then tentatively, '*Español?*'

A woman in a long patched skirt and a brightly coloured headscarf came out of a huddle of caravans. She was carrying a baby in a grubby linen shift on her hips. She pointed towards a circle of battered-looking caravans in the distance, and Ava went towards it, picking her way through the frost-hardened mud.

Ava had written to her father, asking what he knew about her mother's ancestry. 'I do not know any more than I have already told you,' Otto had replied. 'Your mother rarely spoke about her past, and when she did you could never be sure she was telling the truth. She was a fabulist. Her tales were never the same. She told me once her father had been born in a cave!'

So then Ava had gone to question Tante Thea, who had known her mother before they were married. 'I know she was born in Seville, and her father was from Granada,' Tante Thea told Ava. 'She was always being asked to sing in operas like *Carmen* and *Il Trovatore*, because of her looks and the way she danced . . . she was a most fiery and flamboyant dancer . . . and she used to mock herself as the director's first choice to play any Gypsy witch. But all Clementina ever wanted was a home and a child of her own . . . she said she was tired of always being on the road. That does not sound much like a Gypsy, does it?'

'There used to be a lot of Gypsies in Berlin,' Onkel Franz had mused. 'The Nazis cleared them all out before the Olympics. I wonder what happened to them?'

Ava had asked her singing teacher, under the pretext of discussing *Il Trovatore*, and he said he thought there was a Gypsy camp somewhere in the east of Berlin. Ava had then asked Herr Nadel, the local block warden, in a voice of pseudo-horror, if that was true, and he had told her that there was still a settlement of Gypsies out near the sewage dump in Marzahn, but that he was sure they'd be cleaned up very soon.

So, on impulse, Ava had caught the S-Bahn out to Marzahn to take a look. She had worn her oldest coat, and tied an old scarf over her bundled-up hair. Her papers and a few marks were buttoned safely in an inner pocket, and all her jewellery was left at home. The heavy bag she carried was filled with things she hoped to barter for information – cigarettes, bags of sweets, turnips and potatoes, some tins of peaches and sardines, a dried ham hock.

A long line of women waited with wooden buckets in their hands for a single tap, standing embedded in a murky puddle. They looked at Ava curiously as she went by, and a few called out to her, smiling with broken teeth and holding out their hands in a begging gesture. They all wore skirts so long they trailed in the mud, and bright ragged shawls and head-scarves. Ava held her bag close to her body, and shook her head, smiling apologetically.

Then a bright-eyed, tousle-headed boy danced up to her, flashing an engaging gap-toothed smile. 'Fräulein, you want your fortune told? You come. This way.' He seized her hand and tugged her towards the circle of caravans.

'Español?' Ava asked, speaking the only word of Spanish she knew.

He grinned. 'Sí . . . venir . . . mi abuela leer tu mano . . .'

Ava did not understand what he said, but she went with him. He chattered away to her as he towed her along, in a mixture of German, Spanish and other languages. She understood that his name was Dario, and that his grandmother was the best at reading fortunes. Other children ran out to join them, holding out begging hands, or calling to her to look as they capered about, doing headstands and cartwheels, or twirling in a whirl of brightly coloured rags. Ava had to smile, though she kept her bag tightly tucked into her armpit.

An open fire had been built in the centre of the circle of caravans, and women worked around it, washing clothes in wooden basins, or hanging them over a rope strung between the wagons. A gaunt horse lipped hope-fully at the frost-burnt grass, a bare-legged child sitting astride it. A girl with long black hair stood nearby, playing something plaintive on a violin. One woman plucked a chicken, putting each feather carefully into a sack, while another chopped up limp-looking carrots on a wooden board balanced on her knees. A young woman sat on a log nursing a baby. They all looked far too thin, and their multi-layered skirts were faded and patched. As Ava

281

approached, the women stared at her and muttered to one another in their own language.

An older woman was bent over the fire, stirring a black pot. She was very thin, with a high-boned haughty face and striking amber-coloured eyes. Her long black hair was tied back with a tattered scarf printed with flowers. As Ava was drawn into the circle of firelight by the children, she straightened her back and said something in a sharp voice. The children let Ava go, though they still mobbed all around her, chattering away in shrill voices.

'My name is Ava von Löwenstein. I am looking for someone who may have known of my mother or my mother's family. I . . . I have brought gifts.'

The woman looked puzzled, but indicated Ava should come closer. 'What is your mother's name?'

'Her name was Clementina Flores. She was born in Seville.'

The woman shrugged. 'Flores is a name I know of. My mother's people came from Seville. Perhaps she can help you.' She went to an intricately carved wooden caravan, and put her head in the door. A volley of strange words followed, then she helped an old woman down the steps. Her face was deeply lined, and she moved with great difficulty.

'My grandmother,' Dario said. 'She will read your hand.'

'I am Valentina Amaya Vargas and this is my daughter, Abrienda,' the old woman said. 'You bring gifts.'

It was a statement, not a question. Ava nodded, and showed her the contents of the bag. The old woman nodded and waved her hand to Abrienda, who took the bag. 'You want to know about your family. You want to know if you are a *gitano*. Come, sit by me.'

Valentina shuffled across to the log by the fire, and Dario held her hands as she stiffly bent and lowered herself to sit. Ava perched beside her, her hands pressed together in her lap.

Valentina looked at Ava. 'You fear us. Yet should we not fear you more? You think we want to live like this? In cages, in filth? They have taken away all our men, the Lord knows where. They use us as slaves, clearing away the rubble of streets that have been bombed, for who would care if a shell should go off and blow us all to kingdom come? We are nothing but Gypsies. Who cares if we die?'

Ava was ashamed. 'I'm sorry . . .' she began.

The old woman shrugged. 'You bring food. That is kind. What do you want?'

'I've been told my mother was a Gypsy . . . I want to know if it's true. I found this amongst her things.' Ava drew out the small black velvet bag and gave it to Valentina.

'This is a *putsi*,' the old woman said. 'We make them for good luck and protection. We sell them to *payo* too. Having a *putsi* does not make you one of us.'

She opened the bag, and drew out the charms one by one. Her withered lips compressed, and she shot Ava a quick look from beneath her lowered brows. She laid the charms in a line along the log. 'Hazel twigs for protection. Acorn for new beginnings. Shell for drawing love. A white feather means someone who is dead is looking after you.' Valentina put all the charms back in the bag, and passed it to Ava. 'Keep it safe. If your mother made it for you, it was made with love. She wished you only the best.'

The other women had clustered around, preparing a quick meal from all the food Ava had brought. The potatoes were pushed into the ashes of the fire with a stick, the sweets thrown to the swarming children, the ham hock dropped into the pot boiling on the fire. Abrienda tried to open a tin with her knife, and Ava realised she had not thought to bring a can opener.

'What was your mother's name?'

'Clementina Flores.' Her mother's name was like a flash of warm sunshine in the cold wintry evening.

'Only the one surname?' the old woman asked.

Ava shrugged. 'I know of no other,' she said. 'Her mother's surname was Cortez.'

'Clementina Flores Cortez,' Valentina said, rolling the vowels over her tongue. 'Both Flores and Cortez are common names in Spain. Sometimes they are Gypsy names, sometimes they are not. You have the look of the *gitano*, with those old-soul eyes of yours and your dark heavy hair, but not all *gitanos* are dark and not all those who are dark are *gitanos*. Tell me what you know of your mother.'

'She was born in Seville. She sang beautifully. She died when I was born. They couldn't stop the bleeding and so . . .' Ava looked down at her interlinked fingers, feeling a sudden and unexpected wave of sadness that made her vision swim.

In the silence, a plaintive song rose into the darkness. A grey-haired woman swayed near the fire, one hand swishing her skirts, the other arm raised high, the fingers bent to touch. She sang a cappella, while the watching women began to clap in a complex rhythm. A cluster of little girls behind copied her, stamping their feet, twirling their tattered skirts, their arms raised in graceful arches. Dario picked up an old guitar tied with ribbons, and began to play. His fingers on the strings were as nimble as the girls' feet. The woman's voice quickened. She raised her arms, calling to someone, her voice sobbing. The music was like a thunderstorm, like smoke and ashes. The skin all over Ava's body prickled with pins and needles.

Valentina took her hand, and spread it open so she could look at Ava's palm. The old woman's fingers were cold. 'You are afraid.'

Ava tried to smile. 'We live in frightening times.'

The old woman bent her head over Ava's palm. 'There is no need to fear. You will have a long life. You shall have a child, a girl who shall sing as sweetly as your mother . . .'

As Ava's hand jerked, Valentina's fingers closed on it more firmly. 'You do not believe me. You should listen. Darkness lies ahead. I see blood, much blood on your hands. But you will not die. You will live and you shall learn the deep song and you shall find your road.'

She closed Ava's hand and looked around at the watching women and children. 'Now let us sing and dance and feast, for tomorrow we may starve.'

The Nazi Paradise

'What we want to do,' Herbert Baum said, 'is cover the whole city with graffiti. We want Berlin to wake up in the morning and know that not everyone is burying their heads in the sand. We've got to do it big and loud and red, so everyone sees.'

There was a murmur of agreement. Jutta leant forward, gripped with enthusiasm and dread in equal parts. She had told Herbert about the many nights when she and Ava had gone out with their chalk, and he was keen on the idea. Herbert never liked small actions, though. He always wanted to do things in as large and noisy a fashion as possible.

'What shall we write?' Lotte asked.

'Write "No to Hitler's Suicidal Policies!" Or simply "No! No! No!" if that's all you have time for. Target the main streets, the U-Bahn, any Nazi-owned building. Go in pairs, so one can be a lookout.' Herbert looked around the crowded sitting room, his black eyes burning with excitement. He was thinner than ever – they all were – but the weakness of his body in no way limited the strength of his spirit.

One of the other boys said, 'We should go in mixed pairs, boys with girls. Then, if anyone walks past, the boy can pretend to be kissing the girl.

If they're really close, moaning and groaning, no-one's going to check to see if they're hiding a can of paint.'

'Good idea!' one of his friends cried. 'Anyone want to rehearse?'

The meeting broke up in laughter. Most of the young men and women were already paired off. The intensity of their lives led to grabbing what happiness they could, and so there had been a spate of weddings in the past few months. Jutta got slowly to her feet. She could understand her friends marrying so young. She had just turned twenty herself, and she longed for love.

'We've smuggled out cans of red paint from the factory,' Herbert said. 'But there's not enough for everyone. Use whatever you can. Chalk, grease-paint, lipstick . . .'

'I wish I had some lipstick to use,' Lotte said, grabbing a paintbrush from the pile in the corner of the Baums' living room.

'Be careful! Take no unnecessary risks,' Marianne begged.

Jutta stepped forward to take a small can of red paint. Heinz turned to her. 'Do you want to go with me?' he asked.

Jutta nodded. 'All right.' Her skin felt hot. He smiled at her.

Heinz and Jutta walked the dark streets till well after midnight, painting 'NO! NO! NO!' wherever they could reach. They turned to walk back along the Unter den Linden. Jutta was so tired she could barely trudge along. At last their paint can was empty, and they dumped it behind a trash can. It clanged loudly.

'Attention! Who's there?' someone shouted.

At once Heinz drew Jutta into his arms, kissing her on the mouth. He pressed her back against the wall. Jutta closed her eyes. She wound her arms about his neck. She felt the quiver in his fingers as he slid his hand up her thigh, rumpling her skirt.

A light flashed onto them, then Jutta heard rough laughter. 'Can't you find a bed?' one of the soldiers called. They moved away. Heinz and Jutta stood, pressed together in the darkness, pulses thunderous. Soon all was quiet.

Heinz kissed her again.

*

'We need to do more,' Harro Schulze-Boysen declared.

It was a fine spring evening, and their apartment was crowded with people. Music played on the gramophone, and a few couples were dancing a languid tango.

Ava and Libertas were posing for Elisabeth Schumacher in one corner. Both wore exotic outfits thrown together from Libertas's extraordinary clothes collection. Ava was wearing a black lace dress, a crimson shawl, and had shaken out her hair so it hung in heavy curls down her back. She was clenching a silk rose between her teeth. Libertas was wearing a one-shouldered white Grecian slip, and was smoking a cigarette in a long jade holder. As Harro spoke, they both turned to listen, and Elisabeth put down her camera.

'What do you suggest we do, Harro?' Libertas asked. 'More leaflets to be used as toilet paper for the Gestapo?'

'We need to do something big! Something that will grab people's attention,' Harro replied. As always, he was striding back and forth, so full of nervous energy he could not sit down for long. 'Look at all that graffiti someone painted all through Berlin last month. Everybody saw it. Everybody was talking about it.'

'It's too dangerous.' Arvid took off his glasses and cleaned them carefully, before hooking them back on his ears. 'We are all risking our lives as it is, just meeting and talking like this. What we need is to find some unassailable facts and figures, backed up with irrefutable proof, and then take it to the Allied governments.'

'We've tried that. They don't believe us.' Harro picked up his glass and gulped the brandy down, then unsteadily poured another.

'We need proof. Eyewitness accounts. Photographs. Deportation lists. Death certificates.' Arvid ticked the items off on his fingers.

'We're trying,' Libertas said unhappily. 'We've gathered together a lot.'

Arvid shook his head. 'Rumour, gossip, that's all it is. It's not worth our lives to publish that.'

'That's what you always say!' Libertas cried.

His face was set. 'Is it worth dying for?'

Her eyes filled with tears. 'We have to do something!'

'I've heard Goebbels is putting together an exhibition of Russian life. He plans on calling it "The Soviet Paradise",' Ava said. 'Doesn't he know sarcasm is the lowest form of wit?'

'We could deface all the posters!' Libertas cried. 'Paint them over with anti-Nazi slogans.'

Arvid stood up. 'It's too dangerous! Would you risk your lives for graffiti? No, we have to be patient. Hitler cannot live forever. We have to survive so that there are men of intelligence and integrity to help rebuild Germany from the ashes.'

'Only men?' Libertas mocked.

The room broke up into argument. John Sieg was insisting on trying to contact the Soviets again. Greta was worried that nothing had been heard from them in a while, and Mildred thought it was all too risky.

Then Harro stood up, his voice ringing out. 'It's time we did something bold! The people of Germany need to know that there are people who hate Nazism and all its works. Let's hit this exhibition hard. Leaflets, stickers, graffiti, anything we can think of.'

Arvid picked up his hat. 'You're all fools. You don't think that Goebbels won't have the place under surveillance? Mildred, let's go. I'll have no part in this.'

Mildred stood up, cast an apologetic look at Libertas, and followed her husband out. Many of the older men in the circle left too, frowning and telling Harro not to be such a reckless fool. But Harro was determined.

'We have to do something even bigger now!' Herbert Baum declared. 'We've got to keep the pressure up. The more Berliners see that there are people standing up to Hitler and his thugs, the more they'll want to stand up themselves.'

Everyone had been filled with joy and relief at the success of their graffiti operation, and keen to do more.

'What shall we do?' Jutta asked.

'I think we should blow up the exhibition at the Lustgarten,' Herbert replied.

Everyone exclaimed, some in excited agreement, but most in horror and dismay.

'Blow it up? How!' Heinz cried.

'We'll make bombs,' Herbert said. 'We work in an armaments factory! Surely we can get what we need there. Each of us will smuggle something out over the next week or so . . . we'll work out what we need . . .'

'Maybe we should try and blow up Goebbels as well,' Sigi suggested.

'That might be too much to hope for,' Herbert replied. 'How would we know when he intends to be there? Let's just see if we can make the bombs first, and then think about where and when to set them off.'

'But . . . what about the people at the exhibition?' Jutta asked. 'Mothers might be there with their children, or young people just like us. We don't want to hurt anyone.'

'I doubt we'll be able to make bombs strong enough to actually kill anyone,' Herbert said. 'There's no way we could get enough gunpowder. It'll be more like setting off fireworks. You know, a big bang, lots of smoke, maybe a little fire.'

'I think it's much too dangerous,' Martin Kochmann protested uneasily. 'What if we're caught?'

'We'll just have to make sure we aren't caught,' Herbert replied, clapping his old friend on the shoulder. 'Come on, Martin! Think of it! What a propaganda blow it would be for the propaganda minister. His own exhibition blown up.'

'I've heard they are putting a great pile of fresh dung at the entrance of the exhibition,' Lotte said. 'To give it the so-called "authentic" Russian smell. We should put a bomb in the middle of it, so it blows dung all over everyone.' She laughed.

'We should have some kind of plan for afterwards,' Sala Kochmann said. 'We should try and get out of Germany if we can. Because they are bound to suspect any Jew who works at the armaments factories! The Gestapo will start investigating there, and any missing supplies will soon point to us.'

'We should definitely think about going into hiding,' Herbert agreed. 'All right, let's see if we can make this happen! We'll have to be quick, the exhibition opens in just a few days.'

Somehow, all working together, the bombs were made. Torch batteries were used to make simple detonators. Saltpetre, charcoal and sulphur were stolen in small batches from the factory, and mixed together to make gunpowder. The girls stole wire, wrapping it around their bodies, under their clothes, and simply walking out with it. A young man named Werner worked at the Kaiser Wilhelm Institute. He brought the chemicals they needed.

By the evening of 17 May, the bombs were all made. All that needed to be done now was smuggle them into the Soviet Paradise exhibition.

'No Jews are allowed in,' Sala muttered to Jutta as they huddled together in the Baums' cold living room. 'We'll have to take off our yellow stars and risk it.'

'Then only those who don't look too Jewish should go in,' Herbert said. 'Heinz, Jutta, Martin, I'm sorry, that means you.'

'You look just as Jewish as me,' Heinz grumbled but Jutta could tell he was secretly relieved, just as she was. Much as she wanted to fight the Nazis, setting off bombs in a place where people might be hurt seemed wrong to her. There was no point arguing with Herbert, though. Once he had set his mind to something, it was impossible to change it.

Heinz took her hand, and squeezed it reassuringly. 'Don't worry, Jutta. It'll be a blast.' He grinned at her.

The sun had set, and the streets of Berlin were dark. The smell of the linden trees hung sweet and heavy in the air. Ava tiptoed along the pavement, keeping to the shadows. Her satchel was bulging with leaflets. She could only hope no policeman would call her over and ask her what she was doing out on the streets so late.

Elisabeth Schumacher was close behind her, keeping the light of her pencil torch hidden. In her hand she carried a rubber stamp. It said:

Permanent Exhibition
THE NAZI PARADISE
War, Hunger, Lies, Gestapo
How much longer?

As Elisabeth stamped her message all over the posters for the exhibition, Ava shoved leaflets into postboxes, stuck them up on noticeboards, and tucked them under people's windscreen wipers. She left piles on the seats in bus-stops and on park benches. The two women were as quiet and careful as they could be. They saw several patrols march by, but were able to hide from them in the darkness.

The next day, after her lessons at the conservatory, Ava met Libertas at the Lustgarten so they could wander through the exhibition together. It was a cool spring evening, but the sun was shining and the linden trees along the Unter den Linden were all in bloom. The park was thronged with people enjoying the sunshine. Both women looked around eagerly, but there was not a single leaflet to be seen. The noticeboards were all full of Nazi proclamations, and the streets were free of any litter. Ava examined all the exhibition posters. All the slogans Elisabeth had so painstakingly stamped were neatly painted over.

It was so disheartening, Ava could have wept. All those long hours trudging through the darkness, nerves strung to breaking point, and it was all for nothing.

She and Libertas went through the exhibition, gazing at all the photographs of miserable-looking Russian people and the nasty dark hovels where they were supposed to live. Neither spoke much. They were both tired and depressed.

'Let's go get a drink,' Libertas said.

'Gladly!' Ava responded.

The two women pushed their way through the crowds towards the door. Suddenly a great boom shook the exhibition hall. Clouds of stinking black smoke billowed up. People screamed and ran for the doors. Ava was almost knocked over. She regained her feet, and, clinging to Libertas, hurried out into the spring sunshine. Both were shaken and afraid.

'What was it? What happened?' Ava said. 'A bomb?'

'Who could have done it? It wasn't us!' Libertas exclaimed.

'Sssh,' Ava urged her, looking around.

'This'll cause trouble,' Libertas whispered. She was so pale Ava thought she might faint. 'Oh, Ava, why do we have to live in these terrible times?'

She began to cry. Alarmed, Ava took her out into the Lustgarten and found a park bench where she could sit and mop her eyes.

'I just want to live, I just want to love and be loved. Why is that so impossible?' Libertas sobbed. Ava sat and held her hand. She knew what Libertas meant. That was all Ava wanted too.

Fire engines arrived, and police. Injured people were carried out on stretchers. Crowds stood by, watching. Ava felt on edge. 'Let's go back to my place,' she whispered. 'We don't want to be questioned.'

Ava took Libertas home and made her a cup of chicory coffee. 'Here's your *muckefuck*,' Ava told her, trying to make her smile. It only made Libertas start crying again. 'When is this war going to end?' she wept. 'I can't stand it anymore.'

It took Ava a long time to soothe her, and by that time she was shaken and teary too. At last Libertas left to go home, and Ava was able to go to bed. She could not sleep, though. She lay awake, worrying about the bomb at the exhibition and wondering who had been so bold as to set it off.

Ava spent the next day quietly. She did not go to her classes at the Philharmonie, and had no rehearsals to practise for. The State Opera House on Unter den Linden had been bombed in an air raid, and all performances cancelled. Darkness fell eventually, and she put aside her book with a sigh. She went through to the kitchen, Zeus at her heels, and began to put together a simple omelette for supper. Frau Klein had taught her how, and Ava was very proud to have mastered the art.

Zeus lifted his head from his paws, and stared at the back door. He gave a soft whine and stood up, going to stand by the door. 'Do you need to go out, boy?' she asked him.

Ava heard a scuffle, and then a clink. She stiffened. Her first thought was that someone had come to steal her chickens. Angrily, she grabbed the meat hammer from the drawer. She opened the back door and went outside, standing in the dim fan of light.

'Who's there?' she cried.

'Ava, sssh. It's me,' a voice whispered from the shadows.

'Jutta?'

'Ava, I need your help . . . turn out the light.'

She obeyed. A moment later, she heard limping footsteps. Ava shut the door, then turned the light back on.

Jutta was in a terrible state. Her hair was in a mess, and her stockings were torn. Blood ran down her leg. The palms of her hands were grazed too. Ava drew her to sit down and rushed to dampen a cloth. 'Jutta! What's happened?'

'The Gestapo,' she whispered. As Ava knelt to sponge away the dirt and blood from her knee, Jutta drew in a sharp breath of pain.

'But . . . why? What did they want?'

'You heard about the bomb at the Soviet Paradise exhibition?'

Ava sat back on her heels, shocked. 'You didn't!'

'I knew about it. I didn't plant it. Friends of mine did, though.'

She winced as Ava dabbed away some gravel. 'It all went wrong. The bomb blew up too early, and only made a little fire. And now they've arrested everyone! I jumped out the window and ran. Oh, Ava!'

Ava felt sick. 'Do they know you were part of it?'

'I don't know what they know!'

Ava bit her lip and finished cleaning Jutta's grazed knees. Then she stood up, and went to rinse the bloody cloth in the sink. 'You can stay here. Leo's away, so you can sleep in one of the other bedrooms. You'll have to hide in the cellar when Frau Klein comes to clean. I've got a bed down there, and candles, and some food, so it's not too bad.'

Jutta sagged with relief. 'Thank you.'

'Are you hungry?'

Jutta tried to smile. 'Starving.'

'Do you eat eggs?' Ava held one up.

'As long as there's not a single spot of blood.'

'All right.' Ava cracked the egg into a clean bowl, examined it closely, then gave her the thumbs-up.

'And no meat in it.'

Ava tried to smile. 'I don't have any meat to add.'

It was impossible to get news of Jutta's friends. No announcement was made on the radio, and Ava went to sit in the cinema on her own, watching newsreel after newsreel of death and horror, to no avail. It seemed as if Hitler ruled triumphant everywhere. The newspapers were full of images of bombed cities and smoking battleships, but nothing about one small blast at the Lustgarten. Jutta moped, and would not eat. Ava had great difficulty in convincing her not to go to Gestapo headquarters to beg for news.

'You must lie low,' she told Jutta. 'Please. It'd kill your parents if you were to be arrested too.'

After exacting a promise from Jutta that she would not leave the coal cellar, Ava went to see the Feidlers and tell them that their daughter was safe. Both were drawn and grey. 'The Gestapo came and searched the whole apartment,' Tante Thea said, sniffing into her handkerchief. 'They found nothing! But . . . can you tell Jutta that her friend Heinz has been arrested? And also Lotte and Marianne and Hanni. Franz heard from Lotte's father at the Jewish Community office.'

Ava went home with a heavy heart. When Jutta heard the news, she turned so white Ava was afraid she would faint. She lay on the camp bed in the coal cellar, weeping, for hours. 'Heini, Heini,' she whimpered. 'Oh, God, what are they doing to you?' Then Jutta jumped up again, wanting to go out, wanting to try and rescue her friends from the Gestapo cellars. It was very hard to keep her hidden from Frau Klein when she was in such a state of distress. The housekeeper even told Ava that she should have the rat catchers in to check the cellars.

The days dragged past agonisingly slowly. Ava hardly dared leave Jutta in case she did something mad. After a while, they stopped listening to the radio. It was all too heartbreakingly sad.

They were eating a listless meal one evening when Zeus got up and went to the door, tail wagging.

'Leo!' Ava said in a panic. 'He must be home. Quick, Jutta. You must hide.'

Jutta jumped up, looking frightened. She had never met Leo. She knew only that he was a Nazi officer and part of the Abwehr. She ran to the cellar, while Ava hurriedly threw out her meal, wiped down her plate and put it on the shelf. She just had time to put the extra knife and fork in the drawer when the back door opened, and Leo came in. Zeus whined and capered about on his stiff, silver legs, overjoyed to have his master home again.

Leo took off his peaked grey cap and threw it down, then came straight to Ava, seizing both her arms. 'I had nothing to do with it, I swear.'

Ava's heart accelerated at such a rate she had to press both hands against her chest to hide it. 'Wh ... what?' she stammered. 'What do you mean?'

'Heydrich,' Leo said impatiently. He took Ava into his arms and kissed her hard. 'It was the Czechs.'

'What are you talking about?'

'Haven't you heard the news? It's all over the radio.'

'No. I haven't been listening. Sometimes I just can't bear to listen.' Ava tried to keep her face composed, but a guilty flush crept up her skin.

'Heydrich's been killed in Prague. Someone threw a hand grenade into his car.'

Ava could only stare at him.

'I swear I had nothing to do with it. But I have to say, it's the greatest stroke of luck! Heydrich never forgot or forgave a thing. He'd have hounded you, and tried to provoke me into doing something stupid, and he was determined to bring the Abwehr under his control. We're safe now.' He kissed her again.

'But ... but who did it?'

'It was Czech resistance fighters, parachuted in from London. We didn't know they were coming.' He rested his cheek on her hair. 'I can't lie and say I'm sorry, though.'

'I'm glad!' Ava cried. 'Oh, Leo, I'm so glad! I never thought I could be happy a man died.'

Leo straightened up and moved away, unbuttoning his jacket. 'I can't help wondering if the Admiral had anything to do with it. There's no denying that Heydrich's death is unbelievably good luck for him. There'll be no more talk of the SS swallowing up the Abwehr now! It'd be just like the Admiral to bring about what he wanted in such a roundabout way. He has a most Machiavellian mind. But Old Whitehead seemed genuinely moved at the news.'

'What will happen now?' Ava asked.

Leo looked sombre. 'There'll be reprisals. Hitler will demand blood.'

Hot Coal

Blood was what Hitler got.

Two Czechoslovakian villages accused of harbouring the assassins were razed to the ground. Every man was shot. Every woman and child was sent to a concentration camp. Over a thousand people died, and more than thirteen thousand people were imprisoned or deported.

It was not just Czechoslovakians who suffered. Hundreds of Jews in Berlin were shot, or deported, in retaliation for the Lustgarten bomb. Ava heard that the Gestapo were planning to accelerate the transportations. Not even those Jews who worked as slaves in the factories and sweatshops would be spared.

Ava went as often as she could to the Jewish Community office, desperate for news of Jutta's friends. It was there that she heard that Herbert Baum had died in prison. The official verdict was that he had committed suicide. The rumour was that he had been beaten to death. A few weeks later, Ava found out that ten of Jutta's friends had been found guilty of high treason and condemned to death. Sala Kochmann had flung herself down an air shaft, trying to kill herself. She fractured her skull and her spine, and was taken to her execution on a stretcher. Jutta seemed most distressed about the fate of one of the young men, who she called Heini.

Ava was able to discover that he was not amongst those executed, which comforted her friend a little.

In the meantime, Jutta lived secretly in the coal cellar, in constant fear of being caught by Leo or Frau Wirth, rarely going outside, rarely seeing the sky. She grew thin and pale, her eyes far too big for her emaciated face. All her fire had been quenched.

Whenever she could, Ava gave Jutta her identification papers so that she could walk in the Tiergarten and get some fresh air and sunshine. She went to the cinema for the first time in years, and sat on a park bench without fear of harassment. It was terribly dangerous. Although both had dark curly hair, they looked nothing alike. No policeman would accept that Jutta was the same girl as the photograph on Ava's papers. It was worth it, though, for the look on Jutta's face when she came home.

One day, in late summer, a letter arrived from Switzerland.

Ava seized it with a cry of joy. She always loved letters from her sister and father, and had covered one wall of the kitchen with crayon drawings from Angelika.

'Bertha is getting married!' Ava told Leo, looking up from the letter. 'Can you believe it? I knew that she had been seeing someone . . . but . . . marrying them? She's asked me to come. Oh, I wish I could.'

Leo looked up from the papers he was reading. 'When is the wedding?'

'The end of September.'

Leo rubbed at the fair stubble on his chin. 'It could be arranged. Perhaps.'

'Really?' Ava gazed at him hopefully. 'Oh, that would be wonderful.'

'The Abwehr can arrange safe conduct passes out of Germany.' Leo smiled at her. 'They don't usually do so for weddings.'

'But you could ask?'

'I could. I can't promise anything.'

Ava watched as he put his foot down on Zeus's back, rubbing the dog's loose skin back and forth. 'It may actually be quite useful,' he said at last.

'Really? How?'

'Let me talk to the Admiral.'

A few days later, Leo came home early, startling Jutta and Ava who had been out in the garden, tending the vegetable plot. The sound of the car driving into the garage sent Jutta scrambling into the house. She whisked through the kitchen door just as Leo opened the gate and stepped onto the grass.

He frowned. 'Is someone here?'

Ava shook her head, unable to meet his eyes. 'Oh, no. Just me and Zeus. Look at our eggplants, Leo? Aren't they perfectly beautiful?'

'I have good news for you.'

'You can get a pass for me? Really?'

'Yes. But only if you are happy to work for the Abwehr, in a temporary position, as it were.'

'Work for the Abwehr? What do you mean?'

'Just let me get changed and get myself a beer, and I'll tell you all about it.'

Ava went into the kitchen with him, to wash the dirt from her hands. Two coffee cups sat on the draining board. Ava rushed to stand in front of them, trying to hide the cups from Leo's eyes, but he was too quick for her. 'So you've had a friend over today?' he asked.

'Just Libertas.' Ava tried to answer nonchalantly, but she knew her cheeks were flaming.

'We must have dinner with them some time,' Leo replied. His eyes were steady on her face.

'That's a lovely idea.'

It was a lie. Ava knew it was impossible to spend long in the company of the Schulze-Boysens without beginning to talk about Hitler and the war. Harro and Libertas were obsessed, unable to think about anything else. It was as if the secret of their resistance had dug so deep a groove into their brains, they could sing no other tune. She was the same. It was why she had made no other friends at the Philharmonie. The other music students were like an alien species, so full of pride and pleasure that most of Europe now lay under Germany's boot. It was too much of a strain, being with them and trying to be like them.

Leo regarded her a moment longer, then went to change out of his uniform. Ava put the cups away with shaking hands. Her feelings were in turmoil. Part of her badly wanted to confide in Leo. It would be so much easier if he knew Jutta was staying in their house. Yet Ava dared not tell him. Jutta was a Jew. She was wanted by the Gestapo. Leo worked for military intelligence. Ava was risking his job – indeed, his very life – by hiding Jutta. If only she could be sure that Leo would not turn her friend in. The report Ava had found in his desk still troubled her deeply. *The liquidation had been successfully concluded before 9 am . . .* Such cold, clinical language for the murder of thousands and thousands of innocent people. Ava knew that Leo abhorred the unnecessary slaughter of so many German soldiers on the Russian front. She knew that he and his fellow officers at the Abwehr were involved in some kind of conspiracy to bring down Hitler. What she did not know was if Leo would risk everything to save one frightened Jewish girl. Ava could not gamble with Jutta's life.

When Leo came down, Ava had set up the little table on the terrace with candles and a little bunch of flowers and herbs. She did love to make things pretty. Leo came out with a bottle of beer, beaded with moisture, and two tall glasses.

It was a beautiful evening. In this small, walled garden, it was easy to forget that just streets away houses lay in ruins and hospitals were jam-packed with wounded soldiers whose lives had been blasted apart with their bodies.

'The thing is, we have a group of agents who must travel to Switzerland as soon as possible.' Leo's voice was neutral. 'We need permission from Herr Reichsführer Himmler for any safe passes out of Germany. He has given his permission, but not willingly. He feels he has reason to be suspicious . . .'

'Why?' Ava asked.

He flashed a look up at her. 'Most of them are Jews.'

'Oh.' Ava was surprised. She had not expected that.

'Some of them are quite elderly, and not very well. Others are very young. That is, of course, the point. We don't want all our agents to look like . . . well, like spies. We need someone to travel with them, to look after them and make sure that all goes well. Usually . . . well, usually I'd travel with them, or some other experienced Abwehr agent. But we have other games afoot at the moment . . . and you want to go at the same time. It seemed like too good a chance to pass up . . . if you are up for it.'

'Yes! Of course. I'd love to.' Ava's face was alight.

'It may be . . . a bit chancy,' he warned her. 'You'll need to keep your head, no matter what happens.'

'I don't care. I want to do something to help.'

Leo regarded her closely, then nodded his head. 'Very well. I'll arrange it.'

Ava walked in the Tiergarten with Libertas, Zeus tugging eagerly at the lead.

'I have a friend,' Ava said. 'I need to get her out of the country. I've been offered a safe conduct pass to go to my sister's wedding in Switzerland. Do you know of any way I could get my friend across the border too?'

Libertas tapped her cheek thoughtfully. 'Perhaps. Is she a Jew?'

Ava nodded, and her friend sighed. 'That makes it so much harder. It means we have to get her a false passport and ID papers. And the Gestapo are really cracking down on forgers at the moment. So many Jews desperate to escape the deportation lists. I don't think it's possible right now.'

'Could I hide her somehow?' Ava had a sudden image of trying to squish Jutta into her suitcase, and bit back a hysterical laugh.

'There's an idea,' Libertas said. 'A friend of mine has been hiding Jews in furniture crates and sending them on the train to Sweden. It's tricky, but not impossible. We'd all help. All you need is someone in Switzerland willing to hide her.'

'My father would. He's known Jutta since she was a baby.'

Ava went home, filled with excitement, but Jutta only shook her head. 'Thank you, Ava. I appreciate it. I really do. But I can't leave Mama and Father, and I can't leave my friends.'

'But, Jutta . . .'

'I just can't, Ava. I'd feel I was abandoning them. Please don't tempt me.'

Ava nodded, filled with disappointment and anxiety. 'But what will you do? I'll be gone a few days. I can leave enough food for you . . . but what if there's an air-raid and Leo comes down to the cellar?'

'There's a coal-vent,' Jutta said. 'I can climb out that way.'

'It's so dangerous.' Ava gnawed at her thumbnail, then came to a decision. 'Take my papers, Jutta. I'll go and get some new ones. I'll tell them they were stolen, or something.'

'Are you sure? You'll be put on a Gestapo list if you do.'

'I'm sure. I have to do something to help you.'

A few days later, with her new passport and identification papers, Ava went to the station in a state of high tension. She was leaving Germany for the first time, she was going to see her beloved father and her sister and little Angelika, and she was working as a courier for the Abwehr. It all seemed so strange and so exciting.

Ava was rather confounded when she met the group of people she was accompanying to Switzerland. An elderly man, leaning heavily on a stick. His wife and nineteen-year-old daughter. A frail-looking Jewish woman who guided the steps of her blind husband, two young daughters clinging close behind. A widow in black with two frightened-looking teenage daughters. An elderly doctor and his wife. An anxious-faced young woman carrying a cello. A middle-aged lawyer with pince-nez and his wife and sons, aged about ten and eight. Many of them wore big yellow stars on the front and back of their coats.

They looked most unlikely spies.

The first hurdle came with getting them all onto the train. The police examined everyone's papers very closely and with expressions of utmost incredulity. The teenage girls looked sick with fear, and the old man – whose name was Herr Fliess – tried to bluster. Ava put on what she called her 'Gertrud face', saying haughtily, 'It is not for you to question the Reichsführer's orders. These people are in the employ of the Abwehr, and must be given free passage.'

The police begrudgingly allowed them to board. The train did not leave on time, however, and then two men in dark suits came and began to question them all again. They demanded to know what role each played in the Abwehr. The lawyer, whose name was Herr Arnold, managed to fob them off by talking about secret codes, but then they turned to the young woman with the cello and demanded to know her task.

'Fräulein Baxter is one of our most important operatives,' Ava said sharply. 'She is to travel to New York to give a concert there, and will be gathering information for the Abwehr while in the United States.'

One of the Gestapo men bent and poked the eight-year-old's teddy bear. 'I suppose you have secret documents hidden in there,' he said sarcastically.

'Exactly,' Ava responded. 'Now can we please be allowed to proceed? Some of our agents have important rendezvous to make!'

The Gestapo man grunted, and left the carriage. Ava sank back onto the hard leather seat as the train at last began to puff and wheeze its way out of the station. Her blood was zinging with adrenalin.

It was a long journey, and everyone did their best to sleep. Ava could not rest, though. She talked in low undertones to the others. They made no attempt to pretend they really were spies. The teenage girls confessed they were old school friends of Brigitte Canaris, the Admiral's daughter. Their widowed mother was Jewish, and had received her deportation notice. Renate Baxter, the girl with the cello, told Ava that her aunt was a Protestant who had found out, much to her dismay, that she was classified as a Jew under the Nuremburg Laws. She had worked at the Confessing Church with Dietrich Bonhoeffer, and had escaped to Switzerland two weeks earlier, as a test to see if the ruse would work. Herr Arnold was another Protestant regarded as Jewish by the Reich. Herr Fliess, meanwhile, was a decorated war hero. All of them were escaping deportation to the east.

The sun rose and revealed a beautiful landscape of green meadows, dark forests, and shining lakes and rivers, brooded over by wise-faced mountains wrapped in shawls of white. The two boys pressed their faces against the grimy glass, exclaiming in excitement. Their mother began to weep. 'I can't believe that we've made it! I can't believe that we're free.'

'We aren't free yet,' her husband said.

The Swiss police were just as severe and suspicious as their German counterparts, but Ava had made sure that everyone's papers were in perfect order and was able to pass off any questions with ease. The Swiss were most concerned with how the emigrants were to support themselves once in Switzerland, and Ava was able to show them the proof that the Abwehr had transferred funds to a Swiss bank for their use.

As the party rather shakily made their way off the station and into the street, Ava rummaged in her bag and withdrew a pair of nail scissors. 'Let's cut off those stars! You never have to wear them again!'

Ava's work was not yet over. She had to meet with a Swiss diplomat to pass on a packet of secret documents that she had carried in a false compartment in her shoe. She had asked Leo what was in the documents. He had hesitated, then told her that Hitler found Switzerland's neutrality intolerable and had asked the Gestapo for plans to force it into an Anschluss and turn it into a police state. If the Swiss knew, they could make sure it did not happen.

Carrying those documents had been like having a hot coal burning in her shoe.

It was a joy to see her father – fatter and balder than ever – and a plump and smiling Bertha, looking prettier than she had in years. Angelika was the real surprise. She was a tall, slim six year old, with long plaits and a gap-toothed smile. She ran about as nimbly as any other child her age, and spoke eagerly with only a slight thickness to her diction.

'However did you get permission to come?' Bertha cried, when they had all hugged and kissed. 'Monika couldn't get a pass, and she works for a very important man at the Schutzstaffel.'

'I'm married to a very important man at the Abwehr,' Ava smiled.

All was buzz and bustle ahead of Bertha's wedding that afternoon, but Ava managed to have a few moments alone with her father. He took her hand, and asked her, very seriously, if she was happy.

Ava nodded. 'Yes, Father. Leo is a good man. I've been lucky.'

'Do . . . do you love him?'

'With all my heart,' she answered simply.

Otto's worried expression eased. He squeezed her hand. 'I'm glad. To love and be loved is the most important thing in this world. Your mother taught me that.'

He then began to talk to her with great excitement about the ideas of Herr Doktor Jung, and his theory of the shadow archetype. Ava listened, her heart swelling with love for him.

The wedding was long and luxurious, and the stout, balding bridegroom beamed with pride at his meringue-puff of a wife. Much champagne flowed, and many speeches were made. Ava was tired after her sleepless night, but very glad to see her sister look so happy. Her new husband Herr Bergmann seemed kind, and he was gentle with Angelika and listened patiently as she babbled away.

At last Ava rose and excused herself. 'I have an early train in the morning,' she said.

Otto caught her hand. 'Must you go back? Can't you stay here longer?'

Ava shook her head. 'I need to get home. Leo needs me.'

With a spring of her heart, she knew it was true.

When Ava saw her husband waiting for her at the train station in Berlin, she dropped her suitcase and ran into his arms. All around them, people rushed past, eager to be on their way, but neither Ava nor Leo noticed. Steam drifted past like the exhalation of some fierce iron beast.

'I'm so glad you're safe home,' Leo said, when at last he drew away. 'I've been so worried.'

'Thank you!' Ava cried. 'Oh, thank you!'

He smiled. 'You were glad to see your father? How was the wedding?'

'It was all wonderful . . . but that's not it. You saved them . . . you saved those poor people. Oh, Leo . . .' She took a deep breath, nerves fluttering in the pit of her stomach, then gripped his arm with both hands, looking up into his face with determined eyes. 'You need to know. My friend, Jutta . . . Rupert's sister . . . she's been hiding in our cellar.'

'I wondered who it was,' Leo said.

'You knew?'

'I guessed a while ago,' he told here. 'I was hoping you'd tell me.'

'I . . . I didn't want to put you in a difficult situation.'

'I'm already in a difficult situation. We all are.' He sighed. 'I'm sorry, Ava, but she cannot stay. It's too dangerous.'

'I've been very careful, I've kept her hidden, nobody knows.' Ava's eyes filled with tears at the thought of losing Jutta.

He stopped her with a gentle touch. 'I do not mean it's too dangerous for us, Ava. I mean it's too dangerous for her.'

Ava stared at him. 'What do you mean?'

He fixed her with an intense, frowning gaze. 'You know some of the work we are doing at the Abwehr, Ava. It grows more dangerous by the hour. You'll have to tell her to find somewhere else to hide.'

'There's nowhere. All her friends are dead, or in prison, or on the run. The Gestapo are hunting for her.'

Leo frowned. 'Ava, how can you be so reckless? Don't you know the risks you run?'

Ava nodded. 'Of course I do. The same risks as you.' She looked up into his face, shadowed by the stern field-grey cap. His uniform no longer frightened her. Ava knew it was only camouflage, like a moth with predator eyes painted on its wings. 'I'm sorry I didn't tell you about Jutta. I was trying to protect you. Can you understand that?'

Leo drew Ava close into the safety of his arms. 'Of course. I'd do anything to keep you safe.'

'Maybe it's time we began to trust each other. I'll make a deal with you. I'll tell you my secrets, if you tell me yours.'

His face was troubled. 'But it's better if you don't know . . . if things go wrong . . .'

'I'd rather know. I'd rather face it with you.'

He pressed his cheek into her hair. 'Oh God, Ava . . . I wish we lived in some other place, at some other time . . .'

'But we don't. We can only live the life we've been given as best we can.'

He drew an unsteady breath. 'I am so glad I found you,' he whispered. 'Oh, Ava, you . . . you're the only thing that makes sense in this world.'

'I'm the lucky one.' Ava raised her face to kiss him. 'What would have happened to me without you? I'd be lost.'

Smoke swirled around them, hiding them from the world.

Our Death Must Be a Beacon

In early August, Ava found a message from Libertas hidden at the statue of the Amazon. 'Meet me tomorrow!' it said. So Ava got up early the next day, made sure Jutta had some food and water, then took Zeus out for his early walk. The big dog trotted along the path at her side, tail wagging, enjoying the rich scents of the summer morning. Ava went to the statue of the two German folk singers, surrounded by trees and bushes, and found Libertas waiting there, her fingers twisting and untwisting.

'What is it? What's wrong?' Ava asked her.

Libertas took her arm and began to walk rapidly along the path, talking in a low undertone. 'Ava! You'll never guess. The Russians have parachuted two spies into Germany. They're here in Berlin, pretending to be soldiers on leave. We don't know what to do with them! They need somewhere to stay. Can you take them?'

Ava shook her head, thinking of Jutta who was still hiding in their cellar. 'I'm sorry, I can't! What are they doing here?'

'They've brought us a new radio. You know the last one was broken. They want more information. I don't know what we can tell them. Oh, Ava, what are we going to do? Where can we hide them? Arvid and Mildred have gone away for the summer - you know she's not been well.

If we could get them to their summer house, perhaps . . . but how are we to get them there?'

'It's too dangerous,' Ava said. 'You'll have to tell them you can't help.'

'But if they're caught . . . they'll be tortured and they'll talk. Ava, they had our address! They knew where to come.'

Ava thought rapidly. 'You'll have to hide them, but tell them they cannot stay! They must go just as soon as possible.'

Libertas's blue eyes were filling with tears. She dabbed at them with her wisp of a lacy handkerchief. 'Our apartment is too small . . . and we have such a strict block warden! She doesn't like me, she's thinks I'm frivolous, and she's already suspicious about how many people we have traipsing in and out. Oh, Ava, can't you take them? You have a house and don't have to share an air-raid shelter and the Tiergarten is just across the road.'

'I can't,' Ava said firmly. 'It's impossible. Libertas, my husband works for the Abwehr! How can you possibly think I could hide two Russian spies under his very nose?'

Her shoulders slumped. 'I will have to ask the Schumachers. They're artists, people come and go at all sorts of strange hours there. Surely no-one will notice two more.'

'I can bring you some food,' Ava promised. 'Some potatoes and eggs, at the very least.'

'Thank you,' Libertas managed to say. Her face was very white, her eyes strained.

Ava took her a basket of food later that day, and heard the Russian spies had been moved to the Schumachers. Ava felt uneasy, and could only hope they would soon disappear the way they had come.

On 23 August, the Luftwaffe bombed Stalingrad into rubble. The newspapers were full of photos of the city burning, black smoke rising high into the sky. It was an inferno. Everyone was sure the city must soon fall. 'The Führer cannot lose!' a woman in the bakery queue said. 'He'll crush those Russians like a bug.'

Ava was worried about the Russian spies. It was far too dangerous to have them here, in Berlin. She looked for messages from Libertas hidden at the statues in the Tiergarten, but there was nothing.

A few more days passed. Ava's anxiety was now acute. She talked it over with Jutta, who was sure that it was a sign Libertas had been caught by the Gestapo.

'It's not safe for you here,' Ava told her. 'If the Gestapo come and search the house, they'll find you. Is there anywhere else you can go? Just till I know all is well.'

'I'll go and hide in the old Jewish cemetery at Weissensee,' Jutta said at once. 'It's warm enough to camp out for a few days. I've got your old papers so I should be safe if I'm stopped and questioned.'

Ava filled up a bag of food from the garden and gave her a blanket, then Jutta slipped away into the Tiergarten. Ava bundled all her hair up and hid it under a scarf, and then put on her oldest frock and her plimsolls. She wanted to be as inconspicuous as possible.

It was only a short walk from the train station to the Schulze-Boysens' apartment on Altenburger Allee. Ava reassured herself the whole way there that Libertas would be fine. She was just letting the tension of the city wear down her nerves. Her step quickened as she walked down the street, her eagerness to see Libertas safe and well driving her on.

Then Ava noticed a car parked across the road from her apartment. Two men sat in the car. One was reading a newspaper, the other was smoking a cigarette and looking irritable. Ava walked straight past them, and around the corner. There was a tight pain in her chest, as if she had swallowed stones. She went to the gardens of Charlottenburg Palace, and walked and walked along the winding paths till she was sure she had not been followed.

Ava was hot and tired and footsore by now, but she could not rest. She had to warn Libertas somehow. She drew some paper out of her satchel and scrawled a few words on it with her fountain pen. 'Dear Libs. Getting rather hot in Berlin. Time to take a holiday! X.'

Then Ava went back down Altenburger Allee, the folded paper in her hand. The two men were still in the car. She walked past them, not looking their way. Ava heard the man's newspaper rustle as he lowered it to look at her. She was finding it hard to breathe.

As she approached the front door of Libertas' apartment block, it opened. Libertas came out. She was in a dark suit with sensible shoes and carried a small suitcase. Her fair hair was hidden under a scarf. She saw Ava, and her face whitened. She shook her head, almost imperceptibly, then turned and walked away. She was walking towards the train station.

Ava heard a car door open. Heavy feet hurrying. She bent and pretended to do up her shoelace. A man grunted, 'Out of the way.' Ava stood up and turned. 'Oh, sorry,' she said, and did that silly back-and-fro dance one sometimes does when trying to pass someone in the street. He pushed past her and hurried after Libertas. The other man was right behind him.

Ava followed along behind. Libertas was walking fast, but the two men were catching up. Ava tried to think what she could do. Could she steal their car, race up beside Libertas, fling open the door for her, then speed away? If only Ava knew how to steal a car.

There was a train drawing in to the station. Libertas began to run. The men did too. They were burly men, though, and wore long leather coats. Libertas was fleet and light-footed. She dashed up the steps and along the bridge over the road. Ava pressed both her hands together. *Run!*

Down the steps Libertas bounded, her fair hair flowing behind her. She leapt onto the train and slammed the door shut behind her. The Gestapo men hurled themselves down the stairs. The conductor was blowing his whistle and dropping his flag. Black smoke swirled about the train. Ava closed her eyes. *Please. Please.*

There was no hiss of steam, no sound of train wheels moving forward.

Ava opened her eyes. The train stood motionless. Curious heads craned out the windows. The men in leather coats dragged Libertas from the carriage. One of them wrested her little suitcase from her. She was crying.

Ava could do nothing. She walked away at a steady pace, scrunching the note into her damp hand.

*

One week, the camp was full of Jews.

The next, none were left. Only Rupert and a few dozen others thought essential to the smooth running of the camp. All the others were sent east, a place of darkest foreboding.

Rupert was saved only because of his long nimble fingers, and his skill with a trumpet.

Commandant Koch was gone. Sent east too. There were rumours he was under investigation, for theft, for embezzlement, for murder. It seemed a fine joke. Surely a SS Commandant could steal and beat and kill as he pleased?

The new Commandant was not much better. His name was Hermann Pister. He amused himself by forcing the exhausted prisoners to do calisthenics in the darkness before each dawn.

Rupert wondered where all the Jews had gone. He wondered why he had been spared. He tried to make himself invisible. His yellow triangle was so stained and tattered, perhaps they had not realised he was a Jew at all?

His sardine tin was crammed full of fragments of paper, flotsam and jetsam of words. He wrote now with a quill made from an old feather, and ink made from oak glass and rusty nails. Just keep on writing, he told himself. White pages, white wings.

Heinz Rotholz was executed on 10 December, along with many of Jutta's friends. Harro and Libertas and their friends were executed a few weeks later, two days before Christmas.

Ava found it hard to manage everyday life. The smallest things cut her. Light slanting through icicles. Music through an open window. A child jumping through a skipping rope. Any moment of sudden unexpected beauty. She and Jutta stayed inside, huddled by the fire, reading Rilke's poetry, pierced through again and again with horror, with sorrow, with guilt.

Who, if I cried out, would hear me among the angelic orders? Even if one pressed me suddenly against his heart, I would vanish . . . for beauty is nothing but the beginning of terror . . . every angel is terrible . . . and so I hold myself back and swallow the cry of a darkened sobbing . . . oh, and the night, the night, when the wind full of cosmic space gnaws at our faces . . . fling out of your arms the emptiness . . . maybe the birds will feel the rush of air with more passionate flying . . .

Ava did not know what she would have done without Jutta. The two friends clung together, comforting each other as best they could. Sometimes it was Jutta who broke down and Ava who tended her. Sometimes Jutta was the stronger one. Together, apart, they wept till it felt as if there were no more tears left in their bodies, then wept again.

Jutta understood, in a way few people could, the soul-excoriating guilt Ava felt that Libertas was dead and Ava was alive. She too had lost her friends to torture and betrayal and execution. In those dark weeks, Ava grew closer to Jutta than she had ever been to her own sisters.

One afternoon, in the cold darkness of the winter, there was a knock on the door. Both Jutta and Ava froze. Paralysed by terror. The knock came again. Gentle. Polite. It was not hammering. Not shouting. Ava managed to get up, lay down the book of poems she had been reading, and silently point Jutta towards the cellar. Ava locked her in, hid the key, then opened the door. A man in a chauffeur's uniform stood outside. He bowed to Ava, then went to open the door of a long silver Mercedes drawn up at the curb. An elegant older woman stepped out, wrapped in fur. Her hair was a soft silvery-blonde and perfectly set. Her face was thin and drawn, her eyes a luminous blue. It was Viktoria Gräfin zu Eulenburg.

Libertas's mother.

'She spoke of you to me,' the Countess said. 'I thought you would like to hear of her last days and read her letter.'

Ava made her chicory coffee, and they sat together in the sitting room as snow spat against the windows. The fire was low, and Ava added more of their precious fuel so Libertas's mother would not be cold.

The Countess told Ava that Libertas had refused to speak to the Gestapo, despite all their cruelty. They had found her youth and beauty so disarming that they had been ordered to interrogate her in pairs, so that one policeman could stiffen the other's spine if he was overcome

313

with remorse or desire. Eventually they had tricked her, by putting another woman in the cell with her. The woman had won her confidence, and Libertas had entrusted her with warning other members of the resistance circle. The other woman had, however, been a Gestapo spy. The Gestapo had then taunted Libertas with betraying her friends, so that she went to her death heartbroken and ashamed.

It was just mere chance that Ava had escaped the Gestapo's torture cellars. If Libertas had not seen her just moments before she was arrested, then her friend would have tried to warn her too.

The Countess let Ava read Libertas's last letter.

What I was allowed to experience in these last days is so grand and magnificent that words can barely describe it. I still had to drain a bitter cup: a human being, in whom I had trusted completely, Gertrud Breiter, betrayed me (and you). But 'now eat the fruit of your deeds, he who betrays, is betrayed' . . . I, too, out of selfishness, have betrayed friends – I wanted to be free and come to you – but believe me, I suffered indescribable guilt feelings for my deed. Now everyone has forgiven me. We are approaching the end with a sense of community, which is possible only in the face of death. Without sorrow, without bitterness. I also know now about the last things of faith, and I know that you are strong and joyful in the awareness of eternal solidarity. Your angel, who stabs the devil (you sent it to me for my birthday), is standing in front of me . . . If I could ask you for one thing: Tell everyone, everyone, everyone of me. Our death must be a beacon.

The words danced before Ava's eyes. She had a hot, hard lump in her throat. Libertas, her dear bright, beautiful friend. It seemed impossible that she was dead and Ava was alive.

She read the letter again, and only then did the name of her betrayer leap out at her. Gertrud Breiter. Ava lay the letter down carefully, so she would not crumple it in her hand. Rage like she had never felt before flashed through her.

For the first time in her life, she understood what it was to hate.

Part IV

White Feathers
January 1943 – July 1944

*The dove said to her, 'For seven years I must fly about the world.
Every seven steps I will let fall a drop of red blood and a
white feather. These will show you the way, and if you
follow this trail you can redeem me.'*

'The Singing, Springing Lark', the Brothers Grimm

Evil Incarnate

Reasons Not to Kill Hitler:

1. We have sworn an oath on our honour, and to break that oath is to be dishonoured.
2. Assassination is just another word for murder. Murder is wrong.
3. Killing is too good for him. He needs to be captured, put on trial, and made to realise just what evil he has done.
4. It'll only make a martyr of him.
5. The Nazi Party is a many-headed monster. Cut off one head, and another ten will spring to life.
6. The reprisals will be horrific.
7. It's impossible. The man is surrounded by bodyguards, and rides in an armour-plated Mercedes. No-one except his inner circle can ever get near him.

Reasons to Kill Hitler:

He is evil incarnate.

Leo was used to making lists and plans. It was part of his job. He found that the very act helped to clarify his thoughts. This list he was writing now would have to be burnt. It was too dangerous to keep. Yet it made him feel that he was in control of the chaos that was the world, to neatly and precisely draw up a list. Even a list that plotted murder and treason.

It was long past midnight, and Leo's study was full of young men in uniforms. Their talk seemed to go around and around in circles, spinning about one immoveable point like the painted animals of a merry-go-round.

Should we kill Hitler?

The defeat at Stalingrad had just been announced. It had been the bloodiest battle in the history of warfare. Nearly half-a-million German soldiers had died. Germany now had to face the very real possibility of defeat in this ill-advised war. For the first time, Hitler's aura of invincibility had been pierced.

It's time, Leo thought, *to strike.*

Helmuth James Graf von Moltke, the only man in civilian dress, spoke in a low, grave voice. 'We must realise that not only do we face the very real possibility of defeat, but that we have all been drawn into colluding with evil. What has been happening in our country is wrong, very wrong. And all of us are responsible for each and every terrible deed that has been committed.'

Leo set his jaw. He was afraid the Graf was correct. There was a low mutter. Some of the officers looked angry. A few protested.

'We were just doing our duty.'

'How were we supposed to stop it?'

'It wasn't us, it was the death squads.'

Moltke spread his hands. 'We allowed this evil to take root in our soil, and we fed it the blood that allowed it to flourish. We shut our eyes to its dreadful flowering. We must take responsibility for that.'

Leo thought about the word *evil*. It was a word Moltke had used often that evening. Yet it was not a word many people used anymore. Yet Leo felt sure that if evil had ever existed on the face of this earth, it existed here and now, in Germany. He had seen it.

Moltke was speaking again. 'I cannot tell you what to do, or what to choose. I cannot make your decisions for you. I can only tell you what I have realised. I have fought Nazism from the very beginning, because I loathed what it was doing to our great country, our land of poets and philosophers. But I have come to realise that this is a bigger struggle.'

The Graf was pale and weary. He put one hand on the mantelpiece to steady himself, and looked around the crowded room. All eyes were fixed on his face. 'This is a battle between good and evil,' Moltke went on, 'and if we lose it's the soul of the whole world that will be plunged into darkness. This war is not about which country stands victor at the end. This is about standing up to evil. I had lost my faith. I had thought it did not matter. But I was wrong, very wrong. It matters more than it has ever mattered before. The only way we can defeat this evil is if we believe, with all our hearts, in the existence . . . and the importance . . . of good, and if we fight for it, even to the death.'

Moltke fell silent, then gave a strained smile. 'Thank you for listening to me. I am sure I do not need to remind you how very dangerous this is. Good men have died already for less than this. I hope you are all noble hearted and loyal to each other and our cause. Good night.'

He bowed. All the young men saluted him, in the old way, and clicked their heels together. It was a little thunder. Leo's heart quickened, as if he readied himself for a race. Then the Graf left, accompanied by a small group of men with hard determined faces. They all slipped out the back door, into the frosty starlit night. One by one, the others left too, each being careful to let no snippet of light escape the house.

At last they had all gone. Leo took his list, and dropped it onto the fire. He watched the page curl and blacken and be devoured by flame.

Nazism had seemed like such a grand adventure, in the beginning. He and his brother had been like children, pretending sticks were guns and saucepans were helmets. They had loved wearing the brown uniform, and being taught how to march, and talking big glorious words of blood and soil and fury. Then Alex had died. Leo had been like the back half of a pantomime horse, prancing and playing but not seeing where he was going. Without Alex, half of him – the half that had seen the way forward – was gone. He had to stumble onwards, blind and numb with pain, going where he was told, doing as he was ordered. He had clung to the only thing that had seemed to make sense. The promises of his Führer.

Then he had met Ava. She had been the sugar to his potassium chlorate. Only a spark needed for instant fire and utter transformation.

Ava had blasted open his defences. She had made him feel again, when he had thought he was anesthetised to all emotion.

Now Leo was sickened by his own stupidity.

He and his fellow conspirators had tried hard to stop Hitler. They had smuggled out Jews when they could. Five hundred had escaped Amsterdam thanks to the Abwehr. That had been a victory of sorts. But what was five hundred compared to the hundreds of thousands who had not escaped?

They had only managed to get fifteen out of Berlin. Fifteen. More than fifty thousand had been deported so far, to ghettos in the east, and to concentration camps and killing fields. And saving those fifteen had been a terrible risk. The Admiral had had to confront Himmler directly. 'How do you expect me to carry on with the work of the Abwehr, Herr Reichsführer, if your people keep arresting my agents?' he had said. The wily old fox.

The Abwehr had also tried to sabotage the war as much as they could without revealing the double game they played. They had protected those who resisted Hitler. They had fed covert intelligence to the Allies and to the Pope. Admiral Canaris had tried to negotiate personally with the British and the Americans, only to be rudely rejected. The Allies thought it was a trick, a ruse. Only that week, Churchill and Roosevelt had declared that Germany must surrender unconditionally. Any hope that Canaris or the generals could negotiate a diplomatic end to the war had been crushed.

At least they had managed to stop Hitler invading Switzerland, Leo thought. That was one country that was not being trampled under the Nazis' jackboots.

But the Abwehr had not been able to stop the war. And Himmler was suspicious. Leo was afraid that the Reichsführer had baited a steel trap for the Abwehr, and it could be sprung at any time.

Leo heard a step behind him, and turned. Ava stood in the doorway, dressed in a plain dark frock, her hair falling in a tumult down her back. Her eyes were shadowed with fear, but her chin was lifted with that resolute tilt he so loved.

'You were listening?' he asked.

She nodded. 'What are you going to do?'

Leo shrugged. 'It's an impossible situation. Do we kill the Führer, the man we are all sworn to serve and obey? That would make us traitors to our homeland. Yet if we continue to serve him, we are complicit in unspeakable acts of cruelty and murder.'

'Is there no other choice?'

He rolled his shoulders. 'There was a plan to lock him up in a madhouse at one point! And I believe there's been talk of a British commando troop parachuting in and kidnapping him. The problem is he's so heavily guarded. No-one can get close enough to him.'

Outside a blackbird began to warble. Leo went to the window and drew back the blackout curtain. Fiery streaks marked the eastern horizon like the smear of divine fingerprints.

He looked at Ava. 'Do you want to walk with me?'

At the word 'walk', Zeus's tail began to wag.

'All right,' Ava said, and went to get her coat.

Together they stepped through the stillness of the Tiergarten. Trees rose in black and silver fretwork on either side, silhouetted against the burnished sky. Zeus ran across the lawn, nose to the ground, his paws leaving dark streaks against the frost. A robin hopped to a branch, his red breast the same colour as the fingers of light in the east. A star glinted, latticed in twigs.

Leo was silent, his hands pushed into the pockets of his greatcoat.

'Tell me what you're thinking,' Ava said.

He did not speak for a long time. When at last the words came from his mouth, they were slow and broken, as if forced out.

'After my brother died, I thought nothing mattered. Nothing made sense. There was no God . . . there was no point to it all. We lived, we died, it was all just a . . . a . . . meaningless machine. But then I met you. You said . . . exactly what I was feeling. That the world was going mad. That we were stepping into a void and there was nothing beneath us.'

Ava pressed his arm closer to her.

'But then you said something else. You said that we had to act. We had to try and stop what was happening, or else our lives would have no meaning, our deaths no honour. I knew you were right. I've been trying ever since then to make sure I lived with honour. But Ava . . . I'm so afraid . . .'

When he did not go on, Ava said tentatively: 'Of dying?'

He nodded. 'Oh, yes, of course. Dying. Dying hideously in the cellars of the Gestapo. And I cannot bear to think what they might do to you. But that's not it.' His words began to come more quickly. 'Ava, what Moltke said tonight, about God . . . about the necessity of believing. I have such a longing in me . . . Rilke said it best. "You, the great homesickness we could never shake off . . . You, the forest that always surrounded us . . . You, the song we sang in every silence . . . You, the dark net threading us." That's what I feel. A longing for God. But you say that God is nothing but an infantile delusion.'

Ava did not speak. Her face was troubled.

'So if God is just an infantile delusion, what then of evil? Is that a delusion too?'

'I don't know,' Ava answered at last. 'My father does not believe in good and evil. He thought there were simply instinctual drives to death and self-destruction, or to life and creativity. But if this is true, then Hitler and the Nazis have the strongest death drive the world has ever seen.' Ava was quiet a moment, considering what she had just said. Leo felt such tenderness for her, it was akin to pain. He knew nobody else who would listen as she did, and think ideas through with such gravity. From the moment he had met Ava, Leo had known he could talk to her in a way he could talk to nobody else.

'I do not think the world is a machine without meaning,' Ava said eventually, fixing her eyes upon his face. 'I think love has meaning, and beauty, and music. And if such a thing as evil exists, then surely Hitler is its embodiment? I feel sure that there is goodness in the world, and it's not murder and brutality and force, it's not boots stamping and fists smashing and laughing at people's pain. It's . . . oh, it's kindness and gentleness and trying to understand.'

Leo took her hand. 'What Moltke said tonight . . . it hit me hard. He's right. This is not just about stopping Hitler. It's a battle between good and evil, and it's one we have to fight.'

Ava caught her breath. 'You're going to do it. You're going to kill Hitler.'

Leo nodded, looking away from her towards the fiery dawn. 'I think we must.'

Ava's resistance to the Reich had been reduced to very small things.

She listened to the BBC down in the cellar, wrapping the radio in blankets so the distinctive opening chords – *Ta-ta-ta-dum! Ta-ta-ta-dum!* – would not be overheard. When Ava was forced to raise her arm in the Nazi salute, she subtly spread her fingers in a V-shape. She kept slipping food to the forced labour prisoners, and she did her best to look after Jutta and the Feidlers.

Mildred Harnack was beheaded in mid-February. She had been originally sentenced to six years in prison, but Hitler himself had ordered a new trial and sentence. Ava wept for her gentle, scholarly friend, who had done little more than wish for a better world. Then, two days later, it was reported some university students in Munich had been arrested for distributing anti-Hitler leaflets. After a strident and very public trial, they were guillotined. They had called themselves the White Rose, and were much the same age as Ava. It made her realise just how foolhardy and futile all of their attempts at resistance had been.

Jutta hid one of the leaflets the White Rose had printed in the Wagner statue. Ava folded it into tiny squares and took it home in her shoe so she could read it safely. She sat by the meagre fire, Zeus sitting as close to her as he could get, and unfolded the leaflet.

'Fellow Fighters in the Resistance! Shaken and broken, our people behold the loss of the men of Stalingrad. 330,000 German men have been senselessly and irresponsibly driven to death and destruction by the inspired strategy of our World War I Private First Class. Führer, we thank you!'

Ava gave a shaky laugh. They had been funny, these dead young students.

'We grew up in a state in which all free expression of opinion is unscrupulously suppressed. The Hitler Youth, the SA, the SS have tried to drug us, to revolutionise us, to regiment us in the most promising young years of our lives . . .'

Tears scalded her eyes. Zeus whined and looked up at her.

'Freedom and honour! For ten long years Hitler and his coadjutor have manhandled, squeezed, twisted, and debased these two splendid German words to the point of nausea, as only dilettantes can, casting the highest values of a nation before swine.'

Yes, Ava thought.

'Our people stand ready to rebel against the National Socialists' enslavement of Europe in a fervent new breakthrough of freedom and honour!'

Ava gripped her hands together. It was strange. Although she knew the young idealists who had written this tract were now dead, she no longer felt so alone. Were there truly others out there, resisting with all their strength, like her and Leo?

Leo laid down his pen. He pressed the heels of his hands into his eyes. It was late, and he longed to go home. He had so much work to do, though. It seemed to never end. The Admiral had asked him to compile a report on rumours of atrocities in the East. Leo had been working on the report all week. The thick folder sat before him, neatly labelled, 'Evidence of Breaches of Geneva Convention – Moscow'.

Leo picked up his pen again, and continued his list:

Nikoljskoe – one thousand five hundred psychiatric patients poisoned.

Ershovo – one hundred people blown up in the village church.

Strelechje – four hundred and thirty-five spiritually ill people shot.

Vysoko – ninety burnt alive.

Dubna – forty-two civilians hanged.

Kolodeznaja – fifty civilians shot.

Slobodino – fifteen women raped and killed.

Volokolamsk – six hundred wounded Soviet soldiers burnt alive.

Boljshoe – fifty-six burnt alive.

Worjushino – twenty-six civilians shot. Ten were children.

The file was full of photographs. Young soldiers hanging in rows. Dead people sprawled in streets. A dead woman lying, limbs akimbo, blonde hair matted with mud. A boy lolling against a wall, hands folded as if he was resting. Stiff and blackened corpses flung in a pile. An old man lying on his back, his face bruised and discoloured, his hands flung up in a beseeching gesture, frozen forever.

The photographs haunted Leo. He saw them even when his eyes were shut, even when he slept. He did not think he would ever be free of the horror.

38

Street of Roses

Ava leant her bicycle up against a pole, and looked around quickly to make sure no-one was watching. The lane was empty. She took a small sack of food from her basket and nimbly scaled the high stone wall, using a dangling branch to help her. She lowered the sack down into the cemetery, hiding it behind one of the tall trees that pressed their weight against the wall, causing it to bulge outwards. Then she scrambled back down into the street, mounted her bicycle, and rode swiftly away.

Jutta was living in the cemetery. She slept on the marble floor of a mausoleum, wrapped in blankets, and foraged for food on the streets. Ava brought her supplies whenever she could, but it was difficult in winter when her vegetable garden was lying under snow. The shops were emptier than ever, and food rations had been cut again.

It was a cold evening. The wind from the east was sharp with teeth. Ava bicycled towards the paint factory where Onkel Franz worked. He finished so late that he was unable to get to the shops before they shut, and so Ava hoped to slip him another small sack of food. He and Tante Thea were suffering terribly that cold winter. All Jews had been ordered to surrender their winter coats and blankets, to be sent to the soldiers fighting on the Russian front, and their food ration was barely enough to keep them alive.

Ava turned the corner, and then braked hard. Huge lorries were pulled up outside the paint factory, and SS officers were standing guard, barking dogs on leashes. A long line of Jewish workers shuffled towards the lorries, heads bent. All wore the yellow *Judenstern* on their coats.

'Faster, faster!' a guard bellowed. The weary Jews broke into a stumbling run. They were shoved up into the lorries, the guards clubbing anyone who was too slow.

Ava coasted past, looking desperately for Onkel Franz. He was helping another old man who had been struck in the face. She whistled a few notes from Beethoven's Ninth Symphony. Onkel Franz looked up and saw her. His face lit up at the sight of her. 'Tell Thea,' he mouthed silently. Ava nodded and rode away.

She had to push her bicycle through the crooked laneways of the Scheunenviertel quarter. The streets were crowded with people being marched away from their homes, black-uniformed policemen shouting orders over the babble of cries and protestations. Children wept, or stared uncomprehendingly, women argued, some even fought. One woman was being carried down the steps on a chair, her hands clamped on the seat, refusing to get up. One young man lay on the ground, being kicked. Ava had to turn her face away, unable to bear the sight. She padlocked her bicycle to a street sign, and ran through the maze of little courtyards and alleyways to the apartment block where the Feidlers lived.

Tante Thea was searching through the crowds, calling, 'Franz! Franz!'

Ava rushed up to her and embraced her. 'What is it? What's happening?'

'They're evacuating us all!' Tante Thea sobbed. She grasped Ava's arm with a claw-like hand. 'They say Berlin will be Jew-free by the end of the week. Ava, Franz has not come home from work. None of the men from the factory have come home. I'm so afraid!'

'I saw him being arrested. I'm so sorry.'

'He's a decorated war hero,' Tante Thea said in an unsteady voice. 'They promised he'd be exempt from deportation, they promised.'

'What about you? Are Mischlinge to be deported too?'

'I don't know! I'm only a Mischling of the second degree. I was meant to be safe.' Tante Thea was trembling.

'Let's get you out of here.' Ava steered Tante Thea away from the crowd, looking over her shoulder to make sure no SS officers were watching them. 'Tante Thea, here's my key. Go to our place, heat yourself up some soup. I'll be home as soon as I can.'

'What are you going to do?'

'I'll go and leave a message for Jutta, and then I'll go and talk to Leo. He might be able to find out where Onkel Franz is being held.'

Ava rode back to the Wiessensee cemetery as fast as she could, climbed over the wall, and crept through the graveyard. It was a jungle of towering trees, hanging vines, mossy vaults and broken tombstones, stretching for more than a hundred acres within its tumbledown walls. Ava knew the way to the crypt where Jutta had made her base. She slept there with an ever-changing collection of other Jews who had gone underground. They were called U-boaters.

Ava found Jutta there, and quickly told her what had happened. In wild distress, Jutta started up. 'I'll meet you at home,' Ava told her. 'Be careful, the SS are everywhere.'

Then Ava cycled to Leo's office at the Bendlerblock, where the Abwehr had its headquarters. It was almost fully dark, and snow was falling down from the leaden sky. It melted as soon as it hit the pavement. The city was as lightless as if a blanket had been thrown over it.

Even though it was so late, the Abwehr offices were a hive of activity. Women with frowning faces worked at telephone switchboards, or ran about with arms piled with folders. Young men in uniform worked at desks in rows. As Ava was taken along a long corridor, she saw one officer sleeping on a camp bed in the hallway.

Leo had his own office. He sat surrounded by files, with three telephones on his desk. He looked pale and tired. He closed a folder as Ava came in, and stood up, his face full of worry. 'What is it? What's wrong?'

'There's some kind of major action going on. Onkel Franz has been arrested. Tante Thea is beside herself.' A sudden, unexpected rush of tears suspended her voice. Ava pressed her fingers against her eyes. 'Oh, Leo, can you find out what has happened?'

'I can try. Don't cry, sweetheart. Let's get you safe home, and then I'll see what I can learn.'

'Tante Thea is there.'

'Is she going to move into our cellar too?'

'If she needs to.' Ava smiled at him through a mist of tears.

Goebbels had declared total war.

Rupert and the other prisoners had been forced to stand in the wintry air, wracked by a punishing wind from the east, listening as the Propaganda Minister's shrill voice echoed from the loudspeakers at every corner of the Appellplatz. As Goebbels worked himself up to a high pitch of excitement, his audience had responded with cheers, bursts of wild clapping, and shouts of 'Sieg Heil!'.

'Rise up and let the storm break loose!' Goebbels shrieked, his voice drowned in a gale of relentless applause.

The war had seemed far away and unreal to Rupert, like everything that existed outside the high walls of the camp. In the early years, he and the other prisoners had been forced to listen to many a vainglorious announcement through the speakers. Gradually such broadcasts had faltered. But with Goebbels' declaration the war had again come to Buchenwald.

The prisoners had been busy building a great factory on the outskirts of the camp. In early March, it opened. Rupert was drafted into labour there, thanks to his long and nimble fingers. At first no-one knew what the vast factory was for. Everyone was warned to only look at their own work, and not to ask questions or tell anyone about what they were doing. Sabotage would result in immediate execution.

Each night, though, the men would talk quietly amongst themselves in the hour between their soup and lights out. It soon became clear the factory was producing parts for some kind of new wonder weapon.

'Whatever this weapon is, it is very delicate,' said a French prisoner of war named Lucien. He was small, dark, quick, and had only recently come to Buchenwald, having just been arrested for being a member of the French resistance. 'A bolt not properly fastened, a loose connection, and *boum*! It blows itself up.'

'If they suspect sabotage, they'll kill us all,' said a big Czech.

Lucien shrugged. 'We are soldiers, *n'est-ce-pas*? We fight Hitler wherever we can. And I tell you something more. Where it is I am working, there they make parts for . . . how do you say? *La télégraphie sans fil* . . .'

'Wireless,' Rupert said.

Lucien glanced at him. 'Yes, that is it. Wireless. I take a little here, a little there, and *voila*! I can make us *la radio*. We can listen to the news, play a little music. Maybe even we can use it to send out messages, no?'

Rupert leant forward. 'You could do that?'

'*Oui*. It may take some time. But I have nothing better to do.' He grinned, a quick flash of white teeth in his narrow, dark face.

'What if we are discovered?' another man asked, his hands clenched tightly between his knobbly knees.

'We must make sure we are not discovered. It would be better, though, if we had a cache . . . is that the right word? A cache of weapons. So we can fight back. Yes?' Lucien looked around with bright, expectant eyes.

Rupert gazed at him, speechless. Only then did he realise how much his spirit had been broken. He felt a faint flicker of defiance deep within him.

'They are making rifle parts where I am,' another man said thoughtfully. 'My clothes are so baggy, no-one would notice if I hid a bazooka beneath.'

'They think there is no danger from us, that we are slaves,' Lucien said. 'Well, slaves can revolt, can they not?'

The block elder shouted, 'Lights out!' and the men hurried to their bunks. As Rupert rolled up his ragged trousers to use as a pillow, Lucien stepped towards him. '*Parlez-vous français?*'

'*Je parle un peu de français*,' Rupert replied carefully.

Lucien smiled. '*Bon.* We speak French together, *oui?* They say, do they not, that German is the language to speak to your enemies, French the language to speak to your friends, and Spanish the language to speak with God? We shall be friends and so . . . *comment puis-je dire en francais.*'

As the lights turned out, Rupert felt the sudden, quick pressure of the Frenchman's hand on his shoulder.

Leo did not get home till it was almost dawn. He woke Ava gently.

'Ava, I've found him. It took me a while. They've arrested thousands. He's in the Jewish welfare office on Rosenstrasse in the Mitte.'

She sat up, pushing her hair out of her eyes. 'Can we get him out?'

'I don't think so. I'm sorry, Ava, but this order comes from the top. Himmler is determined that Berlin be Jew-free.'

Ava got up, swallowing her misery. 'I'll let Tante Thea know.'

She woke Tante Thea and told her the news. Tante Thea began to put her shoes on.

'What are you doing?' Ava asked in surprise.

Tante Thea pinned up her hair. 'I'm going to get my husband out.'

'But . . . they won't let him go.'

'I have to try.'

Jutta sat up, her hair sticking out in different directions. 'If Mama is going, then I'm going too!'

'But . . . the SS . . . you might be arrested . . . they'll deport you too!'

'I'd rather be deported with Franz, than stay here, not knowing where he is or what's happening to him.' Tante Thea put on her coat and hat.

Ava threw up her hands. 'I'd better come with you.'

The Rosenstrasse was crowded with women. They clamoured around the SS guard on duty outside the front door. 'Is my husband here? Herr Abromov?'

'You had no right to take my Benjamin! He's exempt! He has the papers to prove it.'

'I want to see my husband! Let me see him!'

'His name is Herr Schwatz. Is he here?'

'You better not have hurt him!'

The SS guards were looking harassed. They gripped their guns, and made no reply.

Somebody began to shout. 'Let us see our husbands! Let us see them now.'

The crowd jostled and pushed at the guards. They pushed back. A woman screamed as she fell. A dozen hands helped her up. The guards shouted, lifting their weapons, warning the women to keep back. The women all ignored them, jostling forward, calling for news.

'It's no use,' Ava said to Tante Thea. 'They won't tell us anything.'

'I'm not leaving here without my husband,' Tante Thea said obstinately. 'They have no right to arrest him. He's done nothing wrong!'

Neither have any of the other thousands of Jews already arrested and deported, Ava wanted to say, but held her tongue. Ava knew Tante Thea did not mean to accuse.

As the day passed, more and more women began to gather outside the welfare office. They began to clap their hands and chant, 'Let our husbands go!' The sound swelled into a roar. Ava felt her throat close over, and her eyes blur with tears. Jutta and Ava linked their arms through Tante Thea's and joined their voices to hers.

One of the policemen shouted back, 'Go now or we'll shoot!'

The crowd cried out in fear and scattered, running to hide. Ava helped Tante Thea as best she could. No shots were fired, though. One brave woman got up from the ground and screamed. 'I don't care! Shoot us! Go ahead and shoot us, you cowards!'

The policemen did not shoot.

Slowly the women came back. The crowd in the street expanded till there were hundreds there, their arms linked, shouting. Tante Thea stood with them, her grey hair straggling round her exhausted face. At noon, Ava went and bought bread and cheese, and shared them out among the crowd.

Again and again the policemen threatened to start shooting. Again and again the women scattered in terror. Each time they came back, and each time the throng grew noisier and more defiant. 'We want our men! Give us back our husbands!'

Night fell, and still the women shouted. People in the surrounding houses and apartments brought down blankets and cups of soup for them. The women quietened at last, but did not leave the square. Many sat on the cobblestones. Some went home, promising to return the next day. Ava tried to persuade Tante Thea and Jutta to leave, but they refused. 'They might try to sneak them out to the railway station if we are not here,' Tante Thea said. 'As long as we stand here, our men cannot be deported.'

Ava went home, but came back with a pail of hot soup, some blankets and pillows. It was a bitterly cold night, but the three women huddled together and talked and laughed and cried. Their tears froze on their faces.

At last the pale dawn light seeped into the sky. The crowd of women stood and stamped their feet, and began to chant again. Many more women came, armed with wooden spoons and saucepans, and they banged away, shouting till they were hoarse.

Trucks rumbled up, loaded with SS soldiers holding machine guns. 'Clear out, or we'll shoot!'

'Go ahead! Shoot!' Arms linked, the women braced themselves.

The soldiers did not shoot.

Emboldened, the women all began to shout and sing again. 'Let our men go!'

They stayed, chanting and shouting, for three days. At last, the men locked up in the old welfare office were released. Onkel Franz was filthy and exhausted, with straw in his hair and beard, but Tante Thea flew into his arms and hugged him close.

In punishment, he and many of the other men released from the Rosenstrasse detention centre were sent to clear unexploded bombs from the rubble of damaged houses. The other eight thousand Jews who had been rounded up that day were sent to a camp Ava had never heard of before.

It was called Auschwitz-Birkenau.

39

The Man Who Would Not Die

L eo's hands were steady, though every muscle in his body was rigid with tension. Carefully he lowered the delayed-action explosives into a nest of straw within the wooden box.

Rudolf Freiherr von Gersdorff had managed to procure the explosives for the conspiracy. They were of English make, so that if the bombs were discovered, suspicion would fall upon British agents rather than the Abwehr. Leo and Fabian von Schlabrendorff, adjutant to General-Major Henning von Tresckow, had tested the bombs several times to see if they would explode. Each time the devices had worked as expected. Now it was just a matter of getting the explosives onto the Führer's plane.

Leo gently slid the lid onto the wooden box. It was stamped with the mark of Cointreau & Cie. He nodded to Hans von Dohnányi, who rather gingerly lifted the box and carried it out of the room. He was setting off to the airport, flying to the Russian city of Smolensk more than a thousand kilometres to the east. Hitler was in Smolensk, preparing to fly back from the Soviet Union. It was Dohnányi's task to get the bomb on board his plane.

General-Major von Tresckow called their conspiracy 'Operation Blitz'. The idea was that Hitler's death would be the lightning flash that would lead to rebellion and the overthrow of the Nazi Party, and so the ending of the war.

The problem was, Leo thought, *igniting the spark.*

He and his fellow conspirators had been trying to get close to Hitler for some time, but the Führer had grown increasingly secretive and mistrustful. He changed his plans with only a moment's notice, and his bodyguards had been doubled. But now Tresckow had heard that Hitler was to fly to his military headquarters in the Ukraine, which the Führer called Werwolf.

The General-Major thought that the remote forest setting of Werwolf was the perfect place to ambush Hitler. At first he suggested intercepting the Führer as he drove from the airfield to the bunker. This would have involved a shootout with his bodyguards, however, and no-one liked the idea of German officers killing German officers.

The second plan was to shoot the Führer as he sat at dinner, but there was something so cold-blooded and deliberate about that. It felt too much like murder.

So Tresckow had decided that they would blow up the Führer's plane. The bomb would be given to an officer on Hitler's staff, saying the Cointreau was a pay-off for a lost bet. When the plane exploded half an hour later, it could be blamed on a Russian missile strike.

No work was done in the Abwehr offices that afternoon. Leo sat with Admiral Canaris and General Oster, watching the hands of the clock creep forward. His nerves were strung almost to breaking point, the palms of his hands sweating. When the telephone rang, all three men jerked. Leo listened as the General spoke into the receiver. Only a few words were exchanged. Oster put down the phone and slowly shook his head. 'The Führer's plane landed safely,' he said.

'But . . . what of the bomb?' Leo exclaimed.

'It failed to ignite,' Oster replied.

'But the box . . . if anyone opens the box, they'll find it!' Leo could not believe the plan had failed. It was as if some malevolent force protected the Führer.

'Tresckow will send his adjutant to try and get the box back. We must hope no-one feels thirsty this evening.' General Oster's face was expressionless, but a single bead of sweat rolled slowly down his lean cheek. He looked at Admiral Canaris, who was thoughtfully packing tobacco into his pipe.

'That was rather a close call,' the General said.

'We shall have to make a new plan,' the Admiral said. 'A foolproof one, this time.'

A week later, Leo received word that the Führer was coming to Berlin for an exhibition of Russian battle trophies at the arsenal. 'We have to try again,' Leo told Ava. 'He is so rarely seen in public anymore. This might be our last chance.'

'What are you going to do?' Ava put one hand on the table to steady herself.

He hesitated. 'Do you know Rudolf von Gersdorff? He's Fabian von Schlabrendorff's cousin.'

Ava shook her head.

'He's a good man. He has been asked to show the Führer around the exhibition. He is going to carry the bomb in his pocket and set it off just before he begins the tour.'

Ava sat down, her face white. 'But . . . that means he'll be killed too!'

Leo nodded.

'He's going to kill himself, so he can kill Hitler?'

'It's the only way.'

Ava had one hand pressed to her mouth. 'My God,' she whispered. 'Oh, Leo, this is all so terrible.'

He knelt before her, taking her hands. 'It's the only way, my love. We have to stop this war, and the only way to do that is to kill Hitler, however we can manage it.'

The day of Hitler's visit to the arsenal was even more nerve-racking than the day of the bomb in the cognac box. Göring, Himmler and General Keitel, the head of the Wehrmacht, were accompanying the Führer to the exhibition. If all went well, the Nazi monster would have its most important heads lopped off.

As the afternoon passed, Leo could bear it no longer. He went out into the city.

The exhibition was being held at the Zeughaus, the old arsenal which had been turned into a military museum. Leo walked quickly towards it, his hands clenched inside the pockets of his greatcoat. He reached the museum. It was hung with red swastika banners. Heavy tanks lined up along the square, flags poking out of their guns. All was as usual. Soldiers marching, loudspeakers blaring, people trying to go about their everyday business. Leo went to find Gersdorff.

His friend was pale and shaken, but trying to pretend all was well. He had detonated the bomb in his pocket as planned, he told Leo, then shown the Führer and his retinue around the exhibition. But Hitler had suddenly decided to leave. He had walked out, after only two minutes in the museum, and all his retinue had followed him. Gersdorff had to race to the bathroom and rip the smoking fuse out of the bomb. He managed to defuse it with only a few minutes to spare.

It was as if the Führer had some strange sixth sense, warning him of danger.

Leo was frowning over a pile of paperwork one morning in early April, when he heard the unexpected march of boots on the stairs. He stood up, feeling for his pistol. The Admiral came out of his office and gave him a warning glance. 'Easy, my boy.'

Two men in civilian clothes strode in. Gestapo. They announced themselves as Manfred Röder and Franz Sonderegger, and showed a warrant from Göring. Leo felt a prickle of unease. Röder was known as Hitler's blood judge. He had been the one to investigate and prosecute Harro Schulze-Boysen and his circle.

'Admiral Canaris, we demand access to Herr von Dohnányi's office,' Röder ordered. 'He is suspected of currency violations and other crimes. The Gestapo has been watching him for some time.'

'This is an outrage,' Dohnányi cried. 'How dare you accuse me?'

'Goodness,' the Admiral said mildly, stuffing his pipe with tobacco. 'I'm sure it must just be some misunderstanding. It'll all be cleared up soon, I'm sure.'

'There's no misunderstanding.' Roeder pushed past the Admiral. 'Herr von Dohnányi is under arrest. Now open up his office!'

'Then arrest me too, for he has done nothing that I do not know about,' General Oster said, standing before the office door, his arms crossed.

'That can be arranged, Herr General. Now out of my way!'

The General stood aside, and the two men went into the office and began to search through the desk. Dohnányi stood by helplessly, his hands clenched. Canaris puffed on his pipe. He raised one bushy white eyebrow, and Dohnányi shook his head imperceptibly. He made a small gesture to a sheaf of papers on a side table. Leo's heart sank. The Admiral had heard a rumour that the Abwehr offices were to be raided by the Gestapo, and ordered all incriminating evidence to be destroyed. Dohnányi had been so preoccupied with Operation Blitz, however, it looked as if he had not had time to destroy everything.

Oster went to stand by the side table. The Gestapo officers were rifling through the safe, all their attention centred on the files they had discovered within. Oster picked up the sheaf of papers and nonchalantly tucked them inside his uniform jacket. Sonderegger saw the movement out of the corner of his eye, and looked around.

'Halt!' he cried.

The General paused, his hand halfway out of his jacket. Sonderegger searched him roughly, pulling the papers out. He flicked through them hurriedly. 'A-ha! Here we have it. Evidence that you, Herr von Dohnányi, transferred money to Switzerland to support a load of dirty Jews! You think we don't know what you've been doing?'

'Cuff him,' Röder ordered. As Sonderegger obeyed, the Gestapo officer thrust his face into Dohnányi's. 'Just so you know, I have sent men to your house. Your oh-so-lovely wife has been arrested too, and her traitor of a brother as well.'

Dohnányi cried out in horror. The Admiral flicked a quick look at Leo, who at once went out of the office and ran down the hall. Dohnányi's brother-in-law was Dietrich Bonhoeffer, the Lutheran pastor who had been working as a courier for the Abwehr since he had been forbidden to preach. He was one of the most active participants in the Abwehr's secret resistance.

Leo reached Bonhoeffer's office, only to see the stout young man with his hands cuffed behind his back. His spectacles had been knocked askew. The office was a shambles, every drawer and every filing cabinet emptied and set in piles by the Gestapo men within. Leo met Bonhoeffer's gaze, trying to reassure him. *The Admiral will fix this*, he messaged silently.

But Leo did not see how the Admiral could possibly fix it. Dohnányi and Bonhoeffer, two of the men most active in the plot to kill Hitler, were in the hands of the Gestapo. There was little doubt they would be tortured. Surely, soon, the Gestapo would come for the Admiral himself, and all who worked with him.

'You must get out of Berlin,' Leo told Ava. 'If they find out that you were the courier who took the Jews to Switzerland . . . I cannot bear the thought of it. Go to the schloss. My mother will look after you. Or go to Switzerland to your father. I can try and smuggle you out, though it'll have to be secretly. The Abwehr's normal routes are suspect now.'

Ava clung to him. 'I don't want to leave you! Leo, can't we both escape? Please?'

He shook his head. 'I can't, Ava. Not now. It would be wrong.'

'Then I must stay too.'

He saw the grim determination on her face, and drew her closer. 'Then promise me that, if I'm arrested, you'll get out then. Promise me, Ava.'

'Only once I've got you out too,' she said, trying to smile.

But Ava could not lighten his mood. 'If I'm taken by the Gestapo, there'll be no getting out,' he said.

The next few days were agonising. The Admiral did not lose his head. He dismissed General Oster from his role as deputy head of the Abwehr, then did his best to ensure the Gestapo thought Dohnányi's and Bonhoeffer's only crime was helping Jews escape from Germany. The Gestapo believed him. The assassination plot was not exposed.

Leo could not relax, though. The two men might break and speak at any time.

On 20 April, it was the Führer's fifty-forth birthday. Everyone in Berlin was ordered to hang their swastika flags out the windows. Leo felt sick at heart as he shook out the red banner, marked with the black-clawed swastika. He had hoped to have burnt the hateful rag by now.

That night the British sent a squadron of Mosquitos to bomb Hitler's birthday party. All those celebrating had to run for the public air-raid shelters, as the sky was filled with the black darting shapes of the tiny planes. Leo hoped Hitler had had to scramble too. He hoped the bombers' aim was good, and the Reichstag was flattened and everyone in it.

No such luck.

Hitler was not flattened.

Meanwhile, news of the war kept going from bad to worse. It seemed as if Germany was fighting – and losing – on all fronts.

Ava dreamt she heard a woman singing. She had never heard such a sorrowful sound. She looked for the singer, but all she could see was mist and darkness. Other people were nearby. Sobbing. Praying.

The mist parted as if on an exhalation of breath. Valentina, the old Gypsy woman, was walking towards her. Her long skirts hung in tatters around her bare feet. Her white hair formed a matted cloud about her wrinkled face. She held a snow-white feather in her hand. *Remember*, she whispered. Then Valentina passed the feather to Ava.

The old Gypsy woman then turned, gathering her ragged shawl about her. She walked away into the darkness. Others walked with her – her daughter Abrienda, her grandson Dario, the young woman who had played the violin with such heart-searing beauty, the little girls who had danced. Ahead of them loomed a building without any windows. A massive square chimney vomited black smoke into the sky. The air was so thick with ashes that Ava could not breathe. She was being suffocated.

Ava woke with a jerk. She struggled upright, gasping, her chest as sore as if she had been pressed with stones. For a moment she did not recognise where she was, but soon realised she was safe, at home, in her own bed. Her pillows and eiderdown were all twisted and damp with sweat. She straightened them out and lay back, trying to rid herself of the horror of her dream. She wished Leo was home so she could press herself against his strong back.

Ava lay for a while, then got up, knowing she would not sleep again. She opened the curtains and stood, looking across at the Tiergarten. It was not quite dawn, and the forest was a dark, sombre, rustling congregation, heads bent together to whisper secrets under a sky that was the colour of frost. Ava watched as the sky warmed and the city was etched in gold. With a weary sigh, she turned back to her room and washed and dressed. As she shook out her eiderdown, a white feather floated down to the floor.

Ava picked it up. It was no bigger than a single joint of her smallest finger, as frail as a wisp of mist.

Her skin prickled. Carrying the tiny white feather, Ava went down the stairs, and down again into the coal cellar. She found her mother's old chest, hidden away under tarpaulins. She tucked the feather safely away in the black velvet bag.

Leo knocked on the Admiral's office door, then put his head in. 'Sir! I'm sorry to wake you. But it's important.'

Canaris sat up, his white shock of hair rumpled, the blankets of his camp bed twisted about him. 'What is it?' His gaze sharpened. 'Good news or bad?'

'Good. I think. Mussolini has been arrested.'

Canaris sat on the edge of the camp bed. To someone who did not know him, the Admiral would have looked rather sleepy. Even stupid. But Leo knew that the Admiral's shrewd mind was running through all the implications of the news. Mussolini's arrest was the first defeat of fascism in twenty years. Italy was bound to abandon Germany and change sides. Even though Italy had never been a particularly useful ally, it was a blow for Hitler.

'Right. Type me up a report, there's a good boy. And get me news of Hitler's response. This could be interesting.' Canaris lay down again, covering himself in his blanket.

Leo went away to gather together every cobweb of rumour, every frail thread of hearsay, to see what sense he could spin of it. He came back to Canaris the next day. Hitler had ordered German troops into Italy. That was to be expected. But of far more importance was a report that Hitler had conceived a mad plan to kidnap the Pope.

That made Canaris sit up. 'Better pack a bag, my boy, and kiss your pretty wife goodbye. I think we need to go to Italy.'

The next month was intense and difficult. Leo flew to Venice with the Admiral, and took part in meetings with the head of the Italian secret intelligence in which steps were taken to ensure that the Pope and Italy's king, Victor Emmanuel, were kept safe. The meeting was treason. No doubt about that. If Hitler knew, he would have Canaris shot without a second's hesitation. And Leo too.

Italy surrendered to the Allies, as expected. Most unexpectedly, Hitler sent a company of paratroopers into Italy to rescue the imprisoned Mussolini. The Duce was set up as the leader of the German-controlled parts of Italy.

Canaris fed as much information as he could to the Allies, taking every opportunity, using every channel, no matter how fraught with danger. He even went into occupied France and, blindfolded, met with the head of the British Intelligence, begging to know the terms for peace if Germany was able to get rid of Hitler. Churchill's reply was unequivocal. Unconditional Surrender.

Leo barely had time to sleep. In the few moments of repose he snatched, he worried over the Admiral's behaviour. He had always been so clever, playing the double game with skill and finesse. Yet Canaris was now acting so blatantly against Hitler's interests, it was impossible for him not to be caught. Leo wondered if his boss was gambling the future of the Abwehr, indeed his own life, on the hope that Operation Blitz would succeed, and Hitler would die.

When Leo returned to Berlin in late September, it was to find a new conspirator had joined Operation Blitz. His name was Colonel Claus Graf von Stauffenberg. He had lost his left eye, his right hand, and two fingers on his left hand in the Tunisia campaign. Unlike many of the other officers, he was utterly sure of the rightness of the plot to kill Hitler, and utterly decisive about the way to do it.

The clockwork of the conspiracy quickened.

In mid-November, Leo's old friend Axel Freiherr von dem Bussche agreed to be the key player in another assassination attempt. Bussche was only twenty-four years old, the same age as Ava, and the absolute image of a perfect Aryan specimen. Tall. Blond. Blue-eyed. Strong-jawed. He had been chosen to model the new Wehrmacht winter uniforms in a display for the Führer. The plan was for Bussche to hide a landmine with a quick-detonating grenade trigger in his pocket. He would embrace Hitler, pull the trigger, and blow himself and the Führer up.

The night before the display, an Allied air raid on Berlin destroyed the railway truck that carried the new uniforms. Bussche was sent back to the front instead.

Another friend of Leo's, Ewald-Heinrich von Kleist-Schmenzin, volunteered to replace him in the rescheduled display of the new uniforms. Kleist planned to hide a bomb in his briefcase. All was prepared. The bomb was primed and ready to be ignited. Kleist waited, in an agony of expectation, for the Führer's arrival. But Hitler did not turn up.

The man just would not die.

In Hell

Jutta crept through the tangled undergrowth of the old cemetery, keeping to the shadows. She heard the sound of melodious chanting, and drew aside a vine so she could see more clearly.

A thin man dressed in shabby dark clothes and a white prayer shawl was standing, head bent, by a newly dug grave. An elderly man leant on his spade nearby, his boots stiff with clay. A woman and child stood next to the rabbi, holding hands. Their clothes were ritually torn, their faces contorted with grief. After the casket was lowered into the grave, the woman threw some clods of earth on top, then told the boy to do so as well. He was aged about ten, with two curling forelocks on either side of his thin, pale face. As he dropped in the earth, his face crumpled. He tried to choke back his sobs, as the gravedigger filled in the pit.

Jutta had seen many funerals since she had begun hiding in the cemetery. Many times the grieving families had nothing but a box of ashes, or an urn. Sometimes there was no-one to grieve the dead. Jutta had even seen the Gestapo drive up in a lorry and deposit a dozen coffins at once, which the rabbi would do his best to honour and bury properly on his own. If Jutta heard his thin, mournful chanting, she always came to watch, to bear witness.

The rabbi began to recite the kaddish. Then Jutta heard the ring of boots on the stone path. She shrank back, tiny alarm bells zinging all over her body. She knew the sound of SS jackboots all too well. She watched as two men in long coats came up, followed by their usual impassive, black-clad followers. 'You're under arrest,' one of the Gestapo said. 'You are to be deported.'

The woman was white faced and shocked. 'But . . . my husband . . .'

'Your husband was a second-degree Mischling and so you were exempt from deportation due to your marriage to him. Now he is dead, you are no longer exempt. You are expected to hand over all papers and valuables. Come with us now.'

'But . . . he's barely in the ground . . .' The woman gestured towards the grave.

'So? Come now.' He seized the woman's arm, dragging her away.

The boy suddenly flew at the Gestapo officer, kicking and punching him with wildly flailing fists and boots. The officer slapped him to the ground. The woman tried to get to her son, but was held firmly. Crying, the boy sat up, his hand to his bleeding face. 'Get up,' the officer ordered. Sullenly the boy stumbled to his feet, and the two were marched away.

The rabbi had protested, but now stood, his head bent, his hands twisting uselessly in the fringe of his shawl. The Gestapo officer said to him, 'Once Berlin is truly Jew-free, you'll be next, old man.' Then he laughed, and walked away.

Jutta watched him go, her blood seething with futile anger. He paused by the wall, and spoke briefly to a young blonde woman in a long coat with a fur collar. Jutta saw him pass her a wad of folded notes, before he went through the archway and out of the cemetery. As the blonde girl turned, Jutta's eyes narrowed.

She knew her. It was Stella Goldschlag.

The air-raid alarm screamed into the dead of the winter night.

Ava woke groggily, and stumbled around in the dark looking for her coat and shoes. It had been so long since Berlin had been bombed, she had stopped leaving her clothes and satchel ready. Zeus howled. He hated the noise. Leo had to drag him down the stairs into the cellar. Ava lit the candles, and they sat, one on either side of the old dog, arms around him. As the planes whined overhead and the bombs fell, she hid her head against the Great Dane's warm flank.

The RAF came again four nights later. The sound was indescribable. The low hum on the horizon, slowly swelling into a tremendous roar like a beast that did not stop to breathe. The flak guns firing a hail of bullets high into the air. Shrapnel clattering. Windows cracking. The whine of the bombs falling. Then: *boom!* Everything in the house shook. Pictures fell off walls. Glasses smashed inside their cupboards. Debris rained down.

It went on and on and on.

Then Ava heard sirens. Fire engines racing past. Shouts and screams. Then another high-pitched whine.

Boom!

Ava screamed. A percussive blast blew her backwards. She hit the ground hard. Ava opened her eyes dazedly, feeling the back of her head. It was tender to touch. All was dark. The candle had blown out. Zeus whimpered. She groped out in the darkness, and felt his fur. 'It's all right, boy, it's all right.'

'Ava!' Leo lifted her into his arms. 'Are you hurt?'

'Only a little. What happened? Were we hit?'

'Not us. It was close though.'

'Let's get out of here! If I'm going to die, I'd rather be in the open air.'

Grabbing their bags, they groped their way through the darkness and up the stairs. Ava heard glass crack under her boot. Zeus was at their heels, whining low in his throat. They stumbled through the house and out into the garden.

The night sky was lit up from horizon to horizon with stabbing rays of white light. Hundreds of planes ducked and dived through the beams, avoiding the sprays of shooting sparks from the flak guns. Smoke billowed everywhere, garish and orange. Ava could see black domes and spires and chimney pots silhouetted against leaping scarlet flames. The air caught at the back of her throat, making her cough.

'Half the city is on fire!' Leo stared around, his face grim. In the orange glare, Ava could see him clearly, Zeus pressed against his leg.

Clinging to each other, they stumbled onto the street. People blundered through the smoke and the dust clouds, their faces blank with shock. Ava did her best to help, binding up bleeding cuts as best she could with torn strips of Leo's shirt. Still the planes roared overhead, hundreds of them, and the bombs rained down on the city.

The worst of the bombing was near the zoo. Leo and Ava were helping dig a family out of a wrecked home when another bomb landed so close, they tumbled to the ground in the hot wind. Then came the most spine-chilling shriek Ava had ever heard.

She stared towards the sound. An elephant staggered towards her. His trunk was lifted high, and one of his tusks was broken. Blood streamed down his side.

Ava screamed her husband's name.

Leo looked up. He scrambled away, dragging Ava. The bull elephant loomed over them, his heavy feet shaking the ground. Then a shot rang out. The elephant jerked, throwing up his trunk. Another shot. The elephant folded to his knees, screaming again in pain. Then he fell to his side. Dust bloomed up around him. He lay still.

Ava stood, shocked and numb, staring at the great creature lying dead only a few metres away. The zoo was on fire. She could hear the animals squealing in agony.

'My God, this is hell!' Leo whispered. 'We are in hell.'

Berlin lay in ruins.

Tumbled buildings. Broken roofs. Blackened walls. Smoking ashes. Bodies laid out in rows on the Tiergartenstrasse. Whirling clouds of smoke, black as *Götterdämmerung*.

All day, Leo and Ava worked, digging through the rubble, pulling out bodies both alive and dead, binding up bloody wounds and shattered limbs. Again and again, the world tilted and swayed, and Ava heard the hissing of vertigo in her ears. She steeled herself, forcing herself to stay on her feet, to face the rupture of skin and flesh, the red ooze of blood through the death-grey dust that covered everything.

Nightfall. Too dark to see. Ava stumbled and fell to her knees. Leo bent and picked her up, carrying her through the piles of broken stone. He managed to get her home, but was too exhausted to carry her up the stairs. They crawled up together, and fell into bed as they were, filthy with soot and dirt.

Ava plummeted into nightmares. She could hear the sound of planes again, snarling through the darkness. She could hear bombs falling. The elephant screamed in agony. Then someone shook her. 'Ava! Wake up!'

Ava woke with a jerk. It was no nightmare. The planes were back. The bombs were falling again. Sobbing in terror, she clutched her satchel and stumbled down to the cellar. Leo was dragging the terrified dog. As Ava reached the cellar door, a bomb detonated so close that all the blackout paper in the kitchen windows turned a dull crimson. She was knocked off her feet. Trying to catch her breath, she crawled down into the cellar. There was no need to light candles. Red was glaring around the lid of the coal hole.

Ava pressed her back to the wall, covered her face with her arms, and endured. At last the sound of the planes died away, and the all-clear siren was sounded. She and Leo staggered into the dawn.

Ava could only stand and stare. The Tiergarten was gone. All that was left was a few black smoking sticks stuck in a snow of ash.

Nothing could be done, but try and save as many people as they could.

The Reich set up tents amongst the broken houses and blasted parkland. People sat on the frozen ground, clutching whatever they still owned in their arms. Children played in the wreckage. Long queues of people waited for cups of soup. The dead elephant was carved up and cooked, and Ava was told they were eating roast zebra on the Unter den Linden. One woman told her the heat of the flames had cracked the glass of the snake house, and giant pythons had escaped into the fleeing crowd. 'They'll be down in the sewers now,' she said. 'Feeding on the rats.'

'There are no rats left,' another man retorted. 'We've already eaten them all.'

Leo had set to work rebuilding their side wall, which had collapsed inwards.

'I have to go and see if Monika is hurt,' Ava told him. 'The telephone lines are down so I cannot ring.'

'Should you go? The whole city is in chaos.'

'I have to make sure she's all right. And Jutta and Onkel Franz and Tante Thea. I can't bear not knowing!'

'All right, Best Beloved. Be careful.' He gave her a brief half-smile, and drew her close to kiss her cheek.

The roads were strewn with rubble and pitted with bomb craters. It took two hours to walk to Monika's apartment, a journey that normally took less than twenty minutes. Monika was not there. She had gone to work. 'She was so worried about the Oberführer, she went as soon as it was light,' her flatmate said.

Ava was cut to the bone to know Monika had gone into the Schutzstaffel offices, but had not troubled herself to see if her half-sister was hurt or killed. Ava blundered back out into the street, dashing away tears. As she climbed over one mountain of rubble after another, as she skirted great holes torn in the ground, and passed rows of corpses laid out in the parks, she fought for composure. And lost.

At last, in the red smoky dusk, Ava reached the Scheunenviertel. She had been scrambling for hours. Her legs were like jelly. A stitch stabbed her side. The heels of her hands were lacerated and bleeding. So too were her knees. Ava reached the apartment block where Onkel Franz and Tante Thea had been living. It was nothing but a pile of broken bricks. Ava gasped. Her knees gave way. She dropped to the ground. Everything was a blur. She struggled up and began to search, calling their names.

People's faces everywhere. Gaunt. Grey with dust. Red with weeping. Smoke. A smell like cooking meat.

Ava found them in the end. Both were dead. Tante Thea was dressed only in her nightgown, her spindly legs bare, her bare feet folded in on each other. Someone had crossed her hands on her breast, and laid her grey plait – furred with dust – over her shoulder. Her nightgown was torn and bloodied. Onkel Franz wore only one slipper. This distressed her. Ava searched for a while for his missing slipper. It was no use. All was lost.

Ava had to find Jutta.

Then the siren began. High, low. Near, far. Howling. People ran in a panic. Ava ran with them. She fell. Someone dragged her up. She lurched into the air-raid shelter. It stank of sweat and bad breath and the overflowing latrine. Ava leant her head against the wall and wept.

In the morning, she was allowed out. Ava wanted to go home badly, but she felt she had to find Jutta. She limped along to the old Jewish cemetery at Weissensee. Maybe Jutta would be there, hiding among the gravestones.

'Ava!'

Ava turned at the sound of her name, her heart *acciaccatura*.

It was not Jutta. Ava stared at her for a while before she recognised her. Stella Goldschlag. Jutta's Jewish friend, who had always done her best to look like Jean Harlow. Stella's blonde hair was not quite so perfectly set as before, and her face was free of make-up, but she was nicely dressed in a good coat with a fur collar. She wore an elegant pair of blue gauntlets.

'Stella,' Ava said stupidly.

'As I live and breathe,' Stella replied cheerfully. 'What are you doing here?'

'Looking for Jutta,' Ava said.

Stella's gaze sharpened. 'Oh? Is she here?'

'I don't know. I can't find her.' Ava swallowed hard.

'How long since you last saw her?'

Ava's brain refused to work. 'I don't know. How long has it been? Too long.'

Stella was asking a lot of questions. Why had Ava come to the Jewish graveyard? Was Jutta hiding here? Why did Ava want her? Did Ava know where else she could be?

Ava leant her arms on the wall and bent her head down. Something felt wrong. She lifted her head and looked at Stella. 'You weren't deported?'

Stella looked away. 'They tried. In February, you know, that last big action. The SS raided the factory where I was working, but my mother and I hid under a cardboard box. They didn't find us.'

'You went underground?' Ava could not believe it. Pretty Stella Goldschlag, living on the streets, hiding in a cellar? She looked too clean.

'I've got papers.' Stella had turned red. 'I met a man . . . he can make whatever you need.' Her voice quickened. 'Tell Jutta. If she needs papers, I can get them for her.'

Ava's head ached, her whole body ached. *Jutta has papers. She has mine.* Ava thought of telling Stella so, but she was too tired, she could not frame the words. She sat down abruptly on the ground.

'Are you all right, Ava?' Stella reached down her hand. Ava took it. The blue glove Stella was wearing was deliciously soft. The cuff was decorated with intricate fretwork. Ava stared at it.

She had seen those gloves before.

Ava remembered a day, long ago, when a golden laughing girl had brought a suitcase of clothes to the Jewish Winter Aid office. A coat with a fur collar. A pair of elegant blue gauntlets.

Ava stared at Stella. *How did she get Libertas's gloves? I thought they were meant for charity . . .*

'I escaped the Gestapo twice,' Stella was boasting. Her voice was shrill. 'Once when I hid under the cardboard box, and then again. Later. They found me and took me to prison. But the prison was bombed. I clambered out and escaped.'

'That's amazing,' Ava said. 'You're lucky.'

A peculiar expression crossed Stella's face. Almost like a grimace. 'Oh, yes. I'm lucky. But enough about me. Where is Jutta? I can help her. I'll get her papers. I'll help her hide. Just tell me where she is.'

. 'I think she's dead,' Ava answered and stumbled away. Weaving like a drunk. All Ava could think: *She's so clean. She's so pretty.*

Jutta came, a week later, at midnight. Leo and Ava were huddled in the cellar, leaning against each other, Zeus lying at their feet. Ava was so wrung out with exhaustion that she no longer flinched at the whine of bombs falling. She just wished dully that the RAF would get it over and done with, so she could go back to bed.

Then Ava heard a scraping metallic sound. Zeus lifted his head and gave a little *whuff* of welcome. His tail beat on the filthy floor. The metal lid covering the coal hole was lifted away. A skinny body dropped through, landing in a crouch at their feet. By the light of the candle, Ava saw a dark eye staring through a filthy tangle of black hair.

'Jutta!' Ava leapt up and hugged her fiercely. 'I'm so sorry. Your parents . . .'

'I know.'

Ava's eyes had filled with tears. Jutta, however, was dry-eyed and fierce.

'Are you hungry?' Leo did not wait for an answer, but got down the tins of sardines and the box of crackers Ava kept on the shelf. Jutta fell on them, scooping out the sardines with her fingers, cramming them into her mouth.

Ava told her how she had found her parents. 'I searched for you at the cemetery but couldn't find you.'

'I've moved bases,' Jutta answered shortly, ripping open the box of crackers. 'The Gestapo search the cemetery now.'

'Jutta, I saw Stella Goldschlag . . .'

Immediately Jutta stilled, looking up at Ava through the tangle of her hair. 'What did you tell her?'

'Nothing . . . I said I thought you were dead. Why?'

'She's a Jew catcher,' Jutta answered. 'In the pay of the Gestapo. She buys her own life with the lives of other Jews.' She paused for a moment, her chest rising and falling rapidly. 'If I see her, I will kill her.'

*

The dissolution of the Abwehr came about because of a tea party.

Afterwards, Leo could hardly believe such havoc could be caused by something so innocent. He tried his best to reduce it all down to an official report, a list, a catalogue of events, but all the time he knew that his simple record of dates and names and happenings was an inventory of betrayal, deceit and death.

On 10 September 1943, Elisabeth von Thadden, formerly a headmistress of a famous girls' school, invited some friends to a tea party to celebrate her birthday. Among her guests were Hannah Gräfin von Bredow, the granddaughter of Otto von Bismarck, the famous Chancellor of the German Empire; Albrecht Graf von Bernstorff, nephew of the one-time German ambassador to the United States; Father Friedrich Erxleben, a Jesuit priest; Otto Kiep, a diplomat; and the former State Secretary Arthur Zarden and his daughter Irmgard.

Fräulein von Thadden invited a new acquaintance to her party. A charming, handsome Swiss doctor named Paul Reckzeh. He engaged them all in conversation. What did they think, he asked, of the Mussolini affair?

They answered truthfully.

In mid-January, Elisabeth von Thadden and her aristocratic guests were all arrested, interrogated, and condemned to death. The Gestapo seized more than seventy of their friends and relations. Arthur Zarden flung himself from the window of the Gestapo offices, and died on the pavement below.

Helmuth James Graf von Moltke tried to warn them to flee. He too was arrested. Leo's own circle of resisters was paralysed with horror. If the Graf was tortured, who would he betray? How long would it take for him to break?

The Gestapo summoned two friends of Otto Kiep to appear in Berlin for interrogation. Erich Vermehren and his wife, Elisabeth Gräfin von Plettenberg, were Abwehr agents working in Istanbul. They had been fervent supporters of the resistance for a long time. Instead of returning to Berlin, they defected to Great Britain. It was rumoured they took the Abwehr's book of secret codes with them.

Hitler summoned the Admiral. Leo was not admitted to the meeting, but - waiting outside - he could clearly hear the Führer's harsh voice ranting on. Words to open wounds. Incompetence. Failure. Stupidity. Then, the words Leo had been dreading. Betrayal. Sabotage. Treason.

The Admiral stood firm. 'It is hardly surprising the Abwehr is in trouble when Germany is losing the war,' he said in a clear, strong, carrying voice.

Leo set his jaw, staring straight ahead. He tried not to reveal, with a single quiver of a muscle or twitch of a nerve, his realisation that all was lost. The Admiral had survived as head of the Abwehr for almost a decade by never, ever, admitting what he truly felt. At that moment, Canaris had declared his hand.

The Admiral was dismissed, and the Abwehr was taken over by Himmler. Intricate networks of spies and informers that stretched over all of Europe were, in a moment, torn asunder. Canaris was banished from Berlin, but he was not accused or arrested. No-one could believe the mild-mannered old man, with his shabby coat and chewed pipe, could possibly be of any real importance.

Leo resigned from the Abwehr.

'I shall not work for Himmler,' he told Ava. 'I don't care what happens.'

His wife only nodded. 'I know,' she said.

Leo fully expected that he would be sent to the Russian front, the assignment all soldiers dreaded. But then Colonel Claus Graf von Stauffenberg came to see him. He wore a black patch over his left eye, his damaged right arm tucked inside his immaculate uniform.

'I know all that you've done,' Stauffenberg said. 'Operation Blitz is not defeated yet. Come work for me, and I swear we'll find some way to kill that madman!'

For Ava, music had always been the way to heal herself. When she sang of loss and love and longing, she brought those feelings out of the darkness and into the light. She had always thought that she would die if she could not sing, as if music was a part of her body, like her heart or her lungs or her liver. Now Berlin lay in ruins. The Philharmonie had been bombed. The Deutsche Opera House was destroyed. All was in such chaos that Ava's final year exams seemed of little importance to anyone, not even herself. And, truthfully, she had not found much joy in music since the Christmas Eve she had heard Reinhard Heydrich play his violin. She went to her exams, though, and performed like an automaton. She passed, and was invited to join the Reich Culture Chamber.

Ava declined.

She did not want to be in Goebbels' employ. She did not want to sing for the war effort. She was not sure that she ever wanted to sing again.

Ava spent her days trying to help those in need. She volunteered for the Red Cross, and was given a striped uniform and starched apron that was never white by the end of the day. She did not tell anyone that she fainted at the sight of blood. Instead she struggled each day to conquer her fear.

Train-loads of wounded soldiers from the Russian front. Families dug out of rubble. Women giving premature birth in the midst of a bombing raid. Prisoners who had been smashed and broken, and needed to be patched up to be sent back to their torturers. Desperate souls who had tried to commit suicide, but failed. Ava saw it all, and stiffened every muscle in her body, refusing to give in to the vertigo that whirled about her. She learnt to turn away, to breathe deeply, to wind tight the steel wire of her resolve.

As the winter passed and summer came, bringing with it more death than the world had ever seen, she fought her own private battle with her fear. It was a Pyrrhic victory.

For Ava did not sing.

41

Crack of Light

On Midsummer's Eve, Monika married her SS officer.

She wrote Ava a note to inform her. It said: *Ava, getting married next week. Hope you'll come. Last representative of the family and all that. See you at eleven on Saturday 24 June at the Reichsführer's villa on Schwanenwerder Island.* Enclosed with the note was a formal invitation, printed in gold upon opulent cream paper emblazoned with a swastika.

Leo did not want to go. 'The place will be crawling with officers of the Schutzstaffel. That sister of yours is marrying one of the worst of them.'

'I have to go. She's my sister.'

He said nothing.

'Please come with me. It's only a few hours. And maybe we'll pick up some useful gossip. An upcoming sighting of our elusive Führer. Please, Leo.'

'It might be useful,' he agreed, after a moment's frowning thought. 'And it could be a clever double bluff. Would anyone working against the Reich really go to a SS wedding? They wouldn't think so.' He sighed. 'If I could, I'd take that blasted bomb with me and blow the whole lot of them sky-high, but security will be tight if it's at Goebbels' house. We'd be lucky to be able to smuggle a pin in.'

He was right. Hard-faced guards with machine guns were at the gate to the Reichsführer's mansion, and Leo was searched thoroughly. Even the inside of his cap was examined closely, and Ava's bag was emptied out and the lining felt with probing fingers.

Ava wore a cream silk dress, with the von Löwenstein pearls gleaming around her throat and wrist. She had carefully confined her hair in a sleek roll, making sure not a single errant curl could escape. The dress hugged every curve and line of her body, with billowing chiffon sleeves that revealed the smooth skin of her arms. Nonetheless, she was patted all over as well, the guard's hands lingering on the curve of her breast, the flare of her bottom. Ava saw Leo grow tense, and shot him a warning look.

At last they were permitted through the gates, and walked up the long drive to the villa, a great white building with heavy Grecian pillars and a lofty pediment. It looked over formal garden beds and a lawn as svelte as velvet to the glittering blue waters of the Wannsee. Yachts bobbed up and down at their moorings.

'All these villas used to belong to Jews,' Leo told Ava in a low voice. 'All the great Jewish families had homes here – the Goldschmidts, the Israels, the Monheims. When the Führer came to power, the Brownshirts invaded the island and hoisted the swastika flag over the water tower. Now it's the playground for Hitler and his thugs. I heard Goebbels bought this villa from the Schlitters for a pittance.'

Servants greeted them, handing out tall crystal glasses filled to the brim with honey-coloured champagne. A small orchestra was playing Mozart. Men in uniforms stood everywhere, their hair sleek with pomade. Ava had been afraid her silk dress was too formal for an afternoon wedding. She had no reason to fear. Every woman there wore a dress that could only have been designed and sewn in Paris. Jewels flashed from ears and necks.

Ava recognised Goebbels at once. He looked like a dark dwarf beside the giant blond SS men, who were all almost two metres tall. He had the narrow face of a ferret, but his dark eyes were intelligent. He moved awkwardly and Ava remembered he had a deformed foot. His wife, Magda, stood beside him in the receiving line. Although she positioned herself on a step below him, she was as tall as he. She was a perfect Aryan wife, blonde and blue-eyed. It must have taken hours to have her hair set in such stiff and perfect waves.

Ava shook hands with Himmler and his wife, Margarete. He looked like a mild-tempered man, with small glasses and small moustache. It was hard to believe he was one of the most powerful men in Germany, and the mastermind of the Gestapo. His wife was big-boned and plain. They did not look at each other.

Ava felt Leo stiffen. She glanced at him. He was staring across the crowded lawn. She followed his gaze.

Gertrud Breiter stood on the edge of the crowd, her golden-red hair catching the light. She was wearing a tight black dress that showed off her voluptuous figure to perfection, and a tight choker of dazzling diamonds. A gold swastika was pinned to her breast. She clung to the arm of a black-clad SS officer. He was about fifty years old, and his sparse grey hair had been carefully combed to hide his balding pate.

Sweat dampened Ava's palms. Yet she felt shivery and cold. She turned away abruptly, spilling her champagne. She did not know what to do. She could not confront Gertrud, here at her sister's wedding. She could not scream at her, or accuse her, with SS officers standing all around. Ava could not ever reveal she knew how Gertrud had tricked and manipulated Libertas into betraying her friends. Gertrud must never know that Ava had known Libertas, or any other of those courageous men and women who had dreamt of a better Germany and had been tortured and killed for it.

Ava looked at Leo. His face was pale, with deep dents on either side of his mouth. His hands were fisted. Ava put a hand on his arm. 'Careful,' she whispered.

He glanced at her. Ava had never seen him look so angry. The tendons in his neck were standing out like cords. She tried to warn him with her eyes.

Gertrud saw them. Her eyes widened. She tilted her head, smiled, and whispered something in the ear of the SS officer. He turned and stared. Ava felt colour mount her face. They came across the lawn, smiling, smug with utter assurance that they were the masters of the world.

'Leo, darling!' Gertrud reached up to kiss his cheek. Her lips left a red imprint on his skin. She ignored Ava.

'So lovely to see you,' Gertrud went on. 'Where have you been hiding yourself lately? I heard about what happened at the Abwehr. Shocking. Just shocking.'

Leo said nothing, though his lips tightened.

Gertrud smiled up at Leo, her hand still on his arm. 'Let me introduce you to my fiancé, Max. He may be able to help you. He's something very important in the SS.'

'Obersturmbannführer Max Kranz, at your service.' The SS officer bowed his head. His eyes were so pale they appeared colourless, his skin marked with deep lines from his nose to his thin-lipped mouth. 'I am the adjutant to the commander of the labour camp at Flossenbürg.'

Leo had not responded to Gertrud's greeting. He saluted the officer, however, and greeted him politely. Kranz only had eyes for Ava, however.

'And who is this beautiful creature?' he asked.

'My wife, Ava.'

'It's a pleasure to meet you.' Kranz bent to kiss her hand. His fingers stroked the soft skin of her palm. Ava jerked in surprise, and he smiled. 'You're a lucky man, Löwenstein.'

'Thank you,' Leo replied.

'Very exotic. You don't often see such black hair here in Berlin. Not any more, anyway. What is your ancestry, Frau von Löwenstein?'

'Her mother was a Spanish singer,' Gertrud cut in, her voice poisonously sweet. 'Known for playing the roles of gypsies and prostitutes.'

'Indeed? And do you follow in her footsteps?' Kranz asked.

'I beg your pardon?' Leo said in a dangerous tone of voice.

Kranz smiled. 'Oh dear, how clumsy of me. I simply meant: do you sing?'

'I do,' Ava answered coolly.

'I'm surprised your husband permits. If you were mine, I'd want to keep all that smouldering beauty for myself.'

Ava tried to smile, but her lips were stiff. Something about the way Kranz spoke made her very uncomfortable. He was standing so near, she could smell his cologne. Ava stepped closer to Leo, taking his arm.

'So you were one of Old Whitehead's pups, were you?' Kranz asked. 'How's the old man doing?'

'He's not much enjoying his retirement,' Leo answered diplomatically. 'I believe his wife and daughters are glad to have the chance to spend some time with him, however.'

'About time the Abwehr was cleaned out and taken over by Reich Security,' Kranz said. 'I imagine you're in need of a new role. Else they'll be packing you off to the Russian front. And then who would keep your lovely wife warm?'

It was impossible not to find his insinuations offensive. Ava could feel how taut Leo was beside her. Ava felt sure the Obersturmbannführer was trying to provoke Leo into losing his temper. They knew Leo had worked for Admiral Canaris and so must suspect him of being involved in some of the Abwehr's double dealings.

Ava had to deflect their suspicions somehow. She tried to imagine she was a good Nazi wife. She'd be overawed to be here at Goebbels' private residence, and dazzled by all the uniforms and medals. She'd be ambitious for her husband, and disappointed that he had lost his job at the Abwehr. She'd worship the Führer and believe all the propaganda that said Germany was winning the war. She'd want a piece of the glory and the booty.

Ava pouted, and looked up at Kranz through her lashes. She begged him for advice. Ava wondered what Leo had to do to get a job like his. Surely it must be a very important role?

Kranz smirked. 'There is always work for smart young men in the Third Reich,' he told Leo. 'Flossenbürg has more than doubled in size in recent years and we never have enough men. I'm sure we can find something for you to do, and then we would have the pleasure of seeing you and your beautiful wife more often.'

Ava dropped her eyelashes. 'I'd like that.'

It gave her fierce pleasure to see the jealous anger on Gertrud's face.

*

The wedding was held at noon, in the garden under an ancient linden tree. The sun filtered down through heart-shaped leaves the colour of a cat's eyes. Ava stood with Leo near the front. To her distaste, Himmler was to officiate at the wedding. He stood next to a medieval wooden lectern that had been hung with a swastika banner and garlanded with oak leaves. If it had not been for his black uniform with the red swastika armband, he would have looked just like a typical pastor. Round glasses. Neat hair. High starched collar.

Monika's fiancé stood before the lectern, holding a copy of *Mein Kampf* in his hand. Oberführer Emeric Jaekal had a brutal, square face, a heavy nose and brown hair combed straight back from a low forehead. His mouth was fleshy and wet. He did not seem at all the sort of man to appeal to Ava's fastidious sister.

The orchestra struck up the 'Bridal Chorus' from Wagner's opera *Lohengrin*. Two long lines of SS officers raised their arms in the Nazi salute, creating a tunnel for Monika to walk down. She was dressed in an elegant and tight-fitting gown of white satin, and carried an immense bouquet of white edelweiss and oak leaves. Edelweiss was said to be Hitler's favourite flower, and only grew in the Bavarian mountains. Ava wondered how Monika had managed to get so many, so early in the season. It must have cost a lot of money.

Monika was attended by Gudrun Himmler, a tall rather gawky girl of fourteen, and the five little Goebbels girls, aged from four to twelve. They were all dressed in the brown uniform of the League of German Girls – even the littlest – their blonde hair in neat plaits. The Goebbels boy carried the ring. He was dressed in the Hitler Youth uniform. All six of the Goebbels children had names that began with 'H'. Ava thought it must be a peculiar compliment to Hitler.

Himmler made a long speech about the importance of race and family life, and then read a passage from the Edda: 'And I said to him that I had made a vow in my turn, that I would never marry a man who knew the meaning of fear.' Then the orchestra played Haydn's 'Deutschlandlied', and the newly married couple walked away through the tunnel of outstretched black-clad arms.

'Can we go now?' Leo murmured in her ear.

'We can't go till after dinner,' Ava whispered back.

He made a face. 'Can you eat fast?'

'I can try.' Ava smiled up at him, then realised that Gertrud was watching. Her eyes narrowed. Ava smiled sweetly.

Dinner passed slowly, with the crowd entertained by endless self-congratulatory speeches. As Ava looked around at the tables groaning with food and drink, the women in their satins and jewels, the men laden with medals, it was hard to believe that little more than half an hour's drive away, Berlin lay in ruins with people starving on the streets. Rome had just fallen to the Americans, the British were marching towards Paris, and the Russians were inexorably pushing the Germans back. Yet toast after toast was made to the Führer, and all the talk was of Hitler's genius and how he would soon secure total victory. They all seemed utterly sincere. Ava thought her father was right. Her country was in the grip of some kind of collective madness, and she did not know the cure.

Monika's new husband was boasting of his work. Ava only half-listened. It did not sound very interesting. He was talking about something called the Hygiene Institute, and places he called the bunkers.

'Since we fitted the gas-tight doors and the new ventilation equipment, we've been able to accelerate the rate of extermination greatly,' he said. 'We have vents for the prussic acid in the roof, so all we need to do is herd them in there and dump the pellets through the vents. It does all the work for us.'

Ava looked down the table at Leo. He was sitting next to Gertrud. She was speaking to him in a low voice, and his head was bent close to hers.

Jaekal drank a mouthful of his fine French brandy and then drew out a fat cigar from his inner pocket. 'I don't know how we would cope with the workload otherwise,' he went on. 'They're sending up to twenty thousand of the sub-humans from Hungary every day.'

That caught Ava's attention. She looked up. Germany had invaded Hungary only a few months earlier. Naturally, as soon as Hitler had seized control, he had started shipping out the Jews.

'We're gassing so many now the crematorium cannot cope,' Monika's husband went on, leaning forward to light his cigar from one of the candles on the table. He puffed luxuriously. 'It's a real problem. We're having to burn the bodies in the open air. And the noise they make once they realise what's happening! We have to keep truck engines revving to try and hide the sound so the new arrivals don't get in a panic.'

A wave of sickness washed over her. Ava got up, muttered something, and stumbled towards the bathroom. She hid in the toilet, eyes closed, her head resting against the wall. She could not go out there, pale and red-eyed, her face showing her revulsion. She had to be calm and in control.

Ava could not bear the thought of her sister marrying that monster. Monika worked in the SS offices. She must know all about what was happening in the concentration camps. How could she do it? How could she?

At last Ava was composed enough to face the party again. She picked up her bag and went out onto the lawn to look for Leo so that they could quietly slip away home. She could not find him. Many people stopped to congratulate Ava on her sister's marriage. It was all she could do to smile and be polite. Panic compressed her ribs. She felt she could not breathe in the hot, scented night. It was dusk, and the stars were sparkling in a luminous violet sky. People danced to the sweet music of the orchestra.

And yet they must know about what was happening to the Jews. Oberführer Jaekal had had no hesitation talking about it, here amongst the Nazi elite.

How many had he said?

Twenty thousand a day. Exterminated like rats.

A hand caught Ava's arm. It was Gertrud's boyfriend, Kranz. He drew her into his arms. 'No . . . sorry . . .' Ava tried to release herself. 'I was just looking for my husband.'

'Surely you can spare me a dance?'

Ava submitted, looking anxiously around for Leo.

'I thought you'd relish the chance to persuade me to help your foolish young husband?' Kranz whispered. 'I have connections. I can help get him out of Berlin before it gets too hot for him.'

'Thank you,' Ava murmured, her eyes flicking over the crowd. Where was Leo?

His hands slid down her back to her bottom. Ava tried to step away, but he pressed hard against her.

'Excuse me!' Ava leant away from him with all her strength. 'Do you mind?'

His arms were like steel. 'Don't pretend you don't like it,' he whispered, and squeezed her bottom harder.

'I don't, and neither will my husband!'

'Oh, I told Gertrud to keep him busy for a while so we could get better acquainted,' Kranz murmured. 'Gertrud is very willing to do all she can to show her loyalty to the cause. Are you?'

Panic raced through Ava's blood. His hands on her body sickened and frightened her, but Ava did not know how to get away. 'Please, let me go. My husband will see!'

His fingers only tightened on her buttocks. He was dancing her towards the edge of the lawn, towards the shadowy bushes.

'Does it not excite you? The chance of being discovered? Do you not love the thrill of the forbidden?' He put his tongue inside her ear. Ava jerked violently, and he made a small sound of satisfaction.

'Oh, but I'll enjoy this,' he murmured. 'I love a hot little darkie. I bet you taste sweet. The darker the flesh, the sweeter the juice.'

'No,' Ava said, turning her face away, struggling to be free. 'Please . . . my husband will be looking for me.'

'He'll be in the bushes with Gertrud sucking him off like I told her to,' he answered.

Ava was so shocked she could not speak.

'Gertrud does not like to ever admit defeat,' he told her. 'The harder the chase, the more she likes it. We're similar in that way. She's told me all about you. She knows I like forbidden fruit.'

As he spoke, Kranz ran his hands over Ava as if they were alone in a bedroom, and not standing at the edge of a dance floor at her sister's wedding. Over his shoulder Ava could see couples moving to the music, and waiters carrying trays laden with full glasses. If she screamed, if she slapped him, everyone would hear, everyone would see. What would they do? Surely he'd let her go? But then . . . later . . . what would be the consequences? Ava was paralysed, unable to think what to do. She dared not cry out or make a scene. It could not end well for her or for Leo.

'Please . . . not here . . .' Ava managed to say. 'My sister's wedding . . . she'll be looking for me . . . Leo will be looking for me.'

Kranz backed her behind a tree, pressing her into the trunk so hard it bruised her shoulder blades. His hands were on her breast, dragging up her dress to expose her bare thigh.

'Gertrud told me she denounced you to Heydrich himself,' he whispered. 'There's only one thing that would stop him from shipping a Gypsy to the camps. Well, whatever you gave to him you can give to me.'

He fumbled at the fastening of his trousers. White-hot rage flashed through her. *They are all the same, these Nazi bullies. They think they can take what they want, anytime, anywhere. Everyone is too afraid to resist them.*

Ava pushed him away so violently, he staggered. She rushed past him, back into the light. Monika swayed through the crowd, slopping champagne from the glass in her hand. 'Monika!' Ava called. 'I'm here.'

Monika turned, stumbling a little in her high heels. 'Ava, there you are.'

Ava took her arm, walking away as quickly as she could. She did not look back.

'Wasn't it a fabulous wedding?' Monika slurred. 'Weren't the little Goebbels children simply divine? Such an honour to have them attend me. And to have my wedding here! At the Goebbels' private residence. Weren't you impressed? Such a shame that Father and Bertha couldn't come. It's such a stupid law, keeping the borders closed. I told the Oberführer to do something about it, but he said the Führer was rather occupied with other business at the moment . . .'

Ava hardly listened to her. She was staring into the shadows under the trees, searching for a glimpse of her husband. She realised many had taken advantage of the darkness to creep away for some kissing and fondling. Ava heard a man moan in pleasure, and tensed with anxiety. *He wouldn't,* Ava told herself.

Monika kept on talking. 'I told you the Oberführer was big in the SS! He's been promised a promotion. We'll soon have a house like this, and servants like this, and a yacht . . .'

'Do you hear yourself?' Ava cried, goaded beyond endurance. 'Don't you realise what your husband is doing? He's a murderer!'

'Don't be ridiculous,' Monika snapped back. 'We're at war. We're fighting Germany's enemies.'

'Old men and women? Children? Being herded into bunkers and gassed to death? That's not war, that's murder.'

'You're always so holier-than-thou. How can you speak so to me? You can't tell me your husband's hands are clean.' Monika's voice was shrill.

'Leo's not like them! He wants nothing to do with torturers and murderers. He's trying to stop them!' Even as she spoke, Ava wanted to grab the words back out of the air.

She could only hope no-one else had heard what she had said. Ava turned, scrubbing away tears, and saw Leo and Gertrud right behind her, coming out of the hidden darkness of the night.

Gertrud's expression was one of triumph.

She had heard every word.

42

Dying Is Strange and Hard

Leo and Ava stood in the garden, under the pear tree. The stars spread above them, blazingly bright in the darkness of the shrouded city. She clung to him with all her strength. Once again, he marvelled at the fortitude of that long and delicate body of hers. She was all bone and sinew and nerve and spirit.

'I'm so afraid,' she whispered. 'Gertrud heard what I said. She'll tell that swine of a fiancé of hers. Oh, Leo, can't we try and get away? There must be somewhere that'll be safe.'

'We have to risk it,' Leo whispered into her hair. 'We're so close to the end now. All we need is the right opportunity.'

'You've been saying that for so long. What will happen if you fail again?'

He gritted his jaw. 'I must see this through.'

She nodded, but did not speak. Her face was damp with tears. Leo drew her closer. He had such a lump in his throat, it was as if he was swallowing a stone.

Leo thought about dying. One of Rilke's poems said, 'Dying is strange and hard.' Leo tried to remember the rest of the verse.

Dying is strange and hard

If it is not our death, but a death

That takes us by storm, when we've ripened none within us.

For the first time, Leo thought he understood what Rilke meant. If he was to die now, Leo would never become all that he could be. He would be like a pear dropped in summer, never ripening to its full purpose. He would never hold a child of his own in his hands, or see a seed he had planted grow into a rose. That was an unbearable grief.

He kissed Ava's mouth. She tasted of honey and salt. She slipped her arms around his neck, and he threaded his fingers through her hair, finding each pin and slipping it free, kissing her wet eyes, her throat, the back of her neck, the first small knots of bone in her spine. Very gently he undressed her and lowered her to the ground, spreading his coat on the grass. This was where he had first made love to her, in the garden, under the hanging branches of the pear tree. He prayed it would not be the last time.

Her naked skin was like warm silk. She smelt of flowers and of woman. Leo shuddered at the touch of her hands. His release was swift and urgent, her own cry of abandonment as quick.

Leo and Ava lay together a long time, watching the stars wheel overhead, listening to the owls hunt. Leo never wanted to let her go.

The secret radio made all the difference. Rupert could listen to news untainted by Nazi propaganda, and play music that was not forbidden by the Third Reich.

Every night, he and Lucien and a few others would meet in the latrine to smoke, talk and listen. If the block elder came to find out what they were up to, the radio was quickly wrapped in a piece of oilskin and thrust into the stinking pit.

Lucien talked a great deal, waving his hands in the air, punctuating his speech with French expressions, and making wry jokes about everything.

Rupert was happy just to sit near him, watching the change of expression on his face, listening to the torrent of words.

He was like a slant of sunshine after a terrible hailstorm. Everything Lucien touched, he brightened and warmed. It was true Lucien had been in the camp less than six months, not five years like Rupert. And he had not been beaten and humiliated as Rupert had been, for Lucien was not a Jew. Even his work for the French resistance had not attracted the anger of the guards, for he had been arrested along with men of greater importance to the Third Reich, including Léon Blum, the Jewish former Prime Minister of France. It was not all that which kept him so lively and optimistic, however. It was just Lucien's nature, and Rupert hoped desperately nothing would happen to break him.

One night, only Rupert and Lucien were listening to the radio, all the other prisoners wearied by the long and arduous day. The two men sat on the doorstep, the radio turned down low and held close to their ears, so that the sound of it would not travel through the night. Then BBC Radio announced, with great excitement, that the city of Caen in Normandy had been taken by the Allies, and the Germans were in retreat.

'They've done it!' Lucien cried in high excitement. 'They'll save France now! Soon it will be Paris that will be free, and then I can go home.' He flung his arm around Rupert's shoulders, hugging him close.

Rupert sat motionless, shaken and giddy. Blood rushed through his body. Lucien stilled. For a moment they sat quietly, Lucien's arm still around Rupert. Then he very slowly stroked down the curve of Rupert's spine. Rupert turned a little towards him, and Lucien began to caress him more boldly. Rupert lifted his own hand and shaped the curve of Lucien's bicep. Clumsily they kissed, acutely aware of the danger.

But all was dark and quiet. No-one could see.

Killing Hitler was not getting any easier.

The Führer's world had narrowed down to a mere pinprick, and those who could step within that dark hole found it difficult to hold their nerve. Once, twice, thrice, in early July, one of the conspirators came close enough to the Führer to smell his foul breath, and each time they found themselves unable to pull the trigger.

On 17 July, Leo got word that a warrant of arrest had been issued for Carl Goerdeler, the former mayor of Leipzig who had resigned after the Nazis took down a statue of Mendelssohn. Goerdeler had come to Berlin to help set up a new government once Hitler was dead. He went into hiding at the Anhalter Bahnhof Hotel, near the ruin of the train station where so many thousands of Jews had been deported. Stauffenberg had to strike soon.

On 19 July, word came that a meeting with Hitler would be held the next day at his headquarters at the Wolf's Lair, near Rastenburg. The conspirators made ready. Stauffenberg would fly to the Wolf's Lair with the bomb in his briefcase. He would detonate the bomb, leave it in the conference room, then make some excuse to leave. Surely the plan could not fail this time.

Leo did not sleep. Bombs rained down on Berlin all night, the darkness filled with the drone of RAF bombers, the stutter of the flak guns, the whine of the falling missiles. He lay on the camp bed in the cellar, Ava tucked in close beside him, her breathing hurried and uneven. Occasionally she scrubbed at her eyes with a wet, scrunched handkerchief.

In the red glare of the wounded dawn, Leo dressed himself in his field-grey uniform, drew his cap down over his eyes, and said goodbye to his wife.

'Oh, Leo,' Ava whispered. 'I am so afraid.'

'So am I.' Leo found it hard to speak, his jaw was so stiff with tension.

'At least you tried,' Ava said. 'Whatever happens, at least you know you tried.'

'Promise me you'll get away if you can,' he said in a low, urgent tone. 'I can bear my own death, but not yours, Ava. Not yours.' Ava nodded and promised him, kissing him again and again. He had to break her hold to go.

In the Bendlerblock, the circle of conspirators waited. Some paced the floor, some read the Bible quietly, some sat and doodled. General Beck, the former Chief of Staff, was wearing his uniform for the first time since his dismissal in 1938. He sat stiffly, his hands clasped, looking at nothing. General Olbricht worked away quietly at his desk. Leo tried to emulate his calm. But it was difficult to concentrate on lists and reports. The heat was stifling.

Shortly after one o'clock, the telephone rang. General Olbricht answered it. He was the main architect of the plan called Operation Valkyrie, which the generals hoped to use to seize control of Berlin once Hitler was dead. His hand began to shake, his face was stiff with his effort to show nothing of what he felt. The receiver rattled when he put it down in the cradle. 'The bomb has exploded. Hitler is dead.'

There was a sigh and a rustle all over the room.

'I shall go and inform General Fromm that Operation Valkyrie must be put into action,' Olbricht said. 'Löwenstein, bring the Valkyrie orders.'

Leo did as he was told. It was hard to stop his excitement and jubilation from showing on his face. He had to set his jaw hard, and tense every muscle in his body. A nerve twitched in his thumb, making the papers he carried shiver. Leo put them in his other hand.

General Fromm was the head of the Reserve Army and, although aware of the conspiracy, had never been a part of it. When told that Hitler was dead, he frowned at General Olbricht and snapped, 'Who told you so?'

'Fellgiebel,' Olbricht answered. 'In Rastenburg.'

'We had better get confirmation,' Fromm said. He rang the Wolf's Lair, and demanded to know if Hitler was really dead.

Then he slammed down the phone and glared suspiciously at General Olbricht. 'The Führer is not dead! He's barely wounded at all.'

Olbricht stood as if turned to stone. 'That's ... that's good news, General. Are you sure it is correct? We have had news of an explosion.'

'I spoke to Keitel himself,' Fromm answered.

'Very well. We will wait for orders then.' Olbricht turned and left the General's office. Leo followed him, his jaw stiff with tension. His thoughts were in tumult. His strongest emotion was one of utter disbelief. How could Hitler possibly have survived such an explosion?

Once Olbricht informed the rest of the General Staff what had happened, a tumult of questions arose. 'What do we do? What will happen now? Do we go ahead with Operation Valkyrie?'

'We must go ahead! No time can be lost,' Leo cried.

'No! We must wait for news,' General Beck responded sharply. 'If Hitler is barely wounded at all . . . we must try and save ourselves.'

'There's no saving ourselves now,' Leo replied. 'Our only hope is to act nonetheless.'

General Beck hesitated, his thin face furrowed with fear. 'Let us wait for Stauffenberg. He will know the truth of what has happened.'

Claus von Stauffenberg arrived at the Bendlerstrasse after four o'clock, and was astonished and furious to find nothing had happened. He refused to believe that Hitler was not dead. 'Keitel is lying. We have to declare a state of emergency! Send out the orders.'

The teleprinters all began to chatter as the secretaries ran to obey. For the next few hours, all was busy. Leo worked the telephones, ringing allies, trying to convince them to stand by Operation Blitz, speaking to the conspirators in Paris and urging them to act.

Then Hitler himself spoke on the radio. Leo turned the volume dial up. 'I speak to you today so you can hear my voice and know that I was not injured . . . this crime was the work of a tiny group of ambitious and unscrupulous army officers . . .'

At the sound of the Führer's harsh voice, a groan could be heard all through the busy offices. Till that moment, everyone had tried to hope that Hitler was indeed dead.

Olbricht sent the secretaries home, and ordered the officers to secure the building. Leo obeyed. His friend Ewald-Heinrich von Kleist was sent to find some troops to defend the garrison. 'We'll stay and defend ourselves,' Olbricht said. 'It is most likely we will be crushed within the hour. I intend to die a soldier's death.'

Stauffenberg drew Leo and the other young officers aside. 'You must get out. Our fate is sealed, but you may be able to escape and try again. Swear to me on your honour that you will not rest until Hitler is dead and Germany at peace.'

Leo swore. His eyes felt hot, and his throat stifled. He and the other officers – about five in all – went out a back window and down a drainpipe.

Leo was the last to leave. As he put his head out the window, he saw lorries full of SS officers arrive, skidding to a halt out in the Bendlerstrasse. They all had machine guns held ready.

Then Leo heard a shout from within. 'Treason! Treason!' A shot rang out.

Leo slithered down to the ground, and ran off into the night. His heart was pounding so fast he was afraid it might burst. Behind him, the swift rattle of machine-gun fire.

Ava had been restless and unsettled all day. She walked Zeus in the scorched wasteland that was the Tiergarten, then went to queue for food. She thought she had best be prepared for any eventuality.

The morning was quiet enough, but around one o'clock in the afternoon there had been a gradual change in the atmosphere of the city. Tanks began to rattle along the streets, soldiers marching behind. Potsdamer Platz was cordoned off with barbed wire, and traffic stopped and searched. 'What's happened?' Ava asked a gaunt-faced woman in a shapeless old frock, a scarf tied over her hair.

'They say that the Führer is dead,' she answered brusquely. 'But of course it cannot be true.'

Ava had to guard her face. She could not show either her joy or her fear. She went home, trudging past bomb craters and piles of rubble, and went down to the cellar. Crouching on the camp bed, Ava turned on the radio. She listened all afternoon, Zeus sitting beside her, his head tilted in bemusement. She heard Hitler's announcement, and pressed her hands against her mouth in horror.

The assassination attempt had failed.

Ava could not believe it. What would happen now?

She could not eat, or settle down to read. She paced the floor of the kitchen, while Zeus sat nearby, whining with fear. Ava bent and fondled his silky ears. 'It's all right, boy, it's all right,' Ava lied.

She packed her satchel, just in case they had to flee in a hurry. Her papers and passport. All the housekeeping money. The von Löwenstein pearls in their velvet case. All the food she had bought. Her satchel was bulging, but she managed to squeeze in her father's book of fairy tales and Leo's book of poems as well. She could not bear to leave those behind.

Soon after ten o'clock, the front door banged. Ava rushed into the hallway. Leo came in, his face white. He threw his cap on the floor. Ava flung herself into his arms. 'Oh, Leo, what's happened?'

'Stauffenberg failed,' he said shortly. 'The bomb went off but somehow Hitler survived. He's protected by some malign force, Ava! The SS raided us. I think Stauffenberg and the others are dead.'

'What are we going to do?' Ava clung to him.

'We'd better get out of here. I've filled the car with petrol. Grab what you can.'

'Where shall we go? They'll search at the schloss, won't they?'

'We'll head into the mountains, try to get to Switzerland or Liechten-stein.' Leo had gone into the study. Ava could hear papers rustling. She ran into the kitchen and seized her satchel, putting the strap over her head.

Leo called, 'Ava, I need to burn all my papers. Can you pack me some clothes and we'll get out of here?'

A sudden crash of splintering wood. Ava ran towards the hall, then stopped short, her hand over her mouth. Soldiers had kicked in the door. They burst into the house, guns in their hands. Leo ran from the study, drawing his pistol. Without hesitation, they charged him and beat him to the ground. Zeus leapt for their throats. He was shot down. 'No!' Leo shouted.

The old Great Dane lay where he had fallen, blood seeping from his silvered hide. A wave of such dizziness washed over Ava, she could see nothing. Black stars sparkling in her vision. She put out a groping hand, and caught hold of the door jamb. Head bent, she tried to catch her breath.

The soldiers did not see Ava. The hall was dark, and they were too busy kicking Leo. He fought back. The hall table smashed. A china bowl broke. Leo was punched down again. His nose was bleeding, his shirt was torn.

'Ava, go!' he shouted. 'Get out of here.'

Ava could not move. He flung her an agonised look. 'Go!'

The soldiers had seen her. Two started towards her, ugly looks on their faces. Ava ran back into the kitchen, slammed shut the door and jammed a chair under it. Then she ran into the narrow scullery, opened the cellar door and scrambled down the stairs in the darkness. She had spent so many hours in this dark, stinking hole in recent months, she moved swiftly and surely. She found a chair and dragged it under the coal hole, then climbed on top of it. Her reaching hands found the metal coal lid. She heaved with all her strength and managed to push it up. It fell over with a clang.

The cellar door opened. A powerful torch flashed. She was pinned in its beam. 'Halt!' a voice shouted.

Ava grasped both edges of the coal hole. She dragged herself up, the muscles in her shoulders screaming. A shot rang out. She jerked as fire glanced across the back of her bare leg. The chair fell with a crash. She heaved herself out into the night. A strong hand grabbed her ankle. She kicked her other leg with all her strength. A bellow of pain. Her ankle was released.

Ava scrambled to her feet and ran into the darkness.

Part V

Flesh and Blood
February – April 1945

. . . The girl took courage and said, 'I will continue on as far as the wind blows and as long as the cock crows, until I find him.' And she went on a long, long way, until at last she came to the castle where her lover was held captive by the enchantress who had cursed him.

She dressed in the gown that glistened like the sun itself. When the enchantress wanted the dress, the girl said: 'It's not for sale for money, but only for flesh and blood.'

'The Singing, Springing Lark', the Brothers Grimm

43

Angel of Fire

Ava crouched in the ruins of a bombed-out house, her arms about her knees. Snowflakes drifted down from the blackness.

She was hungry. Shivers racked her emaciated body. She hugged herself more tightly. Her skin was damp with fever, her temples pounding like drums.

Six months had passed since Hitler did not die. Ava lived on the streets, in ruined cellars and abandoned factories. Jutta helped her when she could. Jutta was living underground too. Submerged. They lived on what they could forage or steal. Sometimes kind shopkeepers would toss a heel of bread or a potato. More often they grubbed about on the ground for fallen beechnuts or tore up weeds to stuff into their mouths.

Ava did not know if Leo was alive or dead.

Most of the conspirators had been hanged on piano wire from meat hooks. Some had been sent to concentration camps.

Ava did not know what Leo's fate had been. She had no way of knowing. She tried to listen to the radio when she could. It still blared from loud-speakers on street corners. If anyone ever left a newspaper folded on a park bench, Ava would snatch it up and read it from cover to cover before using it to feed her little campfire. The official news was all lies and propaganda,

379

she knew, but it was better to know a little of what was happening, rather than nothing.

So Ava knew things were going badly for the German army. Paris had been liberated. Florence. Brussels. Athens. Warsaw. All had shaken off the German jackboot.

Germany itself had been invaded. Allied forces had crossed the Siegfried Line to the west. The Russians were advancing steadily from the east. They were now less than eighty kilometres from Berlin.

And the Führer?

Hitler had gone underground, just like Jutta and Ava. He had gone down into his concrete bunker in the garden of the Reich Chancellery in mid-January and not come up again.

Meanwhile, the British and the Americans bombed Berlin day and night.

Ava could not seek refuge in an air-raid shelter. She had no papers. She had burnt them the night she had escaped. Ava von Löwenstein was wanted by the Gestapo. Ava was her no longer. Ava was nobody.

Her constant companion was hunger. Ava had fought others for a handful of potato peelings thrown in a bin. She had stolen bread from a street barrow. She had begged a child in the street for his apple core and crammed it into her mouth with tears of joy streaming down her face.

She heard the familiar hum of approaching planes. She crouched lower. The siren began its awful scream. Ava shielded her ears. The darkness was sliced by stilt-walkers of light. White on black. Like a thousand inverted swastikas. Even when Ava shut her eyes, she saw them. Burning.

Planes soared and spun overhead in a deadly ballet. The flak guns rattled. Bombs whistled. Giant chrysanthemums of flame blossomed from smoke. Somehow Ava was untouched, humming with silence, noise exploding all around her.

An angel of fire strode overhead. Wings of rustling flame. Legs like pillars of smoke. A face of darkness.

All angels are terrible.

Ava stumbled to her feet. She stood, looking up into the blazing sky. It seemed the whole universe burned. Firestorm scarlet with trumpets, gilded with flutes, darkened with brass.

Sparks stung her face and arms. Her hair was whipped behind her in a blast of fiery breath. Her whole body glowed with heat, her skin a lantern. *Is this is how I shall die?* she thought. *Please . . . I want to live . . .*

For a moment, Ava stood, one foot in shadows, one foot in flame. Then, with a turn in the wind, the angel of fire stepped away from her. A whirl of ashes and cinders, a final heavy footfall, and then – to her left – a house exploded into flame. Ava was flung backwards.

Screaming. People ran down the street, arms flailing. Some were on fire. An air-raid shelter had been hit. A mother was carrying a limp child. Mouth gaping. An old woman tottered forward. She wore a fur coat. Handbag on her arm. She fell to her knees. Shrapnel rattled in a deadly hail. She jerked and fell. Smoke billowed. Ava darted forward. Seized the old woman under her arms. Dragged her behind a mound of rubble. She was dead. Ava hauled off her fur coat. Her arms flopped and dangled. She had good stout shoes. Ava tore at the shoelaces. One was knotted. Ava bit it through. Wrested the shoes off her bony feet. Thick woollen stockings. Ava pulled them off her thin white legs. The old woman's dress was soaked with blood. Ava tugged it over her head and clutched it to her. Smiling. Caught up the old woman's handbag. Ran. Left her lying there among the rubble in her satin slip. Withered limbs akimbo.

Shouting. Close. Ava scrambled over the rubble. Found a hole. Crawled in. Huddled down in the warmth of the fur coat.

Smiling.

For months, Ava had scuttled from hole to hole like a rat.

Now she had papers. The old woman's name had been Rosamund Gärtner. She had been born in 1879. The typed numbers had faded with time. With a burnt stick, Ava was able to make it look more like 1919, her own birth year. The photo was more of a problem. She did her best to darken the image's grey hair with dirt and charcoal. At least Rosamund had had a thin face like Ava's. Her eyes had been hazel. Ava's were green. But hazel was one of those words. She thought she could carry it off.

With papers, Ava could walk the streets. She could use the old woman's ration card to buy food. She could take refuge in a public air-raid shelter. Rosamund had had a little money. Best of all, she had had an apartment.

Everything felt strange the day Ava first went there. The air was garish with smoke. Bodies loomed towards her out of the blur. Faded away. Shouting sounded far away. People lurched at her, carrying stretchers. Ava thought she must be light-headed with hunger. Or fear.

She climbed the rickety stairs, keeping her head down. When she reached the apartment door, Ava looked all around. No-one to see. She turned her key in her lock. She walked into the apartment. Ava locked the door behind her.

It smelt stuffy. A bedroom, a tiny gallery kitchen, a flushing toilet and sink. Luxury. She washed and lay down on the bed. She slept. When she woke, Ava ate the food left in the cupboards. She thanked Rosamund for dying. Then she went in search of Jutta.

Many U-boaters took refuge in the dead woman's apartment. They came. They left. Often Ava did not know their real names. Not all were Jews. Some were Communists. Once Ava and Jutta had a family of Jehovah's Witnesses. They never fought back, no matter what Hitler's thugs did to them. They had had a hard time. Ava gave them a floor to sleep on. False papers when she could. Jutta knew a man.

Ava knew – any day now – a neighbour or one of the old woman's friends might see one of the U-boaters coming in or out of her apartment and wonder. Might report them to the block warden. Everyone slept lightly.

On 3 February, American bombers attacked Berlin more virulently than ever before. The Gestapo headquarters were bombed. So were the Reich Chancellery and the People's Court. The Nazi judge Roland Freisler was killed. Hitler was not.

The fire from the bombing lasted four days. It reduced everything in its path to ashes. The Unter den Linden was just a sea of rubble.

The houses of giants had at last been toppled.

Ava heard a rumour that Judge Freisler's body had been found with the files of Fabian von Schlabrendorff in his hand. Schlabrendorff had been one of the men Ava had met at the Admiral's house. He was the one who had smuggled the bomb in the box that was meant to hold cognac bottles. She had thought he must be dead.

But he was alive. Ava could not help the wild hope that Leo was alive too. She had to find out. She had to know.

Ava went in search of her sister. She had not seen Monika since the night of her wedding. She had never wanted to see her again. But only Monika could help her.

It took Ava a long time to find out where she was. Ava waited outside her house for hours, just like the Gestapo, till she was sure Monika was alone.

But Ava knocked politely.

She hardly recognised Monika when she opened the door. Her sister was almost as thin as she was, and her eyes were haggard. Ava was dressed in an old lady's stolen clothes, however, while Monika wore a black silk dressing-gown.

'You've got to help me,' Ava said. 'I need to know if Leo is alive. Please. Help me. I'll come back in a week.' Ava turned and hastened away.

Monika cried, 'Ava! Wait!'

But she did not wait.

That week, US and British forces crossed the Rhine. The Red Army entered Austria and captured Danzig. General Eisenhower called upon Germany to surrender.

Hitler's response?

He sent the Hitler Youth to fight tanks with panzerfausts mounted on bicycles.

When Ava went back to Monika's house, her sister had evidently been keeping watch for her. Monika opened her front door, walked down the street and – not meeting Ava's eyes – tossed a screwed-up piece of paper at the rubbish bin. It fell short. Monika's high heels clacked away down the snowy street. Ava bent and picked up the piece of paper.

It had one word scribbled on it.

Flossenbürg.

Ava dug through the charred ruins of their house with bare hands. She did not know when it had been bombed. Perhaps, if Leo had not been arrested and she had not fled, they would both have died as its walls fell.

Ava found the coal hole. She dragged up the lid and lowered herself through it into the darkness below. Half the cellar had collapsed. Ava moved bricks and rubble until her hands bled. She found her mother's old chest of clothes and dragged it free. Hard as a nut, it was unbroken, though it was heavily powdered with white like an aristocrat's wig. She looked inside. Her mother's dresses lay within, safely folded in tissue. The little velvet bag was safe too, with its charms of love and protection. Ava tucked that inside her dress.

Then she had to try and climb out of the cellar. All the chairs were broken, and the chest was cumbersome. Ava made a staircase of rubble, and clawed her way to the top, the chest resting on one hip like a basket of washing.

Filthy, exhausted, Ava carried the chest down the road.

Berlin at night. An animal in so much pain it could not rest. It whimpered and moaned. Paced back and forth, uncomprehending. Tail lashing. It scratched at its own sores until they were wounds.

Ava had to be quick. Silent. If she was not careful she'd be robbed. Or raped. Or both. Yet her breath came harshly, her feet were leaden.

The church was a ruin. Once-fine villas gaped open to the sky. The forest was matchsticks burnt to the nadir. But there, crouched among the tottering piles of scorched bricks, was Leo's little ramshackle garage. Its window was cracked and veiled in cobwebs. Its chain hung rusty. Intact. Ava found the key, hidden as always under the step, and wrenched it around in the lock till it clicked open. She dragged the wooden doors apart. Within was a dark hulking shape. Ava pulled off the dust-sheets. Gilda gleamed at her through the shadows, her eyes round and friendly as a happy doll's. Ava stroked her curving fenders as if she was a living creature. Loyal to the end. One of her tyres was flat. Ava had never changed a tyre before. She had watched Leo do it. Once. A long time ago.

And Ava needed petrol. The tank was full, but Ava remembered that it had not been enough to get the Mercedes to the schloss after their wedding. She would need to make sure she had extra.

Jutta could get anything on the black market. But petrol?

Ava could only ask.

She put the chest in the Mercedes, locked the garage up safely again, and crept away through the wreckage.

Jutta and Ava were still using the dead woman's apartment as a bolthole. So were four other fugitives. Marlene, a thin young woman with dyed blonde hair that contrasted oddly with her thick black eyebrows. Krista, barely out of her teens but with a six-year-old daughter named Annaliesa. Neither ever spoke about the father, and Annaliesa was a strangely still and silent child. Finally, there was Trudl, a belligerent older woman who had nothing good to say about men or Gentiles. Trudl had not spoken a word to Ava since she had found out Ava was not Jewish.

Krista and her daughter shared the bed, Trudl had taken over the couch, and Marlene lay on a makeshift mattress of cushions and pillows on the floor. Jutta was already awake, sitting at the table with black market contraband spread out before her. Cigarettes. Canned ham. Condoms.

'Jutta, I've found where Leo is,' Ava whispered. 'He's in the camp in Flossenbürg, in Bavaria. I have to go and get him out. Will you help me?'

'What do you need?' she whispered back. Ava told her. Jutta considered for a moment, then nodded. 'I have a secret stash of cigarettes I can trade for petrol. I have one condition, though.'

'What?'

'Take me with you. As far as Buchenwald, anyway. I need to try and find Rupert.'

Ava nodded. 'Of course I'll take you. By all accounts, the Russians will be here any day now. Even if half the rumours are true, we don't want to be in Berlin then.'

'What about the others?' Jutta indicated the sleeping women about her.

'Gilda has only two seats . . . but if they can hang on to the fenders . . .'

'All right.'

'It'll be dangerous,' Ava warned her. 'The roads will be full of people trying to escape Berlin. I don't know how close the Russians are, or which way they are coming.'

'I'd rather take my chances on the road than stay here in Berlin.'

Both Ava and Jutta fell silent. The newspapers had been full of the horrors of the Red Army advance into East Prussia. Civilians had been shot. Women raped, then crucified on barn doors. Babies had their heads bashed against walls. Even though Ava was used to thinking that all the news Berliners received was lies and propaganda, it was impossible not to be shocked and frightened by the pictures. And Ava knew of the atrocities German soldiers had committed in their advance into Russia. One had to expect rage and revenge.

'We'll need food,' Jutta said. 'And water.' She stood up, scooping the contraband towards her.

'Do you know how to put a wheel on a car?' Ava asked.

Jutta stared at her. Suddenly she began to laugh. She bent over, wheezing and wiping her eyes. Ava found herself laughing too. She caught at Jutta's hand, trying to control herself. The friends clung to each other, laughing, unable to stop.

Ava did not understand why.

Barbarossa's Cave

Ava and her friends started out in the grey hush before dawn.

Somehow Jutta and Ava had managed to get the spare wheel onto the Mercedes. Their hands and faces were streaked with oil by the time they finished. The other women had gone to fill up water bottles at one of the street pumps. Although it was not yet dawn, there was already a queue of women waiting.

Ava and Jutta had no more than the clothes on their backs, and knotted sacks of whatever food they could scrape together. They had lost everything else long ago. Ava had grabbed two long-handled shovels and some other tools from the garage. She expected the road to be rough. They had to clear broken bricks and charred timber from the rear lane, but then – once the car reached the Tiergartenstrasse – the road was relatively clear. Krista sat with her daughter in her lap in the passenger seat, with Jutta seated on the boot behind her, holding onto her shoulder. Marlene and Trudl stood on the fenders, holding on as best they could.

Near the zoo, a roadblock had been set up with barbed wire and wooden trestles. It was guarded by rheumy-eyed old men with silver bristled chins, and a handful of frightened boys who looked about twelve. Ava smiled, and said they were going to her mother-in-law's house to the south. After the guards had checked their papers (all of which were fake or stolen), Ava was allowed to drive on. It had been a long time since she had last driven, so Gilda moved in jerks and hops and once or twice stalled, before Ava remembered the rhythm of it.

It was early April. Snow lay in white mounds in the shadow of broken walls, and the ruts of the road glistened with ice. A lilac tree hung heavy purple blooms over a mound of broken bricks and splintered timbers. Children played some kind of war game in the ruin of a school. Smoke smudged the horizon, and turned the sky to orange cellophane.

Gilda's progress was slow. Many of the side streets were blocked with barriers made of warped steel girders and rubble that would have taken hours to dig through. The main roads were choked with cars and jeeps and shabby old carts pulled by horses that were little more than tents of bone and skin. Most people trudged along, pushing wheelbarrows and prams piled high with baggage, or dragging along toy wagons. Babies wailed. Children grizzled. Prisoners of war with sullen faces were digging trenches. Ava nosed Gilda through the crowds. Most people made way. Berliners had always respected authority, even if it was simply a hand pressed on a car horn.

A row of bodies strung up from lampposts. *Cowards! Deserters!* Hastily scrawled placards hung about their necks. One was a boy of only fifteen or so. Too young to have hair on his upper lip.

Ava drove the back ways, trying to avoid the autobahn. Every mile was hard-won. Her hands were tight on the wheel. Shoulders ached with tension. Occasionally an angry pedestrian would refuse to move out of her way. Marlene and Trudl would shout and wave their shovels about, and Ava would toot the horn, till at last they stepped to the verge of the road and let the Mercedes pass.

Once the car reached the forest, they were able to move along more swiftly. Although there were still many people trudging along, carrying suitcases, Ava found her best approach was to put her hand on the horn, and her foot on the accelerator, and force people to jump out of her way. Otherwise they banged on Gilda's bonnet and grabbed at her passengers, trying to force their way aboard. Once Marlene hit a young man over the head with her shovel. Dazed, he let go of the car and fell back on the road and Gilda was able to race away.

Ava was pitiless. The angel of fire had taught her that.

Around noon, a Russian airplane zoomed down low over the road and began to shoot at the refugees. People screamed and flung themselves to the ground. Some did not get up again. Marlene was hit in the head. She fell backwards onto the road, blood spurting. Ava did not stop. With her foot down hard on the accelerator, she veered off the road and away over a muddy field, the tyres skidding. The Mercedes bounced and rattled, then swerved over a ditch and a low stone wall. Ava did not stop until the Russian planes were far behind, and found a narrow laneway that led them south-west, away from the refugees.

Annaliesa would not stop crying. Her tiny bunched hands were blue with cold. Trudl wrapped her in the shawl, but Annaliesa only wept harder. Her mother tried to comfort her with food, but the little girl refused to eat. Even weeping, she made no noise. Her contorted mouth was silent. Only the tears kept squeezing from her scrunched eyes and, occasionally, she would gulp for air. It was a relief to leave Krista and her daughter near Leipzig. They hoped to find a cousin there who would shelter them. Trudl then sat on the boot, a shovel in her hands, as Ava did her best not to skid on the black ice of the roads. Dusk came early, but Ava kept on driving, peering ahead. She dared not stop for anything.

Sometime during the night, Trudl said in a gruff voice, 'I'll drive. You rest.'

Everyone rearranged themselves. Ava sat in the passenger seat, wrapped in a blanket. Incredibly, she slept.

Rupert and Lucien lay under the kitchen bunker, in a hole dug carefully out of the dirt over many weeks. It was almost dawn, and they should be creeping back to their bunks. But it was hard to leave the little haven they had built for themselves.

All order in the camp had broken down. Guards were disappearing without leave, or simply not turning up for their watch, too drunk or too frightened to show their faces. The ever-present rumble of guns in the distance was growing closer. The sky was brazen with smoke. Panic reigned. The camp Commandant, Oberführer Hermann Pister, had told the camp leaders that he intended to surrender to the first Allied forces to reach Buchenwald. He begged them to speak well of him.

The camp was bulging at its barbed-wire seams. For weeks, train-loads of prisoners had been brought to Buchenwald as camps to the east had been liberated by the Russians. The prisoners had come, mere skulls and bones dressed in skin and rags, from Majdanek and from Auschwitz. Those who could still speak had terrible tales to tell. Feverish rumours flew.

Everyone in Buchenwald was to be exterminated, some said. The SS had giant flame-throwers and planned to set the whole camp on fire, with all the prisoners still in it. No, only the sick and the weak would die, others said. The rest would be marched south. Himmler wanted the Americans to find no evidence of what had happened in the death camps under his control. It's the Jews Himmler wants dead, someone else said. They'll kill all the Jews, and then let the gates open for everyone else to escape.

Rupert had thought it prudent to have somewhere to hide. After six years in the camp, he knew every hollow and every crevice. He had hidden in this hole before, and over time had dug it deeper, and concealed it better. He and Lucien had secreted food and blankets and weapons in their hideout. Rupert had his trumpet, and his sardine can full of scraps of poems and songs. He carried them with him everywhere he went.

To feel your touch in the midnight hour, to know the burn of your secret kiss, to hear your groan in my ear, to feel you clench about me . . .

He looked at Lucien, who smiled back. His lover was as thin and bare as bone, but his black eyes were still bright with life. 'We should get back, *mon ami,*' he said. The sound of marching feet. Rupert shrank back down, Lucien close beside him. They peered out the gap between the earth and the hut.

A thickset man was being manhandled down the path by two SS guards, another dozen tramping behind. He was dressed only in trousers and shirt but Rupert recognised him at once. It was Karl-Otto Koch, the former Commandant of the camp. Rupert stared in utter disbelief. He had heard rumours that Koch was locked up in the Bunker, and was to be shot. If that was true, then perhaps the Americans really were only fifty kilometres away. Perhaps the war really was nearly over.

'Who is that?' Lucien whispered.

'Standartenführer Koch. He used to be our Commandant.'

'Where are they taking him?'

'The SS shooting range is down there. I'd heard a rumour he was to be shot. I can't believe it's true.'

'But why?'

'Not for his cruelty to us,' Rupert whispered. 'No, he embezzled funds from the camp finances, so he could live a life of luxury. And there's rumours he killed the camp doctor. Either because he was having an affair with Koch's wife, or because he knew Koch had syphilis, I don't know which.'

The rows of boots marched right past their hideout, and Rupert ducked down. A minute or so later, they heard a fusillade of shots.

'The world is falling apart,' Rupert whispered. 'Now anything is possible.'

Lucien put his arm across his back. 'Like a world where two men are free to love?'

They kissed tenderly.

Soon they heard the drag of a heavy body being taken back to the crematorium.

'If we can just stay safe a little longer,' Rupert murmured. 'Just a little longer.'

When Ava woke, the Mercedes was pulled in under a tree. Jutta and Trudl were sleeping on the ground next to Gilda's wheels. Ava woke them.

She could not bear the idea of sitting still. Everyone clambered back into the car, and Ava started the engine. It sounded diabolically loud in the quiet of the forest. As she drove away down the road, a single star hung in the lightening sky to the east. The sky to the west showed a false sunset of red flames. That way, Ava knew, was the American army.

Trudl left them at Rottleben. She said in her usual abrupt way that she needed to go and find her son. Ava had not known she had a son. Trudl looked her in the eyes. 'Thank you,' she said. Then she melted away into the snow-dusted forest.

Jutta and Ava drove on, into the cavernous night. The whole horizon, all around, was marked with orange scratches. Claw marks of flame.

'While you were sleeping, Trudl told me a story,' Jutta said. 'Not far from here is a cave, where Barbarossa is meant to lie sleeping. His beard is growing around a table. When it has grown around it three times, he will wake. He will hang his shield on a dead tree. If leaves sprout, then better times shall come.'

'And if the tree does not sprout?'

'Then the world will come to an end.'

Ava looked out at the bare trees, starkly outlined against the flaming sky, and shivered. It seemed to her that the end of the world had already come.

The loudspeakers on the Appellplatz called all Jews to report.

Rupert looked at Lucien in horror.

'You can't go,' Lucien whispered. 'Whatever they mean to do, it'll mean death one way or another.'

'They'll search. What if they find us?'

'We'll be careful.'

'What about the boys? How can we hide so many?'

Lucien shook his head hopelessly.

'We have to try.' Rupert clenched his bony hands into futile fists.

The two men hobbled slowly down the hill, keeping in the shadows of the huts. Both were half-crippled by months of near-starvation and brutal treatment. Rupert's feet were numb and black with frostbite, and Lucien had a nasty sore on one leg.

It was still early, and the sun was only just showing a red rim above the smoke-hazed horizon. Down in the curve of the valley was the little camp. A place of mud and filth and disease, where the Jews were locked in quarantine barracks or crowded into tents and makeshift shelters. Typhus had raged through the camp for the last three months. More than thirteen thousand people had died, too many for the crematorium to burn. Their naked bodies were still stacked in piles, waiting to be buried in shallow graves in the forest. The stench was almost unbearable.

Lucien covered his nose with his hand. '*Dégueu!*'

Ducking and weaving through the huts and tents, Rupert and Lucien reached Block 66, a small wooden barrack in the squalid heart of the little camp. There were no guards down here. The SS tried to keep away from there as much as possible. Rupert knocked on the door, and it was opened a crack. A man's weary face peered out.

'Quick, come in!'

The door was opened wider, and Rupert and Lucien slipped in.

The interior of the hut was crowded with children. Some were as young as five, a few as old as fifteen. All were scrawny and filthy, with eyes that had seen far too much. They were dressed in striped rags, with yellow triangles or stars sewn to their chests. Most had come to the camp in the past six months, from camps in Poland, and the prisoners had done their best to help and protect them. A rough kind of school had been set up, and Rupert had come often to sing songs and tell stories and teach them music. Lucien was a great favourite too, for his card tricks and silly faces, though few of the boys spoke French and he could not speak Polish.

'They have called all Jews to report to the Appellplatz,' Rupert said, without preliminaries.

'What are we to do?' The block elder was a kind-faced Czech named Antonin. He twisted his thin hands together. 'Another deportation will kill the boys. It is still so cold . . . and those cattle trucks . . .'

'Can we hide them?' Lucien asked.

'One or two, perhaps. But this many?' Rupert indicated the crowds of boys, all big-eyed and anxious.

'If we could take off their yellow stars . . .' Antonin murmured.

Lucien looked at Rupert. 'The clothing depot . . . so many dead people . . . surely there will be spare uniforms?'

'Let's go.'

The two men went through the camp at a stumbling run. They could hear the barking of dogs and the shouting of the SS guards. 'Out! Out! All Jews report. Hurry!'

Everywhere in the little camp, men were scrambling to hide. Some lay down amongst the stacks of corpses. Others slipped into the latrine pits, or crawled under the bunkers. 'We must be quick,' Rupert panted.

They came to the clothing depot. Usually it was busy with prisoners on laundry duty, but all work in the camp had ground to a halt some days ago. There was just too much panic, too much confusion.

Rupert and Lucien rummaged through the shelves, grabbing armfuls of uniforms marked with the red triangle, a symbol of a political prisoner. Then they crept out and made their way back down into the children's bunker. They helped Antonin dress as many boys as possible in the new uniforms. They did not have nearly enough.

'I will put a typhus sign on the door,' Antonin said. 'That'll keep the guards away.'

'At least some of the boys will be able to go out and get food,' Rupert said wearily.

Their arms full of jackets marked with the yellow triangle, Rupert and Lucien made their way through the outlying huts towards the kitchen and their hideout. Both were tired now. It did not take much to exhaust their reserves of strength.

Dogs barking. Men shouting. The sound of blows. 'Out! All Jews, now!'

'Come on,' Lucien whispered, putting his arm under Rupert's. 'Run.'

Rupert tried, limping along on feet damaged by frostbite. The kitchen block was not far ahead. Lucien lifted up the plank of wood that hid their secret entrance, and slid down into the hole. 'Hurry!' he implored.

Rupert began to crawl through the tiny crack. The trumpet tied at his waist clanged against the concrete pillar.

'Halt!' a voice cried.

Then hard hands grasped Rupert and dragged him out into the light.

Ava drove on into the day. The road was deeply rutted. Sometimes the Mercedes's wheels spun in mud, and she had to jam her foot on the accelerator to drive the car out again.

Ava did not know the way to Buchenwald. All she knew was that it was on the flank of the mountain behind Weimar. There were no street signs. She navigated by trial and error, keeping off the main roads, heading south and west and south again. As the day slowly revealed itself, it grew easier. Ava saw through the bare forest a great pale hulk of a building, built on baroque lines, which she guessed might be Ettersburg Castle. All she knew of it was that Goethe had once stayed there, and that it was near Buchenwald. Ava gripped the wheel harder, her stomach twisting with nerves. What would they do once they got there? How would they find Rupert? And how was she meant to rescue Leo?

Her tired brain could find no answers to the questions.

The road wound upwards through bare winter trees of oak and beech, with the occasional flash of silver birch. Higher up the hill, the forest was all evergreen pine. Then she saw something like a desert through the trees. A vast stretch of cleared earth, shaped like an open fan, and lined with wooden huts. High walls. Coils of barbed wire. Tall watchtowers.

A column of men were trudging down through a heavy gate and along the road. Stick-thin. Clad in stripy rags. Thousands more just stood in rows in the square, lifeless as scarecrows.

'Is that it? Is that where Rupert has been all this time?' Tears began to rush down Jutta's face. 'My God. Oh my God.'

'Wait!' Lucien cried. He scrambled out of the hole and ran after Rupert, stumbling away in the grip of two SS guards. 'Take me too!'

Lucien had dragged off his own jacket, marked with a red triangle, and was pulling on another, marked with yellow.

The guards seized him. 'Right! Two more Jews. Get going.'

Rupert's vision swam with tears. 'You shouldn't have. You'd have been safe. The Allies are almost here.'

'I'd rather go with you,' Lucien said, and put his arm about Rupert's shoulder. They limped on together, towards the iron gate that now stood open.

'Hurry up!' Jutta nudged her hard. 'Drive on. We have to find out what is happening.'

Her hands were shaking, but Ava managed to drive the Mercedes down the long winding path towards the camp. In flashes, through the trunks of trees, she saw concrete walls. Wooden barracks in rows. Prisoners in striped shirts trudging along, heads sunk down. They were so thin. Living skeletons.

She came to the gate into the camp. The iron bars stood open. Alsatians on leashes snarled. A long line of emaciated prisoners stumbled away down the road, urged on by guards with rifles. When the guards saw the golden Mercedes, with her beaming headlights and luxurious curves, they shoved and kicked the prisoners off the road to make way for it.

The men were all wearing yellow triangles or stars on their prison garb.

Ava saw a young SS guard, with a face a little less brutal than the others. She pulled over and tried to smile at him charmingly. He came over, and Ava asked him what was happening.

'We're evacuating the camp,' he told Ava. 'The Americans are only days away. We've been told to clear the camp out and leave no evidence. But it's impossible. There are too many of them! And the railway has been bombed. It's almost two hundred kilometres from here to Theresienstadt. They'll never make it.'

He sounded tired and bewildered. His black uniform seemed too big for him.

'We are looking for a prisoner,' Jutta said urgently. 'His name is Rupert Feidler.'

The young guard looked puzzled. 'Don't know any names, Fräulein. Only numbers. And there's too many to count now. Almost fifty thousand in there.'

'Fifty thousand,' Jutta whispered. Her shoulders slumped.

'Er . . . thank you,' Ava managed to say. She drove on before the guard could get suspicious, or start asking questions.

The long line of stumbling, emaciated prisoners went on for miles. Ava drove slowly along, looking desperately for any sign of Rupert. But the haggard, bruised faces were hardly recognisable as human. They could be mummified bodies dug up out of bogs. All bone and blackened skin. Jutta was finding it hard to breathe. There were a few stick-figure children, stumbling along with blank eyes. Jutta gave them all the food left in the sack. Constantly she asked, 'Rupert Feidler? Do you know him?'

The prisoners only stared back vacantly, shaking their heads. Ava drove on. The fur against her skin made her feel sick.

She reached the bottom of the hill. Both felt faint and nauseated. They tried not to show it in their faces. SS guards were everywhere. On their caps: silver death heads.

'I have to get out here,' Jutta said. 'I have to try and find Rupert.'

Ava gripped her hands. 'I want to stay. I want to help you. But I have to go. Leo . . .'

Jutta hugged her. 'I know. You love him. I hope you find him.'

'I hope you find Rupert.'

'When I find him, we'll come to find you.'

'Leave word at the schloss.' Ava told her the address.

It was terribly hard to leave Jutta there. Ava was terrified at what might happen to her. But Ava also shielded a frail flame of hope. Perhaps Rupert was alive. Perhaps Jutta could find him. Perhaps they could all be reunited after the war.

How Ava wished for it to be true.

45

Skylark

Skylarks sing on the wing.

Skylarks sing in the darkness before the dawn, and in the last chill weeks of winter before any hope of spring. Skylarks sing to guard their loved ones. They sing even hunted by hawks. They sing more joyously, drawing the hawks away from their delicate nests hanging in the grasses. Higher and higher the larks soar. Higher and higher they sing, till the hawks fall away.

Their song pierces the sky.

Ava had not sung in months. But she would sing to save her love. Ava would sing like she had never sung before.

The mess hall for the SS officers at Flossenbürg was a vast hall built of stone, with deer antlers on the wall and deep leather chairs. A fire roared on the hearth. Small round tables set with candles in red glass glowed invitingly. A battered upright piano stood on a small stage, under a huge portrait of Hitler in silver armour, mounted on a prancing horse, a swastika banner held high. A fat man in a stained apron worked behind the bar. Ava had begged him for the chance to sing tonight, and – once he had heard her – he had agreed eagerly. Ava told him she wanted to make her SS lover jealous.

It had taken her two days to get from Buchenwald to Flossenbürg, a journey that usually would be less than three hours. She had driven cross-country over the fields and through rutted country lanes, avoiding the highways and the towns. *I need to save Leo, I need to save Leo*, was the goad that drove her on. The Mercedes was muddied and dented and had bullet holes shot in her bonnet. Ava remembered with a pang how Leo had once begged her to be careful. 'Gilda bruises easily,' he had said.

Flossenbürg was a tiny medieval village nestled into the Bavarian mountains, less than fifty kilometres from the Czechoslovakian border. The landscape was dominated by the ruin of an ancient stone castle on a high hill. As Ava had driven up the road to the village, it had risen out of the morning mists like something out of an old tale. She had parked the car and found herself an inn to stay overnight, and then she had gone to prowl around the perimeter of the camp. It was huge, surrounded by high concrete walls and barbed wire, and guarded by squat watch-towers. Flood-lights illuminated a vast square in the centre. Ava saw rank upon rank of prisoners lined up, all wearing loose blue-and-black-striped pyjamas. They were thin as matchsticks. There were tens of thousands of them. Ava groaned aloud. How was she meant to find Leo in such a crowd? How could she possibly get him out?

Ava needed help. She had spent the afternoon gathering as much infor-mation as she could. This was not easy. The people of Flossenbürg were suspicious of strangers and not inclined to gossip about the camp. The cook at the mess hall had not been so shy, though. He had poured them both a glass of schnapps and told Ava much about the place. It was in utter chaos, he told her. Prisoners pouring in from every direction, and not enough food for them all, or enough guards to police them. God knew what was to become of them all. They said the Americans were only weeks away.

Ava poured him more schnapps and encouraged him to tell her more, and he settled down happily for a cosy chat. By the time he was drunk and snoring, she had formulated a plan of sorts.

So now she stood on the little stage in the officers' mess hall, wearing her mother's golden dress. The von Löwenstein pearls were hidden inside her little gold bag, and her mother's charm bag was tucked inside her brassiere.

Ava sang a sultry Billie Holiday song called 'Lover Man' that she had heard on the BBC the previous year. A skinny, terrified Jew did his best to play the tune on the piano for her. Ava needed to use her body in other ways. She leant on the piano, her hair flowing loose and wild down her back. She had a flower in her hair. Something white she had plucked from the side of the road. Her audience was mesmerised.

Gertrud's fiancé, Max Kranz, was sitting just below her. Ava leant forward, allowing the low-cut bodice of her golden dress to reveal the curves of her breasts. His eyes were fixed on her. Ava smiled and beckoned at him, singing in her deepest, most seductive voice. Kranz half-rose, then looked around him. He saw all the other men, in their crisp black uniforms, leaning towards her, bodies tense. He smiled and rose, coming up the steps to be near her. Ava seized his tie and pulled him closer. Kranz reached for her. Ava evaded him easily. Still singing. Still letting her eyes play over the crowd. Her body swayed. Twisted. Writhed. Like a flame.

He leant forward. 'How much do you want?'

Ava raised an eyebrow. She turned a shoulder to him and sang to the crowd.

She could feel his seething anger and frustration.

The door opened. Gertrud came in. She was dressed in uniform. Black. Buttoned up. At once Ava swivelled back towards Kranz. She sang to him alone. He gripped her wrist. 'How much?'

She ignored him and sang. Gertrud took in the scene in a single glance. Blood rushed up her fair, freckled skin. Ava smiled at her, dragged her fiancé up, then – a scant second before his lips met hers – pushed him away.

Then Ava beckoned up another man.

Ava sang the sultriest songs she knew. She flirted. She teased. Then Ava let them buy her drinks and compete for her attention.

Gertrud came and stood close to her. 'What are you doing here?' she hissed in Ava's ear.

'I've come to seduce your man.'

Gertrud turned scarlet. 'You can't have him!'

'Really?' Ava turned to Kranz and smiled at him. Instantly he was by her side.

Ava pouted. 'Have you no French champagne? I came all this way to see you and you have no champagne for me?'

'Hans! The best French champagne! Now!' he hollered.

Ava turned and smiled at Gertrud.

Gertrud dug her nails into Ava's arm. 'How can you come and try and seduce my man when yours is here! I'll tell him! I'll tell him what a whore you are.'

Ava's smile widened. 'I'll make a deal with you. I'll let your man go if you let mine go.'

There was a sudden flicker of comprehension on Gertrud's face, followed by something Ava did not fully understand. A flare of anger, perhaps. Or laughter.

'You know Leo is here?'

Ava nodded.

Just then Kranz arrived, with a frosted bottle of French champagne. He tore off its golden foil and popped the cork theatrically. He poured Ava a glass. She toasted him silently. He poured himself a glass and drank it, eyes on Ava. She smiled at him, and touched his glass with hers.

It was as if Gertrud did not exist. And though she dug her nails into Kranz's arm and hissed into his ear, he only shoved her away.

Ava drank deeply, keeping her eyes on Kranz. Everyone was begging her for another song. She pretended to hesitate, then allowed herself to be persuaded. She sang another love song, making every word, every gesture, a promise.

Ava had always known she must use her beauty. She was surprised how easy she found it. She was not the same innocent girl who had given herself to Leo. Ava knew so much more about her own body now. Its uses. Its purposes.

Kranz slid his arm about her waist. He whispered in her ear. 'I must have you. Come on, come with me now.'

Ava looked at Gertrud. She bit her lip. Ava raised her eyebrows.

Gertrud rushed forward, gripping Ava's arm, trying to haul her away. She pretended to laugh. 'Now, now, Max. Ava has come to see me.'

He frowned.

Ava smiled. 'Excuse me, gentlemen. I must just go powder my nose. I'll be back soon, I promise.'

Gertrud and Ava left the mess hall, arm in arm. Only a few strides away was the gatehouse into the camp, a long three-storey building with a steep peaked roof. On the stone gatepost was a sign reading 'Work Makes You Free'. Ava could read it clearly in the white lights flooding down, but where Gertrud and Ava stood was in the shadows.

It was cold. Ava's breath hurt her ribs. Her bare arms were blue and goose-pimpled. She said, coldly, 'Help me get my man free or I swear I'll take yours. Forever.'

'He's a special prisoner,' Gertrud said frantically. 'It's no easy task to get him out.'

Ava pushed Gertrud away so hard, she stumbled. Ava turned and headed back to the mess hall. 'Then you're no use to me. I'm sure your loving fiancé will help me.'

Gertrud came at her fast. 'No! I won't let you. What's wrong with these men? Don't they realise how they degrade themselves?'

'I'm sure they do,' Ava answered at once, laughing and shaking back her hair. Gertrud's breath hissed.

'I want my husband,' Ava told her. 'But if I can't have mine, I will take yours, I promise you. Because I hate you. I want to hurt you. I want you to suffer. I want it almost more than I want Leo. Decide now.'

Ava had spoken Gertrud's language. She nodded. 'What do you want?'

'Your uniform. And information.'

In the shadow of the mess hall, Gertrud stripped off her uniform and gave it to Ava. Even in the darkness, Ava could see her fair skin was marked with bruises and red livid stripes that looked like whip marks. Gertrud heard her sharp intake of breath and gave a twisted smile. 'My fiancé likes to play games.'

Ava almost exclaimed in sympathy and concern, but she bit back the words. She slid out of the golden silk dress and gave it to Gertrud in return for her uniform. In moments, Ava wore her skin and she wore Ava's.

Ava slipped the pearls into her pocket, then tucked her mother's little pouch of charms back inside her bra. She felt she needed every bit of love and protection she could get.

Hurriedly Gertrud told Ava where she had to go, and what she had to do. Flossenbürg was being flooded with prisoners evacuated from Buchenwald and other concentration camps. With so many strange guards accompanying them, no-one would know Ava had no right to be there.

Leo was being kept in solitary confinement at the Bunker, a square of cells at one edge of the camp. Along with the other Abwehr prisoners. Ava's heart slammed at those words. 'Who? Who else is there?'

Gertrud shrugged and listed their names. Admiral Canaris. General Oster. The pastor, Dietrich Bonhoeffer. A few other names Ava didn't know. The cells were guarded by the SS, she said. How on earth did Ava think she was going to get him out?

Ava did not know. But she did not tell Gertrud that.

It was much easier to get into Flossenbürg camp than Ava had anticipated. In Gertrud's uniform, with Gertrud's papers, Ava was let through the gate with no questions at all.

Once within, though, Ava had no idea where to go. It was so big. Great floodlights lit the perimeters. Barbed wire like rolls of steel brambles. Rows and rows of wooden barracks.

Ava had bundled her hair up, and wore Gertrud's cap tilted down over her eyes. As far as possible she kept to the shadows of the huts. But no-one took any notice of her. Columns of exhausted, emaciated prisoners were being herded into barracks by hard-faced, impatient guards. Women in uniform were guarding female prisoners. Ava saw they did not carry guns like the others, but long truncheons. They did not hesitate to use them. More guards patrolled the perimeter, guns at their hips, some with dogs on leashes.

She followed the fence around to the right, as Gertrud had instructed. Soon Ava came to a row of concrete bunkers. Small windows with bars. Her heart quickened. Was this it? Was Leo in there? Ava moved forward as quietly as she could, keeping to the shadows.

The cells were built in a U-shape about a courtyard. Six gallows had been erected just outside. They seemed fresh. Ava could smell wood shavings. Nearby was what seemed like a firing range. The concrete wall was pockmarked with bullet holes. A strong smell of cooking meat hung in the smoke-hazed air. Down in the valley below was an orange glow. By its glare, Ava could see what looked like a tall brick chimney, spewing black smoke into the night sky. Bonfires were lit all around it. Men in black uniforms threw long sticks onto the fire. *It's not Walpurgis Night*, Ava thought dazedly. *Why are they building a bonfire?*

It took her a while to realise that the sticks were actually corpses. They were so thin, so stiff. Yet Ava saw spindly legs, skeletal arms, lolling heads. Bile rose in her throat. Ava threw up till her stomach was empty, and still her stomach heaved.

At last she was able to creep forward to the edge of the cell block. She moved along the outside, trying to peer through the tiny, barred windows into the cells. Most were illuminated only by a thin line of light coming in under the heavy steel doors. A few of the cells were empty, but then Ava saw a slouched shape, shackled to the walls. She could not see a face. Ava whispered Leo's name, but no-one responded. She dared not speak louder.

Then she heard the quick pound of feet. At once Ava straightened and stepped away from the window. She walked forward, trying to look confident. An SS guard rounded the corner. He saw her and stopped abruptly. 'What are you doing here!'

'I'm looking for the infirmary,' Ava lied. 'I've got an upset tummy. They told me it was over this way.'

He pointed over her shoulder. 'Back that way.'

'Oh, thank you.' Ava did not turn to go, but smiled up at the guard. He was a big, fleshy man, with his hair cut so short Ava could see the gleam of his scalp. 'I'm new here, you see. I don't know my way around yet. It's like a maze. I don't suppose you could show me the way?'

'I can't,' he said reluctantly. 'They'd use my balls for bullets if I was found missing from my post.'

'Oh, that's a shame,' Ava simpered. 'Not even for a little while?' She laid her hand on his arm.

A lascivious gleam lit in his eyes. He leant closer. 'I can't. There's some bigwig judge come in from Munich. They're putting the men who tried to assassinate the Führer on trial tonight. We're all commanded to come along and watch. It should be a bit of fun. Why don't you come along too? Then afterwards we can go and have a drink.'

'You mean those traitors are here? You're their guard? You must be very important.'

He preened. 'I guess I am.'

'Can I see them?'

He hesitated. 'Please,' Ava wheedled. 'All the other girls would be so impressed.'

'I guess so,' he answered. 'Come on.'

He led her inside the inner courtyard, and towards a solid iron gate in the middle of the U-shape. Ava's heartbeat banged in her eardrums. He unbarred the gate, and stepped into a whitewashed corridor, lit by bare bulbs and lined on one side with steel-bound wooden doors. Each door had a slit at eye level. 'Oooh, how exciting,' Ava gabbled. 'Who's in there?'

'All the most important prisoners.' He puffed out his chest. 'Prince Philip of Hesse is here, and Admiral Canaris, and General Oster. We have a woman in here too. Some French woman. They say she'll be hanged in the morning too.'

Ava found it hard to control her reaction to his words. He saw her distress, and frowned.

'I'm sorry, I'm just amazed,' Ava said, trying to smile. 'A woman kept in here too? I wouldn't have thought she'd be important enough.'

'She tried to organise a camp uprising,' the guard answered shortly. 'But you wanted to see one of them. Here. Take a look.'

He swung open the grille that covered the peephole in one of the doors. Inside was a small cell. A white-haired old man sat slumped in a chair. Blood stained the front of his shirt. His clothes were wet. Ava saw a hose lying in a flood of water on the concrete floor. It was marbling with ice. It was so cold in there that her breath came in short white puffs. The guard shone his powerful torch in the old man's face. He blinked his bruised eyes and tried to raise his head. Ava saw his nose had been smashed. Blood was caked all over his mouth and jaw.

It was the Admiral.

Ava backed away quickly. She could not risk the Admiral recognising her. Her stomach roiled. 'I'm sorry,' Ava gasped. 'I really am not feeling very well.'

'The interrogation room is enough to turn anyone's stomach,' the guard said. 'I've been known to lose my dinner too. They've given Old Whitehead a good going-over, but he's told them nothing. Too late now. He'll be dead come morning.'

'But I thought you said a judge had come . . . that there was going to be a trial . . .' Ava hardly knew what she was saying, she just knew she had to keep him talking.

The guard snorted. 'A drumhead trial, that'll be. The Führer has ordered all their executions. They'll be hanged at dawn.'

'All of them?' Ava faltered.

'Most of them,' he answered. 'We only have six gallows, so we'll do them in groups.'

'Who . . . who will be hanged first?'

He shrugged. 'Not my job to care.' He was looking at her a little oddly. Ava thought she saw suspicion in his little piggy eyes.

She tried to speak gaily. 'So no last-minute pardon for them?'

'Not unless the Commandant of the camp has a sudden change of heart, and he won't be doing that. He loves a good execution.' The guard had led her back down the corridor, but opened another door instead of taking her to the gate. Inside was a small room, furnished with a table, a chair and a bed. 'Now about that drink?' he leered. As he grabbed her and tried to kiss her, Ava smelt the garlic on his breath. She gagged, then threw up a thin bile over his boots. 'Sorry!' Ava gasped and ran towards the gate. 'I think I'm going to be sick again.'

She escaped into the darkness.

The Trial

The trial was that night. Leo and his friends were to be hanged in the morning. She had to get him out. But how?

Ava tried to think, but her mind was frozen.

She stood leaning against one of the wooden bunkers, hidden in the shadows. The smell of the smoke in her nostrils kept her stomach churning, and she was tired. So tired.

Ava ran through all she had to do. Find out what cell Leo was in. Get the keys from the guard. Then get Leo out of the camp. He'd be dressed in those loose striped pyjamas. Ava needed to get an SS uniform for him to change into. Then she needed more petrol for the Mercedes. If it had not been for the jerry cans of petrol Jutta had got for her, Ava would not have made it to Flossenbürg as it was.

She put her hand to her satchel, which she carried over her shoulder. All she had left of any worth was the von Löwenstein pearls. The SS officers had to know how close the Allied forces were. Surely she could bribe one of them to help her?

Ava stiffened her shoulders. One thing at a time. First, find out where Leo was.

She heard loud voices and laughter. A large party of SS guards were headed towards the Bunker. There were uniformed women among them. Many were drinking from silver hipflasks. More came from the direction of the gate. Some were drunk already.

Ava slipped out of the darkness and joined them. Nobody noticed. More guards were hurrying up behind. Everyone went into the inner courtyard, but headed towards one long end of the U-shape. They walked straight past the gallows. Ava averted her gaze.

A door stood open. Within was a long room, set up with rows of chairs. At the far end was a table where a man sat in black robes. He had a pale, supercilious face and thin hair carefully combed across a bald patch.

The room was filling fast. Chair legs scraped across the floor, and a low hum of conversation rose. The audience did not have long to wait. The prisoners were pushed in by guards with clubs. All of them looked weak and gaunt. Leo was at the end. Ava gazed at him in dismay. His head had been shaved, and his face was badly bruised. He could barely stumble along. Dietrich Bonhoeffer, the pastor Ava had once heard preach, tried to support his wavering steps. Leo's eyes were blank and unfocused. He staggered and almost fell. The SS guards lifted him and shoved him into a chair. He dropped his head into his hands.

The audience were all shouting and jeering. Women as well as men. Someone glanced at Ava. She realised she was standing mute and frozen. Ava shook a fist in the air and shouted 'Traitors! Cowards!' like the others, but her voice was nothing more than a croak.

The trial began. It was nothing but a sham. There were no witnesses, no form of defence. The accused all stood in a row while the judge screamed obscenities at them. Admiral Canaris and General Oster had no string to hold up their trousers. They had to clutch at their waistbands to keep their striped pyjama pants from falling down. Ava was sure this was done on purpose to humiliate them. All the men had the marks of violence on their face and body, but none so badly as her husband. Ava feared he was concussed. She could see dried blood in his ear.

When the judge proclaimed the death sentences, the courtroom erupted into wild jeering and cheering. The prisoners were shoved and prodded from the hall. Ava slipped through the crowd, her heart pounding, and followed them down the corridor towards the cell block. She was not the only one to follow, though she was the only one not to torment the stumbling prisoners. They were beaten with clubs, kicked, slapped and spat on. Ava had such a lump in her throat, such burning eyes, but there was nothing she could do without giving herself away. She watched Leo being shoved through the door of his cell so violently he fell to his hands and knees. Ava noted the position of his cell carefully, then turned to go.

Max Kranz stood right behind her. He smiled down into her face. 'I thought it was you.'

Jutta crouched in a ditch beneath a low hanging tree, her eyes fixed on the procession of living skeletons that stumbled along the pot-holed, muddy road. She had a stick clenched in her hand, just in case anyone should attack her. Some of the men seemed hardly human. They howled and gabbled, or tore at their hair and their clothes. Many had tin bowls or plates tied to their belts that rattled strangely as they shambled along. Jutta felt she had stepped through a slit in time, and was back in the days of the Black Death, and lepers that wandered the roads, shaking their alms bowls.

It was late. The moon was a dark bruised orange. Many corpses lay on the side of the road, or were draped over the fence, round bullet holes in the backs of their heads.

Jutta's big fear was that Rupert had walked past her, and she had not seen him. They all looked the same, these bent and skeletal figures in rags with cavernous shadows for eyes.

A motorcycle roared up the road towards her, one black-clad SS guard astride its seat, and another crouched in the sidecar. 'Quick! Quick!' the officer shouted. 'Faster!'

Two stick-thin figures were walking slowly along, supporting each other. One stumbled and fell. As the other struggled to pull him up, the motorcyclist sped past. The man in the sidecar took out his pistol and aimed at the fallen man. Jutta felt an incandescent flash of anger. She darted forward and thrust out her stick. It caught in the spokes of the motorcycle's wheel. It skidded, spun over and crashed. One SS officer went head-over-heels into the ditch, landed awkwardly, and lay still. The other was trapped in the sidecar. His pistol had fallen onto the road. Jutta could see its sullen gleam. She snatched it up and pointed at him. 'Get out of the sidecar or I'll shoot.'

The soldier obeyed. As he got to his feet, he made a sudden grab for the gun. Jutta pulled the trigger. The recoil almost knocked her over. When she recovered her balance, the soldier was lying in the middle of the road, holding one leg and screaming in pain.

Jutta shoved the gun in her coat pocket and picked up the motorcycle. It was heavy and she needed both hands. It had been a while since she had ridden one, but Jutta found she remembered how to kick-start it. 'Get out of my way, or I'll run you over,' she said coldly.

The SS guard rolled aside.

As Jutta raced away down the road, the prisoners behind her closed in around the fallen SS guard.

Ava began to stammer something. Kranz put one finger on her lips. 'Not here, my dear. We don't want to cause any unnecessary fuss. Why don't we go back to my quarters and finish that bottle of champagne? Then you can tell me all about it.'

He clamped his hand upon hers. Then he pulled Ava out past the gallows, through the rows of wooden huts, out the gate and along a well-tended path that led to a row of small stone houses built into the side of the forested hill.

Ava walked passively, not trying to draw away from him, not speaking. He chatted urbanely as they walked, complimenting her singing, and saying what a shame it was she no longer wore the golden silk dress. 'No doubt Gertrud will wear it to try and seduce me later on tonight,' he said.

'She's a fat cow, though. I hope she'll not split the seams. I'd like to see you in it again.'

The houses had been built so they did not look down into the camp, or the smoking chimney of the crematorium, but across the village to the old castle upon its hill.

'Charming aspect, isn't it?' Kranz said, unlocking the door and ushering her in. 'Now let me just get the fire lit. You're shivering.'

He lit the fire, and opened a bottle of champagne that stood waiting in a silver ice bucket. 'I was hoping I'd run into you again,' he explained. 'Come, sit down.'

Ava did not move. His face altered. He put down the glasses of champagne, walked over and hit her hard across the face. She fell to the floor. He gripped the back of her neck, dragged her over to the couch, and flung her down upon it.

'I do not like to be defied,' he said. 'Now, drink your champagne.'

Ava took the glass he passed her and sipped obediently. Her cheek was hot and throbbing, and she tasted blood from the cut flesh of the inside of her cheek. A spark of anger had lit inside her, though, unfreezing the blood in her veins. She took another mouthful. It was very good champagne.

'Now I imagine you have come with some foolish idea of rescuing your husband,' Kranz was saying. 'You must realise now how impossible it is.'

'The Americans are only a few days' march away.'

'Maybe so. They will arrive too late for your husband, though. He will hang in the morning.'

'You could help me get him free.' Ava put down her glass and turned to face him more fully.

'Now why would I do that?' He poured himself some more champagne, then topped up her glass.

'Life will be hard for SS officers once the Reich has fallen. There will be trials and retribution. No matter how fast you burn the bodies, there will still be evidence of your crimes.'

'How very defeatist of you.' He sipped his wine, his cold grey eyes resting on her face. 'A defeatist attitude is treason, you know.'

412

'Germany is in ruins. It will take years to rebuild it. The Americans are coming from the west, the Russians from the east. They'll meet in the middle any day now. You'll be on the run. Hunted down by the Allies. How do you hope to survive?'

'You're beginning to interest me now.'

'I have something that I think will interest you even more.' Ava put her hands into her jacket pocket and pulled out the ropes of pearls, gleaming like little moons. He gave a low whistle and reached out his hand.

Ava pulled the pearls back. 'Only if you help me get Leo out.'

He laughed. 'Oh, my dear. Why on earth would I do that? He's a traitor and a coward and he deserves to die. I am looking forward to watching him twitch very much. You know they plan to hang them with piano wire? An agonisingly slow death, by all accounts.'

Ava could not snatch a breath.

Kranz rose and took off his uniform jacket, folding it neatly and laying it over the back of his chair. He undid the top buttons of his shirt collar and loosened his tie. 'I do thank you for the pearls, however. My car is already packed and ready to go.' He jerked his head towards the back of the house. 'So few of my treasures are portable, though. And they will need to last me a long time. Those lovely pearls of yours will be a great help to me.'

Ava closed trembling fingers over the pearls. 'They are in payment for Leo's life.'

He had taken off his tie and laid it over his jacket. Now he unfastened his belt. 'I don't think so.'

The next moment the belt flicked out towards her. Ava had been waiting for his movement, and flung herself away from him. The champagne glass fell and broke. She landed on all fours and scrambled away from him as fast as she could. The tight skirt of the uniform hampered her.

Kranz frowned. 'Really, my dear, don't be unreasonable. You must know I've been looking forward to this for a while. And a hot-blooded little Gypsy like you must be panting for it.'

Ava barely listened to his words. She was watching the belt in his hand. Nonetheless, its quick flick took her by surprise. It caught her hard across the shoulder. Ava cried out. She tried to crawl away, but in an instant he was upon her. He tore off her jacket, trapping her arms, then ripped away the white shirt beneath. He lashed her hard across her bare back. Ava screamed. She struggled, but he was too strong for her. He set his foot on her buttock, and whipped her again. The steel edge of the buckle tore her skin. She tried to roll away, but was pinned beneath his boot.

Pushing her face down into the carpet, Kranz wrenched down her skirt. He sat astride her, his hand in her hair, holding her still as she struggled. He began to fumble with his fly. Ava tried to throw him off, but she could not move. Then her groping fingers found the broken champagne flute. She seized the stem, and stabbed backwards over her shoulder. He screamed. Ava managed to roll away.

Blood poured down from one eye socket. Ava had stabbed him through the eye. He came at her like a bull. She still had the broken champagne glass in her hand. She stabbed at him again. Tore his cheek. Then her flailing hand slashed the broken glass across his throat. He fell. A horrible gargling sound. Ava stabbed him again. Her hand was so slick with blood she could not keep hold of the glass. She let it go, and realised it was embedded in his throat.

He lay still. He was dead. Ava stood up, panting. Her legs were so weak she had to lean on the couch arm. Blood spread over the floor, and was splattered across her body. She hurt all over. Her back throbbed. Her swollen cheek. Ava staggered away, looking for a bathroom. She washed her face and hands, and pressed a cold damp cloth to the welts on her skin, wherever she could reach them. Her stomach was fluttering with nerves, as if little birds beat their wings frantically within her.

Ava drank some water, and washed herself again and again. At last the water ran into the sink clean.

She needed some other clothes. Gertrud's uniform was torn and bloodied. Like a somnambulist she went into the bedroom. Kranz's bed was folded down, his linen crisp and clean. Ava just wanted to lie down and sleep forever. But she made her way to his wardrobe, holding on to the backs of chairs. She drew off the ruined shirt, and hid it in the linen basket. She re-dressed herself in one of Kranz's black SS uniforms. Her fingers shook so much it was hard to do up all the buttons. His clothes were rather loose and baggy, but Ava pushed the trousers into the tall boots and belted the jacket tightly.

Her hair was wild about her face and body. She searched his drawers until she found a pair of scissors and then hacked her hair off close to the scalp. Ava gathered all her curls up. They filled her hands like the warm body of a kitten. Ava threw the curls on the fire.

Then she bent and unbuckled the pistol from Kranz's waist, and rebuckled it to hers. She felt safer – stronger – with its weight nudging against her hip.

47

To Trust Our Heaviness

A knock on the front door.

Ava stilled.

The knock came again. She crept to the window and peered out. All was dark, but she could see enough to know it was Gertrud standing outside. She was wearing Ava's gold satin dress under a heavy fur coat. Her hair was loosened from its usual rigid setting, and fell about her face in red-gold waves.

'Max,' Gertrud called. 'Let me in!'

Ava scarcely breathed.

Gertrud knocked again, then came to the window to look in. Ava's stomach lurched. Kranz's body still lay on the floor, and blood pooled on the carpet. A chair had been overturned, and broken glass glinted in the light of the dancing flames on the hearth.

Gertrud pressed her face against the glass, cupping her hands around her eyes so she could see more clearly. Ava opened the door. Gertrud turned swiftly. 'Max! I was just . . .' Then her voice died away.

Ava pointed the pistol at her.

'You!' Gertrud cried.

'Yes. Me. Get inside.'

Gertrud went inside as bid, holding up her hands. She uttered a little scream when she saw Kranz lying on the floor. Ava made her sit on a chair, and bound her wrists and ankles with belts and scarves, whatever she could find.

'You need to help me or I'll kill you too,' Ava said. 'Tell me everything I need to know.'

'I won't!'

Ava lifted the gun threateningly, as if preparing to strike Gertrud across the face. She shrank back, protecting her face with her hands. 'What . . . what do you need to know?'

'Everything,' Ava said.

Gertrud told her everything she needed to know. As she spoke, Ava tidied up the mess the best she could, dragged Kranz's body out of sight, and threw together a bag of food from the well-stocked kitchen. Kranz's taste had been expensive. French champagne. Russian caviar. Scottish smoked salmon. White truffles from the Périgord. Vintage cognac.

Gertrud told her that Kranz had a car. Ava went to check it out. It was a big black Mercedes, locked away in a small garage. The petrol gauge was on full, and the seats were piled high with treasure. By the light of a torch, Ava saw oil paintings in gilded frames, little statuettes of dancers, jewellery boxes, silver candelabras, a bundle of silver cutlery. Opening one box, she found it was full of little golden squares. She stared, puzzled, then suddenly realised they were golden teeth. Sickened, she threw the box into the darkness with all her strength. Then a frenzy overtook her. Ava threw everything out of the car. She heard things smash, but she did not care. She wanted it all gone.

Ava then made a bed for Leo in the back seat from pillows and blankets. She filled some bottles with water, added a bottle of cognac, then packed a bag with some plain shirts and trousers for Leo. It would not be safe soon, she thought, to be seen in an SS uniform. She made Gertrud strip off the golden dress, then forced her to climb into the bed, gagging her and tying her wrists to the bedhead.

Then, as quickly and quietly as she could, Ava drove down to the old inn in the village and got her own belongings. She had so little left, she did not want to lose her mother's chest or her father's book of fairy tales. She drove back and parked Kranz's car in the driveway, the nose pointing towards the road.

At last, all was ready. Ava took another black SS uniform for Leo and rolled it tightly, putting it inside a kitbag. Then she went back out into the night, back to the camp.

Raucous singing from the mess hall. A woman's shrill laughter. Ava went to the gate and rattled the bars. A sleepy looking guard let her in. He did not check her papers. Her black uniform and death head's cap were enough for him. Ava lowered her voice to her deepest pitch, and did her best to stride out like an officer. She remembered how she had told Leo's grandfather that women with deep voices like her always got the best roles to play. *Witches, bitches and britches.* A hysterical giggle shook her ribcage, but she managed to compose herself.

Ava had Kranz's wristwatch, a beautiful and precise piece of machinery. Gertrud had told her what time the patrols were, and what route they marched. She had memorised the route to the solitary confinement bunker. She moved quietly from one deep patch of shadow to the next. It was very late now. Every bunker was silent. The air was full of the stench of the latrines, and the filthy smoke spewing from the crematorium. She tasted it on her tongue.

Ava came to the gallows. Large meat hooks gleamed in the faint star-shine. She imagined the men destined to hang there in the dawn, slowly strangling from piano wire. She had to gulp back tears. She could not save them. She could only save one, and that had to be her love. She went to the double doors that led into the makeshift courtroom. They were padlocked. Ava bit her lip. She had hoped to slip in that way. She moved around the buildings, testing the bars on windows. All were secure.

Ava tiptoed to the heavy gate that led to the cell block. It was locked. She rattled it. No-one came. She rattled it louder.

At last the guard came to see what the noise was. He unlocked the gate and opened it just a crack. 'What?' His voice was slurred with alcohol.

With the harsh light behind him, he was just a black hulking shadow. Ava kept well back, so he would not see that she was now dressed in a man's uniform and had hair cropped close to her skull.

'Hi, it's me,' Ava said, in a coy voice. 'You know. I was hoping for that drink.'

'Do you know what time it is?' he began in a surly voice, then seemed to change his mind. 'Sure, sweetheart,' he slurred. 'Come in.'

He opened the gate wider. Ava stepped forward and hit him hard over the head with the wrench she had brought for that purpose. He fell heavily, and lay still. She stepped inside the corridor and quickly shut and locked the gate again. The keys had fallen from his hand, and she bent and picked them up, holding them carefully so they did not jangle. Ava tiptoed down the corridor till she came to the one she knew was Leo's.

Her hands were shaking so much she could not fit the key in the lock. She tried to steady her breathing. At last she managed to unlock the door. She stepped in. The cell smelt rank. Ava went over to the bed. A dark shape was huddled upon it.

'Leo,' she whispered. 'Leo, darling?'

The dark shape stirred. Then she heard a hoarse, incredulous voice. 'Ava?'

'It's me,' she tried to say, but her voice would not work. Ava kissed him, and tried to work out how to unlock his shackles in the dark. She had not thought to bring the torch. She had to go back and get it from the unconscious guard. At last she managed to free Leo. He sat up. 'Is it really you?' His voice was slurred and hoarse.

'I need to get you changed. I have a guard's uniform for you. Can you help me?'

He tried, but he was so dizzy and sick Ava had to do it all herself. His body was thin and bony, and every part of him seemed to be marked with blood and bruises. His nose had been broken again, and all the fingers on his right hand.

It was hard. Ava felt dizzy and sick herself, and he groaned loudly with pain as she tried to manoeuvre his broken hand inside the uniform sleeve. Then she realised, with a swooping fall of her heart, that she had not thought of boots. She had to go back out into the corridor and wrest the boots off the unconscious guard. He stirred and mumbled, and she hit him over the head with the wrench again. Her hands were shaking so much, it was only a glancing blow, but he subsided once more.

Ava could barely manage to creep back to Leo's cell, the boots clasped in her arms. Every muscle in her body was trembling. She was so afraid. What if the guard woke up again? What if a sentry found his unconscious body? What if she was not strong enough to help Leo get out of there?

'Can you walk, darling?' Ava said, struggling to pull the boots on. They were a little small, and Leo's feet had been whipped bloody. Somehow he managed to lurch upright.

Ava put her arm about his waist, and helped him limp to the door. They staggered down the corridor. Leo did not seem to notice the unconscious guard at his feet. His eyes were blank, his head falling onto his chest. Ava propped him against the wall, then dragged the guard down the corridor and into Leo's cell. He weighed a ton. Her arms ached fiercely, and her back was one white column of pain. At last she got the guard inside the door and locked him in.

Leo was waiting where she had left him, leaning his head against his folded arms.

Ava gritted her teeth, and put her arm about him. She led him outside the iron gate, and shut it and locked it. She felt safer once they were out of the white glare of the bare bulbs.

She checked her wristwatch. It had taken her a lot longer to get Leo out than she had expected. The next patrol would be past at any moment. Her heart slammed against her ribs. Thinking quickly, she coaxed Leo to lie down in the shadows of one of the bunkers. He dropped like a felled oak. She lay next to him, her arm about his back. A few minutes later, two sentries marched past, torches flashing about. Ava hid the white disc of her face. Both she and Leo were dressed in black uniforms, black caps pulled down over their faces. She prayed the light would not flash on the metal of their buckles.

*

Jutta roared along the crowded road, stopping often to ask, 'Does anyone know Rupert Feidler? Tall and thin with dark hair?' She infuriated herself. They were all thin, they were all shaven. 'He played trumpet,' she said in desperation.

'Yes,' someone answered her. 'He's here. I saw him before. He was just ahead.'

Jutta's ribs contracted. She could not speak or take a breath. Slowly she rode along the rutted track, calling in a low, rough voice, 'Rupert! Rupert!'

On and one she rode, till her voice was gone, and still the faces that turned to stare at her headlight were faces she had never seen before. The bruised moon sank. The stars were bright above her in a frosty sky, though she could smell smoke and see a kind of creeping fog reaching up from the fields. The sun rose into a glorious paean of colour. Jutta had never seen such a beautiful daybreak. The whole sky was golden and rose and scarlet.

Then she heard it. The halting, lilting notes of a trumpet. Sweet, broken, glad. Jutta jumped off the motorcycle and clambered over a stile. A field stretched before her, furrowed in exact, curving lines. A row of poplars, just touched with flame. A hedge of blackberries and rosehips. And there, lying in the arms of a thin, dark-eyed young man, was her brother. He was playing his trumpet.

Jutta ran up and dropped to her knees beside him. 'Rupert,' she wept.

He turned over-brilliant eyes towards her, deep sunken in their sockets. 'Why, Jutta,' he said, in a croaky voice. 'I thought – if I must die – I'd do it playing.'

'You are not going to die,' she ordered. 'Get up!'

With urgent hands she pulled Rupert to his feet. He was light as a child. Then Jutta put down her hand for the young man who had been holding Rupert so tenderly. 'You too. Neither of you is going to die today.'

The sentries walked on, not seeing the two dark shapes huddled on the ground so close to their boots.

Ava dragged Leo to his feet. He tried to help her, but nearly managed to bring her down again. As they hobbled along through the fading darkness, Ava whispered encouragements to him. She told him about the car. 'We'll go to the schloss. Your mother will hide us. If it's too dangerous, we'll sneak across the border into Switzerland. We'll go and see Father. He'll hide us in his coal cellar.'

She saw his cheek curve, and was encouraged. 'The war is over,' she promised him. 'If I can just get you safe out of here . . . Leo, please! Just a little further.'

Ava had reached the edge of the barracks. The concrete square stretched before her. Birds twittered. The mountains were sharply silhouetted against the rosy blush of the sky.

'You need to walk now, dearest,' Ava told him. 'I cannot support you out the gate. Can you walk that far? Please?'

Leo straightened himself with an effort. He set the death's head cap more firmly upon his shaven head. Slowly but steadily they trod across the square to the gatehouse. The same sleepy, disgruntled guard let them out. Leo walked, slowly but straight-backed, his head lifted proudly, till they had got out of sight of the gate. Then his knees buckled and he slid to the ground. Ava hauled him up, cajoling him, promising him, ordering him. 'Just a little bit further, darling, I promise. Please get up. Leo, get up!'

Somehow they made it up the path and inside Kranz's house. Ava let Leo sit while she brought him brandy and tended the worst of his injuries. She bound his broken hand, and gave him a cold compress to hold against his nose. There was a huge black bruise on his side, and she thought several ribs were broken. She bound him up, using torn sheets, kissing him wherever she thought she would not hurt him. Then she dressed him again in civilian clothes, as best she could. She left his feet bare. Broken and bleeding, it seemed too cruel to try and jam them into shoes that were too small.

Only then did Ava strip off her own hated uniform, and dress herself in an old green frock and a soft cardigan.

'Your hair.' Leo was looking at her in utter dismay.

Ava lifted a self-conscious hand to her head. 'It'll grow back. I promise.'

He nodded, then winced in pain.

Mmmpf! Mmmmmpf!

Leo turned his bruised face, looking vaguely startled. 'What's that?'

'That, my love, is Gertrud. I'll shut her up if you like.'

Leo gazed at her, bewildered. Ava opened the bedroom door, and waved the pistol menacingly. The muffled cries stopped at once.

'Time to go.' Ava managed to get Leo out to the car. His bare feet made bloody footprints in the snow. She tucked him up on the back seat with soft pillows and blankets. He gazed at her with eyes the colour of the dawn sky. 'Is this real? Are you truly here?'

She bent and gently kissed his torn mouth. 'I'm here. Lie still. We still need to get away from here.'

He nodded and lay back. The crease beside his mouth deepened into a half-smile. 'Ava,' he whispered. 'My Ava.'

She started the car and drove slowly down the road. It was a big car, much heavier than Gilda, and no matter how hard she tried, Ava could not stop it jerking and stalling. She eased her foot off the brake, and let it roll under its own gravitational weight.

As the road turned a corner, she glanced down into the camp. The prisoners were being dragged out to the gallows. All were naked. They tried to walk with dignity, but they were pushed and prodded and spat upon by the crowd of laughing SS officers. Ava thought she recognised the Admiral, with his shock of white hair, and the pastor, stumbling blindly without his glasses.

She looked away, focusing all her energy on driving the car down the road. Swifts were flying high in the silvery dawn sky, darting and swooping. Ava fixed her eyes on them, willing the tears away. She thought of a line of Rilke's poetry that had haunted her for a long time. *This is what the things can teach us; to fall, patiently, to trust our heaviness. Even a bird has to do that before it can fly.*

The things.

Stones. Blossoms. Stars. Trees.

Children.

Ava put one hand on her belly. She had not wanted to bring a child into a world that was mad with war. But maybe, now that the war was over, perhaps she and Leo could bear to make a child together. Perhaps they could find some way to rebuild all that was lost.

Ava heard Leo moan with pain.

'Lie still, my darling,' Ava whispered. 'We'll be home soon.'

48

Summertime

Leo had been afraid he was damaged beyond all hope of healing. The morning after he bore witness at the Nazi trials, though, he woke and realised he had not dreamt.

He rose from his bed and limped across to the window. It was summer. He had slept a long time. Beyond the glimmer of the moat, the garden lay fresh and green and bright with sunshine. Ava was singing, 'One of these mornings you're gonna rise up singing, and you'll spread your wings and you'll take to the sky.'

She was sitting by the lily pond, tall and slim in a pale green dress. On the blanket beside her, two babies kicked their bare legs vigorously. One had a soft tuft of fair hair, the other a halo of dark curls. Feeling Leo's gaze on her, Ava turned and smiled and lifted a hand to him. A big-pawed Great Dane puppy lay nearby, chewing on an old stick.

The garden at the schloss was no longer a wilderness of thorns and weeds, but smooth and verdant, the hedges all neatly clipped, the roses bending tightly furled crimson petals over bright blue forget-me-nots. Leo worked long hours in the garden every day, and took great pleasure in watching his seeds grow and flourish.

It had been more than a year since the end of the war. He did not remember much of their homecoming. Only pain and fever and nightmares. It had taken a long time to recover. Ava and his mother, Isabelle, had nursed him as best they could. They had been too afraid to try and find a doctor. Germany had still been at war, and her fate undecided.

Then Hitler and his new bride committed suicide in his bunker. A day later, Goebbels and his wife killed their six young children, then themselves. The German armed forces surrendered. Berlin lay in smouldering ruins.

The schloss itself was not untouched by tragedy. On hearing of the Führer's death Leo's grandfather had taken down Hitler's portrait, broken it over his knee, then shot himself. Leo had been recuperating in a downstairs room. He had woken at the sound, grasped his crutch and limped into the study, to find his grandfather slumped over his desk, blood and brains splattered on the old Aubusson carpet.

His grandfather's suicide had been hard to deal with, after so much death and suffering. Leo blamed himself, for not coming home earlier, for not listening. Then he had to manage all the business of death and estates and taxes at a time when no-one even knew what the laws of the land were anymore. He was thin and nervy and found it hard to eat or sleep. Sudden noises made him jerk so violently it felt as if his heart would stop.

It was almost unbearable to read the newspapers. Concentration camps were liberated, mass graves discovered, rapes and reprisals enacted, Nazi criminals hunted, arrested, accused. Each photograph, each headline, brought Leo days of sickness and suffering and nights filled with vivid hallucinations.

He worked in the garden, repaired broken gutters and cracked tiles, and hammered and painted and washed, focusing all his energies on rebuilding and restoring the schloss. Isabelle taught Ava how to cook, and Ava filled the old castle with music and song.

At night, Leo and Ava rediscovered each other in the secret darkness of their bed. Soon her belly was swelling with their child. Leo loved to lie and rest his head on her stomach, listening for a tiny echo of a heartbeat, feeling the flutter of growing limbs.

Then Jutta had arrived, helping along two skeletal young men as best she could. Both were sick and damaged almost beyond repair. But Isabelle had made them nourishing soups and played piano to them, and Ava had cleaned and sewn up their suppurating sores, and bandaged their damaged feet. Slowly, in the peace and beauty of the schloss, Rupert and Lucien had healed.

They hated Leo at first. But he spoke French to them, and lent them books to read from the library, and brought them small things to mend, and gradually Rupert and Lucien forgot to fear him. Rupert had an old sardine tin full of scraps of paper. Jutta began to type them up for him, and Rupert composed tunes to go with them, and Ava sang his poems as best she could.

For a long time, no-one knew what had happened to Ava's sister Monika. Neither her father nor Bertha had heard a word from her. Ava even went to Berlin, looking for news. She found that Monika's husband had been shot for cowardice and desertion the very week that Ava had last seen her. She remembered how haggard Monika had looked when she had opened the door and how Monika had called to her. Ava had not turned back. She had refused to listen. Ava was wracked with guilt, which Leo understood all too well. He had his own burden of guilt and regret to bear.

Then, in midwinter, Monika had suddenly turned up at the schloss. The elegant, self-possessed woman Leo remembered was gone. She was gaunt, grey-haired and wild-eyed, and in her arms she carried a screaming bundle. A newborn baby boy. Monika insisted the child was her husband's, but Leo knew it was impossible. The boy had been born ten months after her husband's death. Privately he wondered if the baby was the result of a rape, for they had all heard terrible accounts of what had happened in Berlin after its fall. But he could not ask such a question of Monika.

She had been shocked at the sight of Rupert, so bent and gaunt, his ruined feet in soft carpet slippers. Monika had hardly spoken a word all evening, only arranging and rearranging her cutlery and crockery till they were all perfectly aligned, and barely eating a mouthful. She was gone the next morning, leaving the child behind her. There was nothing to do but take the boy in. Ava and Leo had named him Rainer, after their favourite poet, and he was now a fair and sturdy baby cutting his first tooth.

Leo and Ava's daughter had been born two weeks later. They had called her Libertas Isabelle Clementina. A good name for a child born in peacetime. She was as dark as Rainer was fair, and had eyes of the most angelic blue. She was not nearly as sweet tempered as Rainer, however, developing such a strong set of lungs that Ava was sure she would grow up to be a singer.

The Nuremburg trials had been in process for some months, under a blaze of world publicity. Leo found the trials disturbed his fragile peace. He fought flashes of intense white-hot anger and long periods of darkness and depression. If it had not been for Ava, the children and the garden, Leo may have found it all too much to bear.

Then he had been asked to testify. At first he refused. Leo did not want to talk about it. But then Ava had told him that the best cure for those wounded in the soul was to speak.

So he had gone to Nuremburg. It was hard. Nightmares and flashbacks had tormented him. But he had found some ease in telling his tale on the witness stand. Even better, Leo was at last able to speak out about his and his friends' secret struggle against Hitler. The mask was finally stripped away forever.

Then Leo went to Dachau, and testified at the trial of the guards at the Flossenbürg Concentration Camp. Forty-six men had been charged with beating, starving, abusing and murdering prisoners. Leo's legs had trembled as he walked in under the cruel ironic motto, 'Work Makes You Free', and sweat had sprung out all along his hairline. The eight months he had spent at Flossenbürg were still raw in his memory. But he had faced his torturers, he had told his story, and now, he hoped, he could begin to heal.

Pulling on a shirt and some trousers, he went barefoot down the stairs and out into the garden. The schloss basked in the sunshine, its windows gleaming. His mother was playing the piano, and the soft notes filled the air. Bees hummed in the rosemary, and tiny white butterflies danced over the forget-me-nots. Ava was leaning on one elbow, her short curls tucked behind her ears. She smiled up at him. 'You slept a long time.'

He nodded and sat down beside her.

'No nightmares?'

'Not even a small one,' he answered.

She put her hand on his arm. 'I'm so glad. Do you think . . . do you think all will be well now?'

He drew her forward so he could kiss her. 'I think so. In time.'

'I've been thinking,' Ava said. 'Perhaps we could open the schloss to others, to people in need, so they can come and stay for a while. We could play them music, and feed them your mother's soup, and let them work in the garden. Perhaps it might help?'

'I think that's a beautiful idea.' He kissed her again, unable to stop his sense of wonderment that he was here, alive, and she was here, safe in his arms.

Their kiss deepened. The babies laughed. Rainer waved at the clouds and Libertas tried to suck her toes.

Leo had, more than once, wished that he could die.

Now he hoped that death would be a long time coming.

Afterword

It is always difficult to explain how an idea can come to grip your imagination with such deep claws and demand that you turn it into a story. I don't always fully understand it myself.

I think this novel all began when I was about twelve and read *The Diary of Anne Frank*. Her words moved me unbearably. I had never heard of such cruelty and suffering before. I began to write my own diary as a consequence, and now have about sixty notebooks recording the minutiae of my life and work.

I also began to read any book I could find set in World War II. I remember studying the period at school, and watching an old black-and-white film about the liberation of Auschwitz. I was chilled through, and sickened to my stomach, and kept wondering how such things could have been allowed to happen. It all made a deep and lasting impression on me.

As an adult, my fascination with the period deepened. I read many novels set at that time, and watched films and documentaries, and began to collect memoirs and firsthand accounts, particularly ones set amongst the Resistance. I knew I wanted to write a novel set during the period, and sometimes talked it over with my sister. One day, I was at a country book sale with my brother and wanted to buy a whole boxed set of illustrated textbooks on every aspect of World War II. I didn't have enough cash, and so my brother lent me the money then carried the box to the car for me. 'What do you want with so many books about the war?' he asked. I said I was looking for my story.

The years passed, and it was always in the back of my mind.

Then I wrote a novel called *The Wild Girl*, which tells the story of the forbidden romance between Wilhelm Grimm and Dortchen Wild, the young woman who told him many of the world's most famous fairy tales. I had been working on the novel for a long time, and had read and studied closely all the tales Dortchen had told him. One of my favourite stories of hers was 'The Singing, Springing Lark', which she told Wilhelm Grimm on 7 January 1813. It is a variant of the well-known French fairy tale 'Beauty and the Beast'. The first half of the story is very similar, except that the father steals a lark and not a rose, and the beast is a lion. However, the ending is very different. The heroine does not break the spell on the enchanted prince by simply promising to marry him. Instead, she has to follow him for seven years as he flies the world in the shape of a dove, and then must outwit the enchantress who had cursed him. This ending does not appear in any other 'Beauty and the Beast' variant, though it does have echoes of the ancient Greek myth 'Cupid and Psyche', sometimes called the first fairy tale.

'The Singing, Springing Lark' was the second tale in the second volume of the Grimms' *Children's and Household Tales*, published in 1814. Once the two volumes were published together, it was Tale 88.

I thought Dortchen's version of the tale was much bolder and more beautiful than the better known French story, and I began to play with ways of using it within *The Wild Girl*. At that time, I was struggling with the thematic structure of the novel, and searching for ways to draw upon Dortchen's tales. Trying to distract myself from all the worry, I went to bed and read a World War II thriller, one of my favourite genres of fiction.

As I fell asleep, my thoughts circled back to the challenges of the novel I was writing. I told myself, *It's all right, trust the universe, the answer will come, the answer will come.*

The next morning, as I lay in that hypnopompic state between sleeping and waking – a place I call the shadowlands – the idea of retelling one of Dortchen's fairy tales in a Nazi Germany setting just came to me. I had a vivid image of a girl wearing a golden dress and singing to a room full of Nazis. I knew that she was some kind of resistance fighter, risking her life to overthrow Hitler.

I woke in a state of high excitement, and scribbled down several pages of ideas in my diary. I spent the day reading up on the German under-ground resistance, ordering research books, and building an idea of the plot. For about four months, I worked feverishly on the idea but slowly I began to realise that what I had was two separate books. It was very hard, but I resolutely put aside the German resistance idea and worked solely on the story of Dortchen Wild and Wilhelm Grimm. Meanwhile, the other story simmered away in my subconscious. As ideas came, I wrote them down. Slowly *The Beast's Garden* grew.

As always, many hands have helped me. My family and friends all suffered through two years of obsessive research into Hitler and the German underground, and all the emotional turmoil that caused (in particular my poor, long-suffering husband and children, who watched many a documentary with me and suffered many a conversation about the nature of evil).

I need to give especially heartfelt thanks to my agents, Tara Wynne of Curtis Brown in Australia, and Robert Kirby of United Agents in the US; Jill Grinberg of Jill Grinberg Literary Management in the US, and to my Australian publisher Meredith Curnow and editor Patrick Mangan. They all read an early draft of the novel and gave me incredibly helpful and insightful comments. Thank you also to my sister Belinda Murrell, who talked the book over with me at a crucial stage in its development and helped me make a difficult but ultimately rewarding decision.

One of the difficulties in writing *The Beast's Garden* was that everyone – apart from Ava, Leo, Jutta and their families – was a real person. Once I began to research the German resistance, I learned about so many brave men and women, who risked their lives to speak out, to help, and to try and strike back. It would have been much easier to have invented characters and events, but I wanted to try and honour the truth of their extraordinary stories. Some of their stories are well known, and some have been forgotten or ignored.

I had decided in the very earliest drafts of the novel to set the story in Berlin, the nerve centre of the Third Reich. This is where Hitler's inner circle lived and worked, where the headquarters of the SS and the Gestapo were located, and where the Third Reich finally collapsed in flames.

There were many people in Berlin who tried to resist the Nazi regime, sometimes in small acts of futile bravery, sometimes working actively to rescue Jews and other victims of the Holocaust, and sometimes planning outright rebellion, particularly in the case of the secret plot to assassinate Hitler.

Many of the differing circles overlapped with each other.

Operation Valkyrie is usually known as the 20 July Plot, or the Generals' Plot, but was called the Black Orchestra by the Gestapo. Many officers were involved in the numerous attempts on Hitler's life, but I chose to focus on the work of Admiral Canaris and the Abwehr. I read many books on the subject. The most useful to me were *Germany's Underground: The Anti-Nazi Resistance* by Allen Welsh Dulles, who was OSS chief in Bern during the war (the precursor to the CIA); *Operation Valkyrie: The German Generals' Plot Against Hitler* by Pierre Galante; *On the Road to the Wolf's Lair: German Resistance to Hitler* by Theodore S. Hamerow; *Countdown to Valkyrie: The July Plot to Assassinate Hitler* by Nigel Jones; and *Confront! Resistance in Nazi Germany*, edited by John J. Michalczyk. I also read the biography *Canaris: Hitler's Spy Chief* by Richard Bassett many times.

The Gestapo called the circles of resistance that centred on Harro and Libertas Schulze-Boysen the Red Orchestra. This has led many to the mistaken belief that they were all Communists and Soviet spies.

The truth is that the group had many different political and religious affiliations. Some were Communist; most were not. Some were Catholic, some Jewish, some Protestant. Some were aristocratic, some came from poor, blue-collar backgrounds. Harro and Libertas's friends included diplomats, countesses, artists, writers, sculptors and actors. Arvid and Mildred's circle was more serious and scholarly, and they disapproved of some of Harro's wilder schemes, with good reason as it proved. Mildred Harnack was the only American woman to be executed by the Nazis. John Sieg, a journalist, was one of the few to be a member of the Communist Party.

The best books on the topic are *Resisting Hitler: Mildred Harnack and the Red Orchestra* by Shareen Blair Brysac and *Red Orchestra: The Story of the Berlin Underground and the Circle of Friends Who Resisted Hitler* by Anne Nelson.

Helmuth James Graf von Moltke was the leader of the Kreisau Circle, and advocated non-violent opposition to Hitler. He was connected to both the Red and the Black Orchestras, and also knew many in what came to be called The Solf Circle. Although he was executed, his wife, Freya, survived and wrote a memoir of her experiences, *Memories of Kreisau and the German Resistance*.

Similarly, Irmgard Zarden was one of the few guests at the infamous Solf Tea Party to live. She wrote a moving account of her experiences entitled *Memories*.

The attack on the Soviet Paradise exhibition by the Baum Circle is important because it is the only significant resistance action by Jews. Many of those arrested, tortured and executed were only in their twenties. My primary reference was *Berlin Ghetto: Herbert Baum and the Anti-Fascist Resistance* by Eric Brothers.

For trying to understand the psychology of Hitler and the Third Reich, I am deeply indebted to *Hitler* by Ian Kershaw, *The Dark Charisma of Adolf Hitler* by Laurence Rees, and *Hitler's Willing Executioners: Ordinary Germans and the Holocaust* by Daniel Goldhagen.

My key reference books for understanding the impact of National Socialism on the lives of Jews were *Between Dignity and Despair: Jewish Life in Nazi Germany* by Marion A. Kaplan and *Jews in Nazi Berlin: From*

Kristallnacht to Liberation, edited by Beate Meyer, Hermann Simon and Chana Schütz.

Berlin at War by Roger Moorhouse was my constant companion as I tried to imagine Ava's life in Berlin, through the rise of the Gestapo, the air raids and the ultimate ruin of the city.

Finally, I read dozens of first-hand accounts, diaries and memoirs. *Letters from Berlin* by Margarete Dos and Kerstin Lieff and *Berlin Diaries* by Marie Vassiltchikov helped me imagine the everyday life of women in Berlin during the war. *An Underground Life: Memoirs of a Gay Jew in Nazi Berlin* by Gad Beck gave me a keen insight into the lives of the thousands of Jews who managed to survive the Holocaust by going underground, i.e. hiding in cellars and sheds and attics, or on the streets.

In My Hands: Memories of a Holocaust Rescuer by Irene Gut Opdyke helped me understand how an ordinary young woman could risk her life to save others (and made me cry so hard on a plane the flight attendant brought me tissues and a glass of wine).

The scenes set in Buchenwald would have been impossible without The Buchenwald Trilogy, three books written or edited by Flint Whitlock, including the memoir *Survivor of Buchenwald: My Personal Odyssey Through Hell* by Louis Gros.

Different Drummers: Jazz in the Culture of Nazi Germany by Michael H. Kater helped me understand the lives of the Swing Kids of 1930s Berlin, while I was given great assistance in visualising what the German officers wore by *German Army Uniforms of World War II* by Wade Krawczyk, who also helped me understand the varying attitudes to Hitler amongst those who served in his armed forces.

Thanks also to Mary Hoffman, who took me to see the graves of three of the Mitford sisters, at St Mary's Church in Swinbrook, and told me the story of Unity Mitford's tragic obsession with Hitler.

I am indebted to *Hitler's English Girlfriend: The Story of Unity Mitford* by David Rehak for information on their relationship.

It took me two years to research and write *The Beast's Garden*. During that time, it seemed as if every time I opened a newspaper or turned on the TV, there would be some kind of reference to the Nazis and the Holocaust. I realised that many other people in the world are as troubled and fascinated by the period as I am.

The Beast's Garden was the most difficult book I have ever written. The material was, of course, emotionally harrowing and the research exhausting and intensive, but it was more than that.

I think, on reflection, that I was afraid of failing to do the story justice. I was afraid to fail all those people who suffered so terribly during the seven years of my story. It felt like some kind of responsibility . . . to do my best to bring their suffering and their heroism to life. To, somehow, bear witness.

About the Author

Kate Forsyth wrote her first novel at the age of seven, and has now sold more than a million copies around the world. Her books for adults include *The Wild Girl*, the story of the forbidden romance behind the Grimm brothers' famous fairy tales, and *Bitter Greens*, a retelling of Rapunzel, which won the 2015 ALA Award for Best Historical Fiction. Named as one of Australia's Favourite 20 Novelists, Kate has a doctorate in fairy tale studies and is an accredited master storyteller. Kate's children's novels include *The Impossible Quest*, *The Puzzle Ring* and *The Gypsy Crown*. Kate is a direct descendant of Charlotte Waring Atkinson, the author of the first book for children ever published in Australia. Read more at www.kateforsyth.com.au.